HURREM

THE SLAVIC ODALISQUE
SECRETS OF THE SULTAN'S COURT

**Part Three – of the Magnificent Century
TV Series**

ΞMET ALTINYELEKLIOĞLU

For Dheyhan

Prologue

Suddenly the shadows disappeared. The voices got silent. The light, glaring in her eyes, dimmed. Darkness surrounded her. She wanted to clap her hands with joy. It was only in the dark that the little girl could leave the body lying on the bed. Only then did the window in her mind open to the light of endless meadows. It was time. The darkness was so thick that it could be touched. You could hear what the silence was saying.

"Hurry up," she whispered. "Come on now."

She tried to hear her own voice, but she couldn't. She was sure, however, that the girl's voice reached her. Now only she could hear her. Maybe she will talk to her this time. She felt a sudden excitement. She wanted it so much. Every time... She ran after the butterflies, her hair, covering her back; she danced. Suddenly she stopped and just looked. She wanted to reach out to the girl, embrace her, but she couldn't.

She loved her blue-green eyes, tiny dimples in her cheeks, and mysterious smile.

"Come," she repeated. "Don't make the butterflies wait."

So, she didn't. Suddenly, an endless meadow full of yellow flowers of broom appeared in the darkness. She sighed to the butterflies dancing over the flowers: *I missed you*. Then the girl came, raising her blue dress and a white apron. Her mom had not tied her hair, so it danced on her back like red sea waves, racing with the wind. The butterflies immediately drowned in a charm of beautiful curls. Now the girl was probably singing a joyful song, nudging the tiny butterfly wings above her head with her hair. She couldn't hear her, nor the twitter of the birds. She looked at a silent paradise as if from the darkness.

The small, freckled girl with red hair, dancing with the butterflies, noticed her. The tempo of her dancing decreased. Their eyes met. God, how beautiful she was! Beautiful and innocent. And how vulnerable! Seeing her, she wanted to chase away the sadness from her eyes. She was determined to try. When the girl was about to turn around and follow the butterflies, she said:

"Don't go."

The little girl stopped among the yellow flowers. She turned and looked at her. The sorrow in her eyes was replaced by curiosity.

"Talk to me."

Blue-green eyes flashed, but she did not break the silence.

"Tell me who you are."

The girl leaned forward and picked a flower.

"Aleksandra. I'm Aleksandra."

"Aleksandra! What a beautiful name. Fits you."

"And you, who are you? I think I know you."

She did not dare say she had a similar impression.

"I am Sultana Hürrem, my beautiful."

"Sultana Hürrem? Who is this?"

"I am the wife of the ruler of the whole world, Sultan Suleiman the Magnificent."

Holding the edge of her blue dress, the girl bent one knee and gently bowed before her, offering her the flower she picked.

Hürrem tried to get out of the darkness and accept it, but she couldn't. She felt her throat tighten. She wanted to sneak out of the dark and dance the butterfly dance with Aleksandra in the sea of brooms, but she could not save herself from the darkness.

A playful smile appeared on the girl's face.

"Hürrem, do you love Suleiman?"

"Of course."

"Suleiman probably loves you too?"

Hürrem smiled to herself.

"How did you know?"

"You are very beautiful."

The girl was distracted. She started to move away and dance with the butterflies again, chattering among the yellow broom flowers. Suddenly she stopped as if she remembered something.

"Do you have a crown and a throne?"

She didn't know what to answer.

"It is good to be Sultana Hürrem," the girl said and started running again. "I have decided. I will also become Hürrem."

She wanted to get out of the darkness that enslaved her, break away from the place where she lay. But she couldn't.

"Don't you dare!" she shouted. "You'd be better to be the sultana of these meadows."

But Aleksandra had long disappeared among the flowers, dancing with butterflies. Hürrem suddenly heard the words of a song.

May it never end, she thought, but suddenly everything began to disappear. First, the colors faded. Then the flowery meadows disappeared, and then the mountains with their peaks covered by fog. The wind and the song of Aleksandra were the last to die out. The windows of her mind were closed. Hürrem was alone again in the dark.

She couldn't stop thinking about the girl's question. 'Do you love Suleiman?' A sudden shiver shook her body.

"Suleiman – is it you?" she asked, checking the other side of the bed.

Nobody was there.

She missed her husband's arms entwining her in an iron grip. She wanted them. She felt Suleiman's hot lips touching the petals of her ears, neck, breast. She felt that she was breathless. *Is it possible?* She asked herself every now and then. *Is it possible?* Could it be that here, between light and shadow, the truth and delusion, hell and paradise, her body would trash in this unspecified desire?

She got scared. There was a silent scream inside her, and she tried to straighten up.

Whose fingers are these? She froze in horror. In the darkness, she tried to see to whom the fingers belonged, which, wandering between her legs, made her lose her senses. She didn't see anything; nobody was there. Stray fingers wandered between her thighs and her pubes like a spider!

"Is it you?" she moaned.

Nobody answered. Hürrem tried with all her strength to get away from those fingers that had already reached all the intimate places, arousing lust, and sealing the sin.

"No!" she shouted. "No! No!"

She jumped up, thinking she would run away in the dark. She ran to save herself, but she had no hands or legs. The spidery fingers disappeared. Now a handsome young man chased her.

"You!" he shouted. "You, you, you! You killed me! And I trusted you so much." He was about to catch her when suddenly a steed with a tossed mane roared up before them.

Hürrem saw a giant riding the horse majestically. He seemed to hold back the darkness.

"Jump on, kid!" said the giant.

Without thinking, she threw herself into his strong arms.

"Take me away from here..." she whispered, embracing him. "Take me to my meadows. Butterflies are waiting for me."

The steed rushed forward like a storm. Hürrem felt his mane mingle with her curls and snake around her face.

Bodies began to move in the darkness. She couldn't see their faces; only incomprehensible whispers reached her ears...

"She has a fever," said one of them.

It seemed to her that she was beginning to see the faces of her children. It was Mehmed.

"Oh, my Mehmed," she whispered. "They didn't manage to kill your mother, so they sacrificed you."

Then Mihrimah came up to her — her only daughter. Selim's light hair... The fervent look of Bayezid inherited from Sultan Suleiman. Slender Jihangir also approached her. At the moment she was about to hug him, the younger son slipped out of her embrace.

She saw a pair of scary eyes; she remembered them. She shuddered under the gloomy, yet penetrating look. The woman's lips did not move, but Hürrem heard her piercing voice.

"It's a poison! Poison!" the woman shouted in a screeching voice.

Suddenly, the darkness dispersed. Shadows took shapes. The voices found their owners.

"Give good news to the Padishah. Sultana Hürrem woke up."

Behind the fog of her eyelashes, she saw the worry on her husband's face. When she tried to smile, Aleksandra's question bothered her: 'Do you have a crown and a throne?'

"Bring Jafer to me," she said quietly. "Right now. Immediately!"

Chapter One
Autumn 1558

Several restless shadows were moving between the trees. These silhouettes belonged to ten men with repulsive faces who, stooping in the pouring rain, slowly moved forward step by step, stopping and listening. The shadows of the trees filled the forest with a darkness more profound than the night. If not for the flash of the cold steel of the swords they held, it would be impossible to notice them. In spite of the bad weather, they had a task to do, as sinister as themselves.

Although they had been walking for many hours, the place for the ambush was still far away. They were soaked to the bone. Not only because of rain, but also because of streams of water flowing from the leaves of oaks, under whose thick branches they found shelter.

At the sign given by a raised hand, everyone froze. Ten pairs of ears listened to the forest silence. Ten pairs of eyes sought to see through the wall of rain. They did not see anyone. They did not hear anything.

The forest had never been so silent. It was certain that even deer and hares were buried in their hiding places. These ten men had a bloody task awaiting them, but every one of them was warmed by the thought of bags filled with gold.

The hand dropped, and ten shadows moved forward with swords ready to cut a belly at any moment. Another shadow watching them from a few meters away did the same.

When they reached the place where the trees grew less densely, they were exhausted. The ten men stopped - and the shadow following them hid behind one of the trees. He had to be vigilant. He couldn't get too close.

The men lied down on the wet ground to catch their breath. The capes they hid under stuck to their bodies. The man whose face was covered tightly by a hood muttered:

"Damn it! This task will be heavier than the conscience of a giaur, those infidel scum. If we don't take off our cloaks, it will be difficult to brandish a sword."

One of them, lying slightly behind with his face to the ground, pulled the hood off his head.

"But it will be easy to fill our pockets with gold." He covered his mouth with his hand to suppress the sly laughter and wiped the water running down his face.

"Even the devil will not stick his head outside in such weather. I think we work hard for nothing. Eloglu is not as stupid as we are. They must have taken refuge in a caravanserai. They'll wait there until morning, snoring in warm beds," another shadow spoke in the darkness.

"Who knows, maybe they dried by a fireplace and are sipping wine now?"

The man who'd given the sign to stop by raising his hand a moment ago straightened up angrily.

"What caravanserai? What wine? What are you raving about, fools?! Hürrem's people got the order, and they will not stop regardless of the weather. Finish this woman-like waif and let's go. We're almost there."

There were murmurs of discontent. Nine of the men moved forward again, and in a short time, they were swallowed up by a wall of rain.

The commander of the gang lagged a bit behind. He waited until the one who followed them got near. A man wrapped in a leather cloak reaching all the way to the ground, said, trying to wipe away the flowing water:

"A real cloudburst!"

"Thanks to this, the blood shed by us will be washed away."

The man in the leather cloak shivered.

"It will wash the blood, but the dead bodies will remain. Everyone will recognize Hürrem's people. And those guys of yours? Have you made sure that they will not attract anyone's suspicions?"

"Don't worry. My people are clean."

The commander of the band stopped, laughing at those words.

"Clean? Don't make me laugh! Everything can be clean in this world, but people, never."

"Be careful anyway," asked the man. "Don't forget about the agreement. We do not leave any wounded. If one survives, do not say he will die anyway - finish the job."

"If I survive," he said and looked back. "If they kill me, who will do it? You?"

The man pretended not to hear.

"They still haven't noticed that I'm following you?"

"How were they supposed to have noticed?" The leader grumbled. "They are soaked to the bone. Everyone is just thinking about getting away from here and finding a dry, warm corner. Who would think about looking back?" He fell silent suddenly. "You wanted to follow us. We would provide you with what you want after all is done. You didn't have to get your hands dirty."

A few drops dripped down his neck under his clothes. The hooded man shuddered and wrapped his cloak even tighter. This night will not only be wet, but long and bloody. He didn't even want to think about what will happen to him if they don't find Hürrem's people. He absolutely must get this purse.

"The man who gave this order to me is very accurate," he murmured. "He must get what he wants. But that's not enough. He wants to make sure that you have completed the task and did not leave a trace."

"And that's what you are here for. To make sure that there is no trace left."

The man did not answer. He just looked in the opposite direction, though it couldn't be seen in the dark.

"Who gave you this unfortunate order?" The commander blurted out.

The man cursed in his thoughts. What a stupid question. Quite ridiculous.

But his companion did not smile, only once again wiped the water running down his face with his hand.

"The man who told me to do it," he just said.

"And if it turns out that they were right? If instead of riding horses in the rain, they stopped somewhere? You know that with the coming of dawn, the danger of failure will increase."

The man shook his head.

"During the day or at night, in rain or snow, the task is to be carried out. This is the order!" he hissed, giving the man a sign to leave. "They will come. You said yourself that Hürrem's horsemen will not stop."

***

He was right. Sultana Hürrem's people did not stop. The five horsemen, dressed in black, plunged into the forest, leaving the steppes behind them. Even if the darkness and trees slowed them down, they were determined to continue the journey. Firmly pulling the reins, they moved forward, bowing their heads against the low growing branches. Only the snorting of the exhausted horses could be heard in the vast forest.

When they reached the place where the trees were sparser, they accelerated again. They had only a quarter of the way through the forest left ahead of them.

Everything happened very quickly. Suddenly the path of the five horsemen was blocked by a tree falling noisily. The frightened animals began to neigh and rear up, and the men shouted in anger.

At the same moment, ten arrows cut through the darkness. Two of the five riders fell lifeless to the ground. The others grabbed their swords and jumped off the horses.

"Show yourselves, Satan's spawn!" one exclaimed.

The bandits had no reason to delay. Ten shadows emerged from behind ten trees. Ten men surrounded the three cavalrymen of Sultana Hürrem. For a short moment, the riders exchanged terrified glances. They moved closer to each other as if to protect one another. Almost immediately, various sounds mixed - the clash of swords, shouts, and curses.

Among the sparks of steel striking against each other, illuminating the night, the screams began to change into moans. First, two attackers fell face down onto the ground and did not move anymore.

One of the Hürrem's men threw himself at the other thugs, shouting:

"Get out of here, Sokollu's minions!" He swung his sword, taking two more lives, but he was wounded in the shoulder.

He grabbed the sword in his good hand and kept striking. He ripped the belly of one of the men attacking him and cut a hand off another one. However, he spotted the man approaching from behind too late. A huge sword sliced through the air and separated his head from his torso. The headless body shook in a spasm and fell to the ground. The cut off head rolled across the wet earth and disappeared into the darkness.

The riders fought bravely. The surroundings turned into a sea of blood. The bodies of the nine ruffians and four men of Hürrem lay stretched out on the ground. The streams of rain washed the blood that was seeping from the wounds. Only two people remained - the leader of the gang and the last of the Hürrem's horsemen. When they attacked each other with the last remaining bit of their forces, a sudden whistle sliced through the air. An arrow pierced the heart of Hürrem's man. Another one followed it. And then one more. The rider rolled into the mud and everything ended. Nothing but rain could be heard.

"That pig nearly finished me off," the leader grumbled to the man coming out from behind the trees. "Your arrows saved my life."

"Spare me," said the man in the leather cape who had been following the band all night. "They fight better than you do. If I had not made it, the whole ambush would be wasted. Search them. You will find a purple purse on one of them.

While the leader was searching the riders, the other man walked among the bodies. From time to time he bent down and checked if someone was breathing.

"There is no purse," said the captain, but he didn't stop the search.

"How come? It must be here. Look again. Maybe they threw it somewhere? They probably hid it." His voice betrayed panic growing in him.

Repeated searching also failed to bring results. He joined the third search himself. He even undressed the corpses to make sure nothing was attached to them, but that didn't help either.

"Damn it!" He exclaimed angrily. "It's a trap!"

"A trap?"

"A trap! These men were a plant. They purposely told us which route they would follow. While we were setting a trap, the pouch reached its destination by another route. We fell into the trap of your Sultana Hürrem. This Ruthenian bug would hoodwink even the devil himself."

"Just think how many of my men died in vain."

The man in the leather cape turned angrily.

"Three are still alive. I moved them under a tree. Finish the job."

The band leader's sword took the last breath of the three men, standing on the brink of life and death. When he wanted to turn around after he had done the task, he heard a sinister whistle - but it was already too late. The first arrow hit him in the stomach, and the man looked with horror at the growing bloody stain. The second arrow ended his life.

The man in the cloak knew that the third arrow wasn't necessary.

"May you go to hell," he grumbled. "Hürrem's message has probably reached its destination already."

***

Two messengers steered their sweating horses in the dark towards the palace gates illuminated by huge torches. Guards stood on both sides of the road, like cypress trees. They rushed like a storm among the clatter of horse hoofs. The rain that had fallen all day had formed small lakes on the road. The wet, wind-swept horses' mane whipped the faces of cavalrymen. Splashing water around them, they dashed like an arrow up to the gates, over which two towers loomed. To hasten the horse, the rider waved his right hand in the air, hitting the long reins at the animal's sides. He looked as if he was cutting down the enemy with a sword.

"Out of the way! Move out! Let the messengers of Sultana Hürrem pass!"

In the midst of the falling darkness, the weary stones of the courtyard were enlivened by the sound of hurried steps. The Palace guards surrounded the visitors, pointing lances at them, and removing their swords. Several soldiers, armed with firearms, got in positions to shoot. The army, which spilled out of the gates opening into the outer courtyard, did not slow down the riders. The two mounts pushed forward, stretching their heads and the voice of the rider in black rumbled like thunder:

"Make way for the messengers of Sultana Hürrem!"

In an instant, the frightened soldiers scattered out of the way of the steeds racing toward them. Two horses, a bay and a gray, fled like the wind, straight into the second courtyard. Sparks from beneath hooves, hitting the stones, shone like fireflies. This time, the soldiers ran to catch the horses that noisily snorted. One of the horses, frightened by a sudden hustle and bustle, reared up. Standing on his hind legs, he kicked the air vigorously with the front ones, letting forth an angry bray. The bay one followed in his footsteps, filling the courtyard with its own neigh. While four grooms tried to subdue the horses, the two messengers, covered in dirt and dust, energetically pulled their legs out of the stirrups, and slid to the ground. The two men stood in front of the gate and tried to cool off, greedily sipping water that the palace servants had brought to them from a well. The messengers bore the Tugra - the monogram of the reigning Islamic monarch's coat of arms, the emblem of the Turkish ruler, Mehmed the Conqueror.

The commander of the chaushes - the court official of the Ottoman Empire - wondered who had disturbed the evening silence. He suddenly jumped out of the guardhouse topped with two conical domes, separating the square from the second courtyard, and shouted:

"Don't you know that one does not enter the palace like it's some common stable?"

One of the cavalrymen put his hand under his shirt, pulled out a purple purse and lifted it. Seeing it, the Chaush pasha calmed down.

The voice of the second rider echoed among the high palatial walls.

"We have news from the Edirne Palace. Do you want proof? Here it is."

Chaush pasha could not control his distracted eyes. Twisting in his fingers through the ends of his lush, black mustache that he rubbed with hazelnut oil every morning, he tried to keep up what was left of his honor in front of the servants. He lowered his voice, though his tone still sounded like an order.

"Speak then. What are you waiting for?"

"We'll only pass the message to Jafer Aga. These are the orders we received."

"Fool, you want to stand in front of the big harem aga like this? Maybe you do not know the rules here, but don't you have any shame? Tell me what you were supposed to say, take your friend, and leave."

The commander of the chaushes looked fearfully and respectfully at the pouch that the messenger still held over his head. He recognized it immediately. Purple was the symbol of Sultana Hürrem. There was no door in the Ottoman Empire that this purple purse would not open. There was also no life that it could not take away. Still, he couldn't resist. He reached out and tried to take the purse. The messenger in black, with a falcon sight, quickly leaped back. His companion's hand reached for the curved dagger he had at his side.

"Don't do this, Chaush pasha," he drawled in a threatening voice. "I told you what orders we got. We have to give this to Jafer Aga. Even if you send an entire army against us, we will not disobey the order."

The commander of the chaushes and the servants surrounding him could see their fierce eyes even in the darkness. Insults were at the tip of the man's tongue.

Damn fools, boors, churl's spawn, Ruthenian minions, flashed through his head. He did not, however, intend to speak them out loud; he knew what it meant to bring the wrath of Hürrem on himself.

"Follow me," he said and turned away.

He moved proudly, resting one hand on a curved saber. The tassel of the white felt fez swayed to the rhythm of his footsteps. He walked confidently in red leather boots as if trying to cover his earlier uncertainty.

Chaush pasha went first, followed immediately behind him by the two black-clad messengers who were surrounded by guards in red and white costumes, armed with lances. As in a procession, they all moved toward the gate that opened to the second courtyard. Two grooms stayed by the horses. No one except a padishah, even a khan or a king, could enter the second courtyard on horseback.

One of the messengers turned and looked back. The stable boys were still trying to calm down the horses that continued to angrily hit the ground with their hooves. The mounts moved their heads, trying to free themselves from their harnesses.

As they passed through the gate topped with conical wooden domes on both sides, four servants holding torches joined them.

They passed the Tower of Justice, in which each day after the morning prayer, the Divan - the council of viziers - would gather to discuss state matters. Apart from the single torches at the guardhouse, the building was dark. The high walls gave the impression of trying to hide all secrets in the darkness. Chaush pasha, guards, and servants went freely and silently. However, the two

Hürrem's messengers, clad in black, seemed nervous now. In the torchlight, their shadows fell on the floors covered with white marble. They were watched from all sides.

In contrast to the Tower of Justice, the building on the right side of the gate was brightly illuminated. A few of the servants hurried in, while one as quickly hurried out, each holding huge trays. The wonderful fragrances of dozens of various dishes prepared every day in the palace kitchen, sweets, syrups, and sherbets reminded the two horsemen that they'd had nothing in their mouths since the previous evening.

Walking through the narrow streets, through the gardens, over which mysterious scents rose in spite of the autumn, they passed a fountain where the inhabitants of the seraglio looked for coolness in the last summer days. They passed the Enderun school, where the non-Muslim children and youths brought to the empire took lessons in religion, science, history, diplomacy, Turkish, Persian, trade, and court etiquette, before finally reaching the door of the harem. That was as far as they were allowed to go.

One of the servants, even though he had shoes with rolled-up tips on his feet into which only his toes could be squeezed, ran to the harem to tell Jafer Aga as quickly as possible that Sultana Hürrem's messengers were waiting for him. The boy ran breathlessly between the palatial buildings and pavilions through the long, winding streets and narrow corridors lined with stones. He was tempted to call, 'Black Aga, Black Aga, a message!' but being fearful, he only whispered that to himself.

Jafer Aga, to whom Hürrem sent a message, was the most important person in the harem. He was called Jafer, even though that wasn't his name at all. He was also known as Black Aga. Of course, he didn't get this nickname because he was as black as a starless night. This Sudanese with a large nose, big and ugly like a fairytale giant, had become Hürrem's trusted confidant from her first day in the palace harem, still as an odalisque. Sometimes he was her servant, but most often a spy. That was the reason he was generally feared.

His neck was completely hidden by his big shoulders. It seemed as if his enormous head was set directly on them. It also wasn't difficult to bump into him at night. After it happened to several odalisques, who woke up the whole harem with their shrill screams, Jafer decided to wear white clothes.

Also, this night, Black Aga, like a headless ghost clothed in galligaskins, walked the corridors of the harem filled with nighttime darkness. He knew the palace like his own pocket, and he'd been there so long, that he couldn't even remember when he was taken from his homeland. He was called a Sudanese, but he probably came from Abyssinia. He only had two memories left of his childhood: a pirate ship and a stinky musty cellar, where he was stripped of his masculinity. He could still hear his own screaming.

Hürrem came to the palace just as Jafer was experiencing his lonely and painful days. Her name was Aleksandra, but this red-haired girl was also called Ruslana. They were probably the same age. Servants mocked her: "Fifteen-year-old cat!" It was similar with Jafer.

While captivity stifled Jafer, it had a different effect on Aleksandra. Everybody called her a Ruthenian odalisque, and that stirred up a growing rebellion in her. This girl from Ruthenia did not let herself be stifled. She glittered at every step, embarrassing everyone. She didn't listen to either the Padishah or the Mother Sultana. Even taking her to the palace's bathhouse turned out to be a problem. She sat in the corner with Tatar girl Merzuka, who had been brought with her from Crimea, and stayed there. Sometimes, Jafer heard her crying as he'd pass by the door of her chamber at night. At other times, at nights, when the moon climbed through the sky and hovered over the waters, somewhere above the Leander Tower, with its light gently filtering through the barred windows of the room, the sounds of songs hummed in a foreign language reached his ears. Sometimes her voice roared like water coming from the spring; another time it shivered like a wounded bird, except it was more doleful - and would fall with a whisper on her lips. It was clear that she was singing about longing. Maybe she missed her country, her village. Maybe, she remembered her parents. Who knows? Perhaps she sang to her beloved, who stayed in distant lands? Jafer would conceal his huge body in the dark or wander nearby, pretending to have a very important task to do, and wait for the last sounds of Aleksandra's song.

It was on one of those nights that they faced each other. When the last verses of the song came out from the girl's mouth, Jafer could see, even from in his hideout, tears dripping on her cheeks like pearls. And she saw him.

He shook it off and wanted to walk away as soon as possible, but the girl, who was just beginning to learn Turkish, said uncertainly:

"Do not go. Who are you?"

"Jafer."

"And I am Aleksandra Lisowska."

"Why are you crying?"

"Simply cly. I not speak."

Jafer smiled.

The girl could not pronounce 'r.' From her mouth came out a charming 'lll...' It's been like that for years now. Even today, when Sultana Hürrem gets angry and screams at her subjects, hitting the floor with her heel, her 'r' still sounds like 'l.' 'Pass it to the agas! This is my oldel!'

But now no one could laugh at it anymore.

But, back on that first night, Aleksandra had said:

"You not tell anyone. Let it be seclet. Oul seclet."

It was the first secret between the Ruthenian odalisque Aleksandra and Jafer. And there would be even more of them to come. Thanks to these secrets, he gained not only the terrifying reputation of Black Aga in the harem but also at a small estate he was accumulating.

How many years had passed already? Thirty, forty? Now, this harem girl was the most powerful woman in the world. Jafer was also no longer that poor eunuch, pushed around and thrown out of the door, at whom the odalisques laughed: 'Did they tear it off whole for you? Really? Show us.' The harem was not a harem anymore either. Ever since Sultan Suleiman sent the girls away at the request of Sultana Hürrem, the harem became the home of the sultan and his family. Although the girls who rejoiced the hearts of the young princes have not entirely disappeared, the harem was no longer the same as it used to be. An Abyssinian refuge, Jafer Aga, had been at the head of such a harem for a long time.

Jafer, sitting in the guardhouse and doing some reminiscing, was brought back to earth by the arrival of a young servant.

"Black Aga! Black Aga!" The boy's cheeks were red from running. He tried not to raise his voice when speaking.

"Hey! What are these screams? Don't you value your life?! How dare you scream at the house of the Padishah? Lower your voice, or I'll have your ears pulled."

"Aga, a message from Sultana Hürrem has arrived. The messengers said they would either deliver the news to Jafer Aga personally, or someone would pay with his head for it." The boy added a bit of color to what he had heard, but the words he breathed were enough for Jafer Aga to go immediately toward the gate.

"If there was a message from my sultana, why did you wait, you pathetic Bosnian? Why didn't you send for me as soon as they said my name?"

The men, seeing Jafer coming quickly, came out of the guardhouse located on the ground floor of the tower rising on the right. One of them said sternly:

"Are you Jafer?"

"Yes, it's me. And who are you?"

"Is it your business, who I am?"

"If you claim you have news from my Sultana, then it is."

"If so, aga, they call me Lightning. And this is Thunderbolt." He pointed to his companion.

When the man sneered to himself, Thunderbolt spoke.

"We will destroy every enemy of Sultana Hürrem."

Lightning picked up the thread.

"If anyone will curse our Sultana, we will tear his tongue out."

Jafer Aga led the men out of the torchlight to under the shadow of a tree. The only white points were now the whites of his eyes and alternately disappearing and appearing teeth.

"No other tongues are necessary. Fortunately, yours are sharp enough," the aga hissed trying to make his thin voice take on the most ominous tone he could muster.

Feeling that the men's bodies were as tense as a bowstring, he spread his huge hands and smiled.

"OK, I'm Jafer. You are Lightning, and you – Thunderbolt. You will destroy everyone. Of course. But how can Jafer be sure that you are sent by Sultana Hürrem? Do you have any proof?"

The man in black did not make him wait. He took out a purplish silk pouch that shone with the glow of a combination of feminine passion and grace. Black Aga respectfully took over the pouch and sniffed it.

The second man said:

"Say the password. Sultana Hürrem instructed to ask you what her first maid's name was. 'If he knows, give him the message, if not, take his life away from him,' she instructed us."

"Merzuka."

The men looked at each other. The rider who introduced himself as Lightning, looked around to see if there was anyone around who could hear them and then leaned into Jafer Aga's ear.

"Tomorrow, before the evening prayer, Sultana Hürrem will come to the palace."

Hurray! Aga thought. *This is what all those tricks and passwords were about? All this fuss just to say that Sultana Hürrem is coming back from Edirne?*

"That's all?" he asked, eyeing them suspiciously.

This time Thunderbolt bent to his other ear.

"Does your coal-black head always think so slow?" he growled. "Do you think that the Great Sultana would send messengers just for this? You are to deliver this purse to the Great Vizier Rüstem Pasha. This is urgent and important, so you must follow this order immediately. His Majesty, the Great Vizier, will know the rest."

Jafer's face darkened.

"All right, but this purse is empty."

The other man in black looked at Jafer with burning eyes. Jafer also turned his eyes, glittering in the dark, on him. He knew what Lightning would answer to him, and a nervous smile appeared on the man's face.

"Whoever heard of giving the Grand Vizier an empty pouch?"

The other man interjected into the conversation, smiling broadly.

"Aga, you must know what to put in the pouch."

This time, Jafer understood the encrypted message of Sultana Hürrem. *Poison...* crossed his mind. *Death again, misfortune again.* These words burned his brain, although, at the same time, his hands became cold as ice.

So, everything would start again.

The night had not yet left Istanbul when the two men in black, who'd arrived from Edirne, set out on their steeds on their way back.

***

Jafer immediately began his sinister duties. He sneaked through the palace's streets, shrouded by the night's darkness, slinking through the shadows of the walls and the eaves, with his head hid under a black cloak. Now, not even the whites of his eyes were visible in his coal-black face. He was as clever as a fox, as crafty as a scorpion, and as dangerous as a wolf. Every now and then he stopped, listening in silence. He could hear the voices of the Janissaries on guard coming from the outer courtyard, and the incomprehensible whispers of two women being carried out of the open harem window, through which a dim light seeped.

After making sure it was safe, he slowly moved forward and then stopped again. He had to deliver the purse content, unnoticed, to the insufferable son-in-law of Sultana Hürrem, the Grand Vizier Rüstem Pasha – the husband of the beloved daughter of Sultan Suleiman, the Sultana Mihrimah. No one must see him. No one must find out that the purple silk purse he had put in the pockets of his ample galligaskins, brought death within its contents; for within the pouch, in a tiny bottle, there was enough poison to kill an entire regiment – the venom of forty vipers.

Whose life was the goal? Never mind, Jafer Aga muttered to himself. He'd already learned that if you live in the palace, your curiosity is the biggest danger. He had lived here for a long time only because he was not too nosy, or rather, he tried to prevent this feature from taking him over. 'One who knows less – lives longer,' he used to say to the novice servants. Jafer Aga knew a lot, but he also knew to forget everything immediately.

Using a secret passage, he passed the outer walls surrounding the palace and immersed his immense body in pitch-black darkness with amazing speed. He was sure that he was moving noiselessly, but his own steps were like a drum beat to him. *God damn it,* he thought. His nerves were taut like tethers. He was ready to beat, kill or tear to pieces now.

In the darkness of the starless night, he started toward the rickety carriage in the grove on the opposite side. Cabmen, who knew about secret harem escapes that happened sometimes, would wait here hoping for fat profits. Fortunately, there was one carriage here that night. The pale light of the candle standing in the window of the coach door appeared and disappeared into the rhythm of the wind swaying the branches that covered everything. Jafer Aga hid behind one of the trees. He checked and double checked if anyone was following him. After making sure he was not watched, he hid his massive body under the cloak and hastened towards the small, two-horse carriage. He opened the door noiselessly and got in, saying:

"Drive straight. I will tell you where to stop."

Another harem fancier again, thought the cabman, grabbing the reins. Two horses started to walk with a slow, lethargic step.

When the carriage started moving, Jafer once again made sure that the bottle was in his pocket. A shiver shook him. Death lurked there. While the carriage was rolling to its destination, Jafer wondered why he hated poisons so much. The very idea of dying from a poison seemed terrifying to him, and he was petrified that this would become the means of his demise. He didn't intend to poison anyone, either. He believed death should be sublime – for both the victim and the murderer. It should come from the front, looking one straight in the eyes. He pulled his huge hands from under the cloak. Each of them was as big as a log. When his hands closed on one's neck, there was no help anymore. Jafer knew the sound of crushed bones well. He also knew how inert the body left breathless became. He couldn't remember how many people lost their life from his hands.

Jafer looked out of the window. He began to hit the carriage door with a fist to a rhythm.

"Aga, don't knock like this. It won't help," the cabman laughed. His words hung in the air. Contrary to his expectations, the joke did not make the traveler laugh.

"Stop on the right side, by the ruins."

The carriage drove a bit further.

"Ho, ho!" he shouted at the horses and pulled the reins. Tired, the horses stopped with a relief. "Who on Earth wants to go to these abandoned ruins at this hour?" the cabman asked and turned back, trying to see the traveler.

But the last thing he saw in this darkness was a dazzling flash and a curved dagger that struck his heart at lightning speed.

No more witnesses were left now.

Jafer cleaned the knife, wiping it on the dead man. He jumped out of the carriage and entered the abandoned building. It was in this secret passage that he was supposed to meet the person to whom he would deliver the death he had brought.

CHAPTER TWO

The harem convoy had been on the road for a long time; the sun was already high.

Although it was mid-October, the sun was strong. The road curving between the fields became invisible among the clouds of dust stirred by carts and horses. Even the blinding black glow of the sultana's carriage disappeared under a layer of gray dust. The six-horse carriage, despite the stern attention of the coachman, bounced over holes' invisible from behind the dust wall.

Inside the carriage, a servant constantly watched her mistress, fanning her tirelessly in the cramped interior, trying to cool her. Sultana Hürrem soon got tired of her vigilant attendant however and threw her out of the carriage to remain alone in it. She didn't even take Merzuka with her; her devoted friend that looked at her from the next carriage. Hürrem wanted to be alone. She was fed up with this already. Her entire body ached from the prolonged sitting on the seat lined with silk rugs. The front of her purple caftan embellished with gold thread, studded with diamonds and rubies, was unlaced. One end of her skirt was rolled up, the other hung from the seat above the floor lined with silks. The stiff collar of the Wallachian crepe blouse reached all the way under her chin. The beautiful wife of the Sultan Suleiman listlessly took off her hotoz – a headdress traditionally worn by women in the Ottoman Empire – that was decorated with precious stones the size of broad beans and intricately pinned up to her red hair and tossed it on the seat opposite her.

The curtains were tightly drawn. Despite the silken, gold embroidered net hanging from the ceiling, which was supposed to protect the interior of the vehicle from dust, a cloud of it still managed to get inside. Even Hürrem's red hair was white with dust. However, this all-covering, yellow-gray cloud did not eclipse the charm of the woman's ocean-deep, blue-green eyes.

Sultana Hürrem pulled the black leather curtains aside and watched the view outside the window. The officer riding at the front of the cavalrymen armed with swords, whose white belt indicated his high rank, did not leave the carriage even for a moment. His eyebrows were taut as a bowstring. A lush, shiny mustache gave a majestic look to his face, tawny from the sun.

He's quite handsome, she thought. She immediately noticed that his mustache was dyed, probably from using black walnuts. She hadn't seen this swarthy youth before. Did he serve at Edirne castle or was he sent as the commander of the guard from Istanbul? From the corner of his eye, the officer noticed the parted curtain and Sultana Hürrem watching him. Embarrassed, he didn't know what to do, so he kicked his horse lightly, making sure that he disappeared from the woman's view.

Hürrem was distracted. Her head was heavy, and her heart was tight. Recently, she often felt that her heart was fluttering in her breast; she couldn't breathe, and her arms and legs refused to obey. And then there were these sudden cramps in her stomach. Thank God it didn't last long. *At this time of year, nights at Edirne are becoming cool. I got a cold probably*, she thought.

Sultana Hürrem was worried. Very worried. The plan that she had been building for years, intricate as a crocheted embroidery, was one step away from failure.

"Why are you doing this, Selim?" she whispered. "Can't you see that the throne of Sultan Suleiman is too big for you? Too big a throne can take a life. Why won't you listen to your mother and open the path to the throne for your brother, Bayezid?"

She looked around thoughtfully for a moment. *Let this throne, which I did not allow to be taken by Mustafa, the son of Gülbahar, go to my brave Bayezid,* she prayed.

The very thought of Gülbahar and Mustafa made her angry. It had been like that for years. From her, she took Sultan Suleiman, from him – the throne of the Ottomans, but she did not leave either hatred for Gülbahar or the curse of Mustafa behind her.

Hürrem loved both her sons that were still alive. She didn't favor either of them. When she thought of Selim's light hair – which he allegedly inherited from the Sultan Bayezid the Lightning – and his brown eyes, a warm smile appeared on her face. If someone asked her, she would say that 'Selim takes after me and Bayezid is like his father.' Everyone knew that the only thing Selim inherited from Suleiman, was his love for poetry. She loved them both, but the state needed Bayezid. Selim was good, but he preferred women and drinking over the affairs of the country. If he took over the throne, the state would be ruled not by Selim, but by the viziers.

"Hmm..." she muttered. "This highlander Sokollu and that Beylerbey of Damascus, Kara Mustafa Pasha, know that if Selim becomes a padishah, they will be able to drive this horse at their will. God forbid, they could even provoke a rebellion and take over the throne."

If anybody is to lead this horse, it must be me, and the rider must be Bayezid, she continued to think. *He was capable. His shoulders are strong enough to carry the reign of the state. He's wise enough to know that I have done as much service to the state as his Padishah father. He's also loyal enough to remain faithful to my goals.*

Hürrem sighed wearily. She had to put into action the plan she'd worked on for years before it would fall apart completely. She should find new pawns and make sure that Suleiman would not be impartial to his sons before the time comes to say 'check.' She wanted to pave the way for Bayezid, and at the same time to save Selim's life. That's why she escaped from the hustle and bustle of the palace. She went to the Edirne palace to be far away from the ears of greedy viziers, from eyes secretly watching her every step, the spies and harem complaints. For several months she had been resting and re-inventing the plan that would allow her to avoid a bloody fight for the throne between her sons.

She didn't regret anything she'd done so far to plant her son on the throne. She had fought for years. Tirelessly. Balanced on the brink of death. Among the many pitfalls, many had died along the way, but she survived. She was now very close to her goal. Face to face with her own conscience, she was saying there was nothing on her chest. Why would it be? These were the rules. The path to power was strewn with blood. What was she supposed to do?

"But the blood that soaked in this path will not belong to my sons," she muttered angrily. - "Isn't it enough that I have already sacrificed two sons for one throne? I don't want to experience the pain of losing a child anymore."

Edirne, this small Ruthenian village, always reminded Hürrem of her homeland and her childhood that passed so quickly. She remembered the smell of crispy bread baked by her mother over a fire made with pine cones. She thought about the local winters and the crazy wind, and how it would rush between the snow-capped peaks of the mountains, rage in the valleys, and hit the walls of the houses. It threw around the smoke from the chimneys and snatched up everything that stood in its way. The roar of the wind even drowned the howls of hungry wolves.

"Quick, get inside. Unless you want to become food for the wolves."

Hürrem jumped. It was as if someone was shouting next to her. But the language was different. It was neither Turkish nor Persian, but she knew and understood it. Of course, she understood. It was the language of her dreams. Although she had not spoken Ruthenian for many years, she still dreamed in that language; even if you did not speak it or hear it, you could never forget your mother's tongue.

Who spoke to her? Mother? She couldn't remember her face or voice. She'd forgotten it, and Hürrem's heart burned with pain.

"Half a century," she said, nodding nostalgically.

Almost fifty years had passed since the day she'd last heard this voice, but even today it was so familiar and alive… She'd heard it a thousand times.

Aleksandra Anastasia Lisowska, quickly, get inside… the voice was imperious, but above all, full of love.

Hürrem was alarmed. The shakings ceased, and now the carriage seemed to glide along a smooth surface. Or maybe it only seemed so to her? She waved her hand as if she wanted to chase someone away. Something constantly knocked around in her head. Hürrem couldn't understand, however, what worried her so much.

At night, listening to the gusts of wind, she'd huddle under her mother's patched coat. She was so little that she didn't know if she was trembling with fear or cold. She was afraid that an evil giant could come into the house at any moment – just like in fairy tales. 'Blessed Virgin,' she'd whispered back then, 'take care of me.'

A picture of a little girl praying appeared before Hürrem's eyes, kneeling by the bed, and staring at the figurine of the Mother of God, carved in wood. Her hair was carefully braided, and her long braids flowed down her back over both shoulders. Their ends were tied with red and blue ribbons. Her hands were tiny, and her fingers kept dancing around her mouth. Who was this little, freckled girl with a snubbed nose? Was it her? She couldn't remember.

Sultana Hürrem sighed. She could not find the cause of her anxiety again.

The only thing that had not changed was the unruly eyes peering at her from the broken mirror. Nobody could say whether they were blue or green. They were full of depth and feelings, hungry, dreamy, shy, haughty, and carefree. They had an expression as if they wanted to ask: 'Will you play with me?'

Hürrem took a small mirror with a short handle and red dots on its back out of her pocket, cleverly hidden in her caftan sleeve. She had many valuable mirrors in her palace chamber, just like the magnificent mirror imported by Sultan Suleiman from India, that was considered a treasure, and the Venetian mirror, which Admiral Hayraddin Barbarossa won as loot at the Battle of Preveza and gave to her. However, this small, inconspicuous mirror, whose only decoration were red dots, paled in comparison to those at the palace, but it was the one that she always carried with her; it was a gift that she'd received from Fryderyk many years ago.

Poor Fryderyk... she thought and sighed deeply.

Although it was hot in the carriage, Sultana Hürrem shivered as if she'd suddenly felt the cold breath of death on her cheek.

"My beloved, Fryderyk," she whispered.

A youthful face of the Polish trader stood before her eyes. For some reason, she remembered him the way he looked on the day they met at the market for the first time; the ruffled, blond hair, falling on his forehead, always taut, thick eyebrows, his amused gaze, narrow, upturned nose, and lips that looked like two thick lines because of his ever-present smile. The lips – sweet, moist lips.

If he knew what was going to happen, he'd probably curse the day their paths crossed. But Hürrem didn't know that either... Just this first look, the first spark, the sudden awakening in the heart, a stolen kiss, and a breakup. How could she know that years later, she would meet these eyes and ever smiling lips on her path again? Fryderyk ran to her like a moth throwing itself in the flame, conscious of the impending death. Perhaps looking into the eyes of death, he also smiled? Hürrem really wanted it to be so. Maybe then the pain of the sin biting her would be a bit weaker.

She lifted the mirror and looked for a long time at the woman who was looking back at her.

No, I'm not that little girl, she thought. She didn't have that freckled face or eyes full of life. Yes, they were still as beautiful and profound, but there was no more liveliness, tenderness, light-heartedness, and devotion that once existed in the eyes of that little girl.

"I'm not her," she whispered. "I am Sultana Hürrem."

She couldn't take her eyes off the mirror. If she was Sultana Hürrem, who was the woman watching her from the shiny surface of the mirror?

"Who are you?" she asked the reflection in the mirror.

She was about to look away from the mirror when she heard the same voice again.

Aleksandra Anastasia... Come here, child.

The voice repeated constantly:

Aleksandra... Aleksandra... Aleksandra...

Hürrem shuddered as if she were awakening from a nightmare. She tossed the mirror on the seat.

"No," she said. "I'm not Aleksandra. My name is Hürrem. I am the beloved wife of Sultan Suleiman, who overthrew and exalted the kings, before whom khans and kings kneel. I am the mother of his sons and of his beloved daughter."

Her body covered with sweat. Her forehead burned.

Pulled by six strong horses, the carriage began to shake again as if it drove into a storm. The vehicle made miserable noises whenever they drove over a hole.

It was just then that she gave a name to this thing, hidden in the recesses of her mind, that had been bothering her for days, months, or even years.

***

She'd spent her entire existence fighting for survival. At certain times in her life, she fell into oblivion; she disappeared as if she'd never existed. She didn't want to be forgotten, and she didn't want to disappear. She wanted to leave a mark. When that day comes for her to say goodbye to this world, she wouldn't like to just become a handful of earth. She couldn't call it a desire for immortality, rather more like she just wants to be remembered... Yes, that's what it was all about. But would it ever be possible? Who knows during how many sleepless nights full of suffering, those never-ending nights from the dusk till the dawn, she sought an answer with her inner child's reasoning.

In the end, Hürrem discovered this secret. In order not to be forgotten, you have to be strong.

This night was coming to an end as darkness was now slowly giving way to the morning light. To Hürrem, it seemed like it was already dawn. When she remembered how it seemed to her that she'd finally solved the puzzle and would find a way to power and fame, a grimace appeared on her face. She thought it was the end of worries, fear, loneliness, and hard tests.

"Only now came the time for real pain," she whispered to herself.

She wondered many times that had she known that the path to power and fame would be so long and tough, full of deadly traps, would she still have decided to set off on it? And every time she answered: 'Of course. I will pay the price, no matter how high.'

She picked up the mirror again and looked at her reflection.

"Whatever you did, you did it to achieve that goal," she said. "It doesn't matter who you were yesterday.

Today you are a powerful ruler. Tomorrow your son will take over the throne of the Ottomans. Sun and moon, heaven and earth, Mohammed and Jesus are my witnesses. Yes, so it will happen, I swear to you."

But when she looked back, she realized that not everything went as it should have. Yes, she became a sultana, but she was just an unknown queen.

"I don't even have a name," she said, hitting her fist. "Hürrem is not a name. It's just a nickname, that's all. It's only my nickname, nothing more."

Hürrem was already the most powerful sultana in the history of the world, as powerful as the Padishah himself, but in state documents, foundation notes, inscriptions of commissioned works, her name was never mentioned. For example, it was written, 'mother of the Prince Bayezid,' or 'mother of Prince Mehmed.' That's all... a queen without a crown or even a name!

A grimace of pain appeared on her face. She will be only known as the 'Sultana Mother' and will disappear like someone unnecessary. She will be mentioned only in a few words. Will all this pain, torment, fear, tears, and death just be in vain? Just so that only a short note about her would appear? After all, Hürrem was to be unforgettable, she could not disappear.

That terrible night, when she was abducted, thrown on horseback, she tried to raise her head and shout:

"Don't forget about me! Don't forget about me!"

However, the barbarian who had kidnapped her, shoved some rag in her mouth, so no one heard her begging. But ever since that night, she felt her own cry with every part of her body. At a time when she lived on the edge of the wilderness when big, disgusting hands wandered around her body like huge spiders, and salivating mouths closed on her, she'd cry inside: *Don't forget about me!* When a dogwood stick hit her back after she was given to the palace harem as an odalisque, and when she was whipped and shoved, the same cry rose inside her: *Don't forget about me!*

Even if they forgot, Hürrem remembered.

Suddenly she spoke to the mirror:

"Still, you leave as forgotten. For a few more years, they will secretly reproach you, calling you the Ruthenian wife of the Padishah. Somewhere, they will write something about the mother of the Padishah, Sultana Mother, and then everything will end. They will remember neither Aleksandra nor Hürrem."

Her eyes filled with a cloud of moisture. Where did these tears come from now? She'd not cried for a long time... not once since the day her heart became as hard as a stone, had she shed a single tear. Was the last time she cried the day when she got the tragic news of Prince Jihangir? Only for a moment, just for one moment, she looked with her eyes wet with tears at the woman who was watching her back through the mirror. A smile appeared on her face, but it wasn't known whether there was joy hiding behind it, or suffering.

"Tell me," she said to reflection. "So many years, so much pain, so many trials, fear, and humiliation, all this just to be forgotten? Is that what you have fought so much for? To appear for a moment and pass away?"

She turned her head toward the window. She parted the curtains and looked with her eyes wet with tears at the fields of sunflowers stretching out to the horizon; sunflowers that looked like big plates as they turned their heads lovingly toward the sun.

In fact, throughout all her life, they wanted her to forget.

First, there was Tacham Noyan in the old caravanserai room near Bakhchysarai: 'Forget what happened, little girl,' he'd said.

Later, in the palace in Crimea, the mother of Khan Mehmed Girey announced: 'Forget about it, child. This is the past already. Now it's time to look into the future. It's your future.'

Future? At that time, Aleksandra didn't know the meaning of the word yet. Did she have any future?

Even when she entered the harem, the girls in the palace wanted her to forget, and they said to her: 'Aleksandra? It's a difficult name. Forget about it. From now on you will be called Ruslana.'

One day one of the women in the harem asked Ruslana: 'Have you heard what they say, my beautiful, you who are crossing the limits of impertinence? At foreign courts, they say that since the Ruthenian concubine of Sultan Suleiman is so beautiful and so predatory, she should be called Roxolana.'

And so, she got one more name.

The drilling laughter of the gossiping women again resounded in Hürrem's ears.

No one could remember Aleksandra anymore. Ruslana was forgotten very quickly, because one day, Sultan Suleiman declared: 'Forget it.'

She was no longer Aleksandra, Ruslana, or Roxolana. Neither Aleksandra, the name spoken by her mother, was left to her, nor the new, difficult to get accustomed to identities of Ruslana or Roxolana. Now she was 'Hürrem,' the Padishah's beloved wife, the Sultana Hürrem.

Sunlight drifted through the leather curtains in the carriage windows. For a moment, Hürrem plunged into a stream of dust that looked like a column of light in the sun. She moved her lips, but she could not hear her voice. In fact, it only resonated in her head: *Aleksandra died, long live Hürrem!*

Suddenly, she remembered the advice of Sheikh al Islam, Ali Jemal Zembill Efendi: 'You've changed, child. You have become a new person. Leave what happened in the past, don't let it cast a shadow over your future. Padishah is pleased with you. Do not fail faith and religion, may God also be pleased with you. You have to forget about the past to live in the future. Let them remember you not in the past, but in the future.'

That's what she wanted - to be remembered not in the past, but in the present and in the future.

***

The Sultana's carriage was heavily shaken again. Hürrem managed, however, to brace herself so as not to hit her head. Despite the unfavorable conditions of the travel, she continued her journey through the ocean of memories.

To forget!

Easier said than done, she thought. Neither suffering, nor horror, nor joy, let themselves be forgotten. The past did not leave a man alone. Even if you say you have 'forgotten,' the blood will not forget. Even if blood does not exert its rights, your origin will always become a bone in the others' throat. Why, even though she gave the Ottoman Padishah four sons and a daughter, was there still whispering behind Hürrem's back – 'Ruthenian spawn?'

"Even that snake's spawn, Sokollu," murmured Hürrem, and hate could be seen on her face. "As if he himself came from the Ottomans, that hateful Croat."

It was Sokollu Mehmed Pasha who kept repeating at the divan meetings:

'An apple does not fall far from an apple tree, gentlemen. It's certain that an 'apple' will always fall down.' Everyone realized that he meant Sultana Hürrem trying to place her son Bayezid on the throne after Suleiman's death.

Well, thought Hürrem, *the Ruthenian apple falls down. And what does Croatian one do? Jumps? Rolls forward? Who do you think you are, Croatian spawn – if that's where you really came from?*

"Yes, exactly," Hürrem said to the mirror. "You see, even the highlander Sokollu says so. A man does not change just because someone told him so. Blood is attracted to blood, soul to soul."

She remembered when years ago, she asked her son-in-law Rüstem Pasha, who was Croatian by birth: 'Do you think that if someone changes their name, religion, writing, the direction in which they pray, they will become someone else, Rüstem?'

She remembered the fear in his eyes. After a moment, it disappeared and was replaced by a devious, devilish spark. Rüstem was also waiting for the right time. If only the opportunity arose, he would raise his tail like a scorpion, and release poison from a spike on its end.

Hürrem saw through the eyes of her imagination the ever-shifty eyes of her son-in-law and how he silently sneaked through the palace corridors, trying to hide his disability under the sable fur coat, falling all the way to the ground.

She tried to escape her thoughts.

I wonder what Black Aga did. Has the package reached its destination?

"I will crush the snake's head," Hürrem drawled, as the carriage continued to bounce on the road. "Until I do it, neither my sons nor I, will be in peace."

Suddenly there was a sound. Sultana Hürrem parted the leather curtain and looked at the riders by the carriage.

"Guard, what's going on?" she asked.

The man pulled the reins and approached the carriage.

"It's the orchestra of the Janissaries, My Lady," he said. "Soldiers celebrate your return. They are playing your favorite melodies."

Apparently, while doing the examination of her conscience, she'd arrived at the outskirts of Istanbul. As the cloud of dust fell, Hürrem saw the towering minaret of the mosque which her husband had ordered to build in honor of their son Prince Mehmed, who died of black pox at the age of twenty-two. Their youngest son, Jihangir, lay beside his older brother.

"We'll stop by the mosque," Hürrem said to the officer. "My princes are waiting for my prayer."

The officer immediately sent people to take appropriate action. Behind a group of soldiers, Sultana Hürrem saw two armed riders. The horse of one of them was gray and of the other, bay. The five guards could not be seen. They exchanged glances. Hürrem read from their eyes and knew immediately that the message had reached Jafer. A crafty smile appeared on her face. Everything had gone according to plan – she'd announced that the guards were carrying important information to the palace to protect herself from an ambush. In fact, those who tried to stop them fell into the trap. It was true that five men lives had been sacrificed, but the two riders carrying a message by another route had succeeded in giving Jafer Aga her order.

Be afraid now, Sokollu. And you order for your grave to be dug, Lala Mustafa, she thought. The helpless, weak woman who had been examining her conscience for so many hours and had an identity crisis, disappeared – Sultana Hürrem had returned with all her might.

There was a spark in her eyes that never bode well for anyone. Now her gaze was taken over by the red of autumn leaves. *You will see what the Ruthenian spawn can do.*

She drew the curtain. She tried to pull herself together so that the soldiers wouldn't notice her fatigue when she would step out of the carriage. She put a pointy hotoz on her head.

When the six-horse carriage stopped in front of the mosque, there was a voice of hasty steps. Harem servants, chaperones, and maidservants jumped out of the carriages following behind her.

The door to the carriage opened.

Sultana Hürrem looked with a flash of lightning in her eyes at the soldier who came out to meet her. Ignoring the helping hand outstretched toward her, she majestically got out of the carriage. She walked proudly straight to the tomb where her two unfortunate sons were sleeping an eternal sleep.

No one could see the storm raging inside her. If anyone heard the two phrases running around in her mind, they would be terrified. *An eye for an eye. A tooth for a tooth.*

That's how Hürrem's whole life had passed.

CHAPTER THREE

Winter 1514

The weak, trembling flame of the bonfire made by the barbarians was not enough to illuminate the darkness that enveloped the cave. A terrible storm threw lightning bolts across the cave entrance, and a wild wind blew the snow inside. At the sound of a thunderclap, the little heart of Aleksandra began to pound as she trembled in fear in the corner of the cave.

Four barbarians led their horses inside the cave. They tried to warm themselves by the fire. Aleksandra couldn't decide whether she was more afraid of the horses or these men. The man who brought her had left her by the fire in the cave. She hugged her legs tightly, and the rag pressed into her mouth, which had long since lost its color, did not let Aleksandra breathe. There was a nasty odor of animal feces and the wet leather that the men wore constantly. She could see the other three women who cried silently, clinging to each other.

One of the giants gathered by the fire took off a huge helmet that covered his eyes – his hair, matted with dirt, reached down to his shoulders. The man then laid his quiver and bow down by his side. Aleksandra thought he looked like an owl. Compared to his face, his nose, almost invisible from under his mustache and beard, seemed tiny.

His mustache fell all the way to his chest. She tried to guess his age, but because she couldn't see his face clearly, she couldn't. His lips, hidden among the hair, moved.

"Your happiness runs faster than you, Tacham Noyan."

The barbarian who kidnapped her stretched out his hands to the fire to warm up.

So, his name is Tacham Noyan.

He turned his head and muttered, "Why is that?"

His companion nodded to Aleksandra.

"Just look. You caught the most mischievous doe," he said and laughed aloud.

Tacham did not react. It was like he never heard it at all. However, a man with hair stiff like goat's bristles disturbed that calmness. Laughing aloud, he reached out and pointed at the three women nestled in each other's arms.

"Look at them! Ours resemble old hens that escaped the knife."

Two other barbarians joined their companion and also burst into loud laughter.

The man waited for the laughter to quiet down, eyeballing his companions for a moment.

"All happiness comes from God. What are you jealous of, Berkul Djan?"

Aleksandra was surprised. This time the barbarian's voice did not sound like a snake's hiss. Now it seemed to be coming from a very long distance away. After a moment he spoke again.

"It is God who gives and takes away life. He gives to each his servant what he deserves."

The cave filled with dead silence. Aleksandra was already cold to the bone. She opened her eyes wide, trying to make sure that no detail escaped her. It was clear that the three men carefully weighed these words. Although she was still a child, she sensed a growing tension in the air. Then, the dangerous silence was disturbed by a slant-eyed man, scratching under his woolen cap.

"Why are you so mad, Cossack wolf?"

"Jealousy is bad. It is 'haram' — everything that is forbidden in Islam. I am telling you that."

"There is nothing wrong with looking at a fresh doe."

"This is a child. A small child."

"If while sitting, she's touching the floor with her feet, there is no problem," Bristly Berkul burst out laughing.

"This is a child," repeated Tacham, but this time his voice was sharp as a razor.

The third man then spoke.

"People told me the Cossacks were fools, but I didn't believe them."

The others nodded in confirmation of these words.

Tacham's hand moved to the woven belt around his waist.

"Did you hear them say how sharp their knives are?"

Aleksandra noticed that the bristly man also reached behind his belt. At the same moment, the slant-eyed Tatar jumped to his feet with joy and began to sing an invented song.

"Everyone cares about their own!"

While two men joined him, clapping their hands, the bristly one grinned widely at Tacham sitting on the opposite side of the fire.

Aleksandra saw a hidden cunning in his eyes.

"The jealousy does not befit the jigits of the Crimean Khan," said the bristly man.

The other one took his arm from his belt and began to dig in the fire with a stick.

From where she lay, she tried to look closely at him. He took a scarf off his head. The man they called Tacham Noyan had long hair, like the others – however, his hair seemed cleaner. In the light of the fire, Aleksandra could not judge what color it was: Black? Fawn? Red? Or maybe white, like Uncle Vladimir's? Certainly, his thick eyebrows, whose ends stretched like a bowstring and reached to his beard, were raven-black. Just like at the moment she saw him for the first time, his eyes flashed with lightning. Flames danced in his pupils, so it was also difficult to tell what their color was, but she was convinced they were black too. His nose resembled an eagle's beak. Thick lips were visible from under the beard covering his cheeks and jaw. His body was so large that he couldn't hide anywhere. He looked about forty years old... He was almost like her father.

The first time she saw him was when he'd opened the door to her room with a creak. She was between dreaming and waking, so she thought that this huge silhouette in the doorway was just a dream. She wrapped herself tightly in her quilt as the giant figure approached. It stopped, listening. When the giant leaned over her, she felt his repulsive breath on her face.

No, it's not a dream, she'd thought. She tried to shout, but she couldn't. At the same moment, with a lightning-quick movement, the big man covered her mouth.

"Quiet or I'll cut your throat." The man's voice was like a snake's hissing.

The black-bearded barbarian, covered with a large bearskin, threw her on his back like an empty sack and headed straight for the stairs. Aleksandra struggled to get out of his steel arms. She beat his face with her small hands.

"Mom, dad, help! Help me!" she shouted at the top of her lungs.

But no one came to help her.

"Dad! Help me!" she cried out with the last of her strength.

The barbarian understood that the girl would not be silent. He pulled her from his back and slapped her face.

"Shut up, or I'll kill you!" the serpent voice said again.

Aleksandra felt her face burning. She'd spun around and fell to the floor under the force of the sudden blow. Her body twisted in pain, and she could barely catch her breath. The man jumped at her with lightning speed and put a rag in her mouth. Although she tried to fight, he bound her hands and legs with a piece of leather. When Aleksandra saw the man's eyes, glowing like coals, she was even more terrified. This barbarian was a devil incarnate. In the evenings her father, who was a priest, told her stories about Evil; and this certainly was the devil.

"Be afraid! Every evil, every sin comes from him!" her father would shout to the people as they gathered in the small village church every Sunday.

Having cast Aleksandra on his back, he quickly walked down the stairs. He opened the door with a kick and threw himself into a storm whipping with icy wind. That's when Aleksandra saw the other men. A wind coming from the direction of the mountains threw snow swirling around with a terrifying howl. Shadows of men, with blades of curved daggers shining in their hands, tried to reach the place where they'd left the horses, pushing women, barely keeping upright, in front of themselves.

When the giant began to rush his horse to shield himself from the storm, Aleksandra cried out a muffled groan, "Our mother, Mary..." as she was bobbed painfully around on the horse's back. Maybe her mom was also among these women? She tried with all her might to shout, "Moooom!", but her desperate cry was suppressed by that rag pressed firmly into her mouth.

The deafening howl of the wind took over the night. Aleksandra and six or seven other women, pulled along by men, looked like phantoms as they jerked their way through the clouds of snow, whipped up by the wind. Their lace scarves slipped from their heads, and in the darkness, their fair, wind-tossed hair seemed to be begging for help.

If any of them tried to escape, the man riding at the rear would catch her and drag her back – but the women were not giving up. They tried to sneak away, crawling in the snow. Aleksandra wondered where her daddy had gone. For sure, he and the men from the village were waiting behind one of the walls for the right moment to jump out and save them. Sibigniyev, who helped her father in the church, was nowhere to be seen either.

Don't even think about it, she scolded herself, because she had a terrible premonition, and suddenly worried that they could have killed her father. Aleksandra shuddered, but after a moment she pushed those black thoughts away.

The barbarian who had kidnapped her reached the bushes, where he'd tied his horse. They stood face to face. Furious clouds of steam billowed out from his mouth. He tossed the girl face down on the rear saddle of a soaking wet gray horse, which turned his head as if it wanted to check what he'd carry on his back. Aleksandra saw sadness in his big, black eyes. The steed neighed as if to say, 'I don't understand, but don't cry. Don't be afraid.' He fumbled with one leg in the snow, and when he shook his head angrily, his wet, lush mane mingled with Aleksandra's hair.

When the man jumped into the saddle with a swift, agile movement, the animal reared up. He kicked the air with his front legs. The girl thought she would slip and fall, saving herself from the hands of this monster, but it didn't happen – the giant held her in an iron grip.

Aleksandra's tears began to freeze. She looked at everything from behind a thin curtain of ice crystals forming on her eyelashes. Black men fought with white ghosts gliding through the snow. Every now and then a blade flashed in the air, and each time a ghost fell to the ground, flaying its hands. Even if one shouted, no one but the wind heard him. Nobody ran to help. The other three ghosts had long been thrown into the saddle, just like Aleksandra.

A voice shouted over the howling of the wind.

"Let's go! We're leaving!"

Thick leather shoes nudged firmly into the horse's sides. The horses started trotting, then galloped through the darkness.

Aleksandra looked at the people lying motionless on the ground. Her mother was not among them. But she did not feel even a hint of joy in her heart. She recognized Anna, and Tatiana among them, and Natalia too, who got married less than a year ago... and Duniashka... her friend with whom she played by the fireplace even today – all dead now. Her tears fell on the blanket that the man had put under the saddle.

"I will never forget you," she said through tears. "I swear. I won't forget."

Turning her head, she looked at the pale-yellow light of the house disappearing before her eyes.

Mom! she shouted. *Mom! Dad! Don't forget!* Her voice couldn't be heard, but Aleksandra heard it in her head and felt in her heart. *Don't forget about me! Do not forget! I will not forget about you!*

***

Aleksandra was exhausted from crying and from fear. She was cold, and her whole body ached from lying still. She struggled to not fall asleep with all her might.

I can't fall asleep. I can't fall asleep, she kept repeating in her mind. However, it was much easier to order something to others than to yourself. The three men fell asleep. She didn't notice when the barbarian got up from his place by the fire and lay down beside her. He was looking at her, but his thoughts were somewhere far away. Slowly he pulled the dirty rag from her mouth and covered it with his huge hand. He put his fingers to his lips, ordering her to be quiet.

"If you promise not to scream, I'll take my hand away." Then the man slowly uncovered her lips, not once taking his eyes off her. After many hours, she could finally take a deep breath.

"If you shout, they'll kill you," the man whispered.

Aleksandra nodded.

Tacham Noyan looked at the three men lying by the fire. They were sleeping soundly, snoring.

He turned back to the girl again. When he extended his hand to her legs, Aleksandra jumped in horror. Their eyes met, and the wild flash disappeared from the man's eyes. Or maybe it only seemed so to her? The barbarian freed her hands and legs. Aleksandra felt an unpleasant tingle in them, so began to move them because they were numb.

"Try to sleep." The deep voice did not seem terrifying to her anymore. "Just don't think about escaping," he said, pointing to the sleeping men. "Even if you make it out of the cave, you'll become the food for a pack of hungry wolves, or you'll freeze before you take three steps."

"I won't run away," Aleksandra whispered.

It seemed to her that a shadow of a smile appeared on the man's face.

"Sleep. You need to be rested by morning."

He laid the leather tethers on her arms and legs so that they looked tied down. Putting his finger on his lips again, he returned to the fire as silently as he'd appeared. After making sure everything was under control, he leaned his back against the saddle; his head dropped on his shoulder, and after a while, he joined the other men with his snoring.

Her eyelids grew heavier. The images that played before her eyes began to blur. Aleksandra's last thought was: Where to?" Even if she tried to escape and get out of this hell, where would she go? She didn't know where she was. They'd traveled for hours in a constantly raging storm. There were no stars or moon visible. In the darkness of the night, she would lose her orientation anyway. She sighed softly. It was her first night away from the smell of her mother.

Aleksandra dreamed. She was playing tag with a bunch of colorful butterflies on green meadows. Suddenly she saw

Dunyashka. The hair of both girls fluttered in the wind.

"You haven't died!" Aleksandra shouted happily.

"Die?" Dunya's laughter echoed around. "A man dies when he is forgotten," her dear friend answered. "If you don't forget about me, I will never die."

Holding hands, they ran down a flowered meadow following the butterflies that fluttered with yellow wings.

She heard her mom's voice coming from far away. She was singing her favorite song:

Volga girls, Volga girls,
Keep their heads high like mountains.
With a sickle in their hand, they cut the golden ears.
How beautiful they dance and sing among the fields.

Dunyashka also sang a song, clapping her hands:

Hey, the Volga girls, hey, hey!

People gathered by the water in front of the church. Young people danced to the lively sounds of Sibigniyev's balalaika. Girls rested one hand on their hip while shaking the tambourine bells with the other. Rhythmically hitting the ground with their feet, they circled around the boys. Aleksandra and Dunya also danced. The sounds began to recede, and the pictures faded... And then she saw her mother standing in the doorway of the church. Dad was standing next to her. They both were extending their hands to her.

"Aleksandra Anastasia Lisowska, come here, child."

Aleksandra wanted to run to them, but she couldn't. A black man stood in her way. He had a fire in his eyes, and his arms that resembled snakes, wrapped around her body. His stinking breath made her sick. He brought his mouth, dripping with saliva, close to her face. His wet, bold hands, as rough as the bark of a tree, pulled up her skirt in a lusty rush...

Suddenly Aleksandra woke up in horror. She tried to free herself from under the heavy body of the slanted-eyed man with a weasel face. Covering her mouth so she wouldn't scream, the man whispered to her in a rough voice:

"I love resistant young does. You'll see, you'll like it too."

Aleksandra bit with all her strength, the hand with which he covered her mouth. The barbarian fell to his knees in pain.

"You little bitch!" he screamed.

Immediately, everything was turned upside down. The first one to get up at her call for help was 'her' barbarian. The wild man who had kidnapped her from her home was her only rescue. He got to the ugly, bristly man sleeping by the fire. At the same moment, the horses and the three semi-conscious women, sleeping a little further along the wall, woke up. The cave filled with tears, screams, and the neighing of frightened horses.

The man who untied Aleksandra's legs jumped like a spring hearing her scream, grabbed the neck of the hideous thug, and hurled him against the wall of the cave.

"Didn't I tell you?!" he roared. "She's still a child. A small child."

The man got up angrily.

"Where I come from, girls like her give birth to children!"

A large, curved saber shone in his hand. His companions also drew weapons and joined the Tatar.

Tacham Noyan reached for his weapon, covering Aleksandra.

"To the rest of women!" he shouted.

Aleksandra immediately carried out his order and ran to the three women that were crying in fear.

The men lunged at each other.

During the earlier quarrel, Aleksandra had learned that the bristly man's name was Berkul. Now, he was drawing circles in the air with the saber.

"Since when are the spoils owned by one?!" he shouted, furious that he'd failed to achieve what he wanted. He squeezed his saber tighter. "All the spoils are common property. Delicate meat of young does too. That's what tradition says," he added.

The bald barbarian, silent until then, picked up a spear ending with an iron arrowhead, grinning with satisfaction. He watched Tacham, glad he would be able to split his skull.

"No one, who has not respected the tradition, has survived in the lands of the Golden Horde. Be damned," he said.

Bristly Berkul and his companions tried to go around Tacham Noyan on both sides and reach Aleksandra but the long saber of the Cossack soldier, ending with a handle in the shape of a wolf's head, cut their path every time. The weasel-like man was not as stupid as the others – he was clever and cunning. He knew that if a fight started, the man would not give up his life before he took another, only it wasn't known whose life would it be. Trying to scare the enemy, he yelled:

"We won't let you enjoy this doe alone! We have the right to her too! Either you agree that we feed on her together, or leave her to us and go your own way. We can also take both what we deserve and your soul. This is what tradition requires."

"One can't reach out his hand for a child!" roared Tacham Noyan. His deep voice echoed from the walls of the cave. "That's what my faith and tradition say."

All at once, their swords made of double-hardened steel, crossed. Cries and threats mixed with each other. Aleksandra prayed that the man who had abducted her would win in this fight. This barbarian had become her savior.

"Get out of my way, wicked man," thundered Tacham Noyan. "I won't consider the fact that you are the descendants of Genghis Khan, the men of Jochi, Genghis Khan's eldest son, the jigits of Toka Temur. If our ancestors, our khans, our lord Temur saw what you were doing, he would take your life himself."

"Kill this traitor!" the weasel-like shouted, but he didn't finish.

The Cossack turned on one leg and sank the blade in his stomach. Weasel man's heavy saber fell to the ground, and his hands went to the wound in surprise. He touched his insides in horror and slumped to the ground lifelessly.

"May the devils take your soul!" yelled the Cossack jigit while he pushed the saber with a terrifying move into the second man coming at him.

The blade reached his neck, and he fell breathless to the ground.

Now only Tacham and Berkul were left. Their swords crossed once more, and a burst of sparks flew into the air again. More threats and curses resounded, and laments broke out. When the bristly man's sword reached the arm of Tacham, Aleksandra and three women shouted in fear. The man bent quickly and sank his saber in the enemy's belly.

"Go to hell!" Berkul stepped back.

The tormented arm could no longer hold the saber. The battle was over.

Tacham immediately grabbed a saddle lying by the fire and ran to Aleksandra.

"Quick! Let's go!" he shouted.

He saddled his horse, put the girl on it and took his place behind her. He grabbed the reins and moved forward. He turned back and looked over his shoulder at the three abducted women.

"Don't stay! Flee! There are robbers everywhere. If you are lucky, you will survive!"

Leading the horse on which he'd placed Aleksandra, he moved towards the snowy glow visible at the exit of the cave.

CHAPTER FOUR

The terrifying storm that had raged through the night died away, leaving knee-high snowdrifts. The bitter cold cut faces like an ice blade. The snow lying on the branches of pine trees shook loose under light gusts of wind and the gentle fluttering's of starving starlings seeking food in vain and fell on the heads of the three travelers passing under them. The angry breath of the steed, trudging through the snow with difficulty, dissolved the icicles forming around his mouth. Before he could puff out another bundle of hot steam, however, the moisture around him would turn into the ice again.

Aleksandra was cold. Hugging herself, she did her best to warm up her small body, but to no avail. So, she clung to the horse's back instead to try to warm herself up that way – all in vain. The snow falling on her from the branches of the trees dampened her clothes completely; she shivered with cold.

The man sinking in the snow took out a huge piece of fur from his horse's pack and handed it to her.

"Here. Wrap yourself."

Aleksandra pretended not to hear. She couldn't forgive him for killing those three men. If this barbarian hadn't kidnapped her, she'd be sleeping at home right now, in a warm bed, wrapped in the scent of bread being baked on a pine fire.

Without stopping, the man poked the girl with an elbow.

"Here. Wrap yourself."

Aleksandra thought that maybe it would be good if she didn't turn away his gesture of goodwill. Her reason was telling her 'take it,' but her suffering soul didn't want to receive help from the man who was the cause of all this misfortune. However, she was terribly cold. She had the impression that she was being overtaken by a mortal sleep. She wanted to fall asleep. Immediately. A deep sleep filled with sweet dreams. If she fell asleep, maybe in her dream she would see her home again. Mom, dad, Dunya, the golden rooster on the clock tower of the white painted church. But already, the previous night had taught Aleksandra just how dangerous a sleep can be.

"Don't sleep!"

Did she really hear that, or did she just think so?

Swaying on the horse's back, slipping between waking and sleeping, she tried with all her might to hold her drooping eyelids open.

The giant barbarian thought that the girl had not heard him, so he nudged her again. This time stronger.

"Here. Wrap yourself."

"I don't want to."

"You'll freeze."

"I won't. I'm used to cold."

The pertinacity, growing in her childish spirit, showed itself for the first time. She sneaked a glance at the man trying to trudge through the snow. His hair and beard, sticking out from under the scarves, were frozen. His bushy eyebrows and even his eyelashes were white with ice, and only his black eyes could be seen in the white covering everything. Suddenly Aleksandra began to wonder why, even though the snow was already reaching his waist, the man did not get on his horse. Last night, he tied her up and threw her on the horse's back, then jumped himself on the saddle to rush the horse, racing like lightning amidst a thundering storm. He could do the same now, so why didn't he get on the horse?

The barbarian stopped his horse and extended animal skin toward Aleksandra. This time his voice was more severe.

"Take this immediately and wrap yourself. Otherwise, I will put you over my knee and give you a proper beating."

Maybe because of fear, or perhaps because in this cold she no longer had the strength to resist, Aleksandra leaned over and took the skin from the man.

"It stinks terribly."

"You'll get used to it. The stench is better than freezing."

While she tried to wrap her small body with the skin in disgust, she saw a long rope in the man's hands.

"Will you bind me?"

"No, you'll bind yourself."

He gave the rope to the girl. A dashing grimace appeared on the cold-cut face of the man.

"Tie the skin well around yourself, so it does not open. Just like me. Look. Do you understand?"

Of course, she understood. Who did this savage think she was? She tied the rope tightly around her waist. Slowly, a wonderful warmth began to embrace her body.

This time, the man pulled small scraps of fur from the horse packs. He stopped the horse.

"Don't squirm."

"What do you want to do?"

He thoroughly wrapped the girl's right foot with a piece of fur. Her fingertips had already begun to freeze. He went to the other side and did the same with the other foot.

"Now your feet will be warm too."

Aleksandra sought help for her freezing hands. Putting her fingers to her lips, she tried to warm them with her breath. Finally, she slipped them under the fur.

The man noticed that the girl became calmer. He pulled his horse and set off on the way.

"Why didn't you tie me down?"

"It's not necessary."

"But you did it last night."

"You were my loot yesterday."

"And today?"

"A companion for the road."

"You hit me and tied me down."

"If you didn't yell and try to run away, I wouldn't have done it."

"What if I try to escape again?"

"Escape? Where to?"

The horse, ejecting steam from his mouth and nostrils, suddenly stopped and took a deep sniff of the cold air – something clearly worried him. The man also started to listen.

At the very moment he took a step forward, a whistle cut through the air, and an arrow struck him in his left shoulder. If he hadn't moved, the bolt would probably have hit him in his stomach, or it would have pierced his heart. He let out a cry of pain.

At the sight of the huge arrow protruding from the man's arm, Aleksandra was overcome with horror. What was she supposed to do?

"In the name of the Father, the Son, and the Holy Spirit." Aleksandra quickly got out her cross. "Holy Mary, Mother of God, protect me."

"Jump down! Fast!" the man ordered her.

Aleksandra fearfully slid off her horse's back. While he tried to shield her, a second arrow darted over them and dug into the trunk of a large pine tree. The man tugged at the horse's bridle and laid him on the snow. The animal seemed to smell the danger because he lay on the ground without objection. The Cossack hid the girl behind the horse's body and told her not to stick her head out. He drew his saber with a wolf-shaped handle out from behind his belt.

"Damn you! Does a jigit hide in tree branches like a woman? Show yourself, devil's spawn!" he shouted.

Nasty laughter came from the trees.

Aleksandra immediately recognized this terrible voice. *The bristled barbarian!*

Yes, it was him, Berkul, whom Tacham had pierced with a saber and left in the cave, thinking that he was dead.

"If I knew that you have nine lives, like a cat, I would've immediately torn your head off, Berkul Jan."

Laughter again – this time it was much closer.

"He's no more arrows," the man whispered to Aleksandra.

"How do you know?"

"Otherwise, he would have tried to pierce me through with them long ago."

The man wanted to reassure Aleksandra, but he knew that they were in greater danger now than the night before. He was still bleeding and getting weaker; he knew he could faint at any moment. This scoundrel was probably delaying showing up until he would be completely weakened, and this would happen soon. Tacham was slipping into unconsciousness.

However, what he feared, did not happen.

With a broad smile, Berkul came out of his hiding place. As Tacham guessed, he didn't have any more arrows.

Berkul threw his empty quiver and bow from his back, then grabbed a long-curved saber. He'd wrapped the wound opened by Tacham, with a blue cloth. Tacham recognized this bloody material – it was a piece of the dress of one of the three kidnapped women, whom he'd ordered to run away that night. Whose blood was on the dress - the bristly man or the poor woman?

"I'm not going to give you this young doe," Berkul growled. "My hens turned out to be stale."

The bristly man leaned his back against the tree. When he shook the branches, snow fell on his head.

He's also weak, thought Tacham. He hadn't considered another fight. Since he'd come so far despite the wound, the others could have stayed with him. Maybe they too were hiding behind the trees. It was possible that they were the ones who shot the two arrows, and they could be waiting for Berkul's sign to send a hail of arrows at him.

The men stood there for a while, staring at each other. Tacham strained to hear even the quietest sound, to see the slightest movement.

Finally, the bristly man spoke again.

"If you didn't try to ruin our plunder by untying the women, I could've sold those hens to some stupid slave trader. But who'll pay for dead bodies?" The man laughed again, but his face was immediately distorted by a grimace of pain. He raised his hand, pointing at Aleksandra.

"Now I have to take this young doe. Give the girl to me."

Tacham noticed that the man's voice was getting quieter. This time Berkul spoke to Aleksandra.

"Come to me, chick."

Hidden behind the horse, Aleksandra could also see the sparks in the man's eyes going out.

Suddenly Berkul was shaken by a loud cough. His body shook with spasms and his face contorted in pain. He leaned against the pine tree and this disturbed its calm. In response, a portion of snow fell on him. Berkul looked up at the powder. A child's smile lit up his face for a moment. He'd stopped two of the women left by Tacham with arrows, and he'd taken everything he could from the third one and sent her to hell, too. Despite the wound, the desire for revenge led him all the way up here, but that was the end. Death reached out for the bristly rider. There was no escape.

Seeing Berkul wracked with tremors, Tacham decided to try his luck. If the others were with him, they wouldn't be saved anyway. They'll kill him and take the girl. However, if the bristly is alone... He turned and looked at Aleksandra. He made sure that the girl behind the horse was safe – yes, her small body was hidden behind the powerful beast. He turned to Berkul again.

"You wicked rascal!" he exclaimed and threw himself at him.

He managed to reach the man, though he had the impression that they were separated by a greater distance than to Mount Kaf. The man stood still. Nobody came to help him either.

"You wicked man," repeated Tacham. "Don't you know what the law of the Golden Horde says?"

Berkul was no longer able to stay on his feet. First, he dropped the saber in the snow, and after a while fell to the feet of his former companion.

"I do," he muttered. "Do not raise the saber at the begging and defenseless."

"What else?"

"Do not rape."

Aleksandra, trying to hear the man's voice as it began to turn into a whisper, came out of her hiding place and ran to Tacham Noyan.

How strange these barbarians are – they talk while fighting and dying, she thought.

"And what did you do?" Tacham also struggled to stay up on his feet.

He turned his head slowly. The hot blood dripping from his arm melted snow, drilling a red hole.

"I raised my saber at the begging and the helpless," Berkul groaned.

The other soldier also fell to his knees. Sweat beaded on his forehead. In spite of the overwhelming cold, his body was burning.

"What else?"

"I raped."

"Didn't you trample the law of the Golden Horde?"

"I trampled." Then Berkul looked at the man with dead eyes.

Tacham looked with amazement at the arrow in his arm as if he'd just noticed it. A look of joy appeared on his face.

"You will follow me too, Cossack wolf," he said, smiling with an effort. "You won't leave your companion alone on your way to hell. You are dying, too."

Hearing this, Aleksandra twitched. The feelings of joy and fear mixed in her. The death of both men meant her survival. But what will she do if Tacham dies? Where will she go? She thought about the steed. The horse will take her somewhere for sure. Suddenly, hope filled her. She felt stronger.

Tacham was wounded in the left arm, but the pain had already spread throughout his entire body. The saber became so heavy that he could no longer lift it. It was worse because he couldn't even move his hand. He wanted to remain faithful to steppe traditions though. He spread his fingers and dropped the saber with the wolf's head handle. He grabbed the bristly man with his good hand.

"And do you know how our ancestor Genghis Khan ordered us to deal with those who do not respect the law, Berkul Jan?"

The man tried unsuccessfully to open his eyes.

"I... I kn... know," he stammered in a whisper. "D... death a... waits... them."

Tacham let go of the man. His hand slowly moved to his waist. Aleksandra shook with fear at the sight of the curved dagger that the barbarian had put next to her throat last night.

There was a long silence. Berkul's breathing became faster, and his chest moved like blacksmith's bellows. Then his head fell to his chest, and he struggled to lift it with the last of his strength. He opened his semi-conscious eyes and... with unexpected agility put his hand on Tacham's bleeding shoulder.

"An order is an order," he whispered. "It must be carried out."

Aleksandra watched with amazement as Tacham Noyan lifted the wounded hand with a great effort and put it on Berkul's shoulder. One could see the pain in each wrinkle on his face. Aleksandra felt her teeth clench as if she too was feeling the pain.

The two men were now hugging each other. Their breaths merged. The horse, as if sensing the impending disaster, slowly approached his master, pulling the harness with him, sniffed him, and tried to push him away – she was sure his horse wanted to stop the man from this bloody blow. It turned his head and looked at Aleksandra. Now the steed approached the girl as if to shield her from this terrible sight. Aleksandra understood what was about to happen, but she couldn't look away from the two barbarians; regardless of everything, she wanted to see it. The animal became restless and shook his head. He stepped forward, but seeing that the girl wasn't going to move, it backed away.

This scene dragged on forever. This time the silence was interrupted by Tacham Noyan.

"You are right, Berkul Jan... Genghis Khan did not set the law for nothing."

The men crossed their gazes once more. To Aleksandra's renewed surprise, an expression of peace and joy appeared on Berkul's face. Suddenly she saw the powerless body of the bristly man fall to the ground. At the same moment, the unfortunate dagger quickly sank into his gut. Berkul's eyes widened, and a sigh escaped his lips.

"God..." The last word came from his mouth.

Both men fell on the snow. White powder poured down from the tree again and two birds jumped up from the branches... Then there was silence.

Aleksandra wasn't afraid and did not scream. Her heart had become hard like a stone. Not even eight-year-old Aleksandra had witnessed the harvest of death yesterday evening, and now she still had the judgment of Tacham over the bristly one before her eyes.

"I will also get justice if someone wrongs me," whispered the girl.

She looked at the great barbarian lying still on Berkul. She wondered if he really was dead. Even if he hadn't died, he would not have survived long in this cold with a significant wound on his arm. And, even if he's still alive, the wolves will not leave him alone. But Aleksandra Anastasia Lisowska will survive. She must survive to bring justice.

She grabbed the horse's harness and stroked its forehead with her small hand. The horse did not want to leave his master.

"From now on you will be called Hope," said Aleksandra. "I need hope so much now." Her sweet voice was like music, soft and warm.

The horse looked at Tacham Noyan, stretched out on the ground, and then at the girl stroking him on the head. Aleksandra read sadness in his eyes.

"I know," she whispered into her horse's ear. "You are sad that you must part with your master. He wasn't as bad a man as he first seemed. Look how he wrapped my feet."

Aleksandra looked again at the pieces of fur which Tacham had recently tied on her feet so that they wouldn't get cold. Life passed so quickly in wild nature. She was still only a child, but it seemed to her that she'd lived a thousand years during that one night – the same for the giant rider too. Just a moment ago he roared in full majesty, and now he was dead or was about to die. Her heart squeezed in pain. Why was she sad about the death of the barbarian who abducted her and turned her life upside down? *Come on*, she thought, *let him die*.

It took a long time, but in the end, Aleksandra managed to saddle the horse.

"Come on, Hope, take me away from here. Only you know the way to my home."

The animal first looked at his master as if he wanted to say goodbye, then casually moved forward.

At this moment something happened that Aleksandra did not expect.

"Don't leave," she heard.

Sitting on the horse's back, she turned and looked back.

Tacham Noyan was reaching his arm out to her. The snow falling from the tree began to cover him with a down quilt already.

"Don't leave me," he whispered, but Aleksandra could hear his words with her whole body as if it were a cry. "Don't leave me, child."

CHAPTER FIVE

Spring 1518

Aleksandra, dressed like a bride, stood at the window looking out at the trees. Spring in all its glory had settled in the gardens of the palace in the Crimea. Red and yellow butterflies flew everywhere, just like when she was a child, and they fluttered their wings with joy. The only difference now was Aleksandra had to look at them from the window, from behind the tulle curtain. She wanted so much to fly with them. When she looked at them, on the one hand, her heart was full of joy, and on the other, she felt deep sadness. Four winters had passed since that dark night and two years since she was handed over to the palace in the Crimea. Aleksandra was already twelve now.

She watched the branches decorated with white and purple flowers for a moment; they looked as if they were proud of their beauty as they gently swayed in the wind. Yes, the redbuds had their charm, and they transported Aleksandra to another world. Sometimes they were mysterious, sometimes full of majesty. Sometimes they were like a loud scream, and sometimes like a woman's laughter. She adored yellow flowers, but two years ago, on that hot summer day when they reached Bakhchysarai, she saw the purple and red buds of the bougainvillea and daturas. She was enchanted by the magnificence of their colors. Thanks to them, the world became more beautiful, subtler, more passionate, and compassionate. Whenever they bloomed, she felt like singing.

Aleksandra expressed her desire to Sultana Güldane, the mother of her master, the Crimean Khan, Mehmed Girej.

"If my master allows me, I would like to embroider a purple muslin handkerchief."

"Can you embroider?"

"Yes, my mother taught me."

"Does it necessarily have to be purple?"

"I like this color very much."

The elderly woman looked attentively at the girl's blue-green eyes. She liked that little smiling Ruthenian. She immediately found the purple crape and looked closely at the girl as she passed it to her.

"Purple is the color of power, glory, emperors, and empresses," Sultana Güldane told her. "I wish for your life to pass in purple."

So, from that day forward, purple became Aleksandra's color.

As soon as she was brought to the palace, the sadness in the eyes of a ten-year-old girl, in which all her painful experiences could be read, won the heart of Sultana Güldane. Although all the buyers wanted her, the man who had kidnapped her refused to sell her at all. The sultana could not understand it. Why did the man who kidnapped the girl, break the hands of those who wanted to buy her for good money? She ordered to have them watched.

One day she was following them secretly. From the very first moment, she liked the girl.

She called the man to the palace. Then he told her that he loved the abducted girl like his own daughter, and would rather die than see her in the hands of slave traders.

"But I don't want her to be a slave, jigit Noyan."

"Aleksandra is used to freedom, mountains, forests, rivers. Here she will feel like in captivity, Sultana Mother."

"For how long will you protect her? Have you considered this? The girl is growing up."

Yes, he'd often thought about that.

On that day, Sultana Mother and Tacham Noyan talked for a long time, and the next day the man handed the girl over to the people sent by the sultana.

"You sold me! You sold me!" she shouted at the man.

Just like on the first night, she punched at the giant with her small fists. She resisted the guards who came from the palace. She even scratched a few of them, but eventually, she gave up. When the carriage that was going to take her to the palace started forward, she heard Tacham Noyan call out.

"Be happy, child."

"And you be damned!"

"I have done this for you."

"Don't leave me... I didn't leave you. You don't leave me either."

The carriage drove away, but Tacham still stood in the same place. The big Tatar watched with great emotions as the girl who turned his life upside down was leaving.

Are you crying, jigit? he asked himself. *Let her go, that blabbermouth. Men don't cry. Can't you see? Dust fell into my eyes.*

He was crying. Angry waves rose up in his ossified heart while Tacham Noyan watched until the carriage disappeared.

"I will never leave you, child," he whispered, and hastily wiped away the tears that welled up in his eyes.

***

When Aleksandra arrived at the palace, her eyes were swollen from crying, and just like when she was being put in a carriage, she fought bravely when getting out. Several guardians and three servants of the Mother Sultana suffered.

For many days, she sat quietly in the corner, terrified. When someone tried to open the door, she would throw at him whatever she could find at hand. The servants told the sultana that Aleksandra prayed at nights: 'Please, our Mother, Mary, take care of me.' It was as if she was waiting for new suffering.

On one particular day, Aleksandra, absorbed in thoughts, heard hurried steps outside. When she got up and opened the door, she saw Sultana Güldane walking hand in hand with her daughter-in-law Aj Bala, surrounded by a group of servants. At the sight of Aleksandra, the veil of sadness that covered the woman's face from the day her husband Khan Mengli Girey died three years ago, briefly gave way to joy. Sharing this happiness, Aleksandra bowed with respect and greeted the old woman. As Sultana Güldane rarely left her rooms, it wasn't often possible to meet her. The woman sometimes called for Aleksandra and sank in thoughts, listening to the songs the girl sang.

In the first days after arriving at the palace, the servants warned her:

"Never speak first. You must not speak to Khan Mehmed Girey's wife or to his mother, Sultana Güldane."

"Why?"

"Because it is improper. Do not even raise your head until they speak."

"Why is that?"

"Because these are the conventions."

"What are conventions?"

"Respect, upbringing, good manners, rules."

However, when Sultana Güldane called Aleksandra to her presence for the first time, in defiance, she acted completely differently. She looked carefully at the beautiful, slant-eyed old woman.

"Why did you buy me?"

"Was it the wrong thing to do?"

Aleksandra was surprised that the woman had such a clean, gentle, and soft voice.

"I don't like it here."

"Why?" the old woman compassionately asked the ten-year-old girl who was watching her boldly.

"They beat me. They tore out my hair."

In an effort to prove that she was telling the truth, she tried to show her red, waist-length, wavy hair.

Hearing this complaint, Sultana Güldane turned her head in a determined gesture and looked at the servants. One of them fell to the ground and kissed the woman's robe.

"She did not want to wash herself, Sultana Mother," she whispered. "We could not bring her to the bathhouse. Let God..."

Sultana Güldane gestured to silence the woman, who trembled with fear.

I'll pay for it now, thought Aleksandra. But it didn't happen.

"What did they do to you?" the old woman asked in a gentle voice.

"They beat me on the hands and head, they punched me with a comb, poured boiling water on me."

Seeing that the girl's eyes were filling with tears, the woman whispered:

"Come closer. Sit by me."

Aleksandra, having taken revenge for the beating she'd received, came up with a sure step among the surprised looks of the servants, and settled herself comfortably beside the mother of the Crimean Khan. She was tall for her age, but when she sat on the large sofa, her legs did not reach the floor.

"Don't you like washing?"

"I like it very much," Aleksandra answered without thinking.

"If so, why didn't you want to go to the bathhouse?"

"I couldn't wash myself in front of others. They were looking at me."

The woman turned her head away and covered her mouth with her hand, trying to hide her laughter. Seeing that Mother Sultana's anger was over and that she was smiling, the servants also calmed down.

"Well," said Sultana Güldane. "If you like washing yourself, you will be left alone from now on. Nobody will look at you. You agree?"

Aleksandra nodded.

"Do you want to know, child, why I brought you here?"

The girl nodded.

"I had a daughter like you. If she were alive, maybe she would be similar to you. God loved her more than us and took her to himself. She wasn't even five years old. My second daughter, Aishe, is very far away, at the court of the Ottoman Sultans. She became the wife of Sultan Selim." Swallowing tears, the old woman continued. "I think that dingy chambers in caravanserais and wineries, with swarms of drunks and robbers, is not a place for beautiful young girls. They need a mother's arms. Of course, I can not replace a real mother for you, but you need someone to protect you." Saying this, the woman wanted to caress Aleksandra's silky hair, but the little girl turned her head in fear.

"My jigit will protect me," she said decidedly.

Sultana Güldane read the pain and horror in the girl's eyes.

She is not even ten yet, and who knows how much suffering and fear she has already experienced, she thought.

"I know," she said in a soft voice. "I heard that at the market, the slave traders were afraid of getting close to you because of their fear of Noyan. It was only my request that convinced him."

"He sold me!"

"Sold you?"

"He didn't sell me to slave traders, but he did to you."

Sultana Mother shook her head.

"You're wrong," she said and looked into the girl's eyes. "Tacham Noyan did not accept even a single akce for you, Aleksandra. He did not sell you. He saved you."

Aleksandra was silent.

"You can't hate Tacham Noyan, on the contrary, you should love him. Am I wrong?"

Love? It never occurred to her. She was supposed to love the barbarian who snatched her from her own home? Was it even possible?

No! Never! Something screamed in her.

Why didn't she feel hostility toward him? Was that love? Not being enemies?

"Answer me, child," the Sultana asked.

Aleksandra nodded unconsciously.

Bearing in mind that the girl may be scared again, Sultana Mother reached out and stroked her hair, this time very slowly. Aleksandra had already forgotten what it was like to feel a woman's touch. It had been four years since her mother stroked her hair. The hand of the Sultana became a mother's hand for her. She didn't want it to ever release her hair. The woman lifted Aleksandra's chin with her forefinger and turned her face toward herself. She looked into her eyes for a long time. Deep, blue-green eyes began to well up. She was impressed by how the little girl fought, biting her lips to stifle crying. She struggled to stop herself from taking her in her arms. At the same moment, Aleksandra saw compassion in the eyes of the elderly woman.

"I think you both miss each other," said Sultana Güldane. Turning to the servants, she continued, "Send a message, let jigit Noyan come and visit his daughter. They will heal their longing, and the soldier, seeing that the girl is not in any harm, will calm his heart."

Daughter? Aleksandra thought.

"He is not my father," she whispered quietly. "He kidnapped me. My dad is very far away."

That day something stirred in Aleksandra's petrified heart – a gentle beat that she had not felt for years. She trembled.

"If you don't want it, I will not send for him," said the woman.

"Let him come," she said hastily, taking the old woman's hands.

"Well, it's settled then. We'll send for jigit Noyan. But I have a condition; you will tell me about your adventures. Agreed?"

Ah, how much this hardened heart had softened.

"Yes," Aleksandra promised.

"You promise?"

"I promise. But what happened to Aishe?"

At the moment nothing could surprise Sultana Güldane more. She was impressed by the girl's attention. She told her so many different things, only mentioning Aishe once – but she remembered it. Furthermore, she waited for an answer, looking at her. The woman's thoughts traveled far, to the other shore of the Black Sea.

"It's a long story," she whispered.

"That's fine. I will listen to it. I like long stories."

"But this one is sad."

The girl pursed her lips.

"I'm used to sadness."

The stubbornness and words of the girl shook the old woman. She tried to smile.

"But this story is sad for me. You don't want me to be sad, do you?"

The girl shook her head.

"I promise you that one day I will tell you the story of Aishe. OK?" Sultana Güldane said slowly.

Aleksandra nodded.

***

That very day, Sultana Güldane took Aleksandra from the servants' rooms and moved her to her own chambers. She ordered a room to be prepared for her, and appointed a Tatar servant to take care of the girl - a servant who was also still a child herself; Merzuka was only seven years older than ten-year-old Aleksandra. While one would not call her ugly, she wasn't beautiful either, but she was very talented. From that day, Sultana Güldane – the beautiful wife of Crimean Khan Mehmed Girey – Aj Bala Hatun, and Merzuka, tried to make a real lady from this little Ruthenian who had experienced so much pain and fear, despite her young age. The girl was very clever and quickly learned everything.

Tacham Noyan visited her often. Sitting opposite each other, they talked for hours about various topics.

"Why did you leave me?" Aleksandra asked him harshly on his first visit to her.

Tacham remained silent. He kept his eyes on the girl.

"You... are growing up."

This girl, once always ready to fight anyone who stood in her way, had finally found a place where she felt safe. She quietly walked the corridors, shuffling her slippers, and she flooded the residents of the palace with a hail of questions. She even interrogated the Khan himself, Mehmed Girey. Time went by, and she ceased to be a child anymore.

***

One day, the palace filled with joyous laughter, reminiscent of a spring stream. From the day she was brought there, despite all the attention and care she was surrounded with, no one had managed to bring a smile to her lips. Now, however, she ran happily around the garden, chasing butterflies that fluttered from flower to flower. Her galligaskins and cute caftan flapped in the wind.

"This girl is crazy!" said Merzuka, who struggled to catch her breath trying to catch up with her.

Aleksandra's laughter, echoing from the walls, was so beautiful that the butterflies didn't even fly away from her. Fluttering their colorful wings, they played in her hair. Sultana Güldane, with her eyes filled with tears, stood at a window and observed the joy and happiness of the girl for a long time.

"Look, the pupil of my son Khan, mother of my grandchildren, my beautiful and good daughter in law Aj Bala," she said. "I won't see it, but you will. It was not given to my daughter Aisha, but one day this girl will win the throne and the crown. I want you to take care of her after my death. You will take care of my little girl."

The old woman removed her hand from under her daughter-in-law's arm. She looked at the girl and reached out her hands. Aleksandra ran to the woman, for the first time giving her a sincere feeling of gratitude and love. At the same moment, she realized that from the first day of her stay in the palace she admired the Crimean women during their walks. Their long dresses reached to the ground, covering their feet, and if they took small steps on their toes, they would look as if they were floating. Now Aleksandra also wore skirts that were long to the ground, but although she tried many times, she couldn't move in that way. She couldn't walk in a different way than her mother, taking the skirt in her hands and lifting it over her knees, raising her two fingers at the same time.

"Aleksandra, my lovely, I have not seen you for so many days."

They hugged. Smelling the rose-jasmine scent of the woman, Aleksandra felt long-forgotten feelings again and buried herself in the sweet warmth of the mother's arms.

***

It was freezing cold outside, and it seemed that the snow wasn't about to stop falling soon. Although the servants constantly added wood, the fireplace couldn't warm the large chamber. Sultana Güldane sat on her magnificent sofa again, and Ai Bala had covered her mother-in-law's knees with a huge skin. Aleksandra sat opposite the sofa on a thick blanket. The time had come for Sultana Güldane to hear Aleksandra's story.

"Aleksandra," said the Sultana, breaking the silence, "tell me about what you have lived through with Tacham Noyan."

The girl told her about everything. About the abduction, the stormy night, how the women who tried to escape from the barbarians died, and about hiding in a cave. Sultana Güldane and her daughter-in-law listened to her story breathless, and with their mouths wide open.

How fast time went? Two winters had already passed since that night when Tacham Noyan had whispered to her, 'Don't leave me, child.' At the mere memory of it, Aleksandra shuddered.

That day she'd jumped on the horse of the barbarian who had kidnapped her and turned her life upside down.

"Go," she'd said to the animal. "Take me away from here."

And she turned away as if she was going to leave, not hearing this begging request, and not turning back. But where to? She didn't know herself. She'll go where Hope will take her. Maybe toward a life, or maybe toward a death. But could she leave after hearing his voice? It meant he hadn't died – he was alive! Her little heart told her that if she would leave him there and ride away, she would not be any different from the barbarian who had taken her to the mountains. Even if she didn't want to turn back, Hope wouldn't allow it. As soon as the animal heard his master's voice, he stopped immediately. They turned back.

Aleksandra slid off the horse's back and went to Tacham, who lay face down on top of the body of the bristly barbarian. He stretched out his hand as if he wanted to hold on to life at all costs. His big fingers drowned in the shadows. He turned his head with a great effort, and his face, black eyebrows, and eyelashes were covered with snow. When he saw Aleksandra's feet wrapped in the fur, a smile appeared on his pained face.

"I knew you would come back," he whispered.

"What should I do?"

"Don't leave me!"

"I won't."

"Take me away from here."

Aleksandra looked around helplessly and knelt beside the man.

"I'm small, and you're huge. I can't lift you up."

A smile appeared on the man's face again.

"I'll tell you what to do. I'll help you."

The words came out of his mouth with difficulty. When he spoke, his face grimaced with pain.

"You have to put me on Storm."

"His name is Hope now," Aleksandra said.

Tacham Noyan smiled broadly.

"Fine, let it be so. You must put me on Hope. There is another cave in the area. We will go there."

She watched as he crawled to the nearest tree, leaving a bloody trail on the snow. Moaning in pain, he stood up, holding the rough trunk for his support. She watched with admiration as Hope approached his master and knelt down to take him on his back, and how the giant man staggered two steps forward, then, biting his lips in pain, climbed to the saddle.

Sitting on the horse's back, he breathed out deeply.

"Pass me the saber," he slowly spoke to the girl.

The weapon with a wolf-shaped handle was so heavy that she had to raise it with both hands.

"Now you, get on."

After several unsuccessful attempts, Aleksandra finally settled in front of Tacham on the horse's back.

"Go, Storm," the giant groaned.

The girl turned her head and looked at him with relentless eyes.

"Go, Hope. Take us away from here," he corrected himself.

The animal moved forward with effort. Aleksandra thought the man was inhaling the smell of her hair. Trying to stop from screaming, she turned quickly, only to discover that it wasn't what she thought – she saw the tears flowing from the man's eyes! The barbarian was crying, and he was crying aloud.

Is he crying in pain? she wondered. *Or maybe the cause of his tears was different?*

"You did not tell us what happened in the cave the night they kidnapped you," Sultana Güldane said suddenly.

Aleksandra was ashamed. She didn't want to talk about it.

"What happened?"

The girl looked ahead, moving her finger along the embroidery of her straitjacket.

"Why did you fall silent, child?" Sultana Mother said. "Tell us. You must keep your word."

"I don't want to talk about it."

"Did they do something even worse to you in the cave?"

The elderly woman stole a glance at her daughter-in-law. Ai Bala answered her gaze with a questioning gaze. *What worse can be done to such a small girl?* After a moment she understood the woman's doubts. A chill ran through her spine... *It's impossible*, she thought. *Such a little girl? No, it's out of the question*. It was true that the robbers' lives passed in the mountains. They lived on war spoils. There was no love in their lives, there were no women, but there was a law. It was allowed to take away wealth, but not virtue or honor. Besides, Aleksandra was still a little child.

She stroked the girl's bowed head with compassion.

"Tell us, honey. You are safe now. Don't be afraid. Let us know the whole truth so those who deserve it could be punished."

"Those who were at fault, have already received what they deserved."

There was something in the girl's eyes that the women couldn't understand and frightened them at the same time.

"How come? Did you...?"

The girl shook her head and told in detail what had happened that night in the cave. When she told them how the bristly man had attacked her, the words could barely pass her throat. Her cheeks burned. At her words: "He pulled up my skirt and touched me here," both women in shame, fear, and excitement gave a short cry: "My God! My God, did he...?" However, when they heard that Tacham Noyan got to him, snatched the man from her, and threw him against the wall, they felt a great relief. Real life was so different from the one they'd led.

Sultana Güldane also felt the bitter taste of captivity, because her husband, Mengli Girey, broke the promise given to the Ottoman Sultan Bayezid, and did not send troops – so the sultan had taken them from the Crimean Khanate to Istanbul as hostages.

"Blood was shed, but I did get something out of this," she said.

Admittedly, she had a house, maids, and servants at her disposal, but it was captivity all the same. If they were not in the Ottomans' captivity, would she give Aishe to Selim?

"Ah, my Aishe..." she sighed wistfully. "Who knows what she has experienced so far?" *And what else awaits her?*

Hearing that Tacham Noyan saved Aleksandra from rape, Ai Bala could not resist. She clapped her hands, letting out a cry. Meanwhile, Sultana Mother sank in her thoughts. She took the girl's hand.

"You must have been very scared."

"Yes, I was scared."

"Divine judgments are unknown. The man who once snatched this unfortunate chick from the nest now protects her like a father. Tell me, honey, what happened next."

Aleksandra looked at the women.

"He killed those three men. He actually killed two, the third one was still alive. He found us later."

Both women clung to each other and waited for the rest of the story with a mix of curiosity and excitement. The maids also trembled and cringed in their places, maybe because the room was still chilly, or because of Aleksandra's story.

Suddenly Aleksandra quickly cut the air with her hand.

"Bzzz, an arrow dashed by and stuck in his arm," she said intensely.

"What happened next? What was next?"

The girl was focused again. Her child's memories carried her back to that place. She drew marks on the silk upholstery of the sofa with her forefinger.

"What was next? What was next?" Aj Bala Hatun asked.

Aleksandra shrugged.

Sultana Mother, noticing that this story completely absorbed the girl, slowly took her hand and stroked it.

"What happened then, child?"

Aleksandra shrugged again.

"Did Tacham Noyan kill him?"

"How could he do it with a huge arrow stuck in his shoulder?"

The women trembled. How could such a little girl talk about death and killing with such calmness? While the women exchanged glances with horror, Aleksandra rose from her seat. Pretending to pull a dagger from behind a belt, she threw herself on her knees and played out with awkward movements, the scene in which Tacham Noyan's dagger sank in the bristly man's body.

The women did not know whether they should laugh or cry at the sight of this performance. That was death. If one looked too often into its eyes, even a child became accustomed to it. Sooner or later, it just became a game.

"Thank God, he died in the end. Unfaithful..." emotional, Sultana Güldane whispered unknowingly.

"And what about the other one, jigit Noyan? What happened to him? Was he wounded too?" her daughter-in-law kept asking.

Aleksandra, still kneeling on the floor, just like Tacham Noyan who'd fallen into the snow, dropped to the floor face-down and remained motionless.

The women watched the lying girl breathlessly. After a long wait, the old woman whispered:

"He died?"

For a moment, Aleksandra did not answer. Then she slowly raised her head and looked at the women who clang to each other.

"He'd collapsed." Then, to the great surprise of Sultana Güldane and Aj Bala, she jumped up from the floor and cried with joy: "Are we going to play the shadow theater?"

"A shadow theater?"

"Yes, shadow theater. Birds, butterflies, wolves, and other creatures. I can also do priest Vassiliy... My mother taught me..."

Her gaze was full of happiness and joy as if she had not even experienced these horrible memories anew just a moment ago.

"Please, please." She jumped around them and danced.

That's how a child's joy saved the old woman and her daughter-in-law from horrors of the story. They were in the palace; they did not lack for anything. They were not afraid of either robbers or that they would fall victim to rape. Fate was so kind to some, while to others it showed its scariest face. Some laughed and enjoyed themselves, others experienced the greatest tragedies. How much pain and suffering were there in this world, and how little happiness. How is this all arranged?

Aj Bala Hatun was a deeply religious Muslim woman, but she couldn't resist the question: *God, why did you give so much pain for this child? What was her fault?* She tried to cheer herself up with the thought that since she had survived hell on earth, a paradise would wait for her after her death. This girl had been balancing on the brink of death. She'd been a witness to bloody battles, persecuted by savages, and she'd seen more dead bodies than springs in her life.

The daughter-in-law wanted to share this childish joy.

"I've never heard of playing shadow theater, Aleksandra."

"It is wonderful. My mother taught me."

Sultana Mother also joined them, trying to straighten her sore back.

"Where will we make this shadow theater?"

"Here."

"Here?"

"Of course, but first we will move these candles."

She did as she said. She set the candles on the table correctly. She checked everything and observed where the other women were carefully.

"Now shut your eyes and don't open them until I tell you. Otherwise, you will ruin the fun."

The daughter-in-law smiled, and the mother-in-law let out a sigh: "Ah, sweet child," pursing her lips in a mock complaint, and then both did what Aleksandra had asked them.

The girl, giving a particular shape to her hands and fingers, placed them in front of the candles and watched the shadow appearing on the wall.

"Open your eyes!" she shouted with excitement. "Look, a butterfly!"

The women watched with admiration at a butterfly moving its wings.

"A wolf."

Now a hungry wolf appeared on the wall. He opened his mouth and moved his ears.

"And that's father Vassiliy," Aleksandra laughed.

Now the shadow of a long-bearded man with big ears was walking along the wall.

That night the whole palace was filled with Aleksandra's joyful laughter. Accompanying her were short, shy, delighted cries of Mother Sultana and Aj Bala Hatun.

CHAPTER SIX

One night, Sultana Güldane could be heard crying out: "I can't believe it!" The sultana couldn't understand how Tacham Noyan wanted a little child to take an arrow out of his shoulder. It was incredible that she could deal with such a difficult and bloody task, when so very young.

Moving her tiny hands across the purple silk embroidered with various flowers according to what women taught her, Aleksandra was continuing her tale.

Embroidering was just one of the activities she learned in Bakhchysarai. She was also slowly beginning to speak Tatar and learning how a lady of the court should sit and talk. She also took music lessons from a stout matron, learning to play the oud and kanun stringed instruments. Whenever the woman entered the room with the oud in her hands, Aleksandra could barely contain her laughter – because every time she wondered what was bigger – the woman's stomach or the oud box. If only matron Nurben Kalfa would let her, she'd take the oud in her hands and try to play beautiful Volga chants, or pluck the kanun's strings, trying to recreate the love songs that the boys from her village played on balalaikas. But the woman insisted on only playing exercises and scales. Fortunately, she had evenings for herself. A few months after she'd begun to take music lessons, one could hear simple but touching melodies from Aleksandra's room every evening. With her delightful, beautiful voice, Aleksandra sang Ural songs:

> *The hunters told Katja's mother*
> *that they haven't seen her daughter anywhere.*
> *Now the waters of our Volga*
> *will flow alone.*
> *Tell me big, snow-capped,*
> *ice-bound peaks,*
> *how are flowers to open*
> *in this world without Dunya?*

"How could he ask you to do this?" Sultana Güldane asked that evening. One could feel the anger, disbelief, fear, and the will to punish in her voice.

Aleksandra didn't know what to answer to that. She couldn't say, 'There was no other way.' She wanted to explain, 'If I didn't do it, he would surely die,' but she gave up. She finally answered in a manner as stupid as the question – she just shrugged.

In addition to lamps and candles, the room of the sultana's daughter-in-law was illuminated by the flames of two large logs burning in the fireplace. Aj Bala Hatun was also embroidering, but she used a wheel. She'd dip the needle in the fabric with her skillful fingers and pull the thread at the end, and then do the same in the other direction. She was very focused on her work.

"He wanted you to take the arrow out of his arm? Really?"

"Yes."

"But you didn't do it?"

"I did."

"What? You didn't have enough strength to get that arrow out."

"I pulled it out." Aleksandra's voice was firm. "And he helped me," she murmured.

The faces of the women were frightened again.

"'Listen to me. We'll both grab the arrow. Pull it out slowly. Do not wave your hand left and right. Pull slowly,' he'd said. 'If you move the arrow, the tip will break and stay inside. If it breaks, there will be no help,'" Aleksandra reported with a tremor in her voice, re-experiencing the moment.

Sultana mother watched the girl carefully.

"Well, child. And didn't you think about breaking the arrow?"

"I did," Aleksandra said without thinking.

"Then why didn't you do it?" her daughter-in-law asked, without taking her eyes off her handiwork.

"Then we would both die." She remembered with horror the howling of the wolves coming up to the entrance of the cave. "It was lots of snow, and it was very cold outside. There were also lots of hungry wolves and maybe bears, too; big, hungry bears.

"You were little. How did you find that much strength in yourself?"

Strength? In fact, how did she manage to get the arrow stuck in his body out?

Tacham Noyan's face, wet with sweat, stood before her eyes. *Press your feet against my chest*, his voice echoed in her ears again. She could hear that horrible sound again, when the flat, sharp arrowhead tugged at the muscles and nerves, sliding across the bones.

"I found it," she said, greedily plunging the needle into the silk fabric. "I pulled it out slowly. Very slowly. He didn't even shout, though I knew it hurt him a lot."

This time, she remembered how he had clenched his teeth in pain, and that his suffering had made her feel happy. *How was that possible?* she suddenly thought. *How... while helping someone who was face to face with death, could I've felt joy over his suffering? How was it possible that two conflicting feelings could be born in one heart?*

Then a more important question arose in her head: *How can a person get so savage in just a day and a half?*

When the man fainted in pain, Aleksandra had taken out her cross and begun to pray in her mind: *Holy Mary, help us both. Jesus, our Father, help me, and this unbeliever. Do not punish him for abducting me. Don't let him die. At least not now. Please... God, for the sake of me, let him live.*

While Aleksandra was experiencing these terrible moments again, she heard Aj Bala Hatun speak.

"What happened when you took the arrow out?" she asked thoughtlessly, opening her dark brown eyes wide. The woman put the needlework aside and looked at the girl carefully.

"Nothing." She shrugged. "Black blood spurted from the wound." *And when we managed to take out the arrow that had torn his body, he'd whispered, 'My God,'* she remembered; for Aleksandra, that whisper had echoed through her like a scream. "Black blood was flowing all the time. It didn't stop. He told me then..."

"What?"

This time the question of Aj Bala upset her mother-in-law.

"What could he say, child? He probably thanked her."

Aleksandra clicked her tongue on the palate and shook her head.

"He wanted me to heat his dagger and press it to the wound."

"That's too much!" Aj Bala exclaimed. "Such a little girl. What was this man thinking? It's like torture. How could you do something so horrible? It was his wound – he should've burnt it himself."

"He couldn't do it," Aleksandra cut her short. Her thoughts flashed back to the cave again, seeing Tacham Noyan still falling in and out of consciousness, and her fear back then that she was losing her senses, fearing that the man would die.

Open your eyes, she'd begged. *'Don't die! Don't die! He can't die now! Holy Mary, please, help him!'*

"What did you do, child?" The older woman's question called her back to reality.

"I begged God."

"God listened to the prayers of a little girl. Your prayers saved you and jigit Noyan."

Aleksandra re-lived that moment, and her tears dripped onto the silk fabric. She looked at the two women from behind her wet eyelashes.

"I put the dagger in the fire and heated the blade until it was red. I was shaking with fear. Then I turned and looked at him. His face was chalk-white, and his eyes were glassy. I don't know if he saw me or not, but his wound was still bleeding. I approached him and knelt down. He stared at me. He moved his lips, saying something, but I couldn't hear it, so I brought my ear to his lips and listened to his whisper. Only then did I understand him."

"What did he say?"

Aleksandra swallowed.

"'Forgive me. Fff-or-g-give m-me', he moaned, and his voice was breaking."

"What did you say?"

"Nothing."

What could she say? The iron of the dagger she had raised was still glowing with heat. Aleksandra thought that a smile brightened Tacham Noyan's face.

"I mumbled something like, 'you'll suffer a lot, again,' to him. I really said those silly words in the hope that he'd tell me: 'In that case, stop it. Don't do it.' But he didn't. So, then I whispered in his ear: "Just don't die. Hold on.""

Aleksandra didn't know how to tell the man balancing on the edge of life and death, that she'd forgiven him. But he probably understood that. When she brought the red-hot dagger close to the wound, she'd been filled with horror, but a weak smile appeared on the man's face.

She had no idea that while he writhed in pain, the man had pondered that unfortunate night when he'd invaded her room. He remembered how he froze when he saw that the girl had woken up terrified. At first, he wanted to turn around and leave, he hadn't intended to take her away. But what would it change? If it weren't for him, those merciless and cruel men would have abducted her. No human feelings were left in their stone-hard hearts. Maybe God himself put him in Aleksandra's way as her savior...? Who knows?

Suddenly there was a core-piercing roar, and Aleksandra smelled the awful smell of charred meat – she sensed it with her whole body. Tacham Noyan shouting echoed in her ears:

"Oh, mother! Oh, mother!" he'd yelled.

The man closed the girl's tiny wrist in an iron grip, fearing that Aleksandra would take the dagger away too soon in pity, and he pressed it firmly to the wound. He devoted all his remaining strength to do it. After a moment, his fingers relaxed on her wrist, and his arm dropped. He looked pitiful. Aleksandra cried, taking the glowing blade away from the wound – she'd cried out of terror, disgust, and fear of making a mistake. But above all, she'd cried because she'd just given so much pain to another human. She felt the man's suffering with all her heart. She had the impression that it was her body she was burning with a hot iron.

Later she told the women who listened to her story with bated breath, how she made a dressing from her apron. She told them about dressing the wound and sitting in beside him for hours, feeling very scared.

"Finally, I fell asleep," she said slowly. "I jumped in fear when after some time I felt a touch on my hand. Tacham Noyan was staring at me."

He was exhausted. Suddenly, however, a shy, sympathetic smile appeared in his eyes. The girl didn't know whether the man's great face had brightened, or if he paled because of the loss of a large amount of blood. But she certainly understood that he was grinning at her with gratitude.

"'Forgive me, child. Ff-for-g-give m-me,' I heard him say again."

CHAPTER SEVEN

Time passed, and Aleksandra turned from a little girl into a young lady. First, her breasts began to grow. She was so ashamed of this she even tried to hide them – but she failed, and so gave up after a while.

When she saw the blood between her legs for the first time, she froze in fear, and then she ran to Merzuka, terrified.

"I'm dying!" she started to scream. "Run for the medic. Let the Sultana Mother know."

Contrary to her expectations, Merzuka was calm.

"Calm down, crazy girl. Say slowly what happened."

Listening to Aleksandra, the Tatar girl closed her narrow eyes in laughter.

"God bless you!" she shouted and embraced Aleksandra by the neck. "You're not dying; you're just becoming a woman."

The first one who found it out from Merzuka was Aj Bala Hatun. She ran to her mother-in-law.

"Aleksandra became a woman!"

The very old Sultana Güldane was combing her thin hair with an ivory comb, which she'd received as a gift from her husband. First, joy appeared on her face, but it immediately gave way to worry.

"Now our task will be more difficult, dear daughter," she said in a trembling voice. She took Aj Bala's hands. "I am here today, but I will not be here tomorrow. My visit to this world is coming to an end. Know that even in the future I will be watching the girl closely. She blossoms with each passing day. You must protect her. Although he is my son, save her even from your own husband; God entrusted her to me, and now I entrust her to you, Aj Bala."

The woman looked into her mother-in-law's eyes, now eighty-years-old already.

"Mother," she began slowly. "Do you know something, or did you see anything, that makes you ask me to protect Aleksandra from my husband?"

"Khan Mehmed Girey's father sucked the righteousness with his mother's milk. Me too. I also taught it to my son and my daughter, Aishe, who became the odalisque of the Ottomans Khan – Selim. Your husband considers only you as his wife, and only the prince of Moscow, Ivan, who thinks he has freed himself from the shadow of the Golden Horde, as an enemy."

These words calmed her daughter-in-law.

"But Aleksandra is completely different," the old lady continued. "We both know how much she suffered. Even at her very young age, she's seen more suffering than me, an old woman. What she's experienced, has shaped her strong will, but it has cooled her heart. She has been here for three years – safe and peaceful. After she had to hide in caves and caverns, after the fear she experienced in seedy caravanserais, she's finally found a quiet place. She doesn't need to worry about hunger, either. Put yourself in her place – would you like to lose everything you have now and go back to those days?"

Ai Bala shook her head.

"She doesn't want to either. She will do everything to avoid losing it. Everything."

The old woman stopped. She saw the worry hidden in her daughter in law's eyes.

"You must protect Aleksandra from everyone. Even from herself."

***

The following day, Sultana Güldane called Tacham Noyan to give him the news.

Thanks to the Sultana Mother, the man had been able to give up his robber's life and had secured a job in the palace stables. Both the horse, whom Aleksandra called Hope and he called Storm, and the jigit Noyan, were happy with their new lives. They no longer had to fight for survival, and they were both near Aleksandra, whom they loved very much. Tacham saw the girl often, and although they didn't talk much, they were happy knowing that they both were doing well. Aleksandra now rode horses as well as the Tatar girls too. She'd ride on Hope and run with the wind through the steppes, as if they were a unified whole – they only differed in that she had red hair, and he had a white mane.

There was an unnamed, secret agreement between her and Tacham Noyan – neither of them talked about the past. They never mention the night when Aleksandra was kidnapped, about what had happened in the cave, and about how the girl pulled the arrow from the man's shoulder, saving his life. However, whenever they met, they both remembered each day of these two difficult, shared years...

***

A week passed before Tacham Noyan was able to get on his feet. During this time, they tried to quell their hunger with the dried meat from the horse's packs. In the first days, the Aleksandra would put small pieces in Tacham's mouth, and he'd chew them for a long time as if they were never going to end. He advised her to do the same.

"Chew them for a long time. You won't feel so hungry."

At first, Aleksandra didn't want to eat the meat that was as hard as a leather sole but eventually she tried to when she had no other choice – but she could hardly swallow it. So, she did as Tacham taught her.

One morning, when she woke up, Tacham and Hope were nowhere to be found. Aleksandra panicked. Did the man leave her to a fate that only saw death? How could he do something like that?

Why not? she thought. *The infidel barbarian was capable of anything. I should have broken the arrow in his wound.*

But her worries were unfounded. Tacham returned to the cave with a huge hare, and they had a real feast. Aleksandra ate with such appetite that her ears shook, and then she laughed for the first time. It seemed like years had passed since she'd heard her own laughter. Then she noticed that the man was watching her closely.

"Why are you looking at me like that?" she asked.

"I admire your smile. You look well with it. I wish you to always be smiling."

Aleksandra remembered that very well.

The next day they set off on their way. It was cold but sunny, and by evening they'd arrived at a caravanserai. They headed straight for the room rented by Tacham. The owner of the caravanserai was fat and bald, and even Aleksandra could see the evil lurking in his eyes.

Fortunately, nothing happened that night, and even though the bed was dirty, to Aleksandra, it seemed so comfortable that as soon as she put her head on the pillow, the color of which was difficult to recognize under the layers of dirt and grease, she fell into a deep sleep. In the morning they went downstairs. They filled their stomachs with cheese and bread, hard as a stone, brought to them by the lazy wife of the host. They shared a bowl of buffalo milk.

It didn't take long for the landlord to sit down next to Tacham. His greedy eyes were shifty, and he didn't take his eyes off the girl, not even for a moment.

"Where did you find this youngster, my jigit?"

Tacham responded with a menacing snarl.

"Easy. She must be in your way. If you want, you can sell her to me and go on your way."

"She's not for sale."

"I'll give you whole three akce for her."

"She's not for sale."

"Those who say you're a tough haggler, are right."

"What do you think, woman?" The landlord said to his wife. "Shall we give five akce for this weakling?"

The landlord's ugly wife pursed her lips.

"What do I care? It's your money. Just don't come to me if you can't find a fool at the market that will buy her from you."

The man reached for a pouch hidden behind his belt. He untied it and put his fingers inside.

"What is the child supposed to do by the side of a jigit plundering villages? I will do him a favor. You'll see, one day he'll reward me for my goodness." Then the landlord smiled boldly, his thick tongue appearing and disappearing between his teeth, most of which were missing. "She is of no use for me, but let it be my loss."

He put five coins on the table, watching each coin closely. He tried to move them towards Tacham Noyan, but he failed. Tacham clenched his hand onto the man's hairy wrist with lightning speed and pushed him away together with the money.

"I told you she is not for sale!" he roared.

Stepping back in fear, the man tried to free his hand from Tacham's grip.

"OK, you got it, ten akce!" he finally moaned. But seeing the sparks in the eyes of the guest, he gave up. "Fine. Fine, what can I do? You don't want to sell, that's fine. The ten akce will stay in my pocket."

Aleksandra watched as he pulled his wrist away with difficulty from Tacham Noyan's grip, rubbed it, and cursed under his breath.

In the evening they ate dinner sitting by the fireplace. The room was filled with men with faces as ugly as the night. One could find all kind of characters at the tables.

Aleksandra noticed out of the corner of her eye that the fat, bald landlord talked behind a column to an equally ugly man, gesturing vigorously. His nasty wife carried wine around the room. There was drunk laughter every now, and then and the woman would lean coquettishly over the tables. Men who had not seen a woman for months drooled at the sight of the fat, dirty, dwarf landlady with a huge bust. They patted her on her huge buttocks and stroked her calves. In answer to these taunts, the woman laughed disgustingly. Who knows with which of these savages she would land in bed with, filling her husband's purse?

Tacham Noyan didn't want Aleksandra to witness this show of animal lust any longer. While leaving for their room, they both felt the eyes of the men sitting at the table, follow them. As Aleksandra settled down to sleep, she saw Tacham set a chair by the door and sit down on it; it seemed that he did not trust those suspicious characters' downstairs either.

Aleksandra quickly fell asleep, listening to the whistling of the wind between the wooden shutters.

She was awakened by Tacham Noyan's whisper:

"Don't move and be quiet." He put his forefinger to his lips.

Death knocked at their door again. Someone was in the corridor and Aleksandra could also hear the strange noises. The people outside tip-toed, trying not to be heard – however, they couldn't control the rustle of their clothes and the creaking of the floor.

Tacham Noyan silently returned to the door. First, a cold flash of a saber ending with an eagle-shaped hilt appeared in the darkness, and then Aleksandra caught a glimpse of the familiar dagger.

When the door began to slowly open, Aleksandra's heart pounded like crazy. She saw two enormous, hooded shadows in the trembling candlelight. Noyan stood behind the door as the shadows got closer. Aleksandra closed her eyes tightly. A whole orchestra was now playing in her heart. *Why is the barbarian hiding behind the door? Let him come out and catch those bandits*, she thought. Then she understood exactly what he was doing right now – Aleksandra was the bait. Using her as a lure, Tacham Noyan lured those two uninvited guests into a deadly trap.

As the men, tip-toed closer and closer, Aleksandra noticed that they had a large sheet in their hands. They were already leaning over her, about to cover her head, when Tacham closed the door with a loud bang.

"Ah, you, evil's spawn!" he shouted loudly as he jumped at the men.

The walls shook. Aleksandra didn't know whether the reason for this was due to the force with which the door slammed, falling off the hinges, or because of the thunderous cry that came from Tacham. First, he cracked the skull of the first man, and then, in another flash, he stabbed the other man with the dagger. Among the blood gushing in all directions, Aleksandra saw a third shadow by the door.

"Behind you!" she cried out at the top of her lungs.

Tacham Noyan, just like on the first night in the cave, quickly turned on his heel. With the saber in his extended hand, he cut the belly of the man behind him. Everything was over in the blink of an eye. Leaving three corpses behind, Tacham took Aleksandra by the hand and picked her up. Her face was smeared with blood, so he poured some water from a broken jug and washed it. He stuck the bloody dagger behind his belt. Then, he rushed into the corridor, holding the saber in one hand, and Aleksandra in the other. He moved so fast that she had to run to keep up with him.

Tacham suddenly stopped by the door at the top of the stairs, and Aleksandra saw the same wild flash in the giant's eyes as she did on the first night. She was breathing very quickly, her chest moving like bellows. Tacham forced the door open with his arm, and a horrible stench struck their nostrils. Tacham pushed Aleksandra aside and headed inside.

The landlord was sitting on a dirty bed in the room, with his eyes wide open in horror. His fat, hideous wife tried to reach for the dagger lying next to her. With one blow, Tacham threw the woman to the other end of the room, then he put the saber next to the man's neck.

"You owe me ten akce, you pig."

Even while standing by the door, Aleksandra noticed that the landlord's face had become chalk-white.

"Why d-did-didn't you s-s-sell me..."

"Silence, you pig!" Tacham roared, pressing the blade harder. "It's the payment for the blood. Look what condition my daughter is in because of the three devils that you sent at us."

The man's face twisted in a grimace of pain. The red mark on his neck, where the blade had been applied, grew bigger and bigger. While the landlord tried to sneak his hand under the pillow, Tacham reached for the dirty pouch and called Aleksandra over. He laid ten akce in her hand and threw the purse in the man's face.

"Now you also owe me your life, cowardly pig," he said. "The time will come that I will take it from you, too."

It was dawning when they left the Black Caravanserai in Sarok. Hope's mane flew with the wind, as they headed south.

CHAPTER EIGHT

On the lonely nights in the Crimean palace, the word *daughter* echoed in Aleksandra's head. Why would this wild man who had kidnapped her – or should she rather call him her savior – this killing machine who initiated fights when a slave trader looked at her, call her a 'daughter?'

"Honey, who would believe that such a dark highlander with black eyes, and raven-black eyebrows, be the father of such a beautiful, red-haired, blue-eyed girl like you?" Sultana Güldane said one night, as she stroked Aleksandra's hair and listened to more of her story.

"I don't know," she replied, spreading her little hands and playing with her fingers.

***

And it was true – nobody believed it. In every village they visited, in every settlement, as well as in every caravanserai, they were in trouble. Tacham Noyan was constantly forced to reach for his dagger. It didn't matter where it was; it even happened in the middle of a village.

Actually, that particular village had appealed to Aleksandra. There were two-story houses cut by narrow, winding streets, and at one place, a tall, slender tower rose to the sky between the houses.

"What is that?"

"A minaret."

"Minaret? What is a minaret for?"

"To call Muslims for prayer."

"How do they call them?"

"One person goes up the minaret. Do you see that protrusion? He calls people from there."

While Aleksandra wondered if it was dangerous to climb so high, Tacham Noyan held her hand tightly and walked, carefully looking around.

There was a great deal of buzz at the village market. Colorful fabrics, a large variety of colorful spices that she'd never seen before, copper dishes, beads, sabers, knives, shields, and anything else that could come to mind were spread out on the tables, sheltered with awnings to protect against rain and sun. Everyone was saying something, everyone was trying to buy the best fabric, or the most aromatic herbs, and anything else that could be useful.

Suddenly Aleksandra stopped. In the corner of the bazaar stood a man in a big yellow turban, putting burning torches in his mouth, swallowing fire and breathing out flames. Onlookers gathered around and watched the show with admiration. Some people threw money onto a dirty piece of fabric lying on the ground.

"He won't burn his mouth?"

"I tried it once and scorched myself."

"You tried?"

"Aha," Tacham nodded. "I was a child then. Even before I put it in my mouth, the flame burned my lips. But it doesn't burn him – he has a secret, but he will not reveal it to anyone."

Aleksandra giggled, trying to imagine how such a giant man burns his lips, trying to swallow the fire.

For a moment they stood among the crowd and admired the fire-eaters. Then the man put the torches down and grabbed a big sword. He picked it up.

"And now I will swallow this sword!" he exclaimed.

Cries of disbelief could be heard throughout the crowd.

This is too much, Aleksandra thought. *One can't swallow such a great sword.*

"You won't do it!" she cried out.

The fire-eater turned around, searching in the crowd for the owner of the thin voice. Several people standing in the front also turned around and looked at them.

The fire-eater was already standing by them.

"You don't believe me, kid?"

"I don't. You won't swallow it," Aleksandra answered boldly.

A circle formed around them. Several men nodded, supporting the girl. Others were sharing smiles and nudging each other with their elbows.

"Why wouldn't I swallow it?"

"Because the sword will cut your tongue and throat."

"In that case," said the fire-eater. "Let the giant who holds you by the hand throw a few coppers here. I'll show you then."

Aleksandra raised her head and looked at Tacham Noyan. For the first time, she saw joyous flashes dancing in his eyes. Without letting go of her hand, he reached into his belt and tossed two coppers into the bundle in front of the man.

"I have to swallow a big sword for two coppers?" he laughed insolently. "A man as big like an elephant, but wears a snake in his pocket. Can't you find a few more coppers, jigit? Convince me to show this weakling how I swallow the sword."

A few more coins fell into the bundle, accompanied by laughter among the audience.

The man raised the sword in concentration, holding the blade. He had it exactly at the height of his mouth. At first, Aleksandra looked at him boldly: *He won't do it anyway*, she thought. However, when the sword slowly began to sink into the man's mouth, Aleksandra's eyes widened in amazement. It was unbelievable. She waited in vain for the blood to flow. In the end, the whole blade disappeared. As the crowd applauded, the man slowly pulled his sword out and greeted Aleksandra.

"You believe it now, redhead?"

Although the fire-eater had already gone, the crowd around them didn't thin out, and a group of men surrounded them. Tacham Noyan, holding Aleksandra, wanted to leave immediately but it was too late. A huge man stood in their way.

"Wait, jigit. Why this rush? Let's talk."

"I don't know you, and you don't know me. We have nothing to talk about."

Tacham wanted to clear his way out by pushing the man away. However, the man standing nearby stopped the Cossack soldier and grabbed his hand. Behind them, were three other characters with menacing faces.

"I think we have. Who is this girl? What is she doing here?"

"That's my daughter."

"Look at this," the man laughed, peering over his shoulder at the people standing behind him. "Black-haired man has a red-haired daughter."

The men around him laughed disgustingly. Aleksandra felt Tacham's muscles tighten, and hold onto her stronger. The individual who crossed their path turned around again and looked at him.

"The lie of this jigit is as big as himself," he said to the others, not taking his eyes off Noyan. "What do we do with liars?"

"We cut out their tongue and hand it over to them."

"No, my dear," the man said. "This pertains to hardened liars. I think we can work something out." He took a step forward. "You heard the law. If you like your tongue, leave the girl, and go," he said.

The nasty man stretched out his hand to grab Aleksandra, who now hid behind Tacham Noyan and listened to the conversation in horror. That was enough for Tacham. The Cossack soldier's huge fist hit the man like lightning. The guy fell on his back as if a heavy rock had hit him in the head. In the next moment, Tacham had armed himself with the dagger with the wolf's head handle and started to fight with the other three men pressing against him with knives and daggers.

"Get out of here, devil's bastards!"

The fight didn't last long. One of the men splattered with blood and fell limply on the ground.

"We are finished!" lamented the unfortunate individual who had shouted to cut out the liar's tongue, as he tried to run away.

The last one, after Tacham hit him, fell to his knees next to the man already laying on the ground, and begged for mercy.

***

It was always the same. A huge man wandering with a little girl caught the attention of all slave traders, and they tried everything to take away this tasty morsel from the highlander. And each time, they had to deal with Tacham's dagger. They left behind so many corpses that eventually they had to stay away from towns and villages. Forests and mountains became their place. Some people were more dangerous than hungry wolves or bears.

Aleksandra thought that wherever she went, she brought death. Worse, the constant bloodshed became something normal to her. She no longer had any fear or compassion in her for the dying. During one of the fights, Tacham gave her a small dagger.

"Take it, defend yourself."

She didn't even know what happened to the man she'd stabbed with that dagger. Anyway, what did it matter? She survived. Only this counted – to survive, and not to sympathize. It was important to be strong and courageous, not weak, and timid.

One day, Aleksandra asked unexpectedly:

"Why won't you leave me? Take me to my village, to my mom. You'll become free, and I'll be free. The Blessed Virgin will reward you."

Tacham Noyan looked at the girl for a long time and said nothing. Aleksandra didn't ask him to leave her again.

Suddenly something changed between them. They had long forgotten that one of them was a hunted animal and the other a hunter. These words reminded them of what they had tried to forget – as if it had never happened. They came face to face with the truth. From then on, they didn't talk as often as they used to.

***

When the spring flowers began to bloom, Tacham took a long time to prepare the horse. He even changed his horseshoes. Sitting comfortably on the horse's back, Aleksandra dug her heels into the sides of the animal. Four days and four nights passed. They rode through the dark forests, and over the rocky peaks covered with remnants of snow. They crossed the wild mountain rivers. On the fifth day, when the sun was almost at its zenith, the meadows and trees began to seem familiar to Aleksandra. Suddenly she saw butterflies – flapping colorful wings as they flew from flower to flower.

The girl let out a cry of joy. She turned to the man behind her and, from joy combined with gratitude, gave him a happy kiss. It meant that the barbarian was taking her home. Filled with emotion, she slipped off her horse's back and chased after the butterflies.

"Butterflies, beautiful butterflies…" Out of joy, she began to sing invented songs.

She suddenly stopped. She felt that something was wrong. Something was missing, and it hurt her like a dagger's blade. Of course, Aleksandra knew what the difference was already.

The butterflies! In the past, they would fly around her. They batted their colorful wings over her head and danced as if to say, 'Come on! Catch us!' But now they were all running away. Then she realized she didn't hear birds singing. They also escaped from there.

She looked around sadly. The wheat was just beginning to sprout, but the barley ears were nowhere to be seen either. No one had done the sowing this year? She knelt and touched the soil. It was black, hard, and dry. Apparently, nobody was taking care of it! Nor was there any grain that would breathe life into it – the soil was dead. It died!

Aleksandra raised her head and looked at Tacham Noyan, who sat rigidly on the horse. He seemed to be depressed by this sight as well. In fact, he was crying. Leaning over, he gave Aleksandra a hand and pulled her onto the horse's back. He was silent. The horse bowed his head and sniffed the ground, looking for traces of life in it.

They rode like this over the hill. Seeing the landscape in front of them, Aleksandra couldn't even shout. The village was burned to the ground. More precisely, someone had burned it and leveled it. A few blackened beams stood in the place where the white painted church once stood. There was also no bell tower, only a few sooty planks rising to the sky remained of the house that once stood by the church – the house where she'd been born. Each of them looked like an outstretched arm. They passed through the depressing ruins in silence.

Aleksandra saw a wall standing firmly like a witness of the tragic events. In the window, a curtain that had been hung by her mother still was still there, moving gently in the breeze but its sides were burned. The white fabric was completely black from soot, and the floral patterns had faded.

Tacham Noyan helped Aleksandra get off the horse. She looked for traces of her family through the rubble of the house, which had been filled with joyful laughter two years earlier. A wooden spoon, broken plates, a burned table – nothing else was left. The robbers even took the copper plates. The small brown cross was also missing.

Suddenly, she saw something familiar among the ruins. She made her way through the destroyed remnants and pulled out a small, broken icon – the Virgin Mary – and she was smiling at Aleksandra from under the blackened paint. Only the face of the child she held in her arms, and half of the gold-winged angel above him were left. Aleksandra showed the icon to Tacham Noyan.

"It's the only thing left from my house and village," she whispered.

Her tears fell on the blackened face of the Blessed Virgin. She wiped the icon with her hands first, then with the hem of her skirt, and carefully hid it under her clothes.

Grabbing the man's outstretched hand, she jumped onto the horse's back. Her silent tears turned into loud sobs. Just like on that stormy night, she began to pound Tacham's chest with her small fists. The man remained motionless, not trying to stop the hail of desperate blows. In the end, Aleksandra hid her face in his broad chest and burst into loud crying. The man caressed her hair shyly.

"My beautiful daughter," she heard the desperate voice of the Cossack rider.

They left her nightmarish village in the evening sun, riding through the forested hills bathed in a reddish-purple glow.

The bag attached to Hope's back now contained all of Aleksandra's dowry: a scorched curtain, two wooden spoons, a surviving piece of her mother's plate, and a piece of the icon with the image of the Blessed Virgin.

CHAPTER NINE

Merzuka rushed into Aleksandra's room, dancing with joy.

"Get up, young lady!" she shouted with excitement. "Get ready. We're riding."

"Riding? Where?"

"To the market."

"To the market?" she asked surprised.

Merzuka impatiently pulled the quilt from her and burst out laughing.

"Yes, to the market. Jigit Noyan will come with us. We can't be late. Aj Bala Hatun and a host of servants will not wait for you."

Soon after, they were already at the market. Aj Bala Hatun was surrounded by a wreath of servants. Merzuka clutched Aleksandra's hand tightly. Tacham Noyan stepped majestically right next to them, clearing a way through the crowd.

The sun was strong. The market was larger than the rural bazaar where she and Tacham Noyan had admired the fire-eater. More people and colors surrounded them. On each side of them came calls and shouts:

"Chinese silks, Indian atlas!"

"Must see! Ottoman drapes!"

"My dishes are pretty and durable!"

"Only here spices from India and China!"

In front of one of the tents, Aleksandra saw a woman with a bust so huge that it was difficult to take one's eyes off it. She danced, and her plump body fluttered rhythmically. Merzuka also, couldn't believe what she was seeing, and she stared at the woman's breasts with her mouth open. Aleksandra glanced at Tacham Noyan out of the corner of her eye. The intrepid rider tried not to let it show, but only a blind person wouldn't notice how dreamy he was, looking at the enormous bust. The girls nudged each other and giggled.

Laughing, they ran to another tent. Noyan also had to give up the delightful dreams of a generously endowed woman and run after them.

This time, a half-naked man was calling people.

"See the beast!" he shouted.

Drawings of animals were hung on the huge canvas in front of the tent. One of them depicted a terrifying boar with two giant fangs. But others? Aleksandra had never seen such animals. One of them was very, very big with huge ears – but how to call such a nose? – It reached the ground! It also had two, twisted, sharp, shining fangs as long as horns, growing on both sides of this strange nose. The second giant resembled a cat. It had a lush mane around its head. There was a great, huge lizard on yet another drawing.

Noting that the girls were staring at the images spellbound, Tacham Noyan squeezed a few coppers into the man's hand and led them into the tent. Aleksandra would never have believed that such a stench might exist – and she covered her nose; she wanted to get to the exit as soon as possible. Suddenly, as if wanting something, the elephant stretched out its long trunk in their direction. A lion, staring at the girls with starving eyes, opened his mouth as wide as he could. Seeing two sharp, dagger-like fangs, Aleksandra clung to Merzuka and walked even faster. The crocodile was lying still. Was he dead? He was terrifying and huge, and his jaws showed long rows of razor-sharp teeth.

They hastily left the hideous but awe-inspiring tent. All three of them greedily gasped the fresh air.

If they hadn't noticed a man playing with a monkey a little further along, they'd probably have just stood there, wondering if they had become saturated with that nasty smell. Tacham Noyan pushed his way through the crowd around him, as he paved the way for the girls, then he crossed his arms and stood next to them.

A few people who were behind him were unable to see anything but arms that resembled the walls of the fortress.

"Hey, you! Move aside!" they shouted.

However, when Tacham turned and looked at them with stern eyes, they fell silent.

What a weird creature the monkey was. It jumped, slid, and rolled on a rope stretched by the owner between two pillars. It jumped on the shoulders of those who rewarded it with small coins. The spectators burst out laughing when it fled, taking the hat of one of the children. Only when its owner got another coin, did it jump on the rope and give the hat back. In the end, it stole the man's purse where he'd put the money collected from the spectators. After that, the unfortunate man chased the monkey, shouting: "My money!", and then disappeared in the tent, and the show was rewarded with thunderous applause.

Aleksandra was the one who shouted loudest and clapped most eagerly. She couldn't stand still – she just bounced with joy. Her cheeks were red from emotions and the sun, and there were sparks of happiness in her eyes.

Suddenly she noticed Tacham Noyan watching her display of exuberance with a smile illuminating his dark face. Were there tears in his eyes, or did it just seem so to her?

They turned into a small street in which Aj Bala Hatun looked at all sorts of beautiful fabrics. A little further still and the sounds of music came from a small square. Aleksandra ran toward them, followed by Merzuka. Even Tacham's shouting did not stop them.

A group of men gathered in front of a platform surrounded by red, blue, yellow, and green tulle curtains. Among them were warriors armed with swords, youths, potbellied old men, ugly servants, and men black like the night. For the first time in Aleksandra's life, she saw a black man. Only the whites of his eyes and his teeth were white, and he had huge lips.

The men stood before the platform, blocking the view completely. Aleksandra could hardly see anything. She only managed to see a bald head above the crowd and hear the music flowing from there.

"Come here! Come on! You haven't seen anything so beautiful yet!"

At that moment, a girl came out of the place the man was pointing to. In the crowd, one could hear lusty, lewd murmurs.

"Just look at this hair, those eyes, slender neck, breasts, narrow waist, round hips, and long legs."

Men were watching.

The girl raised her arms and began to dance to the rhythm of the music. It was a reluctant and sad dance. Tens of hungry, wild eyes stared at her.

"Fifty akce!" the bald man exclaimed. "Who gives more?"

In an instant, Aleksandra understood everything.

My God! she thought. *It's a slave market. They sell people here.* Pulling Merzuka behind her, she tried to get closer to the stage, elbowing her way.

"Come on! Open your purses!" the bald man shouted. "This Persian beauty is worth at least a hundred akce!"

"Fifty-five!" a voice could be heard.

"Sixty!" another one shouted.

"Sold!" cried the bald, fat type. "Sold to the honorable gentleman for sixty akce! Or maybe someone will give seventy?"

No one. 'The honorable gentleman' with a satanic face moved forward. He tossed a purse on the stage. The bald, repulsive individual, drooling, began to collect scattered coins, pushing the half-naked girl into the hands of the chap who had been staring at her greedily.

When the man with a satanic face moved away, taking with him the girl he bought, another eight girls were pushed out onto the stage, their legs tied together with chains. Some of them were younger than Aleksandra. They were as small as she was when Tacham Noyan had abducted her, and they didn't even wear decent clothes. The dirty skirts of older girls were ragged. Hungry eyes of the male part of the audience were directed at the legs appearing between the scraps of fabric. One got the impression that before they were pushed here, someone's clumsy paws had tried to smooth their hair. However, because of dirt and neglect, their disheveled hair stuck out in different directions.

All of them, as if they had agreed on it, stared into space. Were they ashamed? Yes, they were. It was visible. Well, but of what? This crowd, staring at them with starving eyes? Maybe they were ashamed of themselves, probably at how inhuman they looked. But it wasn't them that should be ashamed, but rather the drunken mob devouring them with their eyes.

Aleksandra felt that she'd burst into tears at any moment. She bit her lips. The girl standing in front was red-haired. *Just like me,* she thought. *She looks just like I did that night!*

Having arranged the girls in line, the bald, repulsive man shouted:

"Come on! Make up your mind quickly, because the goods will slip out of your hands! You will not find one like this anywhere! Each of them is like a palace beauty!"

"Come on, trader! What palatial beauties?" a voice called out from the crowd. "They are all lousy! You don't sell girls, but lice!"

At these words, the crowd burst into laughter, and the little slaves watched with even greater embarrassment.

"What do you know about palace beauties, horse dealer? You better go look at donkeys and mules," the fat, bald man retorted.

The mob responded with laughter again.

"Come on!" The dealer roared again. "Who gives more? Olga!"

Olga? Ruthenian! My countrywoman! Aleksandra barely suppressed a cry. She didn't even hear when Noyan spoke to her.

"Let's get out of here," he said quickly.

This man was selling her countrywoman about two yards of linen.

A red-haired girl with a wheat-like complexion, standing in front, stepped forward. The slave trader held her by the chin, trying to lift her head. Olga vigorously opposed it.

"She is a real Ruthenian princess. Look at those eyes, at this body. It's an eight-year-old bud, still intact. Reach for your pocket! Somewhere else I would demand two hundred for her, but I got to like you. Come on! One hundred akce for Olga! Who'll give more?"

"One hundred and one!" someone shouted from the crowd.

"One hundred and five!" answered another.

"One hundred and fifteen!" one of the men standing in the back called.

At that moment something happened that no one, not even Aleksandra, had expected.

"You!" Aleksandra shouted with all her strength, pointing to the slave trader with her finger. She felt all eyes fell upon her. "Aren't you ashamed to sell such a little girl?"

While Tacham grabbed her and tried to get out of the crowd, the trader roared with laughter.

"Look!" the trader shouted, and he signaled her to come over. "There is one more bud among us. Come here, beauty. We'll sell you, too. You are worth more than all of them put together."

Trying to get out of Noyan's iron embrace, Aleksandra cursed:

"Damn you!"

But her words did not reach the trader – they were drowned in the crowd's laughter. Aleksandra noticed that Olga watched her with eyes that showed a mix of gratitude, shame, and helplessness. Aleksandra was devastated.

She could have guessed what kind of a place a slave market was. When nightmares haunted her at nights, various images were painted in her head. But now, this was the reality, a truth, not a dream. And standing face to face with the truth turned out to be frightening. She had thoughts that were as sharp and deadly as a dagger.

Would they have also sold me that way too if it weren't for Tacham Noyan...? Maybe at the same bazaar, the same repulsive, fat man would've shouted to sell me: 'Aleksandra. Ruthenian. An eight-year-old bud. Is there anyone here who would like to smell it? Come on, bid! Place your bid.' Who knows in whose dirty paws I would've fallen if it were not for dad, Tacham.

She didn't realize that tears were flowing from her eyes – she just saw what a fate this strong man had saved her from, and she hugged him tightly.

"Thank you," she whispered. "Thank you."

She never thought she'd forgive him the sin he had committed and that she would throw herself on his neck with such gratitude.

The Cossack rider lovingly kissed Aleksandra's hands, wet with tears. The huge man with a heart hardened from many bloody fights cried, and tears seemed to clean his conscience.

"Come," he said, wiping his nose and leading Aleksandra out of the crowd. "Look, there are jugglers."

He couldn't let his little girl cry.

Aleksandra could barely laugh as she watched the juggling tricks. She gripped Merzuka's hand tightly, and both girls still trembled after their horrible experiences. Aleksandra wiped her eyes with the back of her hand. The funny anecdotes of the two jugglers didn't reach her – they failed to make her laugh when they were rolling around on the ground or beating each other's necks. Aleksandra couldn't stop thinking - *was Olga sold?*

Just then Aleksandra noticed that someone among the crowd was watching her closely. A pair of dark blue eyes stared at her without embarrassment. She quickly looked away. She tried with all her effort to focus on the stage where the two jugglers were showing off, but it was all in vain. Now she couldn't stop thinking about a pair of infinite, sky-blue eyes. Who was this young man? Why was he watching her?

His fur hat and a strange outfit indicated that he was not local. *Don't let him know you're looking at him, Aleksandra. He can't notice it*, she kept telling herself.

After a while, however, she suppressed the orders of her common sense.

So, what if he notices?!

She didn't move her head but strained her eyes as hard as she could. It didn't work. The fur hat still was not in her field of view. Or maybe he'd left? She focused her eyes again, but she still couldn't see him.

Anyway, she said in her thoughts, *what do I care. If he wants to go, let him go*.

Suddenly Merzuka nudged her with an elbow.

"Psst, have you seen?"

"What?" she asked.

"That man," the girl whispered.

"I haven't seen anyone," Aleksandra lied.

"He's looking at you all the time."

Aleksandra felt a strange sensation – it was as if a big butterfly fluttered in her small heart.

"He doesn't take his eyes off you."

"Really? What does he look like?" she whispered.

On the one hand, she prayed that Tacham Noyan standing behind them wouldn't hear what they were talking about, and on the other... not to see the man in the hat.

"He is very young... and... Why are you asking me? See for yourself!" Merzuka replied with sudden anger.

"Shh!" Aleksandra nudged her. "I can't. He'll notice that I look at him," she whispered.

"So, what? Let him notice. He doesn't turn his head even for a moment."

Tacham had also noticed the stranger unable to take his eyes off Aleksandra, long ago. From the excited whispers of the girls, he guessed that they too had noticed the stare, but he didn't let it show. What's wrong with the fact that her heart will beat faster?

My God! he realized. *She's growing up.*

For a moment, the girls didn't talk. At that time, Aleksandra laughed loudly, pretending that the juggling performances were very funny to her. Without taking her eyes off the stage, she asked Merzuka in a whisper:

"Is he still looking?"

"He is, and how! What will happen if you look at him too?"

She was right. What was wrong with looking? So, Aleksandra slowly turned her head and saw a man in a cap. Thousands of butterflies fluttered their wings excitedly now.

Is he handsome? she asked herself. *I don't know, I guess so.*

Living in a community where men outdid each other in their ugliness, she didn't really know what it meant to be 'handsome.' When the man noticed that Aleksandra looked at him, he smiled.

My God! Tacham Noyan will see it! Aleksandra thought, and at the same time returned the smile.

The young man seemed quite charmed by its warmth – he'd never seen anything so beautiful before. He greeted her discreetly.

Tacham Noyan noticed it right away, as well as the fact that Aleksandra answered him. He suddenly felt breathless. So, this interest was not unrequited.

Aleksandra did not know what to do. She started looking at the artists again.

"Maybe we'll go now?" Tacham asked.

"Please, let's stay a little longer," she replied hastily. "A little bit more."

She looked at the young man again, trying to calm her quivering heart. The youth in the fur cap gave her a sign with his head.

"Did you see it?"

"Yes."

"What is he doing?"

"I think he wants you to follow him."

"I can't do that. He must be crazy!"

"Certainly. He's crazy for you."

The young man in the cap repeated the sign and began to move to the right of the juggler's tent, towards the long stall, where various sweets were laid out. At the same time, he watched Aleksandra to be sure that she followed him.

It seemed that the butterflies in her heart fled, to be replaced by big drums beating in her heart.

It's impossible, she argued with herself. *I can't do something like that.*

"Can we go to sweets?" Merzuka suddenly asked Tacham Noyan.

Aleksandra felt that her heart would stop at any moment. The huge man leaned over her and looked deep into her eyes. There was a long silence that chilled her veins.

"No," he finally said.

Everything is over, Aleksandra thought.

"I don't like sweets. You go. I will catch up with you," he murmured.

A miracle! Yes, it must have been a miracle! The girls were already preparing to move towards the candy stall when the Tacham grabbed Merzuka's arm in a steel grip.

"Watch my daughter!"

Seeing the light in his eyes, Merzuka understood that he agreed to this meeting.

The young man in a fur cap was waiting. The girls hurried to the other side of the stall. It was enough to look at them to know that they were interested in something completely different than sweets. Tacham also knew what they were thinking about, maybe that's why he did not take his eyes off them.

The young man, who had been watching the girl passionately all this time, took off his cap.

Aleksandra looked up from the sweets and smiled shyly. He was very young. Maybe three or four years older than her. When he took off his cap, unruly, blond curls fell on his forehead. His thick eyebrows were taut as a bowstring, and he had a narrow, upturned nose. His dark blue eyes shone, and his lips that looked like two thin lines stretched in a smile. His chin was covered with youthful beard.

God, thought Aleksandra, *how handsome he is.*

At the same moment, she heard the young man's voice.

"You are very beautiful, young lady."

My God! My God! My God! Aleksandra shouted silently. The man was speaking her language.

"Are you from Ruthenia?" he asked shyly.

"You could say so. I was a little closer to the Polish border."

That was already too much. The man who spoke to her came from her area.

"Me too," he answered with joy.

"Really? Where are you from?"

"From Ruthenia. And you?"

Aleksandra talked to the young man, and at the same time, she looked through dishes with sweets.

"More to the north. From around Kowel."

Merzuka went a bit further aside to leave them alone. The young man sank into the girl's eyes again, and a moment later, as if waking from a dream, he said respectfully:

"Forgive me. I drowned in your beauty and forgot to introduce myself. I'm Fryderyk... Fryderyk Lubański."

Aleksandra stared into his warm eyes, smiling to herself.

"Aleksandra," she said slowly. "Aleksandra Anastasia Lisowska."

How could she say that? Did she really say that? Or maybe she just thought she did.

Ah, heart, she thought. She could barely catch her breath; her emotions were in such a turmoil. She was fascinated by the beauty of her horse Hope, mountains, and plains, but they did not take her breath away like he did. She was afraid she would start to mumble, not able to find the right words.

Fryderyk was like her. In a few words, he told her that he was the son of a trader who came here for business.

Then he politely handed plates of pudding with rose water to her and Merzuka. His hands shook with nervousness. The dessert sprinkled with colorful syrup reminded Aleksandra of a heart.

My heart is shaking and trembling too, she thought.

Aleksandra also mumbled something about herself, but she couldn't admit what she was doing here or how she got here. Was she supposed to reveal that they had abducted her, and she was a slave now? Who was she really? Who was Aleksandra in the Crimean palace? A slave? How was she different from Olga, who was recently sold by this repulsive trader?

You saw the difference a moment ago. Don't be ungrateful. You should be glad that it happened to you, she scolded herself in her mind. The merchant could now be selling her, and handsome Fryderyk could be standing among wild men, undressing her with their eyes and looking at her. Would he look?

The only thing she could say was that she belonged to the court of Sultana Güldane.

"I must go now," she said reluctantly.

Suddenly Fryderyk took out an object from his pocket and handed it to Aleksandra.

"What is this?"

"A mirror."

The girl looked at the small mirror with red dots and a short handle.

"Will you give me this honor and accept this mirror from me?"

"Why do you want to give it to me?"

"So that you would remember me when you look at your beauty."

Her charming smile blossomed on Aleksandra's face again. She slipped the small mirror into a tiny bag tied to her wrist.

"I will remember you," she whispered. Her face burned with fire again. "I have to go. They are waiting for me."

"Will I be able to see you again?"

"I don't know."

"I will look for you at the market every week. With hope and excitement."

"I don't think they'll let me come."

"I will be waiting here, Aleksandra Anastasia."

He went around the table and approached the girl. He reached for one of the flowers scattered on the stall, handed it to her... and placed a short kiss on Aleksandra's lips, then slipped the fur cap over his head, and melted into the crowd.

She didn't talk to anyone anymore about these two events that took place at the bazaar. Neither about the sale of Olga at the slave market nor about the short but unforgettable kiss of Fryderyk – a young man in a fur cap. Nevertheless, both episodes became engraved in her memory forever.

Tacham Noyan didn't embarrass Aleksandra either, with talking about a stolen kiss. He only tried to understand what impression this hot, wet touch of another's lips made on her. There was an expression on Aleksandra's face he'd never seen before – happiness, but also maturity; as if the girl grew up in one moment.

That evening, Aleksandra looked at the mirror she'd received from Fryderyk for a long time. This small mirror with red dots was like an engagement ring for her. Then, she took the bundle of her dowry, and along with the flower she'd received from the young man, she gently placed the mirror into the bundle.

Fryderyk Lubański kept his word. Since that day, he went to the same place at the market every week. He waited for hours, but the girl did not show up. Maybe because the name on the cards of Aleksandra's destination was different.

***

Aleksandra had the bundle with her as she sailed to Istanbul on a galley whose huge sails were filled by the wind of the Black Sea. It was in a place of honor, in a box filled with presents from Aj Bala Hatun, and a few dresses that Sultana Güldane had offered to her before her death...

***

Sultana Mother sat down next to her one day and had her first conversation with her about femininity.

"Childhood is over, Aleksandra," she'd said. "Today you took the first step into adulthood."

Soon after that, she died.

One day, Merzuka came to Aleksandra with her eyes full of tears.

"Come," she said to her.

Aleksandra understood. She'd been waiting with horror for this day for a long time. The old woman was very sick. Entering the room, Aleksandra immediately noticed that death had long ago marked the woman lying in bed.

"It's me, Sultana Mother."

A soft smile appeared on the pale face.

Prayers were made at the head of her bed. Ever since she heard the Koran being recited for the first time, this sound moved the strings of her soul. One night she took out the cracked icon from her bundle and prayed in the flickering candlelight.

"Our mother, Mary, forgive me. I let another religion influence me. Jesus, our Lord, forgive me."

But that's how it was. Even without understanding the meaning of the words being said, she was moved, listening to the Koran. Perhaps it was because the other women were also crying while listening to the Koran. So, she thought it must be something moving; she couldn't determine what it was.

Sultana Güldane outstretched her weak arm. Aleksandra took her frail hand, which now looked like bones coated with skin. She put it to her lips and kissed it. She looked gratefully into the eyes of the old woman that had saved her life, and even if Aleksandra didn't admit it, had become like a mother to her.

"Aleksandra," the woman whispered. "Come closer, child."

The girl brought her ear to the woman's lips.

"The time has come. The Judgment Day has come for me. Pray for me so that God would accept me into Paradise."

"But I don't belong to your religion. You know that."

"For God, there is no you and us. We all come from him."

The older woman's breath did not even reach Aleksandra's ear.

"Take Mother Mary out of your bundle. Pray to her for me. Let Your Blessed Lady put in a word for me. You have been like a daughter to me."

She knows, flashed through Aleksandra's mind. *Sultana Güldane knows that in the evenings I kneel in front of the icon and cry.*

She kissed the woman's hand again.

"I entrust you to Aj Bala Hatun," Sultana Mother whispered with difficulty. "Before I leave, I have to tell you something, Aleksandra. Hear me well and remember what I will tell you. Never forget what I have taught you. You will need this knowledge."

The woman fell silent. She breathed noisily a few times.

"Don't-don't be afraid... Your pa-past is d-dark, but your... fu-future full of light... Bright like stars, Aleksandra. Never loo-look behind you... Don't wait for someone to give you what you want... Reach for it... Take it, even if by force... Hold on to it and do not let it go... I see your pa-path... You are a white dove that will capture an eagle... That's your destiny... Do not let anyone change it..."

Sultana Güldane's voice was getting weaker and weaker. Aleksandra, Aj Bala, and all the women in the room were crying.

Suddenly, the woman's hand strained with incredible strength. She tried to lift her head from the pillow.

"My daughter in law!" A husky voice came out of her throat. "Where are you, child?"

"Here, Mother."

"Give me your hand, wife of my son Khan, mother of my grandchildren, Queen of Crimea and Golden Horde..."

The woman immediately extended her hand to her mother-in-law. Sultana Mother joined the hands of her daughter-in-law and Aleksandra, and three hands clasped together.

"My beautiful, my kind. I entrust to you the country of my husband, the glory of my son's throne, the fate of my grandchildren, and the fate of this undeveloped flower which God has sent to me at such a late age."

Her daughter-in-law looked at Aleksandra with her eyes full of tears.

"I will guard her more than my own life, Sultana Mother." Aj Bala Hatun continued in a voice interrupted by sobs. "It will be my duty to look after my husband the Khan's country, after the glory of the ruler of Crimea and the Golden Horde, after the fate of my children. The penalty for not keeping it will be my life. Know that your daughter will be my sister from today on. A sister will never leave her sister in need."

Sultana Mother squeezed Aleksandra's and her daughter-in-law's hands with bony fingers.

"God help you. Do not let me down. Make sure she gets her crown. My own daughter, Aishe, gave birth to two daughters of the Ottoman Sultan Selim, but none of them wore a crown. Selim put the crown on the head of another beauty who gave him a son. Make this girl wear a crown whose radiance will illuminate not only the lands of the Golden Horde, the legacy of Tuka Timur, the grandson of Genghis Khan, but the whole world. Let the Ruthenian princes bow their heads before her glory. Tell Sultana Hafsa, the mother of Suleiman – the son of Sultan Selim, that Aishe's mother sends her youngest daughter to her. Let her help the white dove catch the eagle."

That night Sultana Mother left to join her husband, Khan Mengli Girey.

"I missed him," she'd said.

Aleksandra cried all night.

Did they meet? she wondered. *Has she seen my parents?*

Later, she had remorse that she thought so. Maybe her parents didn't die, maybe they survived? And if they did live, did they sometimes think about their daughter, Aleksandra?

* * *

In those days, Aleksandra realized for the first time how strong a woman could be.

I can not believe it, she thought. She could deal with the Crimean Khan – he followed her instructions without hesitation. Aj Bala Hatun had also influence on Mehmed Girey. The last word always belonged to her.

Suddenly, she remembered Sultana Mother's advice:

'Remember it well. Behind every man, even the strongest one, there must be a woman. A woman who will know how to guide him.'

How was she supposed to guide a man? Sultana Güldane left before she told her this secret.

* * *

It had been two years since the death of the old woman, and fifteen winters and fifteen summers since the birth of Aleksandra. The girl flourished; she became even more attractive, and her hair shimmered red. Her beauty and the charm of her eyes had become famous among the Crimean lords and jigits.

One day, the lord of the Azak fortress came to Bakhchisarai personally to officially ask Khan Mehmed Girey for her hand. That same night, Khan told Ai Bala about everything. The woman had no doubts.

"Absolutely not."

"Why?"

"That was not the will of Sultana Mother. I will not give her to the mercy of local lords. I will make sure a crown will be placed on her head, one whose radiance will illuminate not only Crimea but the whole world. That was the will of the Mother Sultana."

"And where is this crown?"

"Very close. On the opposite shores of the Black Sea."

Mehmed Girey could not believe what he was hearing.

"Are you talking about the Ottomans?"

"Yes, the Ottomans. Suleiman has been on the throne for a long time. He went to war right away and took the fortress in Belgrade. Isn't it fitting that the Khan of Crimea, the brother of his father's first wife, would send a gift to Sultan Suleiman for his victory?"

"It is. I've already given orders. They are preparing things."

"In that case, send Aleksandra with the gifts."

"What?" The Khan looked at his wife, worried, then anger appeared in his eyes. "Is this your loyalty to the girl that Sultana Mother has entrusted to you, Aj Bala? Do you want me to give her to the Ottomans as odalisque? My dear father of holy memory, Mengli Girey, gave my sister to Sultan Selim when he was still a prince, and you know what happened. It wasn't enough that she gave Selim two children. He took Sultana Hafsa as his wife, and the harem became her prison. Do you want to send the girl to captivity in the harem? Isn't it enough that our son is imprisoned in Istanbul as a safeguard of our loyalty to the Ottomans?"

The woman looked into her husband's eyes.

"No," she said. "This was your mother's dream: 'the white dove will catch the eagle.' Aleksandra will not be a prisoner in the harem, but the most important woman in the Ottoman state. Aleksandra will wear the crown of the Ottoman Empire that your sister did not manage to get. You will see, the day will come when the Ottomans, confident of our loyalty, will free our son."

Mehmed Girey looked at his wife in disbelief and thought about it.

"The Ottomans will not let my son go. The girl will also be lost in the harem. Either she will grow old before she has the chance to see Suleiman, or they will waste her life by marrying her off to some elderly vizier. Of course, if they don't come up with something else entirely. Can an ordinary odalisque be the ruler of the Ottoman State?"

"She will. It is in the cards for her."

"False hope, wife. Suleiman took a Circassian beauty as his wife. He will not even look at another."

"So, what? Our girl is a Ruthenian beauty. Aishe was also beautiful, but it was Sultana Hafsa who won Selim. In addition, Aleksandra is a flower that is yet to bloom. She is smart, ambitious, consistent, and knows how to fight for what is hers."

"But this Circassian gave Suleiman a son before he became a padishah. There are only two women in Suleiman's life, his mother, and the favorite. Are you saying that apart from waging war and these two women, his attention will still be attracted by some harem odalisque?"

"Do as I advise you, Khan Mehmed, and you won't regret it. Not only will you fulfill your mother's wishes, but you will also act like a wise father."

By saying 'father,' Aj Bala Hatun had tried to give her husband a hidden message. She paused for a moment, then, trying to find agreement in her husband's eyes, she continued:

"This way, you also won't have to follow every step of Aleksandra anymore."

Mehmed Khan, who was considered to be the worst nightmare of Ruthenian princes, was forced to close his eyes to the plundering expeditions for the sake of good relations with the Kingdom of Poland. He was also the heir of jigit Tuk Timur, the grandson of Genghis Khan, and of other beys and khans in the hands of the Cossacks. He was a man who always tried to walk with his head up as the new ruler of the Golden Horde. Yet, upon hearing his wife's words, he couldn't believe his ears! So, Aj Bala knew that his heart was not indifferent to this Ruthenian girl. He could never let it show – it wasn't good for him as a ruler to send the mother of his children away and enjoy a Ruthenian beauty, the same age of his own daughter.

First, he tried to show remorse by staring into space for a moment, pretending to think about something. Then he looked up at the woman with whom he had been putting his head on the same pillow, for so many years. He understood that she was ready to forgive him at any moment. He was ashamed.

"What happens if you keep her here?" she asked meekly. "Once you've enjoyed her, you'll give her away to some soldier, stinking of horses. Let her embark on the path that the Sultana Mother foretold her. Let her try to catch the eagle, and you be the father of your children, my man, and the ruler of Crimea, and not a khan of an odalisque."

The man saw the uneasiness in Aj Bala's eyes and the tears rising in them. So far, Mehmed Girej had seen his wife's eyes fill with tears only twice. The first time was on the day her mother died, and later, when her mother-in-law gave up the spirit in her arms.

He nodded.

"My spouse has never shown me a wrong path yet," he said in a trembling voice. "The wife of my father the Khan of Khans, the Mother of Mothers, used to say: 'Son, listen to my dear daughter-in-law and you will be happy.' She was never wrong. This time she was right, too. Let everyone follow the path of their destiny."

***

Once Aleksandra learned that she was going to go to the Ottoman court as an odalisque, she made a scene.

"I don't know the Ottomans, and I don't want their son. My home is here. Sultana Mother is my mother, Aj Bala is my sister. Do I bother the Khan, the son of my Mother Sultana, so much, that he wants to throw me out of the house?" she lamented day and night. Her wailing put everybody around on their feet. "What did I do that my sister turned her back on me?"

Merzuka's attempts at calming her down brought about nothing but scratches on her face.

The day of departure was approaching, and Aleksandra's resistance had not diminished.

"They want to push me into the bed of some old sultan, Sultana Mother. Get up and see."

These words made Merzuka's patience run out.

"What old man, stupid girl. Suleiman doesn't even have thirty springs behind him. European courts send him the most beautiful girls to win his heart – and you reject such an opportunity. Enough with this pout, get ready."

It wasn't Merzuka's shouting, but her words that the sultan 'doesn't even have thirty springs behind him,' that talked some sense into Aleksandra. She wiped away her tears and remembered the words of Sultana Güldane: 'Remember what I tell you. Take it, even if by force. Reach for what you want and do not let go of it.' Maybe the Ottoman ruler was worth getting? Maybe Merzuka was right? What will happen if she rejects this opportunity? And what if the Crimean Khan, who had been appearing in her way for months, gets upset by her resistance and sends her away? Will she return to the mountains on horseback again? These considerations gave her a lot to think about, especially as images of blackened chambers in caravanserais, dirty beds, rough men drooling at her sight appeared in front of her eyes.

When Aleksandra finished her fussing, peace returned in the Crimea palace again.

Ai Bala, who had of recent not visited the girl fearing her anger, finally gathered up the courage and went to see Aleksandra, who was preparing for the journey to Istanbul. They embraced, but there was some coldness in it, even though all women shared the same fate.

In the end, Sultana Mother had been the concubine of Megli Girey at one point. She, too, despite the girl's cries and pleas, sent her daughter, Sultana Aishe, to the harem of Sultan Selim the Grim, and even though she gave birth to two of Selim's daughters, the place in the heart of the sultan was taken by another woman – the one who gave birth to his son. She became the wife of the padishah, and now she was the mother of the great sultan.

And Aj Bala? How many tears she shed before she saved herself from the life of an odalisque by giving a son to Mehmed Girey? And what was Gülbahar, the current favorite of Sultan Suleiman supposed to say? In the end, she was also a concubine, but she gave Suleiman a son. As a result, she'd become the most powerful woman in the Ottoman state, right after the mother of the padishah, Sultana Hafsa.

Aleksandra was now setting off on the same path. Either she will end up forgotten like the unfortunate daughter of Sultana Güldane, or, like the Sultana Hafsa, she will become the wife of the padishah and the mother of the future sultan.

As if they both were processing the same thoughts, the cold between them warmed up. They embraced like sisters and inhaled each other's smell deeply so as to never forget it.

"Go, Aleksandra," Aj Bala said slowly, stroking her hair. "Leave it to God. Reach for your destiny. I believe in you. Don't let Mother Sultana or your sister down. Those who enter the palace as odalisques give birth to princes. Let the soul of Sultana Güldane, who suffered because her daughter Aishe did not get the crown, get some peace."

***

So, Aleksandra went to meet her destiny, on the galley, whose sails were pushed by a wind from the north. From under the deck, one could hear the rhythmic groans of slaves, who put all their strength into moving the oars, and the regular splash when they plunged the oars at the same time.

Leaning on the railing, she admired the sun disappearing in golden sea waters on the horizon, like a huge red ball.

"I am coming, son of the Ottomans," she whispered, looking at the purple clouds. "Wait for me, Suleiman. I come to share the crown and the throne with you."

Chapter Ten

Spring was like a nightmare for Aleksandra, from which she couldn't wake up. As soon as they arrived at the palace, black men with feminine voices took her and Merzuka to a large hall surrounded by balconies and supported by marble columns. It was dim inside despite it being the middle of the day, and they couldn't tell where any of the light that filtered in came from. Once their eyes grew accustomed to the prevailing gray, they saw that the balconies were full of beautiful women. Several girls passed before them, tapping their richly decorated slippers. They didn't even look at Aleksandra and Merzuka.

After a moment, another woman came; this one accompanied by a black woman with huge lips. The beauty and grace of the first one was as great as the ugliness and weight of the other. Rustling the skirts of her long caftan, and wide galligaskins, the girl passed Aleksandra. She tried to hide her face behind a red silk voile hanging from some fancy headgear, but it didn't work – both Aleksandra and Merzuka immediately noticed her eyes, bloodshot from crying.

They sat by one of the columns and waited. Aleksandra held tight to her bundle, and she didn't know what had happened to the chest with the gifts donated by Aj Bala. The bundle was the only thing left to her in this strange place. Inside it, a few damaged souvenirs, some clothes, and fabrics.

They looked around with surprise. Was this the harem? They couldn't see any stairs leading to the first floor. Was it impossible to get to the higher levels after going down to the lower floors? If that was the case, how was the harem different from any dungeons?

Aleksandra circled the stone floor with her eyes, looking up. Each floor was surrounded by mezzanines. The empty space in the middle was filled by the crying and whining of children, and females shouting. Aleksandra listened to the sounds, but couldn't distinguish them. She could only hear a language she didn't know. The fact that the voices echoed in this empty space made them even more incomprehensible.

They waited for someone to come and take care of them – but so far, in vain. How much time had passed? An hour, maybe five? They only knew that the sunlight now penetrated the dimness from a different angle. When they'd arrived here, streaks of light illuminated the rooms on the left, and now it had moved to those on the right. It seemed to them that the light had begun to change from golden to red. Was it evening already? Aleksandra felt that the anger rising in her would soon explode. She moved toward a girl passing in front of her, who carried a bowl full of hot coals.

"Is nobody is going to take care of me?"

The girl raised her head and looked at her with concern. There was anxiety in her eyes. She was quite ugly, and her gaze could be described by Aleksandra as a bit dumb. She noticed that the girl did not understand her language. Pressing her finger to her breast, she said patiently:

"My name is Aleksandra. A-lek-san-dra. And this is Merzuka. Mer-zu-ka."

The girl was using a utensil with a long handle, she later learned was called a dzezve, used to prepare coffee in the traditional Turkish way, and when she immersed it into the coals, a light briefly appeared in her eyes, but went out immediately. Like Aleksandra, she put her index finger to her chest.

"Io Sophia. Sop- hi-a."

Hearing the conversation, another girl appeared. Her raven-black hair was covered with a white veil.

Are these girls more beautiful than me? Aleksandra wondered. If all the women in the harem were so beautiful, her task was going to be difficult.

The two girls whispered something to each other in an incomprehensible language.

"We've been waiting here for many hours. We're hungry, thirsty, and tired. Is nobody going to take care of us?"

Aleksandra's voice was getting increasingly louder. She couldn't stop the anger rising in her. The girls whispering at the stove did not even pay attention when she raised her fingers to her lips, showing that she wanted a drink.

"My name is Aleksandra!" she shouted. "Aleksandra Anastasia Lisowska. I came from Crimea."

A growing movement was heard on the upper floors. Aleksandra's voice echoed through all the floors. After a few seconds of silence, a beautiful woman leaned out from the mezzanine. However, nothing could be heard except the rustling of her robes. Merzuka ran to her in vain. Aleksandra raised her head and spoke to the woman who was looking at her with curiosity:

"Is this how the Ottomans greet the daughter of Sultana Güldane, who is the mother of Crimean Khan Mehmed Girey, and the sister of her daughter-in-law Aj Bala Hatun?"

Whispered women's conversations were heard from the upper floors.

They don't understand me. I stand here and shout for nothing, thought Aleksandra.

"Is there anyone here who knows my language?"

Curious women, looking down from the upper floors, disappeared just as quickly as they appeared.

"There is!" The roaring-like voice was so powerful that Aleksandra's and Merzuka's hearts leaped into their throats. "Look here, you who dare to disturb the peace and silence of the harem."

After the roar she heard a moment ago, the order sounded like a whisper now. Aleksandra couldn't see them, but she felt that the women filling the floors of the harem secretly watched what was happening. The two girls who had been brewing linden tea by the stove also disappeared, but Aleksandra was sure that they were hidden somewhere too.

Both women slowly turned to the direction from which the voice came.

A black man stood in the dark at the entrance door. The man's skin was hardly distinguishable from the dark caftan and galligaskins he wore. If not for the strange, white headgear, he might not have been visible at all. At first, Aleksandra thought he was alone, but after a moment she saw another, smaller figure at his side. It was equally black, and only the whites of the eyes could be seen. It was a young boy, watching with curiosity.

Aleksandra shyly took a few steps toward the huge figure.

What big lips, thought Aleksandra. *It must be typical for black people*.

"Who are you?" The giant's whisper pierced the air like a whip.

"Aleksandra Anastasia Lisowska."

"Who are you?"

He probably didn't hear, thought Aleksandra.

"Aleksandra Anastasia Lisowska. And this is Me..."

"Who are you?" The same whisper interrupted her.

Was he playing with her? A smile appeared on Aleksandra's face. She tried to read the intentions from his eyes, but they were devoid of luster. In turn, a shadow of worry lurked in the eyes of the black boy as if he was trying to tell her something.

Aleksandra had learned good manners and court customs back in Crimea. She knew how to sit down and get up, and how to talk to the elders but she couldn't understand why this servant was addressing her, the daughter of Sultana Güldane, with such disrespect.

"I've already said. Haven't you heard?"

"I have not heard. Who are you?"

Aleksandra had enough. When she shouted in his face: "Aleksandra Anastasia...", something she didn't expect at all happened. The man's arm moved up as fast as lightning, and a thin stick hit her arm. The girl cried out in pain.

"You're an odalisque.*"

While Aleksandra rubbed her hand that burned like a fire, the man's arm rose and fell down again. This time the stick reached her shoulder.

"Who are you?"

Unable to stop her tears, Aleksandra could say only two syllables:

"Alek…"

She felt a blow again.

"You're an odalisque. Have you heard, Ruthenian odalisque?"

It was only after the fifth strike that Aleksandra nodded in a sign that she understood.

Merzuka knelt at her feet and sobbed. One was crying in pain and the other from fear. Between her damp eyelashes, Aleksandra saw women watching them with a mixture of curiosity and fear. They'd all watched her get the hits, and shame made her pain even more intense. She looked at the man. From behind the curtain of her tears, she tried to remember every detail of his face.

Don't forget this face, Aleksandra, she said to herself. *Don't forget it.*

The man seemed to read her mind.

"Did you say something?"

The girl shook her head.

"You are a Ruthenian odalisque. Do you understand? In fact, you're not even that yet. You will wash and change, and then you will learn. The Ruthenian gadabout will disappear, and the palace's odalisque will take her place. If the Sultana Mother decides that you fit our ruler's harem – you will stay, if not – you will leave." He fell silent. He took the girl's chin and lifted it up. After a moment he added: "If you are lucky, you will go to serve at the house of a vizier or a bey, if not, God help you."

He looked at the blue-green eyes, wet with tears.

"One more thing. One does not scream here. The silence in the palace is a sanctity – it must not be disturbed. Instead of destroying this peace and quiet, you'd be better to go and throw yourself into the sea. Do you understand, Ruthenian odalisque?"

Aleksandra wanted to die. No! She wanted to cut the throat of this man the most. She suddenly missed Tacham Noyan. Where did her jigit go? If he were here now, he would throw her on the back of Hope and take her to the mountains again.

"Do you understand?" repeated the man. There was a familiar threat in his voice – that at any moment he could give her another blow.

"I understand." Aleksandra nodded.

"Let's move on to the second lesson." He shook the girl's chin and let it go.

"You will not give your name unless asked for it. Even if they talk to you, you will not raise your head and look at our ruler the Padishah, the Sultana Mother, or Haseki Hatun until they order you to do it."

Where am I? Aleksandra wondered. *What mistake did I make that Aj Bala Hatun sent me to this prison?* Or maybe it was hell? And that ominous face probably belonged to the demon. Then a desperate thought crossed her mind – *I won't leave this place in one piece.*

"You will do what they tell you to do. You will not be stubborn. You'll wash your clothes and clean your dishes yourself until someone tells you otherwise. If they tell you to wash someone else's stuff, you will not complain either."

The man continued to enumerate her duties, but now his voice seemed very distant to Aleksandra. She heard what he was saying, but she didn't understand it – she did not want to understand. She nudged Merzuka, kneeling at her feet. The Tatar girl raised her head and looked at Aleksandra; tears left dirty streaks on her face.

"Did you understand me?" She woke up when the man shook her.

He'd probably asked this question several times, but she hadn't heard it. She nodded. Now, a completely different expression was on the face of 'Black Face boy' standing next to them. Aleksandra couldn't decipher his gaze. Was it a pity? It didn't look like it. Or maybe he wanted to say to her, 'Don't be sad?' It didn't matter – at least he didn't look at her as ominously as Thunder Arm, who, as he was about to turn away, noticed the bundle held by Merzuka – the bundle with Aleksandra's dowry.

"What is this? It is not allowed to keep such dirt here. Give me that."

The man wanted to take the bundle from Merzuka's hands. Aleksandra stood in his way while pushing away Merzuka, who was trying to protect the bundle.

"Don't touch it!"

A cry full of horror was heard from the women who watched what was happening.

Black Face stood baffled, with his hand outstretched.

"What did you say?" This time his eyes were filled with anger and disbelief. "What did you say?"

"Don't touch it. It's mine."

Aleksandra braced herself for another blow. Their eyes met. For a moment, Aleksandra stared intensely and fearlessly at the eyes that flashed thunderbolts. She squeezed her eyes tight, waiting for the impact.

But nothing like that happened. The man looked for a moment at the girl standing opposite him. Straightening up, he said:

"Well, let it be so, but I don't want to see it anymore."

Aleksandra opened her eyes in surprise. The man and the boy accompanying him headed for the door. The Black Face turned and looked at the girl.

"That's all for today. We'll come back to this. Now I have other things to take care of."

He turned back again and, taking huge steps, started toward the door. Before he left, he asked unexpectedly:

"Who are you?"

Aleksandra's voice, like when he had asked her earlier, echoed through the walls.

"Aga of the harem calls me a Ruthenian odalisque. Ask him, he will tell you who I am."

Horrified whispers of women standing on the mezzanines reached her ears.

The man stopped short. The dark-skinned boy next to him turned and looked at Aleksandra as if to ask, 'Why did you do that?' This time the black giant did not turn around. Instead, he took another step forward.

"Soon, we will get to know each other very well," he threw over his shoulder.

He left, leaving Aleksandra and Merzuka in the stone yard of the harem, amid countless cynical, compassionate but also jealous glances of the women.

That's what Aleksandra's arrival at the harem looked like – the end of a journey which she'd started with the words: 'Wait for me, Suleiman. I come to share the crown and the throne with you.' It was painful, humiliating, and disappointing.

Aleksandra slowly leaned over Merzuka, who was still on the floor. She stroked the hair of her companion in misery as if it wasn't her who'd received the painful hits just a moment before. She straightened up and proudly moved toward the stove, where the two girls had tried to brew linden tea earlier. The girls had left their dzezva and hid as soon as they'd heard the voice of the harem aga. The linden powder had spilled on the coals and hardened, and an intoxicating and warming aroma of the brew now spread around the courtyard. The smell of linden tea instantly dispelled the terrible impressions of the harem. Aleksandra always associated this aroma with home – now here was her home. She raised her head and looked around the mezzanines surrounding the courtyard. Lights, candles, and lanterns were starting to appear in the cells. A few women hid hastily.

Aleksandra and Merzuka sat by the stove. The girl pressed the bundle to her breast.

"A Ruthenian odalisque," she muttered angrily. "This Ruthenian odalisque will become the lady of this house."

CHAPTER ELEVEN

Winter 1521

She was depressed. She learned that the harem aga's name was Sümbül, and the pain of the drubbing she got from him burrowed deep into her mind.

After the man left, two black-skinned women appeared. Both were tall and slender. If she had been in a different mood, she would have died of laughter at the sight of their pointed headgear, pinned on their jet-black hair, curled like sheep wool. However, right now, she didn't feel like laughing. They were dressed in white caftans over green shirts, and loose, yellow galligaskins. They had leather slippers on their feet.

Aleksandra didn't know yet, that the harem was full of dark-skinned slaves called kalfas, whose task was to help the odalisques, and whose most important duty was in fact, watching the other women – and providing information about everything they saw and heard to the aga of the harem – Sümbül.

One of the kalfas, quite young looking, nudged Aleksandra as if to say, 'Come on.' Unfortunately, none of the girls knew her language.

"What's going on?" Aleksandra muttered. "We're hungry. Where will we sleep?"

The black women didn't understand her either. All the effort she'd put in to learn the Tatar language in Crimea was wasted. She wondered where Thunder Arm had learned Ruthenian. True, his Ruthenian was terrible, but nevertheless, they could communicate.

Seeing that the girls were not moving, the other woman grabbed Aleksandra by her arm. The sore girl pulled her arm away with a vigorous movement and got up.

The first maid pointed at herself saying, "Setaret," then introduced the other woman: "Gülbejaz."

Had Aleksandra understood their language, hearing the words *gül* and *beyaz* with regard to a woman with ebony skin, she would certainly have burst out laughing because 'gül' to meant rose to her in Turkish, and beyaz, white.

"Se... ta... Gül... be... az" Aleksandra tried to pronounce.

The woman corrected her, smiling:

"Setaret. Gülbejaz."

She also introduced herself.

"Aleksandra," she said, then pointed to the Tatar girl. "Merzuka."

The woman learned the name 'Merzuka' in an instant, but she couldn't pronounce 'Aleksandra.'

They managed to establish a line of communication, even if very thin. The harem courtyard filled again with noise. These were the voices of curious women speaking all at the same time.

Aleksandra, raising her hand to her lips, tried to show that they wanted to eat.

"We're starving," she said, pointing to her stomach.

A woman named Gül-something raised both hands to her head and began to move them comically as if she were washing raw wool. Seeing that newcomers were looking at her with surprise, she repeated the movement.

"Bath... Bath..." she said.

What was she talking about?

"What?"

The maid started massaging her head with her hands again.

"Bath first, then food," she said. Then the woman's patience ran out.

She pushed the girls, trying to force them to move. Feeling their resistance, she pushed them a bit harder, showing her determination. In the end, they moved in the direction where they were led.

As they passed down a long, dark corridor, they entered a room with a high ceiling, lined with marble. Now they understood what the woman meant – they were supposed to wash.

A marble shelf contained snow-white, thick towels, and thin colored cloths, all folded neatly on them. There were wooden platform wedges on the floor.

"Towel," said Setaret, pointing to the thick white material. "This is a blindfold, and these are clogs."

Seeing that the girls were looking at the wooden clogs with astonishment, she took off her shoes and put her feet in them. Aleksandra and Merzuka watched her in disbelief; how can you walk in something so high? The woman, as if understanding their doubts, pulled up their yellow galligaskins and began to walk around, tapping on the marble floor. Aleksandra thought she would never be able to walk in something like those. What was this strange thing? Setaret, walking around the bathhouse, giggled softly, saying something to the other woman. It must have been something funny because Gül-something also laughed. She covered her mouth with her hand as if to cover the white teeth among her thick lips.

She approached Aleksandra and stopped. She pointed to her clothes.

"Undress!"

"What?"

Taking off her caftan, the woman showed what she meant.

"Undress yourselves!"

Chaos ensued after that. Aleksandra tried to explain to them that she would not undress in their presence. If they wanted them to wash, they would need to leave them alone, and then they would wash in turn with Merzuka. However, her explanations did not bring any results.

The black women began to get upset that the newcomers opposed everything. When Gül-something reached out, trying to undress Aleksandra, the girl screamed. There was a terrible confusion. Suddenly the door opened, and two more women entered. The resistance of the two girls was useless against the strength of four dark-skinned women. Before long, Aleksandra and Merzuka were naked.

Tired from the exhausting struggle, the women didn't pay much attention to Merzuka, but stood as if enchanted, looking at the white as ivory, delicate body of Aleksandra. It seemed that the interior was filled with a moonbeam. Setaret Kalfa constantly expressed her delight, rolling her eyes:

"Mashallah! Mashallah!"

Aleksandra tried to cover herself with her hands, blushing, but it was all in vain. She knew the word Mashallah was Arabic for expressing their admiration, so the women's eyes on her made her feel even more embarrassed.

"Damn you!" she cried, closing her eyes and turning away. "Black witches!"

She felt cool, thin cloths on her burning skin – Gül-something was slowly scrubbing her body. She didn't know how to escape from the big paws touching her delicate, newly blossomed breasts, and the woman kept looking at her. Aleksandra stepped back to avoid her rough touch.

This time, the woman knelt and grabbed the girl's tiny feet. Lifting her slim ankle, she gently slipped on the clogs, slowly scrubbing her calf as well. She did the same with her other leg. With wooden wedges on her feet, Aleksandra suddenly became very tall.

Kneeling on the floor, the woman looked up at Aleksandra.

Why was she looking so strange? Was there a longing lurking in her eyes? Where did this begging look come from? Why was the woman who had just yelled at her, now be stroking her feet and calves tenderly?

She must have noticed my fatigue, thought Aleksandra.

The touch of the ardent hands of the woman on her porcelain skin was beginning to be painful.

In the end, Merzuka, covered with a sash, made two shaky steps in the high wooden flops. She had to stop the intrusive behavior of the woman – she knew those looks all too well.

"Leave her alone! Go away!"

Gülbejaz Kalfa jolted as if woken up from a dream. It seemed that she came back from far away. Confused, she looked at Merzuka. The girl saw anger in her eyes... and jealousy.

Setaret Kalfa went to a large wooden door on the other side of the room and opened it. A cloud of hot steam billowed around inside.

Aleksandra slowly walked to the door in those strange, high wooden shoes. Her legs shook, and the clogs kept sliding off her feet, so she had to stop and adjust them. What was this folly to walk on marble in wooden shoes? What kind of strange habit of the Ottomans was this?

Holding hands, and with the help of Gülbejaz Kalfa, the girls reached the door of the bathhouse. A blast of heat hit their faces. Under the big dome was a tall, marble elevation. Setaret Kalfa came over and lay down on it... She probably wanted to show what it was used for. Aleksandra sat on a warm stone and turned her gaze to the ceiling. In some parts of the dome, she noticed round, colored windows. She also noticed a window above the marble swimming pool opposite. It seemed to her that a lantern burned behind the pane. There was also a lantern above the entrance door, in which two large candles were burning. Gülbejaz ran to the room where she'd just undressed Aleksandra, and brought two more lanterns. Now, the interior of the bathroom, up to now shrouded in darkness, filled with a weak gleam. Setaret Kalfa helped Aleksandra enter the pool. She turned the faucet that glinted in the light of the lanterns and filled the tank, decorated with marble reliefs, with warm water.

Then she took a tin bowl full of water and rinsed the girl's head.

Washing, it seemed, also couldn't be done without Gülbejaz. All attempts to explain to the Moroccan that she could wash herself were futile. The strong woman took off her caftan and shirt. Aleksandra looked in disbelief at a pair of huge, black breasts, that were bigger than a human head. Embarrassed, she looked away. Gülbejaz guessed what the girl was thinking about. Her breasts were huge, and her nipples were the size of nuts.

The woman soaped her body with strong hands. She did it slowly, as if she did not want to hurt her. At one point, as if by chance, in a slick movement, she slid off the edge of the loincloth covering the girl's charms. Relaxed after previous experiences and by the stream of warm water washing over her body, Aleksandra didn't notice that her firm breasts of the size of oranges, were exposed. It was only when she noticed the dreamy look of Gül-something that she realized that her sash had slipped down. The woman watched her bright, hard, and shapely breasts with genuine reverence. They looked like two small snowballs with pink strawberries on tops, and her pinhead-like nipples stuck out. The woman caressed them with her eyes, then her heavy hands began to slide from the girl's shoulders towards those firm breasts. Aleksandra reacted immediately. She pulled up her loincloth and tied it tightly. A damp cloth wandered between her legs, revealing a small triangle concealing her greatest secrets. Aleksandra pushed the woman away. She threw the clogs off her feet and moved firmly toward the door. Setaret, turning angrily to Gülbejaz, opened the heavy wooden door with difficulty, and the girl quickly rushed into the next room.

***

Accommodation of the newcomers in the rooms did not go without incidents, either. In a room occupied by seven or eight women, Setaret pointed to two mattresses stretched out on the floor. The girl's screams of objection ended with a sharp pinch to the arm and caused a tumult among the women in the dormitory. They shouted from their beds in a language that was incomprehensible to her. And the light-haired girl lying on the nearest bed through a shoe at Aleksandra.

She didn't let it go. She grabbed the shoe and threw it back to the owner. If it weren't for Setaret, their first night in the harem would have ended in a great fight. Instead, pressing her bundle firmly to her chest, the girl clung to the window above the bed and cried softly. She couldn't see much through the barred glass, but she knew that there was freedom outside – somewhere there were mountains and rivers – far, far away.

In response to her sobs, there were angry murmurs. She felt helpless, tired, and angry. She pulled the quilt over her head and tried to suppress her crying. This was not a palace, but a real prison.

Who will free me from this prison? she thought as she soaked her pillow with tears. There was no Tacham Noyan here, who would take out his dagger with a wolf-shaped handle, and turn this place that made her cry, into rubble.

Where are you, Noyan, father? Come, look what happened to your daughter. Aleksandra couldn't believe the thoughts that circled in her head. She felt her heart tighten; Noyan was supposed to be her father? It came down to this: that she called the barbarian who changed her life, her father. She had no one else in this great world. Neither mother nor father, nor the village, nor the house, not even a warm corner. Nobody risked their life for her like Tacham Noyan. And so many times. *Where are you, Noyan, father?* she thought again.

She waited for the huge man with his head wrapped in a scarf, with black, wind-ruffled hair sticking out from under it, to break into the palace. He had to come, sitting proudly on Hope, and roar, making the Ottomans tremble: 'I came for you, daughter!' But, she knew her hope was in vain. Nobody answered her silent scream. The harem silence was disturbed only by the whispers of women talking to each other, not counting a child's crying from time to time, and the sounds of the guards reporting:

"Midnight... One o'clock... All quiet."

In this palace, where she'd come to get the Ottoman crown and throne, she was just an ordinary slave. She was beaten, pushed, undressed, watched like the slaves sold at the market, pinched, and humiliated. What else could a slave experience? Were the shoes and beautiful clothes she got after leaving the bathhouse supposed to be a reward for slavery?

"I don't want them," Aleksandra murmured.

She preferred the simple sandals from un-tanned leather that Tacham Noyan put on her feet.

"It can't be like this," she complained.

She made the decision that the first thing she would do the next day would be to go to Suleiman and tell him everything: 'I have not come here to be treated like a slave. You are Suleiman, and I am Aleksandra from Ruthenia. I was brought up by Sultana Mother – mother of your father's first wife. Is this how I should be treated?'

She was so angry and deeply upset that she was sure she wouldn't be able to fall asleep. But a sleep is a sleep, somewhere between life and death, and no one was able to resist that force, not even Aleksandra.

In her dream, she saw a huge eagle with black wings.

CHAPTER TWELVE

Aleksandra had no opportunity to meet Sultan Suleiman the next day, nor over the following days. She lived in the same house as the padishah, under the same roof – but not only did she not see him, she never even heard his voice. That is why she had no opportunity to say the sentence she'd prepared in her mind: 'You are Suleiman, and I am Aleksandra from Ruthenia.'

She not only did not see Suleiman, neither did the mother of the padishah appear – Sultana Hafsa, whose name she had heard so often, or Gülbahar Haseki, from whom she intended to remove from her place of love and position. What would happen if it was different? Her life was passing like a storm.

Every morning she experienced the same anguish in the bathhouse, being undressed by the black women.

"These women touch me," she once complained to Sümbül Aga, for which she received three additional hits. Thus, she learned she couldn't object to the claw-like, impatient fingers of Gül-something, which among the treacherous darkness touched her most intimate places that she herself had not yet discovered.

After the bathhouse, it was time for lessons.

Everything was taught from the very beginning, starting with how to stand, sit, talk, eat, and ending with how to walk in the presence of the padishah. Aleksandra gave her greatest attention to the importance of learning the language – after all, one day she was supposed to face Suleiman. What she wants to tell him she must say in his language.

The only thing that distinguished one day from the next in the harem was the constant quarrels between girls competing with each other for which one of them would win the sultan's favor. Because each of them spoke her own language, one couldn't tell who said what, but it didn't matter anyway because no one listened to anyone.

For the first few days, the turmoil and chaos disturbed Aleksandra. Usually, she didn't understand what the reason was for this quarrel or that. Neither did the screaming girls. At that moment, all was irrelevant to Aleksandra, who couldn't get to sleep until the girls reconciled.

In fact, since Aleksandra came to the harem, quarrels and disputes broke out much more often, and she was the main character in most of them. She never gave up. She didn't listen to what was being said to her, and even a trivial reason was enough for her to attack other girls. Contrary to the warnings she got from Sümbül Aga on the first evening, she always opposed to everything.

But she added a few Turkish words to her dictionary every day. She said, for example, 'Ucly thing.' One who knew that 'ucly' meant 'ugly,' understood. To the black harem witches, who poked her with an elbow or punched a fist into her stomach if she opposed them, she learned to say, 'Break your hands.'

After each dispute, new scratches appeared on her body. Sümbül Aga would appear on the spot right away, his fat belly bobbing rhythmically during his run. However, before his arrival, Aleksandra always managed to give the girls a hard time. Then came the time to endure Thunder Arm's painful hits of the stick on her back without letting out the slightest sound.

***

The biggest fight broke out when Aleksandra caught one of the girls rummaging in her bundle. The girl emptied it, spreading all the destroyed items on the floor:

"Look! Look!" she shouted, laughing.

Four black witches couldn't prize her out from Aleksandra's hands.

That day she met the falaka punishment: she was locked in a restraint to immobilize her, and she had her feet flogged with a stick.

Even though tears gushed from her eyes after every hit to her bare feet, she refused to make a sound, not even the slightest whimper. She clutched her bundle tightly.

After it all, she spread her hands and asked:

"What did I do? What did I do?"

For three days, Aleksandra couldn't stand on her feet. Walking was also difficult. When she had no other choice, she staggered in unimaginable pain, leaning on Merzuka's shoulder. She didn't even think about moving on all fours. Merzuka cried and rubbed oils onto her feet.

Setaret Kalfa also cried, but no one saw her tears.

"One day they will see," was the only thing she said.

Sümbül Aga was the most impressed with Aleksandra's progress in learning Turkish. The girl had long overtaken the novices who came to the harem many months before her. Basically, aga could say with confidence to Sultana Mother that the Ruthenian was ready to leave the novice pavilion. But the man thought to himself: *Wait, let her learn some humility. Let her understand who Sümbül is.*

That was why he lied unscrupulously when the Mother Sultana asked about her.

"A girl came from the palace of Aishe, the first wife of my husband of holy memory, Sultan Selim. Apparently, her mother's daughter-in-law's sent her. Where is she? How is she doing?"

"She is not ready yet for the sultan's chambers, My Lady," he lied. Knowing that the old woman always carefully listened to his words, he added hastily: "How to say it... This is a difficult girl. She has a big mouth, is quarrelsome, and causes turmoil among girls. There is not a shred of obedience in her. But do not worry, your servant Sümbül softened harder stones. Time will come for her as well."

These words satisfied Sultana Hafsa.

"I am counting on you, Sümbül. Show what you can do. I want to see this girl. Aj Bala Hatun sent a message: 'My mother-in-law entrusted her to me, now I entrust her to you.' We can not leave her alone. It is a sin."

Aga of the harem bowed respectfully to the mother of the padishah.

It will be better if I stop beating this Ruthenian girl, he thought. He had to admit that the girl was unusually capable. She behaved as if she were born and brought up in a palace. Her curves charmed anyone who looked at her. She had an unbreakable pride in her. When the light emanating from her eyes combined with a noble attitude, no one could match her. In music, too – she surpassed all the girls. Taking the oud into her hands, she moved the most tender strings of the soul. When she played, the stones from the courtyard rose to the upper floors. Her tunes managed to take the breath away from even the greatest beauties in the harem.

One of the few men with the right to enter the harem was the music teacher Kemali Efendi. He adored Aleksandra. Harem girls even began spreading malicious rumors that this admiration was associated with the girl's blue-green eyes, but none of them dared to say that she played more beautifully than them. The fingers of none of them moved with such speed and mastery on the strings of the kanun. She also added the saz to her musical instrument accomplishments, and when she played this new stringed instrument, it seemed that she had been doing it for years, and not just starting to learn. No one could bring out equally touching sounds from the instruments.

Her voice caused trepidation in Sümbül Aga – he wouldn't lie, saying that he'd not heard such a beautiful female voice. In the evening, when the harem was enveloped in the night's silence, the girls who came from all four corners of the world, one more beautiful than the other, listened to her with growing longing. When everyone left for their own worlds after the evening prayer, the harem, which was a witness to great dreams, ambitions, and disappointments, was filled with the delicate, moving voice of Aleksandra, coming from the pavilion for novices.

Even the frozen heart of Sümbül warmed up when he listened to the girl's songs. These sounds brought the memory of the past, and longing choked him in his throat.

When he realized that his eyes were misting, he immediately tried to shake it off, repeating: "the Ruthenian madwoman, Ruthenian madwoman." That's why he pretended not to see when the Abyssinian assistant, who had accompanied him for three years, listened enchanted to Aleksandra's song at nights. He didn't even react when he noticed them whispering about something secretly. Did the boy cry? Let him cry. If Sümbül Aga could not mourn his fate, at least let Jafer despair over his. Crying cleansed the soul. Sümbül's soul had not been cleansed for a long time; he did not even remember when he'd last cried. Perhaps it was on that unfortunate night when he fell into the hands of slave traders, or perhaps when the damned tongs snapped between his legs, crushing all his dreams? He did not remember.

CHAPTER THIRTEEN

Aleksandra lost track of time. How long had she been in the harem? For ten days? Fifteen? Or maybe twenty? Who knows...? She wasn't aware that almost two months had passed because each day was no different from the previous one.

When she went into the garden under the watchful eye of Setaret Kalfa and Merzuka, the air was crisp. She saw the cloudy sky between the naked branches of the trees, and the sea looked as if it had been painted gray. A white tower rose in the middle of the water, and red, blue, and green boats sailed in the distance. There were huge wooden sailing ships on the left, and a round tower was visible on one of the hills.

The cold didn't bother her, and in fact, she even liked it because it reminded her of her homeland. She strolled between the rose bushes that were waiting with longing for the spring to bloom. She wondered what color they would be: White? Red? As soon as they develop their buds, there will be no need for her to ask such unimportant questions to pass the time.

So... What will I do then? she asked herself. *I guess I'll be wondering how many flowers they will have.*

Were there also her beloved redbuds in the garden? If not, she must tell someone about it. But who? To whom would she say that? The Thunder Arm Sümbül Aga? Or maybe that shameless black witch? As her Turkish was becoming better, she whispered her name in secret: "Gülbejaz... Gülbejaz..." She still called her Gül-something, but the woman didn't care.

Aleksandra's thoughts returned to the redbuds.

What would I say? Sümbül Aga, Sümbül Aga, I like them so much. Where are my redbuds? If you tell Sultan Suleiman about it, he'll order a few trees to be planted here. How many whips would I get as an answer?

"Tsss... Girl..."

A feminine voice. Ruthenian – and this in the harem garden! She turned immediately to the direction from which it came.

"Are you talking to me?"

She was beautiful. Very beautiful. The most beautiful wheat ears would envy her for the colors of her curls. As the Ruthenian girls often did, she braided her long hair and pinned it on her head like a crown. She covered her head with a fur hood. She had beautiful eyes, blue like a spring sky, and her smooth, firm cheeks were red from the cold.

"Yes, to you. Are you this new Ruthenian girl?"

"Yes, it's me. I'm her."

She knew that she was talking nonsense out of pure joy.

"I did not expect anyone else from Ruthenia to be here. I'm so excited."

The girl with blond hair moved on a garden chair lined with large pillows.

"What's your name?"

"Aleksandra. Aleksandra Anastasia Lisowska."

"Are you Ukrainian?"

"Yhm. I come from Ruthenia."

"My name is Ekaterina Ivanova. I'm from the Moscow area."

Aleksandra's heart almost jumped out of her chest. Now she was not alone here. She had a countrywoman in the harem.

Without thinking about whether it was allowed or not, she sat down next to Ekaterina. A little further, Merzuka and Setaret Kalfa tried to communicate with each other, waving their arms. It may have been in vain, but since they did not give up, it had to be something important.

Aleksandra wanted to talk about everything that came to her mind because she wanted to enjoy her native language. She wanted to put her head on the girl's chest and cry, kiss her, smell her. After all these years, she'd finally met someone from her homeland. Novices couldn't go to the floor of odalisques, and neither did odalisques go to the dormitory of the new girls. Perhaps they weren't allowed to talk to each other, either. Aleksandra didn't care – she was ready to take the punishment of ten, twenty, a hundred, and even a thousand blows from the hand of the Thunder Arm.

She was about to start telling her whole story when Ekaterina spoke.

"How long have you been here?" she asked.

"I don't know," Aleksandra replied. "Ten days, I think. Or maybe fifteen? Maybe two months? I don't know.

And you?"

"Three..."

"What?" Astonished, Aleksandra interrupted the girl. "So, you've been here shorter than me?" There was disappointment in her voice.

"No, my lovely. Not three days... Three years..."

Aleksandra opened her mouth in amazement. Three years? My God! Three years!

"Three long winters, three long springs, three long..."

"How old are you, Aleksandra?" asked the girl unexpectedly.

"It's my fifteenth winter."

Ekaterina smiled.

"When I came here, I was a year younger than you."

So, she was seventeen now. She was only two years older than her, but to Aleksandra, she seemed much older, at least she looked so. She was taller, more mature, more experienced. She raised her head and looked tenderly in the girl's blue eyes.

"How did you get here?"

"It's simple," Ekaterina said with a dry smile. "My father was a salesman. He transported goods from Moscow to Kiev. I was with him. The Tatars attacked our transport..."

The rest was obvious. Somewhere around the Azak fortress, the Tatars sold her to the Genoese captain, and he sold the girl to a slave trader. First, she went to the house of some bey, and from there she arrived at the Ottoman palace as a gift.

"And you?" Ekaterina asked, even if she was to listen to the same story.

Although they had a lot in common, Aleksandra realized that her situation wasn't so bad. First of all, she had never been sold. The mother of the great Crimean Khan entrusted her to the Ottomans. She decided that she had the right to boast a bit.

"Crimean Khan gave me to Sultan Suleiman. I'll see him."

This time it was Ekaterina who opened her eyes wide. She looked at Aleksandra with surprise, and there wasn't even a shadow of mockery in her eyes – she believed her words.

"So, you will see Sultan Suleiman," she whispered.

"Yes, but until now there hasn't been an opportunity."

"Do you know what he looks like?"

Aleksandra shook her head.

"Listen, my beautiful," Ekaterina said quietly, hugging her more tightly. "There are certain rules in the harem. You will not see the Sultan – he will see you. You will be honored to be seen by the Padishah. Do you think that you can knock on the ruler's door and say: 'I came to see you?' Do not boast that you are his gift or who knows what. We are all gifts here."

Aleksandra's eyes clouded.

"How do I get the honor of being seen by Sultan Suleiman?"

"You must be on good terms with Sümbül Aga. Here to be on good terms with someone means that you have to give him money or..." The blonde fell silent.

"Or what?!" Aleksandra exclaimed with excitement.

"You have to play with him."

"Merzuka said that they are no longer men."

"They are not, but some of them enjoy love playing. 'It's nice to interact with beauty,' they say." The girl fell silent. She looked around as if she wanted to see if anyone could hear them, and then added quietly: "Most of the girls in the harem before they saw the face of the Sultan, passed through their hands. That's what eunuchs are like. And do not think that kalfas are any different. These black hags also love playing with girls."

Aleksandra couldn't believe what she was hearing. She would never allow anything like that. What will happen to her if she has no money? Does this mean that she will not see Sultan Suleiman? Was the path foretold by Sultana Mother to end here?

Ekaterina read the girl's thoughts unmistakably. In the first months of her stay in the palace, she too, like this innocent girl, had to choose between dreams and morality.

"What did you do?"

Hearing this, Ekaterina sank into her thoughts. Then, she stood up and looked deeply into Aleksandra's beautiful eyes.

"How do you think I got in their favors and ended up in the sultan's bed?"

Instantly, blood rushed to Aleksandra's head.

"You..." she stammered. "Did you get to the sultan's bed?"

Ekaterina's face changed her expression. Aleksandra read on it both pride and shame, anger, as well as dashed dreams.

"Yes," she whispered, nodding. "For one night."

What else was the odalisque to do, if not ignite her master's senses, satisfy him, fill him with pride, give in to his will, and fulfill his wishes? Weren't all of them here to give him a son or at least a daughter? This means that Ekaterina failed.

"He did not call me again."

Aleksandra did not know what to say. Was she sorry? Yes, she felt internal pain, but at the same time, she was happy. If the ruler did not like Ekaterina, she still had a chance. She was ashamed of her conflicting feelings. She stretched out her hands and covered the girl's little frozen hands with hers as if to comfort her.

Along with the honor of communing with the ruler, Ekaterina had gained a higher position. A day earlier, she had been led out of the dormitory for novices, and now she had her own small room in the harem. She wore beautiful clothes and even received money for small expenses. It didn't matter that she never poked her nose outside the harem door; she was allowed to send servants to buy what she wanted. She also had money, which she could give stealthily to the harem agas, if necessary. She waited weeks for a re-invitation, but it eventually became clear that the sultan had forgotten about her. She even gave a bribe to Sümbül Aga so that he could discreetly remind the ruler about her, but that was in vain too. Aga did not have good news for Ekaterina, neither that day nor the next one. She gave him some money a few more times, but since it failed to bring any results, she gave up trying to remind the ruler about herself.

"He didn't want me anymore," she said without raising her face. She was embarrassed to look Aleksandra in the eye.

Why? Aleksandra wondered. *Why doesn't she look at me? I don't understand it. Was it because she shared the bed with the Sultan, or because he didn't like her enough to invite her there again?* After all, all the girls in the harem were waiting, wishing, praying at night, dreaming about spending the night with Sultan Suleiman. Ekaterina had succeeded. So, she had no reason to be ashamed. She wanted it. Very much.

I'm here for this, too. To share a bed with him, she continued to think. If the reason for Ekaterina's embarrassment was that he did not like her, she couldn't say anything to that. *I will not be ashamed,* she decided. *I will share a bed with him, and he will want only me.*

But what should I do to please him, so that he would like me? How could I please a man before whom the whole world trembled? What does it actually mean to give a man pleasure? How should I behave in bed? Except for a few overheard things, she knew nothing about such love. She was worried. *What if I fail, too?*

Both were silent for a moment. In the end, Aleksandra thought with horror that the Sultan might not like her, either.

"What will you do now?" she whispered.

The girl smiled bitterly.

"I have no illusions anymore that our ruler will remember me. I do not expect it. I hope that they will marry me off to some aga, bey, or janissary who has just graduated from Enderun, and I will get out of this harem."

***

That night anxiety kept Aleksandra awake. She had to take care of her destiny.

First of all, she had to see Suleiman or show herself to him, and the rest would go smoothly. She intended to open the way to her happiness. In bed, she'll give her best, too.

She remembered the advice of the Sultana Mother: 'Do not wait for someone to give you what you want. Reach for it, snatch it, if necessary, by force, and do not let go...'

So, that's what she will do. To pave the way to happiness, she would even agree to playing and stroking of these disgusting harem agas, and if necessary, even by the witch Gülbejaz.

CHAPTER FOURTEEN

Aleksandra and Ekaterina met several times.

"You know, we have to change your name," the fair-haired girl said one day.

"My name? Why?"

"Aleksandra Anastasia Lisowska is very difficult. Turks can't even pronounce 'Aleksandra' correctly."

The girl was surprised. She didn't know what to say.

"You need a simple, easy-to-pronounce name."

"Like what?"

"For example... For example, I know! Ruslana. Yes, from now on you will be Ruslana."

"Ruslana?"

"Yes... Ruslana. It's easy to pronounce and suits you."

"Ruslana... Ruslana..." repeated Aleksandra. "Do you think it's necessary?"

"I think so, my lovely. The Sultan can not have difficulty saying your name. He can not forget it. He will break his tongue on 'Aleksandra.'"

"Ruslana... Ruslana..."

"Yes. Don't you like it? After all, you are from Ruthenia."

In fact, Aleksandra did like the name. It sounded nice.

"How do you change your name? Should I just say that I am Ruslana from now on?"

"You will tell it to that pig Sümbül. When he calls you 'Aleksandra,' you won't react. You will only answer if he calls you Ruslana."

"Then he will really beat me."

"This man is a devil. And even worse. You must be on good terms with him, my lovely. If he wants, he can clear your path, but he can also get rid of you from the palace – and no one will know about it."

***

Aleksandra decided she would become Ruslana. At the first opportunity, she told Sümbül Aga about it.

"I am changing my name."

"You are doing what?"

"I'm no longer Aleksandra, but Ruslana."

"Who are you?"

The man's ebony face was unreadable. He began to play with the stick in his hand.

I guess the blows will fall on me soon enough, she thought.

"Rus-la-na. Rus-la-na," she spelled with emphasis.

"Ruslana," muttered Sümbül Aga. It seemed that a smile crossed his face. "Well. It was difficult to say 'Aleksandra' while hitting you with a stick." And then he just left.

Then she went to Merzuka.

"Don't call me Aleksandra anymore, but Ruslana."

Hearing this, the Tatar girl was very surprised. The rest watched her in silence.

"My name is Ruslana, not Aleksandra. Ruslana. Do you understand? The girl from Ruthenia. Ruslana."

Setaret Kalfa and Gül-something were also surprised, but they didn't ask any questions. They only looked at her for a long moment. When Setaret tried to pronounce the girl's new name, opening her huge black lips wide, they all burst out laughing.

After that, everything happened as she had thought it would. Because she did not respond to the name Aleksandra, she got several hits from Sümbül Aga, but that didn't break her stubbornness. Finally, the harem's aga and his helper Jafer also began to call her Ruslana.

After a few days, everyone forgot about Aleksandra. Lying in her bed in the novice's dormitory, she covered herself with a blanket to the tip of her nose and repeated all night: *Ruslana. Ruslana*. Then a thought occurred to her: *I killed Aleksandra.* Now she was to start a new life in the Ottoman palace in her body. She forgot about Aleksandra Anastasia Lisowska. Several times it happened that she didn't react when someone called her by Ruslana, but she quickly got used to it.

Aleksandra's life began in a mountain village in Ukraine, and fifteen winters later came to an end in Istanbul, in Suleiman's palace, she whispered to herself one night in the darkness of the novice's bedroom.

Along with the name, she rejected her past – her village, home, memories, mother's voice, and the sound of a bell in a small church. She erased everything from her memory. The gloom of the past, unhappiness, harm, pain, tears were all to disappear together with Aleksandra.

The girl with great dreams and goals was Ruslana.

She wiped the mist that covered her eyes with the back of her hand. She suppressed the sobs choking her throat.

***

Ekaterina was the first teacher of love for Ruslana. She asked questions, and Ekaterina answered.

"What does Suleiman like best?"

"How do you think, my lovely. He likes it most when the bird flies into the nest."

"A bird? What bird?"

Ekaterina looked at her so that at first Ruslana thought that her question was very stupid, and out of place. But seeing the playful and meaningful look of her friend, she immediately understood what the bird meant.

"I... Yyy... I'm sorry. I'm so silly!"

Both began to giggle. In fact, Ruslana had never seen it before.

"Merzuka calls it a 'one-eyed jigit.' It's a bit longer than a hand," Ekaterina explained.

Ruslana swallowed several times.

"Ekaterina..." she began, but she couldn't get the question out of her throat. She was even embarrassed to look her friend in the face.

"Ask me, my lovely."

"I was wondering how to say... Is it difficult? This first time... Is it difficult?"

"A bit," the girl murmured.

She didn't remember her first time. Out of emotions and fear she'd turned her head away, so now she recalled everything as if through a fog. She did what she was told. When she was told to spread her legs, she did it – and she didn't remember the rest – it was as if she lost consciousness.

If I had been in control of myself, she thought frequently, *maybe I could have charmed the padishah. If I had just kept myself in check.* But, because of pain or perhaps fear, everything was blurred. Did it really hurt?

"How was it? How was it?" the women in the harem questioned later.

"It probably hurt," one said.

"Of course. The first time for a fourteen-year-old must be difficult and painful," someone else added.

The girls before her had also said so, Ekaterina remembered.

Then Ruslana asked about something that terrified her terribly.

"Is... is there a lot of bleeding?"

The girl felt her cheeks burning.

"Pray for the bleeding. If you bleed, the Sultan will know that no one had touched you before, and you will fill him with pride. If you bleed, Sümbül Aga will take the sheet to the Mother Sultana as proof of her son's ability, telling her the good news."

"Good news?"

"Yes, my beautiful. About the fact that the Padishah succeeded, and that the girl was clean. If such a girl gives him a child, she will become haseki."

"Haseki? What does that mean?"

"Oh my, you really have no idea about anything. Haseki is the Sultan's favorite, the one he likes most, who gives him a child."

"What if I don't bleed?"

"You must. You'll surely bleed."

"What if not?"

"Then, even if you give him a child, it won't matter. They will take the child, and they will give you away to somebody, and throw you out of the palace. To become the ruler's favorite, you must protect your virtue, my beautiful one."

Ruslana didn't know anything anymore. If she was to protect virtue, how was she supposed to play with harem agas? Ekaterina told her the secrets of this game every night.

It certainly had to remain a secret. Admittedly, everyone knew that the capable fingers and wet tongues of some harem residents, even eunuchs and black servants, were a remedy – especially for those odalisques who missed love when they were not called again after a night spent with the Sultan – but no one had the courage to say it aloud. Such a secret could be deadly. Who knows what punishment would be inflicted upon those who committed such acts?

"The most dangerous weapon in the palace is the tongue," Ekaterina said one day. "There are lots of spies everywhere, everyone snitches. You have to keep your mouth shut, my beautiful one. Here, you should not say anything if there is no need. You have to solve the problems in sign language."

Ruslana opened her mouth in amazement. That was why when she asked a question, instead of answering verbally, the girls would gesture with their eyebrows and eyes.

***

After Ekaterina's lessons of love, Ruslana's world stood on its head. When the theory was not enough, the girl also gave practical lessons.

At first, Ruslana was very ashamed. She tried to escape from the arms of her friend. But when she felt the hands, fingers, and lips of Ekaterina, her resistance eased. The wandering lips around her neck made her mad. Feeling the lusty hands grasping her breasts, she could see the stars – and especially when Ekaterina's talented fingers set off to search for her most secretive places – Ruslana was breathless. Suddenly her body shook with a spasm. When the girl found the place she was looking for, her fingers began to move faster. A wave of pleasure spilled over her body. She covered her mouth to suppress the urge to shout. Another spasm. And one more! Ekaterina's fingers did not stop, like her suppressed moans. She returned to her bed with trembling legs.

Then she realized that something warm was coming out of her, so she checked with horror – was this blood? Could women's fingers have made this? She saw something sticky and transparent on the fabric. Although she saw it for the first time, she calmed down and swore that it was the last time. She will not allow Ekaterina to do this anymore. But some inner voice ridiculed this resolution. Her resistance was useless and didn't stop Ekaterina's passion. When the storm of passion stopped, Ruslana whispered:

"We shouldn't do this."

"Don't be stupid." Ekaterina laughed softly. "That's how it is in the harem. What do you think all these women can do without a man?"

"But it's indecent."

"Wasn't it pleasant?"

Ruslana tried to change the subject.

"Wasn't it pleasant?" Ekaterina asked again – she wasn't giving up.

When she didn't get the answer again, she grabbed the girl's breast and squeezed her nipple.

"Do not pretend, my beautiful one. You are dying of pleasure. You wait for me to come to you." She paused for a moment, then looked into the beautiful eyes of the girl, reflecting the waves of pleasure. "You drive me crazy too."

Ruslana's face brightened.

"So, I can give pleasure, too?" she whispered shyly to Ekaterina.

"If you manage to get to the sultan's bed, you will bewitch the ruler."

"Really?"

"Yes. But be careful. Do not you dare to shout in the Padishah's bed. Never do that. And never bite a man like you bit me."

Ruslana gently stroked the purple spots that her teeth left on the girl's neck.

She was surprised that passion can enslave a person like that. It changed the water, quietly meandering from the source into a bubbling waterfall. Will she be able to please the Sultan? At the very thought, her heart pounded. It bothered her on long lonely nights.

Then, everything happened so suddenly – in the blink of an eye. She didn't know herself how it exactly happened.

***

One day, Sümbül Aga's strong shoulders squeezed her waist. The man pulled her into a secret room under the stairs. His big hands tightened on her breasts.

"You can't," Ruslana opposed, just as Ekaterina taught her.

Her opposition aroused even greater lust in the men. His thick mouth began to suck her neck.

"Do not pretend to be unavailable. You know that you will rot here without me. You will not even see the face of the Sultan," he murmured.

Do you want me to pay you in love, Sümbül Aga? she thought.

The man whispered something, trying to kiss her on the lips, but Ruslana did not care.

"If I do what you want, will you arrange that Suleiman will see me? Will you tell him about me?" Ruslana tried to close the man's mouth, but her small body started to weaken, faced with his strength. "Tell the Sultan things to make him want to see me."

Sümbül Aga caught the air as if he was about to suffocate.

"Fine," he grunted.

Ruslana was ready to give him the expected payment, but she continued to tease him, pretending to try to slip away.

"Promise. Swear. Say that you promise."

Sümbül Aga was on fire. When Ruslana uncovered one of her full, milk-white breasts, he went mad with lust. Grabbing her in his ebony hands, he whispered:

"I swear. I promise you. Come."

Ruslana suddenly became aware that now she was in control. So... it was so easy to win over a man.

"What are you promising? I won't come until you say it."

"I will tell the Sultan such things about you that he won't even want to look at others. I promise."

"That's all?"

"As soon as possible, I will take you to the Sultana Mother."

"You promise?"

"Yes."

Suddenly Ruslana remembered Ekaterina's advice — *do not tease for too long.* She clung to the man. Her hard breasts touched his hairy torso. She moaned as if it was pleasant to her. Or maybe it actually was? She did everything Ekaterina had taught her to give the eunuch as much pleasure as possible.

When it was over, she assured herself, *I swear. It will never happen again.*

Aleksandra understood there was no use of a dead bird for anyone. That day, for the first time, she said to Setaret Kalfa voluntarily:

"Take me to the bathhouse."

She was disgusted with what she'd done. She felt dirty. Will she feel the same when she finds herself in the bed with the Sultan?

***

At the exact moment Ruslana felt certain that the door to her future was wide open for her, an unexpected misfortune stood in her path. It was in the form of a tall and shapely Greek woman with raven-black hair, black eyes, and a lithe waist. Despina, like Ruslana, was among the novices. From what Ruslana learned, she'd come to the palace a few months before her. They said the Greek girl was thirteen, but she couldn't believe it – her body was more developed than Ruslana's body. Her large breasts looked like they were about to jump out of the caftan, and her hips were also very feminine.

"In my opinion, she has about eighteen winters behind her," her Tatar friend claimed.

"No, she's a little girl. A girl's body develops faster in a warm climate. There's a hot island called Crete, and the pirates have kidnapped her from there.

There were various stories about Despina's age, but her beauty was unquestionable. Anyway, there were no ugly girls in the harem. Some gossiped about her because they were jealous of her. Despina moved like a dream. Her black-olive eyes were incredibly beautiful, but she didn't seem to realize it – her stare was blank, and there wasn't a trace of reflection, flirt, or desire in her gaze. She was just beautiful; that was all.

She was called 'Helen of Troy' in the harem. She was capable and learned Turkish quickly. She sang Greek songs to the accompaniment of a strange saz with a long fretboard and a pear-shaped box, which she called a bouzouki. The songs were beautiful, but you couldn't say the same about her voice. The Sultan probably put up with it because of the rhythmic melodies, when one day he called her to his chamber to sing for him.

Ruslana didn't consider her a threat. She was sure that Sultan Suleiman would choose her, and when that happens, she will make sure that he doesn't look at any other girl. She will succeed because she was prepared to do anything to enchant Suleiman.

There was a quiet but fierce Ruthenian-Greek rivalry in the pavilion for novices, that broke out in the least expected moment when Ruslana, beautifully dressed, waited for an audience with Sultana Hafsa. When the harem servants came to take her to the Sultana Mother, they saw Ruslana and Despina struggling in rage. What could have happened? Nobody knew. Even the strong bodies of Setaret Kalfa and Gülbejaz, and their claw-like hands were not enough to separate the girls that were hitting each other, pulling hair, scratching, and rolling on the floor. Ruslana shouted in Ruthenian, Despina in Greek, every now and then, interjecting with Turkish curses. Both shouted out the same threats:

"I will kill you! Murder you!"

They fought with such fierceness – as if they wanted to put their threats into practice immediately.

Because the efforts of Setaret and Gülbejaz didn't work, a few black eunuchs came to help, but they were also helpless.

When Despina called Ruslana a "Ruthenian strumpet," the quarrel broke out again.

Ruslana lunged at the girl and clasped her hands on her neck.

"Try to repeat it!" she shrieked, clenching her hands tighter and tighter.

If the familiar arms of Sümbül Aga's had not lifted her up, Despina would probably indeed have lost her life. Five fingers of Ruslana left a trace on her neck, and it was clear that there would be a bruise. Blood appeared in the spots where the girl's nails had dug in. Aga held kicking Ruslana in a steel grip.

"Let me go! I will show this primitive Greek woman!"

Meanwhile, Despina writhed on the floor, gasping for breath.

"What happened?" Sümbül Aga roared, passing Ruslana to his young helper, Jafer.

Nobody answered anything. Ruslana put her hand to her breast, that rose and fell like a blacksmith's bellows.

Sümbül tried to stay calm, then the girl's white firm breasts came to his mind.

"What happened?" he repeated, trying to erase those images from his memory.

Ruslana was silent. She thought that Thunder Shoulder would hit her any moment, but she didn't care about any beating. The only thing she was afraid of, was that because of this quarrel, he would give up showing her to Sultana Mother. Clenching her eyes shut, she waited for the blow, but nothing like that happened. When she opened her eyes, she saw that Sümbül Aga was nudging the Greek woman, still squirming on the floor, with his foot.

"You tell me what happened here."

But Despina wasn't able to talk.

Aga didn't find out anything from Setaret Kalfa or other girls, either. Finally, he turned angrily to Ruslana:

"We'll have a talk later!" he shouted, spitting in all directions. "Get her out of here! I don't want to see her!"

When Jafer and Setaret were leading her to the door, Ruslana heard the whistle of a stick. Turning around, she saw Sümbül Aga punish Despina. The proud girl did not even moan so that Ruslana couldn't hear her and it was only when the door closed behind her that the Greek girl screamed.

"Now she will know who she is dealing with," muttered Ruslana. She didn't even try to hide the satisfaction on her face.

Setaret Kalfa, Merzuka, and Gül-something were busy like bees. They ran back and forth. They took Ruslana to the bathhouse again, and after having thoroughly washed her, they tried to give her hairstyle the right shape. They cut her bangs, and they curled her hair over her ears on thin rollers. They tried new clothes, for which they sent young Jafer. They put a white, ankles-long robe over airy galligaskins sewn from a soft flowing fabric, and three beautifully decorated red velvet skirts on top. Ruslana hated the leather shoes with raised toes. She couldn't walk in them and wanted to take them off before she even took two steps in them. As a result, she wore shoes decorated with the same velvet from which the skirts were made.

Merzuka frowned, looking at the girl.

"What?"

Ruslana was afraid she'd done something wrong again.

"May she break her hands. You have marks made by this simpleton's claw on your face."

Ruslana grabbed the mirror. She didn't know if it was because of unrestrained anger or the hot water, but her face was all red. Her eyes flashed with rage seeing two scratches on her cheek and temple – she thought it was all over. How could she stand with such a face before the Sultana Mother? It was out of the question.

"I'm not going," she sobbed helplessly. What would her future mother-in-law say if she saw her all bruised and scratched? "I'm not going! I'm not going!" She hit the sofa with her fists.

"Silence, crazy girl!" Setaret Kalfa said. "I will find a solution. Nobody will notice anything."

The woman kept her word. She mixed up a bit of powder, blush, and a few other ingredients Ruslana didn't recognize and put it on her face. All nail marks disappeared! She put a small silk cap over her hair that fell onto her shoulders. Over the cap, she placed a soft, tulle veil, decorated on four sides with colorful embroidery. She arranged curls on her forehead to cover up the scratches. When she finished, she moved away and admired her work from a distance, like a painter.

"Success. No trace of scratches."

Ruslana didn't even have time to look in the mirror because the door opened, and huge Sümbül Aga came inside.

"Come on, come on, hurry up! Our master's mother will not wait all day to see some snot!" he roared.

He looked at Ruslana and almost flipped. Oh gosh! Was she really this tiger-like girl with lush eyebrows?

When their eyes met, Sümbül Aga still couldn't hide his admiration. This girl took not only his breath away; when the Sultan sees her, he will be impressed. He knew him. He knew what he was looking for in women, what he liked and what attracted him. He had to know, it was his job.

Anxiety began to germinate in his head.

What will happen if Suleiman likes the girl? Then my fate may change too, he thought. *If she becomes the favorite of the Sultan and tells what happened under the stairs, I will pay with my head. If she keeps this secret for herself, then probably my fat purses will be joined by some new ones.*

He realized he had only two options before him: either to prevent the meeting of the Sultan with the Ruthenian novice or vice versa – to find a way to promptly bring Ruslana to the Padishah. The experienced aga made the decision in an instant.

Sümbül Aga walked first, while Ruslana stepped carefully behind him, trying not to slip in the uncomfortable shoes or lose any of them. On her right side were Merzuka, Setaret, and Gül-something, and other white-skinned and black eunuchs. They walked quickly down the long corridor to meet Sultana Hafsa. Suddenly Sümbül Aga slowed down a bit and addressed Ruslana.

"What happened? Why did you fight with that girl?" he asked her in Ruthenian.

"She told me that she saw us under the stairs," Ruslana whispered.

It was fortunate that Aga's skin was black; otherwise, everyone would have surely noticed the blood hitting his face. His body became heavy. Ruslana had tried to strangle the girl, and he again fueled her jealousy and anger with a beating.

Good God, he thought, *why did I do it? Why did I allow myself to give in to my lust and drag this girl under the stairs?* But now wasn't the time for self-pity – he had to finish what Ruslana did not do.

"What happens now?" Ruslana's voice was full of worry. All her dreams could be ruined.

Opening the elegant rosewood door at the end of the corridor, he snorted:

"She will not say anything."

Ruslana walked inside, trying to erase all possible terrifying solutions. Now she had to focus all her attention on making a great impression on the older woman. Her life, future, and dreams depended on this. Simply everything. She must get her mother-in-law to like her.

***

That night, two dark shadows sneaking under the city walls threw something big into the sea. The sack floated on the foamy waves for a moment, then disappeared into the depths. Despina would not be able to say anything anymore.

CHAPTER FIFTEEN

The maids standing in front of the double-winged carved door looked worried at the sight of Sümbül Aga. One of the girls gently opened the door and quickly looked inside.

Ruslana was so nervous that she thought everyone could hear her heart beating. Finally, the moment of truth had arrived. If the woman behind this door likes her, she will be a step closer to achieving her goal. Otherwise, her destiny will again be at a dead end, and she will sink into fear and helplessness.

Ruslana suddenly felt hot as she repeated to herself that she must please her.

What if Sultana Mother had heard about that quarrel? What if she won't allow this 'Ruthenian cat, who throws herself at everyone with her claws bared,' to get to her son's alcove? Then it won't matter that someone recommended me. I'll just be thrown into some dark corner of the palace and left alone, or even worse – given to someone and put outside the door of the Seraglio. Has the Sultana promise me to someone for their son as a wife, or that she'll make me a haseki? No. I'll probably rot in the palace for years. In the end, I'll become an old, grayed odalisque.

I'd rather die, she continued to think.

"Do what I do. Do not dare look at the face of Sultana Hafsa without orders. Do not open your mouth until they tell you. Do not try to raise your voice," Sümbül Aga told her, and in doing so, he brought her back to earth.

I know, she thought. How many days she had been sitting with the black witches and repeating with them: 'I will not look in the face of the ruler without orders. I will not speak until asked. While speaking, I will not raise my voice.' Sometimes she even repeated in her sleep: 'I will not look in the face of the ruler without an order.'

Or maybe it won't be necessary at all. It is possible that in a moment the door will open and the girl who had just entered there will stick her head out and say: 'Sümbül Aga, Sultana Mother says she does not want to see this Ruthenian girl. Go away and take this gadabout with you.'

Don't you dare raise your head. Don't you dare speak. Don't you dare look her in the eye, even if you get an order. Don't you dare forget to bend low when crossing the doorway and disturbing her peace. Damn it! The list. Don't you dare... it was so long. How many of these prohibitions will I remember? What will happen if I forget something? Ruslana worried. *The Sultana will order to take my head, saying: 'This girl looked into my eyes?' It's all so silly.*

Where is this girl? Why isn't she coming out? Let what has to happen be done now.

She couldn't stand the tension. Now she not only had a trembling heart but also had ringing in her ears. She was overcome by even more terrible doubts.

Could Sultana Hafsa really have heard about that quarrel? Of course, she heard about it, she answered herself. *If not the mother of the great Padishah, then who was supposed to hear about it? Those black harem witches probably ran to her a long time ago*, she thought with conviction. *Was it possible that she also knew the reason for it? And if Despina said she noticed me playing with Sümbül Aga: 'I saw them making out under the stairs. I swear.' If this has happened, then I'm finished.*

"Get a grip," Merzuka whispered behind her. "If someone looked at you, he would think you're going to be beheaded. You are white as a wall."

Ruslana immediately pinched herself on both cheeks. She looked at Merzuka as if to ask: 'Better now?' but the Tatar girl only muttered in response.

Just as the new doubts began to overwhelm her, the huge double doors opened.

Sümbül Aga walked in front with the pride of the owner of all mountains and valleys.

"Move," he whispered to her over his shoulder.

Crossing his arms, the man put his right hand on his left arm and the left hand on his right one, then stopped in front of the high threshold in the doorway. Forgetting all his haughtiness, he bowed low and took a step forward.

Ruslana trembled at the doorstep. She tried to cross her arms like Sümbül Aga, but she couldn't do it. Joining her hands on her stomach, she crossed the threshold. She took a few steps. Did she bow?

Damn it! Did I forget? Where is this woman? Why can't I lift my head and look? Or maybe I'm walking in the wrong direction? She felt that the door behind her had closed as silently as it had opened. *So, the rest stayed outside. Where was Sümbül Aga? Is he with me? To my right or left? I want to finally raise my head and look around!*

She didn't know how long she would stand staring at the floor. She did not raise her head, so she could only feel the sunlight falling on her from the window. At the same moment, exactly opposite her, she heard a woman's voice:

"Sümbül..." The voice was not too loud, but imperious. It wasn't high, but feminine. "Did something happen today in the novice's pavilion?"

Too bad! Everything is over! This woman knows! I'm finished! All these words filled her thoughts in an instant. Ruslana didn't even hear Sümbül Aga's answer, she was so overwhelmed by panic. But it was obvious that it wasn't satisfactory for the Sultana Mother.

"Don't you know, aga, that the harem is the home of our Master, the Padishah, and no one has the right to disturb his peace and quiet? What were those noises? What was this disobedience?"

"I know, My Lady."

"If you know it, why did you let this happen?"

"Sultana Mother knows better than me how difficult it is to manage the novices."

"What am I hearing, Sümbül? Were the novices entrusted to an aga who is unable to exercise power over them?" The woman's voice was harsher now.

Things get complicated, Ruslana shuddered. *My dream will end even before it started.*

"Not just one Sümbül, but thousands will sacrifice for our ruler. I am ready to incur punishment if these screams reached your ears, and caused your anger."

Ruslana didn't understand half of what the man was saying, but the calmness and confidence of his statements calmed her.

"Who does not know the basic rules? What is one like this doing in the harem?"

Something sounded like a warning in Ruslana's head again. This woman would not let it go. Everything will come out.

"It was a novice, My Lady."

"I know that, Sümbül. Don't you dare allow something like that again – who was it?"

Sümbül Aga was silent. He couldn't do anything else now. Would he say, 'It's the one who is standing before you?'

Before that would happen, thoughts rushed through Ruslana's mind.

Maybe I should boldly raise my head and shout: 'It was me! It was me! It was me who crossed the mountains and valleys with Tacham Noyan. It was me who faced the unbelieving savages. Should I be afraid of some Greek? Maybe thanks to that I will stop cowering with fear. I will stop my trembling heart.

Just as she made this crazy decision and wanted to open her mouth, Sümbül Aga spoke softly:

"It's a Greek woman from Crete. They call her Despina."

Ruslana pressed her lips tightly so as not to let out a cry of joy. Will Sümbül mention her?

"How long has this Despina been in the harem?"

"Almost a year."

"For almost a year she has not learned not to shout in the Sultan's home?"

Silence. Sümbül Aga was probably staring at the floor now just like she was. Another question asked by Sultana Hafsa made Ruslana's world collapse.

"Who was this rough novice quarreling with?"

In Ruslana's head, already well-known thoughts appeared: *It's over! Everything is over! This woman knows! I'm finished!*

Sümbül Aga had no other choice now. Surely, he will say that it was Ruslana who caused the argument and nearly strangled the girl. Ruslana bowed her head even lower and closed her eyes tight. Her heart pounded furiously in her chest.

"Who didn't she argue with, My Lady. She attacks everyone. I think she is crazy. Nothing gets through to her."

Hurray! I'm saved again!

Sümbül Aga decided not to mention the love play under the stairs.

Of course, she thought, *if the word got out, he would lose his head too.*

"What did this Despina want?"

"What could she want, My Lady? She doesn't like her meals; the bed is uncomfortable... She teases the girls who visit the Sultan's chambers. She gives orders to everyone..." The man fell silent. "If it is allowed, I will say..." He didn't finish.

"Speak, Sümbül Aga. Why are you quiet? What do you need to keep peace and quiet in the harem of Sultan Suleiman – the son of my husband of holy memory, Sultan Selim the Grim?"

Ruslana understood the tactics of the experienced harem aga. Sümbül Aga was saying only what the Sultana Mother wanted to hear. If she could lift her head, she would see triumph in his eyes. Ruslana liked this game. She decided she had to master this skill.

"Let me say that this girl does not deserve the grace and protection of our Sultan."

"What's that supposed to mean?"

"If you agree, I will release her from service. Let her seek happiness outside the walls of the palace."

Silence.

Ruslana watched the patterns on the carpets on the floor. While waiting for the woman's response, she had the impression that time had stopped. Since Sultana Mother was delaying her answer, Sümbül Aga was forced to make another move.

"I'm afraid that... God forbid! One day this girl may threaten the life..." Aga did not finish.

"Tfu, tfu, tfu..." escaped the lips of Sultana Hafsa. "May your words never come true. What is such a mad woman doing in the harem? You have my permission. Take care of it."

Victory! Victory! Victory! Ruslana shouted in her mind.

Meanwhile, Sümbül Aga's face was devoid of even a shadow of a feeling. After all, he'd already taken care of it. If the decision was made to expel the girl from the palace, no one would look for her. But when someone asks, however, he already had a ready answer: 'Who are you asking about, My Lady? That crazy Greek woman? Who knows where she is? I hope luck has smiled at her.'

But Ruslana had no idea what Sümbül thought. She was happy, believing that Despina would be expelled from the Seraglio. Outside, she could say whatever she wanted - who would ever believe a girl who was expelled from the palace?

"I am the mother of the Sultan. Come closer." This time, the woman's voice sounded like the verses of the song of happiness in Ruslana's ears. "I've forgotten about you because of that cheeky girl. But since this issue has already been settled, we can talk."

Ruslana did not even have the courage to move. The woman whose face she had not seen yet, wanted her to take a step toward happiness. Was she only this small step away from reaching her goal? No, definitely not. Even if this woman likes her, it doesn't mean that she would pass the test in the face of Sultan Suleiman.

Sultana Hafsa noticed that the girl didn't even move.

"Come closer, child," she said with tenderness.

Ruslana moved gracefully forward, just as she'd been taught in the Crimea.

"So, you are Aleksandra, the protégé of Aj Bala, the wife of the Crimean Khan?"

The girl, without saying a word, shook her head slightly. How could she tell the mother of the great Sultan that her name was now Ruslana?

Sümbül Aga came to her aid again.

"My Lady, your servant wants to be called Ruslana. She decided that the name Aleksandra could be difficult for the residents of the palace."

"So, you want me to call you Ruslana?"

The girl again moved her head silently, this time in confirmation.

"Let it be that way. It fits this place. Clever idea. The girl from Ruthenia, Ruslana..."

Silence.

The girl knew exactly what the silence meant. The mother of the Padishah observed her attentively, looking her up and down. Perhaps she was comparing the woman in whom the Sultan was so interested, with Gülbahar Haseki. Before the great trial, she had to gain recognition in the eyes of the Sultana Mother.

She's so delicate, Sultana Hafsa thought. *She is not as tall as Gülbahar, but her grace adds her so much charm. Besides, she is very young. Much younger than Gülbahar. She's fresh like a flower.*

"Lift your head, child."

The moment had arrived. She could finally look into the eyes of the mother of the Ottoman Sultan, whose love and crown she wanted to win. She knew perfectly well how important this first look was. First, she slowly bowed with respect.

Setaret Kalfa warned her repeatedly:

'My beautiful. If Sultana Mother asks you for anything, do not do it right away. First, bow to her in greeting.'

'Why?' Ruslana had asked.

'The bow means: 'Your word is an order to me.' First bow down, then do it.'

'If it's an order, I'll do it right away.'

'Absolutely not. These are the rules that apply to women in the Seraglio.'

It doesn't make sense, Ruslana had thought, but since such rules are in force in the palace, she must follow them before the Sultana Mother.

So, she bowed slightly. She lifted her head from staring at the silk carpet straight into the source of light she had not seen until now, and the brightness dazzled her. As their eyes met for the first time, she saw an elderly woman sitting haughtily on a magnificent sofa in front of a window that looked like a pearl against a wall lined with green and white tiles. Because the sun was behind her, the girl couldn't see her shaded face at first.

She gave a short moan. This unexpected sound made the hearts of the ladies of the court and the servants waiting for the orders of Sultana Hafsa come up to their throats in fear. Ruslana tried to prevent anything wrong from happening again, and quickly covered her mouth with her hand.

"What happened, child?"

Ruslana didn't answer. Instead, without realizing it, she took two steps towards the Sultana Mother. A few ladies of the court looked at her with envy – the girl looked as if she were floating above the ground.

Her grace also moved the strings in the heart of Sultana Hafsa. She remembered herself as a young girl.

Ah, she thought, *if only you could know how I was floating then.* It reminded her of the days when Aishe Hatun came from the Crimea to become the odalisque of Sultan Selim, but could not give him a son. She didn't feel resentful toward her successor, Hafsa, on the contrary – she had taught her everything. Also, how to float instead of walking, for which the Crimean women were famous. She was promoted from an odalisque to haseki, then the Sultana Mother, but she'd already forgotten how to do it.

Good old times, thought Sultana Hafsa. *How many years have passed already? Thirty? Forty? Am I still able to glide on my fingertips? Who taught this girl to move like this? Sultana Güldane or her daughter-in-law Aj?*

Taking a small hand away from her mouth, Ruslana looked at the woman from a shorter distance. A few ladies of the court sitting at the Sultana's feet, and the servants standing by the wall whispered with to each other with affection.

"It's unbelievable! How dare she approach so close to the Sultan's Mother? Where did she take the courage from to look her in the eye? Never, ever has a woman shown such disrespect."

One of them looked at Sümbül Aga as if to say, 'Haven't you taught her how to behave?'

"Tell me, child. What surprised you so much?"

The elderly woman watched her with equally great attention. She was so beautiful, so young. Her lush red hair fell in waves over her shoulders, and the white decorated veil she wore on her head seemed to cover her virginal beauty with mystery.

My God, she sighed. *What was in the girl's eyes? Had these eyes enchanted a man; or their gaze?* Sultana Hafsa thought. In the flickering light, her eyes were sometimes blue-green and sometimes became dark as night. And what was she to say about those full lips under the strong-willed nose, gushing with sultriness and passion – lips that would take away the mind of every man? A swan-like neck, slender arms proportional to the slim body, firm, large for her age breasts hidden under clothing, a narrow waist, and inviting round hips. *Maybe she's not that beautiful, but she has some unusual charm,* she thought further.

Having decided that she had looked at the girl closely enough, the woman noticed that Ruslana still had not answered her. She raised her head and looked into her eyes. She couldn't believe it. She looked at the others as if she wanted to make sure they saw it too. Yes, everyone saw it. The Ruthenian novice was sobbing quietly.

"It's unheard of," the servants whispered among themselves.

For a moment, the Sultana Mother, ladies of the court, and servants, all stared at the pearly tears flowing from Ruslana's eyes, resembling the bottomless wells.

Sultana Hafsa was the first one to wake up:

"What happened, child? Why are you crying? Tell me. Don't be afraid."

"You remind me so much of Mother Güldane."

Even if she should not have addressed the Sultan's Mother in this way, there was everything in her music-like voice: pain, longing, surprise, joy.

Sultana Mother, who shuddered when she heard the name of the mother of her husband's first love, tried to find in her voice a shadow of falsehood or hypocrisy – in vain. How much did she have to love this woman?

"They say that people are similar to each other, child. They say so for a reason."

She tried to remember those several times when she saw the face of Sultana Güldane during the forced stay of Khan Mengli Girey in Istanbul. Only beautiful slanted eyes remained in her memory.

"Sultana Güldane has wilted like a rose, child."

Ruslana shook her head and sobbed softly.

"Are you crying like this for a woman who you did not even have blood ties with?"

"Yhy."

"You're shedding tears for an old woman who, even if she was mothering you, was a stranger. Really?"

"Yhy," Ruslana stammered, sniffing.

The older woman looked at her for a long time. She tried again to find something false in the watery eyes, but she couldn't find it. The girl genuinely cried from the bottom of her heart. She was shedding tears just because the Sultana reminded her of the woman who had replaced her mother.

"Tears give you nobility," she said slowly.

Neither Sümbül Aga nor the ladies of the court had heard the most important woman in the Seraglio talk to someone this way before. She didn't even realize that her own voice trembled, and her eyes were misted. They looked at each other, convinced that the tears of the mother of the Padishah did not bode well.

The woman sighed deeply. Ruslana's emotions reminded Sultana Hafsa of her own mother. She did not enjoy having her for long, either.

"Come here," she said. "You cry for the woman you considered as your mother. I have not even thought about my own for a long time. Come closer, let me look closely at these beautiful eyes. Perhaps I will find a trace of my mother in them and will cry because of my own oblivion and disloyalty."

Noticing that Ruslana looked uncertainly at Sümbül Aga, the woman turned to him.

"You are still here, Sümbül? While some primitive girl is trying to disrupt the peace of my son's house, you are standing here and listening to the old woman's sighs?"

Sümbül Aga couldn't believe what was going on. Taking off in a hurry, he heard the voice of Sultana Hafsa:

"Go away, Sümbül. Do what is necessary. Leave us alone with the dear protégé of Mother Güldane."

As Sümbül Aga retreated towards the door, the woman added:

"You'll explain to me later why you brought our girl to us only now."

Cheerfulness mixed with happiness was heard more in her voice, than anger. What's more, it seemed that when she was wiping tears from Ruslana's cheeks with a small handkerchief, an expression of longing appeared on her face.

Sümbül Aga was happy. Bowing three times, he left.

On his way out, he silently saluted Sultana Mother.

You were right on the mark, Sümbül, he thought. *The Sultan himself will soon lose his head for this Ruthenian girl, too. Oh, beware, Mahidevran Gülbahar Haseki! They may call you 'Mahidevran'... 'always beautiful,' but you have competition now.*

CHAPTER SIXTEEN

The news that Sultana Hafsa saw the Ruthenian from the Crimea flew to Gülbahar Haseki as if on wings.

Gülbahar, who had been putting her head on the same pillow as Sultan Suleiman from the time he was still the Sanjakbey of Manis, walked over to the sofa, sweeping the floor with her gorgeous skirts, and sat down. The servants hurried to put the cushions behind her back and adjust her skirts.

"Is the girl very beautiful?"

The maid who had left Mother Sultana chambers and immediately ran to convey the message to the second most important woman in the Seraglio, didn't know what to answer. If she said, 'yes,' it would be bad. If she said, 'no,' her lie would eventually come out, and it would be even worse.

The maidservant, familiar with the palatial customs, also knew a few things about hypocrisy. Bowing deeply before the haseki, she replied:

"My Sultana, is there a woman more beautiful than you? Can any Ruthenian girl compare with my haseki?"

Gülbahar was beautiful – the most beautiful of the beautiful, and it wasn't without reason that she was known as Mahidevran, which meant 'always beautiful.' The blood of ancestors raised among Caucasian mountains, icy waters, and fresh air fragrant with thyme, flowed in her veins. She was a tall and slim Circassian. Her black, waist-length hair reflected even the tiniest ray of light with the brightness of the stars. For this reason, Sultan Suleiman used to call her his Star. Indeed, Suleiman's star shone with Gülbahar, and she'd given him a wonderful son. When his father, Sultan Selim, died, Suleiman sat on the throne of the Ottoman Empire at a young age.

Gülbahar's eyes were large and dark like black grapes, and their corners looked as if painted. Suleiman saw in those eyes both a subtle tremor of love, and a delicate doe, yet ready to fight in defense of her offspring. She was proud of her position. In a palace full of beautiful girls, the ruler of the world did not want to smell any other flower.

"Don't lie. They say she is beautiful. She even charmed Sultana Mother with her beauty and sweet words. If she is endowed with these two qualities, then she is dangerous."

The servants are not stupid either, she thought. *After all, it was also said that she is fresh and translucent like spring water.*

The girl knew that Gülbahar haseki was waiting for her answer.

"But, My Lady, so what that she is pretty?" she faltered. "My haseki is like the sun. If this girl is a spark, then you are a flame of a candle. She will flash and go out. Besides, she's still a child."

"What are you talking about? You call a fifteen-year-old girl a child? When I was carrying Prince Mustafa under my heart, I was fourteen years old."

Gülbahar remembered that winter day. The night she spent with the son of Sultan Selim, Prince Suleiman. At that time, she didn't think about the throne or the dignity of the ruler. Who could have guessed back then that Selim, crushing his enemies in the battles, and being the biggest nuisance of the ruler of Iran, Shah Ismail, and Mameluk Tumanbay, the ruler of Egypt of the Mameluk Dynasty, would not die at the hands of one of his numerous enemies – but would be defeated by a boil on his back! Then, not even twenty-five-springs-old Suleiman would take power in the empire extending from the Caucasus mountains to the Hungarian steppes?

They were happy like children back then. When her husband embarked on an endless journey, Sultana Hafsa moved with her son, to Manisa. She adored Gülbahar, and her affection grew even stronger when she saw her son's happiness. And when she learned later that Gülbahar was expecting a child, it was second to none. In fact, Suleiman, exercising the authority of Beylerbey in the eyalet – the administrative division – in the old Crimean city of Kaffa, tasted lust for the first time as a seventeen-year-old boy and gave evidence of his masculinity in the bed of a Tatar girl, Fulaje Hatun. They also had a son named Mahmud, but he was still a child himself then. Therefore, neither he nor Sultana Hafsa recognized the child he had with that odalisque.

But now everything looked different. The young twenty-five-year-old prince was manly like an eagle, and on top of that, in love. He lost interest in the Tatar girl who gave him a son – only Gülbahar counted now. There were even times when he neglected his duties as governor so as not to leave her embrace. He stayed with her all days long, which was the subject of quiet jokes among his guards.

"Did anyone see the Prince?" some would say.

"Haven't you heard, he set out to conquer Circassia."

Gülbahar's servants would whisper among themselves and laugh stealthily.

"Did you hear that Gülbahar is pregnant?"

"Is it a single or multiple pregnancy?"

"Why?"

"See for yourself, the prince does not leave her bed. You'll see, she'll give birth to twins, maybe even triplets."

The whispers echoed through all corners of the city, turning into laughter. Soon, they also reached the ears of Sultana Hafsa. But Sultana Mother did not laugh.

"Ignorance. What an audacity. Aren't you ashamed to denigrate the Beylerbey who feeds you? Do I need to cut out your tongues?"

The terrified servants fell on their faces in fear. Sultana Hafsa, who recognized Gülbahar as her daughter-in-law, although the girl was not married to her son, was unmoved by the crying and begging for forgiveness. She punished the servants who had been mocking her with a flogging. What's more, to relieve her bitterness, she took the withe and administered several whips herself.

"This time it's a flogging, but know that if I hear something similar again, I will order to have your tongues torn out. You will not spread such slanders when mute!"

In fact, the rumors, which calmed down immediately, didn't bother either Suleiman or Gülbahar. Full of love, exhausted by their passion, the Circassian would sit opposite the window overlooking the forest shimmering with all the shades of green, knitting clothes for the baby that was already beginning to kick. Meanwhile, the prince would listen to the howling of the wind echoing in the steep rocks of the Manisa mountains and stare at the hills overgrown by the sea of trees. There, he would grab his pen and write poems praising the dark brown eyes and black hair of Gülbahar.

Evenings at the Beylerbey's home had a different charm now. At night, Suleiman and Gülbahar sat embraced in each other's arms, staring at the fire that raged in the fireplace. The prince, taking a sip of wine from a chalice made of cut crystal, then asks:

"Can I also taste these cherry lips?"

Pretending to be ashamed, Gülbahar sometimes gave herself into a delicate and affectionate kiss, or sometimes a shameless and lusty kiss of his strong lips. Then she'd groan with the pleasure that the young man's bold movements gave her.

"My Prince," she whispers.

This passionate whisper would then kindle an even larger fire in him, and encouraged him move faster and faster. Gülbahar, embracing his waist with her legs, reached peaks with him. When their tired bodies were rested side by side in the silk bedding, damp with sweat but satisfied, Suleiman would then whisper in her ear the poem he'd written earlier that day:

What is one life for a kiss?
I would give away a thousand lives
For one short kiss of my beloved's lips.

The fourteen-year-old Gülbahar often wondered what more she could possibly want from life.

I think that's complete happiness. My man is young, handsome, and I'm carrying his child. If fate favors him, he will get the throne. My son will become a prince, and I will become the mother of the Padishah.

Actually, at that time Gülbahar didn't even care about the Sultan's title. It was enough for her that Suleiman belonged to her.

***

Sultana Hafsa was happy about this relationship. Suleiman did not see anything but the Circassian girl, and he devoted all his energy to her. What could have been better than that – the mind of the heir to the Ottoman Empire was absorbed by love instead of the affairs of the State? Hafsa didn't even want to think about the horrible things that would happen if he started to be interested in the state. What if he one day asked:

What is our Padishah doing? Because of the wars, society is exhausted and impoverished. Can't father see this?

Ever since her husband took the throne, Hafsa did everything to keep Suleiman out of his sight. She knew that when it came to the State, the cruel ruler didn't care about his wife or son. He wasn't known as Selim I, The Grim, or 'The Cruel,' for nothing. If someone told him, 'Your right hand betrays your State,' he wouldn't hesitate to take out his saber and cut it off. Sultana Hafsa couldn't forget how her husband stood against his father, Sultan Bayezid.

"He is our father, but he doesn't know how to rule the State," he'd said back then. One day he even asked: "What do you think, Hafsa, will our Prince Suleiman be like me and someday come against me?"

This question hit the young woman. She immediately tried to calm him down.

"May your words never come true," she quickly said.

"Who could stand against the great Selim the Grim, who had fought all his life to enlarge his country? Who would dare look at him badly? Blood from his blood, and flesh from his flesh?"

She knew, however, that this doubt deeply penetrated the heart of Selim, The Grim. Sultana Hafsa was afraid that if she made even the smallest mistake, her husband would try to kill Suleiman. Therefore, praying every evening, she thanked God that her son was spending time in the arms of Gülbahar.

When a midwife was called in at Gülbahar's first contractions, the city of Manisa was filled with new happiness. After many hours, the first crying was heard in the corridors from the tiny body of a boy, who came into the world at sunrise. The messengers were quickly dispatched.

"Good news, Prince! Good news! You have a son!" the messengers shouted with excitement.

The streets of the city were filled with the shouts of heralds:

"Let everyone hear the good news! The ruler of the world, our Padishah, Sultan Selim, The Grim, with God's will became a grandfather for the second time! Let everyone hear about it! Our prince Suleiman has a second son! The name of the little Prince is Mustafa. May he have a long and happy life!"

At the other end of the city, another herald also passed the good news:

"May Mustafa Khan live happily ever after! God Almighty, protect our Khan Mustafa! Let our Prophet Muhammad be the protector of Mustafa!"

On the advice of Sultana Hafsa, Gülbahar also did everything she could to keep Suleiman away from State affairs.

***

Gülbahar Haseki remembered the day when they heard that messengers had arrived from Istanbul. The hearts of both women froze in fear. Did the riders bring bad news?

"Long live the Padishah!" they exclaimed.

When the men fell to Suleiman's feet, everyone understood that destiny had set a new path. Sultana Hafsa cried soundlessly for her deceased husband. She thanked God that her safe and sound son sat on the throne, and Gülbahar was silent.

"We need to set off immediately," Suleiman said to the messengers. He hugged his son and then turned to Gülbahar.

"Look, you were the Prince's woman, and now you have become the Sultan's haseki," he told Gülbahar. "You are the most important woman in the Ottoman State, after my mother. Your son, Prince Mustafa, is my successor."

It was certain that Suleiman had crossed his firstborn son, whom Fulaje had given him, out of his life. She didn't know what the reason for this was, and nobody asked about it, either.

Gülbahar still remembered Suleiman's long gaze before he set off on the back of his gray steed, and his words:

"Do not worry about the throne. You will always be my Mahidevran. Remember this, Gülbahar."

Unknowingly, she stroked her cheek that Suleiman had kissed before heading at full gallop for Istanbul.

It seemed that a thousand years had passed since then. From the day he took over the throne, Suleiman's love dissipated. From that moment, Gülbahar had to share him with the countless number of viziers, with thousands of pashas, beys, and agas, but she agreed to that. If you don't count a few night's adventures with harem girls, he always came back to her. Whenever he called her to him, she joyfully ran into her man's arms. The young Padishah kissed her cheeks and savored her scent.

"Your cheeks are like a rose, and you smell like a rose. Come to me."

No, she told herself, *this Ruthenian can be as beautiful and as young as she wants. Suleiman will not move his rose aside to smell some prickly bush.*

So, if this were the case, then she wondered where this internal anxiety came?

The Sultan invariably showers me with compliments, so why is this insidious fear destroying my interior? How should I understand these nightmares?

From the day she heard that the Ruthenian girl had charmed Sultana Hafsa, she dreamed the same scene every night; a raven-black shadow entered her room with a greased rope and snatched Mustafa from her shoulders. She didn't talk about it to anyone.

I have the same fear as the Sultana Hafsa used to have about Suleiman, Gülbahar reasoned in her mind. *Whose life is in danger? Mine or Mustafa's? Or maybe this shadow that haunts me in my dreams is this Ruthenian bug they call Ruslana?*

***

In those days, Gülbahar wasn't the only one looking for the meaning of her dreams. Sultana Hafsa also tried to guess the meaning of the dream in which she saw Gülbahar. Certainly, it had something to do with Ruslana. But what?

Sultana Mother remembered every word of the letter sent by Aj Bala.

'The beloved of the Sultan Selim, the Grim, the venerable mother of Sultan Suleiman,' Aj Bala began her letter. 'I would like you to know that the Ruthenian Aleksandra, whom my husband Crimean Khan's Mehmed Girej sent to the ruler of the world Sultan Suleiman, was entrusted to me by my mother-in-law of holy memory on her deathbed. She told me her dream, just as I will tell it to you now. In her mind, she saw a girl in the Istanbul Seraglio. She was beautiful like a nymph – just like Aleksandra. Suddenly an eagle appeared and the bird circled above the girl's head. Then she extended her hands to the sky and caught it. The eagle hugged the girl with huge wings, and they flew away together.'

The words of Aj Bala echoed in the memory of Sultana Hafsa.

What could that mean? She pondered. *How to explain it? What did the eagle symbolize? What was the importance of the girl catching the eagle? Was it a good sign or a bad omen?*

'You and my mother-in-law's daughter share the same fate. You gave your hearts to the same man, and you gave him children. Mother of your companion, and my mother-in-law, whispered to me on her deathbed, that the girl's destiny was related to the Ottoman family. She said: 'Send Aleksandra to the mother of Sultan Suleiman. If she has as good of a heart, as my daughter said, she will accept her.' That's all. You know the rest. If you do not want to do this, follow your judgment. You can let her go if this will be your wish. Maybe she will return to the mountains where she came from. No, if she does not win your heart, know that Mother Güldane's will was for me to treat her like a sister – send Aleksandra to me, to the Crimea. However, if you want the girl to catch the eagle, with God's permission, you will fulfill my mother-in-law's last wish. My dear Sultana, the noble mother of Suleiman, let the will of God be fulfilled. Make the right decision.'

Hafsa considered everything for a long time, but she couldn't give any meaning to this dream. Finally, she called for the Sheikh of Islam, Ali Jemali Zembilli Efendi.

"I had a dream, my Hodja," she began. She sighed deeply and frowned. "But I am afraid to ask anyone about it."

The man sitting opposite her was white as milk. Right at the edge of his turban, you could see his snow-white, lush eyebrows, and his eyelashes had the same color. Wisdom still emanated from his faded eyes.

"May it indicate prosperity," he said ingratiatingly, though his voice was full of reserve. "Dreams are a narrow passage between our faith and the sins that we hide deeply in our soul. They penetrate into our minds and tell us what the tongue will not say. Sometimes they whisper about secrets from the past, or at other times, from the future. In dreams, Sultana Mother, the divine power and unbelief of Satan face each other. Commenting on a dream is an attempt to understand its meaning; it can be read in the right or wrong way. To claim that the interpretation is certainly right is like trying to equate with God. May God show us the truth and make us understand it. May he not let us come close to Satan."

Ali Jemali Hodja closed his eyes and moved his lips in prayer, and then he blew to the four sides of the room.

Sultana Hafsa, who listened to the man, nodded her head and patiently waited for him to finish his prayers.

"Hence my fear," she said. "Should I put so much hope in this explanation and follow it? If it is wrong, will I commit a sin and cause a misfortune? Or on the contrary? Is it not a sin to ignore orders coming from dreams? What will happen then?"

Wise Ali Jemali Efendi, appointed Sheikh of Islam by Sultan Selim, became worried when he saw that the woman was still considering her dream. What dream could it be if it aroused fear in the heart of the powerful Mother Sultana? Perhaps when he listens to the dream and interprets it, it will let him learn a secret.

I have to consider it quickly, and if necessary, even tell the future, he thought. He turned to the woman waiting for the answer.

"My Lady, can one stay away from dreams in life? Can one avoid trying to interpret them? There are many dreams that show the right way. Did you know that the Sultan Alp Arslan faced the army of the infidels of the Byzantine Diogenes at Manzikert because of the words of a white-bearded sage who told him: 'Go west, take the sun of the east to the west?'

Ali Jemali Zembilli Efendi then fell silent. Right in front of him on a table made of mother-of-pearl, stood a carafe with water, on which rose petals floated. He filled a glass and took two sips.

"I will say more. If our ancestor Bayezid the Lightning, had not listened to his dream but the one that his wife saw, perhaps he would not have suffered a humiliating defeat and would not have ended his life in captivity. Our prophet also told his dreams to his companions, commented on them, and drew lessons."

Ali Jemali Hodja drank another sip.

"I want to say, My Lady, that you should not be afraid of dreams or their interpretation. God has given his people reason so that they would not do wrong. If you do wrong, then it will also be the divine will."

He slowly put down the glass.

"What was your dream about?" he finally asked.

Sultana Hafsa, sitting on her knees, slowly began to tell the dream of Sultana Güldane as if it were her own dream.

"I saw an eagle. A great eagle in a color of ash."

"Eagle means the State. It is strength and power. It may mean prosperity. Did this eagle fly?"

"Yes. He flew continuously. He flew over the highest hills, over snow-capped peaks, among the stars."

The face of Sheikh of Islam flashed with joy.

"That's good news then. God wanted to pass it to the Mother of our ruler. Our master will make more conquests. The head of our country will reach the stars, the sun. Did the eagle land somewhere?"

"No."

Seeing the woman's hesitation, the curiosity of the Sheikh of Islam grew even more.

"And then, Sultana?"

"Suddenly, a girl appeared, walking on the walls of the palace, facing the sea."

"A girl?"

"Yes, a very beautiful one."

"And then?"

"The eagle began circling over the girl's head."

"It certainly means happiness, Sultana."

"Happiness? For whom? For the eagle or the girl?"

"Go on, Sultana."

"Suddenly the girl reached out and caught the eagle."

"Caught an eagle flying over her head? Really?"

"Yes. The eagle spread his wings, embraced her, and they flew away."

Sheikh of Islam, Ali Jemali Zembilli Efendi's jaw dropped in astonishment. Honestly, he didn't expect such an ending of the dream. *What could that mean? What did the girl mean? What did the capture of the eagle symbolize?*

Seeing that the teacher was deep in thought, Sultana Hafsa asked again:

"What does this dream mean? Does it mean prosperity or misfortune?"

For a moment, Zembilli sat in silence. Then his lips began to move again. He closed his eyes. His white eyelashes trembled with fear and excitement as if he were afraid to see what was happening in another world. His white beard was struck by the red of the sun preparing to set, and his robe seemed to be submerged in golden water.

For a moment, Sultana Hafsa waited respectfully for Ali Jemali Efendi to return from the worlds in which he had sunk. In the end, she couldn't stand it any longer.

"Hodja..." she murmured indistinctly.

Zembilli's twitchy eyelids opened. His eyes, once as sharp as steel but now grayed out of old age, looked for a long time at the woman, who waited for what he would say with a mix of impatience and fear. He didn't fail to look around first as if in fear that someone would hear them.

"Sultana," he whispered. "Our ruler will easily make new conquests, however..."

When the man fell silent, anxious Hafsa asked:

"Will something happen to him, Hodja? Tell me."

Ali Jemali Efendi nodded slowly. Keeping the right distance, he approached her.

"Our ruler will win many new lands, but the love of a girl will win him," he whispered in Hafsa's ear.

After the Sheikh of Islam left, Sultana Hafsa sank into her thoughts. What did it mean?

"My God!" she whispered to herself. "If the dream of Aishe Hatun's mother announces glory, I have two paths ahead of me. Which one should I follow? Should I let the girl catch the eagle? Should I protect the eagle from the snares of love? Show me the way. What should I do?"

It was clear that she liked Ruslana. That was her heart's hint.

Or have I let myself be fooled by the girl's innocence? That question had not left her alone since Ruslana left her room.

Nothing like that, she thought. *I may have aged, but my eyes are still sharp enough to see any thin line between innocence and lies.*

As soon as she'd looked at her, she understood that under the girl's innocence there was an iron will – and boundless ambition. She also went through a lot to finally give birth to her son and take Selim from Aishe. Besides, Ruslana was so noble that she had no need to hide it. Otherwise, when she'd asked her, 'Do you have any wish, child?' she answered the Mother of the Sultan without hesitation:

"My only desire is health, peace, happiness, and the success of our ruler. If I become his slave, I will be happy."

Who taught these great words to a girl who could not even speak Turkish correctly? Sümbül?

"He's the devil incarnate," Sultana Hafsa muttered, shaking her head.

Or maybe it was her eyes that charmed her? Those mysterious, sparkling with blue and green, as deep as the sea, big eyes.

It was hard to deny it. Perhaps they were not the most beautiful eyes she had ever seen in her life, but Ruslana had eyes that could enslave in one moment, tie the hands, strike with their beauty, and consume.

If her gaze made such an impression on a woman, who knows what they can do with Suleiman, Sultana Hafsa wondered, unaware that a strange smile appeared on her face. Nobody knew her son better than her.

"When Suleiman sees the Ruthenian, he won't be able to resist her," she giggled.

But she was immediately ashamed of her thoughts.

Was it betraying Gülbahar, who called her a mother? Yes, apparently I'm doing just that.

She stubbornly tried to find a companion for Gülbahar.

How was this possible? Would Gülbahar share her fate?

However, when Sultana Hafsa remembered Ruslana's eyes, the brightness that flowed from her face when she smiled, the dimples in her cheeks, and the snow-white neck, she immediately forgot her shame.

I'm sure of that, she thought. *Ever since Suleiman became a Padishah, he lived under heavy stress. Not a year had passed since he became a Sultan, when he captured Belgrade, standing at the head of the army. He avenged the blood of Sultan Murad I. Who knows what else he plans? Even his gaze has changed.* She couldn't see the old gleam of happiness in her son's eyes.

I know that look well, thought the older woman. Her husband, Selim The Grim, looked at people with the same eagle-like eyes. It wasn't without reason that Selim was called the 'eagle of battlefields.' Now her son was looking like that too. Just like an eagle. An unhappy eagle.

That's what it meant to be a Sultan. It required sacrifices. It made the man reach for the stars but at the same time loose happiness.

"You see, Hafsa, the nation is not what you command it to be," her father had told her one day. "It creates itself. You can put all the Sultans, Khans, Kings and Beys at its head, but it is the real ruler."

Hafiza, whom the Ottomans had called Hafsa for short, had never seen so much suffering in her father's eyes. She didn't know the reason, although of course, she saw that difficult days had come. If it were not so, why else would her mother lock herself in the room and cry? Why was it whenever the arrival of a messenger was announced, the woman always pressed her hand to her chest? Why was her father's face so pale lately?

Her father fell silent and looked into his daughter's eyes for a long time.

"Now you have to serve the nation."

"How can a little girl serve the nation? Tell me what to do."

"I am sending you to the harem of Prince Selim. If you give him sons, fortune will smile at you."

So, she did. She became a woman of Selim the Grim, before whom everyone trembled. It was her who gave Sultan Selim a son that Aishe from Crimea could not give to him. Luck smiled at her, just as her father had foretold. She became the wife of the Padishah and saw her son also seated onto the throne.

And now she was a witness to Suleiman's sadness. The nation had taken her son's life. He was so young, but she knew he was suffering.

Prince Mahmud's death two months earlier shook him more than she expected. Ever since he took the throne, he lived for the State. He wasn't interested in the harem. Even Gülbahar had stopped interesting him. In his life, there were only the Great Vizier Piri Mehmed Pasha, viziers, agas, and soldiers. And this falconer, a convert called Ibrahim – some say he was Croatian, but others thought him Greek. It didn't matter to Hafsa – she hated this man who constantly encouraged her son to make new wars.

Nobody said it to her, but she'd seen enough all these years to understand it. He didn't even get to have a good rest after the conquest of Belgrade before he was already preparing for the next expeditions. She was as sure of it as of her own name; he talked with Ibrahim for hours on end, he met with the Great Vizier, the minor viziers, and the Commander of Janissaries. He was constantly checking the army and the fleet.

Didn't Suleiman have the right to be happy when he carried such a heavy burden?

Gülbahar was good, beautiful, and she was the mother of her grandson, but she couldn't raise new ecstasies and happiness in her son's heart anymore. Ruslana was fresh, childish and full of life.

As the first rays of the sun filtered through the grating, Sultana Hafsa straightened up in bed – she had made her decision – she will tell Suleiman about Ruslana. She will try to arrange for him to see her. The rest will be up to the divine will – either the girl will catch the eagle, or the eagle will fly away towards the snowy peaks.

"Ah, my rosebud, my Güldane; you who share my fate, mother of Aishe," sighed Sultana Hafsa. "So be it. If you still think I am a good person, even though I have taken the man, the future, the crown, and the throne from your daughter, you are like my mother. Watch over me."

CHAPTER SEVENTEEN

There was a buzz outside. One could hear the rhythmic beats of drums vibrating through the air and the penetrating sounds of zurnas and bells.

All the odalisques ran from the courtyard to their rooms, where they tried to see through the barred windows what was about to happen. Actually, the same scene repeated every Friday. A solemnly played celebration after the Friday's prayer.

"Quick, my lovely, quickly," said Merzuka. "Come, look."

Ruslana stopped walking around the vestibule and ran inside. As she approached the bars, she saw him, and a cry spontaneously erupted out of her mouth.

"My God, Jesus our Father, Holy Mary, that's him! Him! The man who will change my fate. The one with whom I want to share happiness and the throne! Sultan Suleiman!"

The young Padishah looked amazing in a large turban and an extremely elegant sable caftan.

"How handsome he is," Merzuka whispered solemnly.

"Not at all. He has a hooked nose. And it's so big."

Ruslana knew that it wasn't true, but for some reason, she was embarrassed to admit that he was handsome. His dark brows and a full beard covering his face could be seen under his huge turban, decorated with pearls and diamonds, that shone in the sun, and rubies flaming red in its rays. Certainly, he sowed fear among those facing him and aroused respect. However, there was something strange in his eyes.

Are they black or brown? Maybe they have the color of ash? Ruslana wondered. Those eyes made her heart burn for the first time since she met Fryderyk. His large, beak-like nose hung over two distinct lines of his mouth, but it gave his appearance a strength that inspired fear.

She'd never seen such a perfectly fitted male outfit. The caftan was lined with sable fur, starting from a colorfully decorated collar all the way to the hem. The Sultan wore a felt robe under the caftan and a red silk belt around his waist. Her eyes were drawn to the diamond-covered hilt of a dagger stuck behind the belt, undoubtedly worth a fortune. Among the sounds of drums and timpani, he looked haughtily at the shouting inhabitants of the Seraglio, turning his head to the right and to the left.

He is self-righteous, crossed through Ruslana's mind, and suddenly panic overtook her.

Why would a handsome and powerful man like him need a country girl who can't even speak Turkish properly? This thought pierced her mind like an arrow. *Also, you are a Ruthenian girl*, she worried. Just like one of the odalisques described her with a grimace, when passing by her: 'You are a giaour.' It was on that day that she learned that the Turks called the dissenters giaours.

Ruslana decided not to give in to the inner voice.

I'm beautiful, she told herself.

So what, that you are beautiful? There are many beauties around him. You don't even know what it means to be beautiful, her doubt answered her.

I'm also smart.

What's the use of your mind for the man before whom the whole world trembles?

Perhaps Ruslana would have continued this internal dispute, but just at that moment, a white-maned steed, equally majestic and proud as the rider who would ride him, was brought in front of the stone elevation, on which Suleiman stood like a monument. The crowd gathered in the courtyard shouted in one voice:

"Live happily ever after! May God grant our Ruler a long life! Long live the Sultan!"

At the sight of the steed, Ruslana felt a stab in her heart. She remembered Tacham Noyan's horse, who'd carried her through mountains and rivers, away from the hands of robbers and slave traders. Where was Hope now? Traveling again with Tacham Noyan across the free highlands of the Ural? Quenching his thirst in the cold waters of the Dnieper and Volga? Walking through the Ukrainian plains and Polish fragrant meadows? For the first time, she wished she had not changed his name to Hope. Storm was more suited to him. It gave him strength and dignity.

I hope dad Noyan doesn't think so, she thought.

As she continued to watch Suleiman bounce off the platform with dignity and move to sit on the horse's back, she had the white mane of Storm, dancing in the wind, in front of her eyes.

Setaret entered the room and also approached the barred window.

"*Mashallah, Mashallah!*" she said. "God protect him from the evil eye. Tf, tf."

"Where is our Padishah's army going? To war?"

"Ah, my silly one. What war? Our master has just returned from the victorious expedition to Belgrade."

The woman noticed Ruslana calmed down upon hearing that the Sultan wasn't going to war. She smiled to herself.

"You know what day it is today?"

Ruslana had already forgotten about days, weeks, and months.

"No, what day?"

"Friday, my lovely. Friday."

"Eee, so what?"

"On Fridays, all men pray together in the mosque. Our Ruler is going to the mosque right now."

While Sultan Suleiman was expertly getting on the horse, several stable boys ran up to him and spread a caftan trimmed with sable fur on the horse's back. Another one helped the Padishah put his feet in the stirrups. The horse was also dignified and suited the rider well. His head was straight, and his ears were high. Although the stable boys held the horse on both sides, he could not stand still. He slapped the stones all the time with his slim legs.

Ruslana looked at the rider who was standing full of the dignity next to the Padishah. A large, precious saber rested on the right shoulder of the man. Its scabbard, decorated with diamonds, emeralds, and rubies, shimmered in the sun.

"Who is that?" she asked curiously.

"He's a sword-bearer," Setaret replied. "He's carrying the saber that our Ruler uses for his victories."

"Can't he carry his sword himself?"

The woman was surprised by the question.

"That's a custom. How should I know?"

When Suleiman's steed together with the rider sitting on him moved majestically across the courtyard, the shouts broke out again:

"Long live the Padishah!"

My God, thought Ruslana, as she took out her cross at precisely the same moment Suleiman passed before her, *he's so handsome. Magnificent*.

In fact, it wasn't their first meeting.

The first one took place three days after meeting with Sultana Hafsa. She didn't even remember how the two following days had passed. Sultan Suleiman, surrounded by his servants, passed through the courtyard of the odalisques. Everything happened so quickly that before Ruslana heard the whispers: 'Sultan is coming,' and ran out before the cell assigned to her, it was all over. Ruslana only saw the man's collar, lined with a sable fur.

When she'd left the room of the Sultana Mother, she'd been immediately transferred from the pavilion for novices, to now living on the upper floor with the girls who were promoted from the novices to the odalisques. She got a two-room apartment. One of the rooms opened onto a gallery surrounded by a balustrade overlooking the courtyard of the novices, on which she had received an infinite number of hits from Sümbül Aga. The room in the back had two large, barred windows overlooking the inner courtyard. At the sight of them, Ruslana had jumped in joy. She would be able to see the sun now, and maybe even look at the clouds racing against each other, even if only through the bars.

Later that evening, her room became filled with women who spread various colored fabrics in front of her. However, Ruslana wasn't in the mood to look at the fabrics – the harem's agas had not agreed to move Merzuka upstairs, so Ruslana was angry. She hit the door with her fists, went out to the gallery and shouted.

Finally, Sümbül Aga appeared in front of her, his face covered with sweat.

"What is it now? Why are you screaming? What happened to Despina hasn't taught you anything? One does not scream like that here," the man said slowly.

Sümbül was furious, but this time the hits were spared. It was evident that he was trying his best to control his anger.

Oh, Sümbül, he said to himself, *control yourself. Do not forget that Sultana Hafsa called her a daughter, so don't try to break the neck of this Ruthenian girl. This head will be useful to you one day.*

Ruslana quickly noticed the difference in Sümbül's behavior. The tribute paid with her body could not be the only reason for this change. Sümbül had seen with his own eyes and heard with his own ears, the closeness that Sultana Hafsa showed to the girl.

Ruslana shouted, stamping her foot:

"Where's my companion?!"

Rage filled the harem aga. His pride was deeply wounded. How dare this insignificant girl look down at him and talk to him like that? And in the middle of the harem? He was close to losing control. He didn't have a stick with him, but it would be enough to hit her in the eye with his fist.

Understanding that the man would strike a blow at any moment, Ruslana looked at him in such a way that Sümbül immediately regained his mind.

What are you doing, Sümbül? he scolded himself.

However, all the odalisques had certainly heard everything, so he had to save the situation somehow. He made the decision that he would also raise his voice.

"How dare you?! Don't you know how severe the punishment for disturbing the harem is? Be quiet, don't shout like that."

It was as if he'd said, 'Shout,' because Ruslana hit the floor again with her heel.

"I want my companion, aga. Immediately. Now. How can an odalisque be without a maid?"

"They'll give you a new servant tomorrow."

The third stamp was even stronger.

"I don't want anyone else. Merzuka is my servant. She was given to me by Sultana Güldane, the mother of Aishe Hatun, who is sharing her fate with mother Hafsa. Send Merzuka immediately."

She spoke their names in such a way that it made a great impression both on the eavesdropping odalisques and on Sümbül Aga. Ruslana, seeing the man's confusion, moved closer to him.

"Please, Sümbül. Am I asking too much?" she murmured like a cat.

Aga once again thanked in his mind that his skin was black. Otherwise, all the harem residents would notice how his face flared. The blood in his veins boiled from her passionate voice. With her sweet games, the girl excited even the eunuch. He looked meaningfully at Ruslana. His lips moved as if he wanted to say something, but no sound came out. What could he say? The Ruthenian was no longer available – he could only experience new adventures under the stairs in his dreams now. He couldn't play with a girl who was taken care of by the mother of the great Padishah. He would be skinned for it, and his flesh would be thrown to the dogs and cats. Or his neck would be broken.

He unloaded his anger on the odalisques gathered in the vestibule.

"What are you looking at?! Get out of here, now!"

He turned and walked away.

An hour later, Merzuka was in Ruslana's room. The friends hugged each other. That night the Tatar girl curled up in the legs of Ruslana's bed – she no longer laid on a mattress spread on the floor – and fell asleep.

The next morning, Setaret Kalfa came with a group of dressmakers. They spent all day taking measurements for new costumes. In the evening, when it began to get dark, three new dresses hung over Ruslana's bed, each more beautiful than the other.

For just a moment, it seemed to Ruslana that she saw Sümbül Aga's assistant, Jafer – but when she looked again, the boy was gone. Was he watching her? Suddenly, she remembered Jafer crying, listening furtively to the song she sang on the first night in the novices' pavilion. When a sobbing interrupted her song, he'd whispered:

"Do not cry, Aleksandra, I will protect you."

In all the recent confusion, Ruslana decided that she would win Jafer, and by rewarding him with a radiant smile when she saw him, she took the first step to put this decision into practice.

CHAPTER EIGHTEEN

That day unbelievable things happened – Sümbül Aga took Ruslana, wearing a beautiful dress, to the upper floor.

The hall was full of chatting women sitting on large pillows along the walls. Some large bottles between them with tubes that connected from the cylinders to their mouths, from which they let out puffs of smoke. This was the first time in her life that Ruslana had seen something like this.

At precisely the same moment that she was about to sit down, a confusion arose; and a fuss like this in the harem always made her heart leap up her throat.

"Move away, go!" a servant shouted, as they cleared the path for someone following them.

A very beautiful woman then appeared at the top of the vestibule among the ladies of the court, a thousand times more beautiful than them. She was tall, with jet-black hair that reached to her waist. Her round, moist eyes were surrounded by thick lashes that were long, like arrows, and her cheekbones gave an unusual attractiveness to her round face. Her lips were narrow but shapely, and except for a bit of blush on her cheeks, she did not have makeup on her face – she had a real, natural beauty. She also exuded confidence, aware of the power of her beauty; she bore a stately and prideful beauty. She walked with a determined step, looking ahead as if she was trying to see something that was on the ceiling.

All the girls gathered in the courtyard bowed when she passed. The woman did not even turn her head to look at them.

Ruslana stared at her so much that despite Setaret's nudge, she bowed too late. But it was too late to fix her mistake. Exactly the moment they were walking by Ruslana, one of the ladies of the court whispered something to the woman's ear. She turned her head and looked straight at her.

Maybe I'm wrong, she thought. *No, I'm not wrong. She looked at me.* It lasted only a short moment, but the woman remembered everything she saw. It was a very significant look – curiosity, anger, jealousy, and everything else were in it.

Then the woman and her ladies left for the opposite end of the room with the same soldierly step they had come by. For a brief moment, the tall woman looked up at the ceiling again, and hesitated, as if she wanted to stop. However, if she had, the girl following her would have bumped into her. She finally gave up, she fixed her eyes on the ceiling again and walked away.

It seemed to Ruslana that a great weight had been removed from over the yard of the odalisques.

The atmosphere in the vestibule relaxed again as before.

"Who was that?" she asked Sümbül Aga, who was still bowing.

The big man jumped as if scalded.

"Shhh..." He let out a fearful whisper, quickly putting his finger to his lips. "That is the favorite of our ruler. The mother of Prince Mustafa."

Well, well! So, that was Mahidevran Gülbahar Haseki! The woman who she'd decided to take Suleiman from!

Black thoughts came over her again.

Difficult task. Those two words bothered her. *The woman is beautiful*, she thought. *Very beautiful. Tall and graceful. Those numerous skirts and even the corset around her couldn't hide her beauty. If Gülbahar was so tall, then how tall must Suleiman be? Will I look like a child next to him?*

Ruslana sank deeper into her black thoughts.

The woman had such firm skin. And her eyes? They were so dark and cold. For how long did our eyes meet? A second? Five? That look in her eyes chilled me to the bone. Did she also look at Suleiman in this way? In that case, I have a chance. Why would a man need a woman with such a cold look? No... she didn't look at him like that. Actually, it was the mystical depth of darkness that was in those eyes. What am I talking about? Since she gave a son to the Sultan, it's obvious she knows how to light up a man. Although... she is twice as old as me, but she's still full of life and healthy. What did I expect? she wondered, recovering. *That I would see a blind, infirm, cross-eyed old woman? It's obvious that the favorite of Sultan Suleiman is beautiful."*

Thinking this, she became clearly sad.

"Ruslana!" someone shouted.

She saw Ekaterina on one of the seats among other women, waving to her.

The girl ran up to her immediately.

"I see that you have learned the lesson well, my beautiful."

They fell into each other's arms, laughing. Ekaterina took her hand and led her a little farther away from Sümbül. She set her down by the stove near the railing. For a moment she tried to revive the fire, stirring the ashes with tongs. Ruslana's face flushed from the warmth emanating from the coals.

"Have you seen him?"

"Who?"

"The Sultan."

"No, I haven't seen him yet."

"How did you become an odalisque so quickly? Did Sümbül get lucky?" Ekaterina gave Ruslana a meaningful look. "I'm kidding." she continued, grinning broadly. "The whole harem talks about how you won Sultana Hafsa. The woman called you a daughter. That's all you need."

"She liked me." Ruslana paused for a moment. "I also liked her. She reminds me of mother Güldane a lot."

Ekaterina interrupted her, covering her mouth with her hand.

"Come on, girl. If the mother of the Padishah likes you, you have success. But know that it is only a matter of time until the Sultan's favorite will hate you, and you will become the target of her arrows."

"But I haven't done anything to her."

Ekaterina smiled.

"What more could you do, my beautiful? You took the favors of the mother of the Padishah from her. It is a great threat for her. Didn't you notice? She passed by like a storm."

"I saw."

"She came here just to see you. Did you understand that? The woman feels it. Mahidevran has started treating you like a rival. Sultana Hafsa has for the first time showed such closeness to a harem girl. Gülbahar certainly knows that the woman will tell her son about you. What's more, she also knows that the Sultan will want to see you. If the Padishah likes you, what will happen to Gülbahar?"

"The Sultan hasn't shared a bed with another girl for all these years?" Ruslana suddenly fell silent and looked her friend in the eyes, then took her hands. "Don't get me wrong. He shared a bed with you too, because he liked you. If he likes me, how will I become a danger to Gülbahar? Today he likes me, and in the morning he won't. You told me that."

It seemed that Ekaterina was sad for a moment, but she quickly pulled herself together.

"Yes, but," she began quietly, "Gülbahar has never before come to the odalisques to see the girl who is a candidate for the Sultan's concubine. She saw you and considered you a threat. I advise you, watch out. Keep your eyes open and do not fall into the Circassian's trap."

There was a stir again in the harem as several Arab servants walked in, hustling and waving their hands.

"Move aside! Make way for the Sultana Mother!" they shouted.

Sultana Hafsa walked into the harem in all her splendor, accompanied by ladies of the court. Sümbül Aga ran immediately over to her and bowed low. The Sultana, along with the servants surrounding her, stopped by a stove along her pathway and exchanged a few words with the odalisques there as they bowed respectfully to her.

Suddenly, Ruslana noticed out of the corner of her eye that the woman standing among the crowd was looking for her. Their eyes met. As she continued to bow before the woman, Ekaterina giggled:

"Your mother-in-law is coming, my lovely."

"How is our girl feeling today?"

When she stood bent like this, she could only see the woman's shoes.

Damn it! Ruslana thought. *I'm fed up with these constant bows; I hate this.* But for now, she had no choice. Until everybody begins to bow to her, she had to bow down.

"I am praying for the health of our Sultana Mother," Ruslana said, without straightening up. Her voice again caressed Sultana Hafsa's ears like a sweet melody.

Slowly, she reached out and took the girl by the elbow. She made a move indicating that she wanted the girl to straighten up.

"Do not hide your beautiful face from an elderly woman, child," she said. "Looking at you, I remember my childhood when in the early spring I used to run on meadows among the blooming crocuses."

Ruslana raised her head and straightened up. She looked into the woman's loving eyes. She didn't know if she did it naturally or if someone had taught her that. Suddenly, she lifted the woman hand marked by age, to her lips, then kissed it and put it against her cheek. Her eyes fogged over again.

The odalisques could not get over their amazement. All the more, they did not expect something even more unusual to happen. Using her handkerchief, Sultana Hafsa reached out and wiped a single tear that flowed from Ruslana's spring-like eyes. Forty, or maybe fifty odalisques gathered around them, gave out a sigh of surprise and jealousy. To better see what was happening, the girls started pushing each other.

"Smile, child," said the older woman joyfully. "Smiling suits you." Seeing Ruslana's face light up, she added: "Just like that. Know, child, that your mother Güldane is also my mother. My desire is to see you as happy as your mother wanted you to be."

Everyone was shocked.

Sümbül Aga's eyes moved nervously - this Ruthenian was certainly a witch. He'd been in the harem for forty years, but he had never seen or heard anything like that before.

Ekaterina opened her mouth in amazement.

It's good that I made friends with Ruslana, she thought. *The girl is very lucky. She'll probably be able to do something for her friends too.*

"Let's sit down," Sultana Hafsa instructed the ladies of the court.

A way for the stove was made immediately.

Ruslana prepared the plumpest seat for the Sultana Mother and put pillows behind her back. The woman, holding the girl's hand, seated her at her feet.

"Sümbül," she said without taking her eyes off Ruslana.

The harem aga moved toward her, making his way between the odalisques, and filled the space before the Sultana Mother.

"Could I exchange a few words with my daughter in private, Sümbül? There is a terrible crowd here. You can't even breathe."

The man pushed back the crowd of odalisques and ladies of the court. The girls scattered, trying to take their seats on the closest pillows, hoping to hear their conversation.

Sultana Hafsa stroked Ruslana's hand gently.

"We were delighted with your song last night," she began to say slowly. "Do not think it was only me. The whole harem was silent. Even the babies in their cradles listened to it. The Sultan could not remain deaf to such a beautiful voice either."

Hearing this, Ruslana felt close to fainting.

Suleiman heard me? What did he do? What did he think? Did he ask who was singing? she thought rapidly.

"God gave you such a wonderful voice, my child. It's not just about making a beautiful sound, either. Your singing is very moving. Not only are you feeling the emotions of your song, you make those who listen to it also go through them. Yesterday evening, even those who do not know your language listened to you in silence."

Do not talk about it anymore. Don't talk about it, Ruslana rebelled. *That's not what I want to hear. What did Suleiman say? Did Gülbahar listen to it too? What was her reaction? Is that why Gülbahar visited the courtyard of the odalisques today – to see the one who was singing? God, is it possible that she came just for that?*

Hafsa was oblivious to the questions flashing through the girl's mind.

"What was that song?" she asked.

"It's the Song of the Volga Villagers, Sultana Mother."

"Its words are filled with longing. I know this feeling well; I know how it can destroy a person from the inside. Your song transported me away and moved me back to the old days."

Sultana Hafsa knew what that longing was, but how could she know the longing of the giant Volga peasants, with huge hands and feet? Arranged in a row along the coast, they moved ships up and down the river by pulling thick ropes over their shoulders. Standing on the shore, they fought against the furious waters of the Volga. The foaming, whirling waves, crashing with all their force on the rocks, would not allow the boats to cross. Gold-haired, blue-eyed men fought a murderous fight to pull the ship on the ropes. Who knows whom they had left, and where had they come from for this work? They didn't know what the ships' holds were loaded with, but their hearts were always filled with longing. It was this longing that put songs in their mouths. They sang them to soothe the sorrow that made their work even harder.

The Sultana Mother began to quietly hum the words of the girl's song, which had moved her to tears.

"Pull, huh, pull, huh, pull, pull!"

Ruslana joined her with a radiant smile.

"Join forces, shoulder to shoulder, pull it!
A little more, and defeat the Volga, pull it!
The Volga's waters will take us home, pull it!
Pull, huh, pull, huh, pull, pull!"

Suddenly they fell silent and looked at each other.
After a while, Ruslana sang on.

"Foam, rage, hit with waves.
Your anger will not stop me, Volga.
Even the black longing did not win with us.
Should we bend before you, Volga?"

Ruslana raised her voice, then she lowered it almost to a whisper. Sometimes its timbre reminded one of a violin, while at other times it sounded like a kanun. Finally, she fell silent. Ruslana and the others sat in silence. Sümbül Aga noticed Ekaterina wiping her eyes. The other odalisques didn't understand the words of the song, but its melody and Ruslana's emotional voice enslaved everyone.

Ruslana waited for the woman to return from the worlds she had set off to.

"You know," said the old woman again, full of childlike joy, "this morning the Sultan said that..."

My heart can't take it anymore, Ruslana shuddered. *God, what did he say? What did he say? What?!*

"He said exactly: 'Mother, in the evening I heard a beautiful voice. The whole harem must have heard it. What a wonderful tone it was. Do you know who was singing?'"

Sultana Hafsa fell silent. The child's joy in her eyes gave way to the gaze of an experienced woman who had seen and survived a lot. She looked as if she wanted to read what was hidden in Ruslana's eyes. What was the girl thinking?

For a moment the odalisque faced this look courageously. She needed superhuman strength not to show her growing joy. If the Padishah asked who sang this song, then Sultana Hafsa must certainly have told him.

What should I do? she asked herself. *Should I throw myself on the woman's neck, or jump up and scream of joy? He already knows about me. Suleiman knows that I exist!*

She was close to losing the fight with herself to control her joy and excitement. She couldn't, however, hide the blushes that appeared on her face. When the flush appeared on her cheeks, she bowed her head, trying to escape the woman's gaze – but the Sultana Mother saw enough.

"I answered that I knew. How could I not know that a beautiful girl came to my Sultan's harem."

Suddenly, the older woman rose in a movement so nimble that she had not expected it herself. She stroked Ruslana on the cheek.

"If I were in your place, my lovely, I would immediately start embroidering a handkerchief. Immediately."

She turned and walked over to the ladies of the court. Moving away, she looked once again at Ruslana who acknowledged her.

"Go on," said Sultana Hafsa in a whisper. "Fly, dove, catch the eagle."

CHAPTER NINETEEN

Ruslana immediately found out what Sultana Hafsa meant by talking about embroidering a handkerchief. The words that the Sultana Mother had addressed to the Ruthenian reached Gülbahar equally fast.

According to custom, any girl who was to be invited by the Padishah to his alcove had to hand over a handkerchief. If the handkerchief came back to the odalisque somehow, it was a message from the Sultan: 'I am waiting for you tonight.' Ruslana, having learned about it, almost passed out from excitement. When the first shock was over, she immediately set to work.

Carefully, she cut out a piece of purple crepe which she had in her bundle. Then she began to embroider it with silken threads, dipping and pulling the needle through the fabric. Both Setaret and the other servants constantly checked on Ruslana's progress at work. At last Setaret couldn't take it anymore.

"Hurry up, girl. Do not let the man wait too long." Thus, saying this in front of everyone, she revealed the purpose of the handkerchief.

Every corner of the harem roared with gossip. News that Sultana Hafsa went to the odalisque's courtyard to compliment the Ruthenian and ask her for a handkerchief, finally reached the ears of the Grand Vizier of the Ottoman Empire, Ibrahim Pasha – the second most powerful man in the country after Sultan Suleiman. He was powerful enough to attract all the anger of the impatient viziers that waited in the queue for the position of Grand Vizier, who all would secretly wish him an imminent falling out of grace.

The gossipers would say: 'We've lived to see the time when the Ottoman State is ruled by two sultans.' This was because he was close enough to the ruler that even his chamber was located next to Suleiman's apartments.

Ibrahim Pasha knew that the Padishah observed the meetings that took place each day at the Divan, from behind a screen, and always listened to him discussing the issues of the state with the viziers. So, after having learned about the episode with a handkerchief, couldn't fail to mention it.

"We must hurry up, agas. I have a feeling that soon our Ruler will be seriously absorbed by matters related to the harem."

The viziers, who'd already heard the rumor, secretly covered their mouths with their hands to hide their smiles. Those who had not heard about the handkerchief looked at each other in surprise.

Gülbahar wasn't idle either. She sent a sorrowful letter to Sultan Suleiman.

'Has my master forgotten his faithful servant? How much time has passed since you could not find a moment for your Gülbahar in the midst of the State affairs? Did I make a mistake, that you have taken away the source of life from me? Why do you spare me the joy of watching your face?'

When Gülbahar went to the room of Sultana Hafsa, she could barely hold her anger.

"I heard that Sultana Mother is very tired lately. I came to kiss her hand and ask about her health."

The woman immediately noticed the tremor in Gülbahar's voice and the spark in her eyes, but she preferred to give the impression that she had not seen them. She reached out her hand to let her son's favorite kiss it.

At the right moment, agitated Gülbahar gestured to the servants to leave the room.

"Can you leave me alone with my grandson's mother?" Sultana Hafsa eventually asked seeing that the servants lingered with the decision whether they should fulfill Gülbahar's order or not.

"Gülbahar, how is my grandson, Prince Mustafa?" she began after the servants had quietly departed.

"You know Mother, he is unruly. He brings his teachers to despair, but none of them says anything out of fear."

"Let them know that I will not let anyone say a bad word about my grandson. Disobedient children are wise. He takes after Suleiman. Our Sultan, too, could not sit in one place. Who said that being the mother of the heir to the throne is easy? Do not complain about my grandson."

Answering with a smile, Gülbahar didn't know how to get to the real reason for her visit.

Sultana Hafsa, however, sensed the purpose of her visit, but she waited for her to start the subject. So, the women chatted about insignificant things for some time until finally, Gülbahar broached the real purpose for her visit.

"Do the girls in the harem disturb your peace, Mother?" she asked.

"I can't say that, Gülbahar. A few days ago, a Greek woman behaved badly. That's all."

"I heard that there was a row."

"Can something like this happen in the Sultan's house? In what times do we live? I told Sümbül Aga: 'Free the girl, let her go, let her go and look for happiness outside.' He did what was necessary."

Gülbahar thought that the woman hid the fact that the Greek woman argued with that damned Ruthenian girl.

"Are you saying, Mother, that she was the only one guilty?"

"I don't understand."

"I mean, who did this Greek woman argue with?"

"Are you interrogating me, Gülbahar? Do you have doubts about my decision?"

Gülbahar immediately withdrew, but she was determined to pursue this topic.

"Of course not. That's not what I meant, Sultana Mother. However, each argument must also have the second side. Who did this insolent girl argue with?"

Hafsa looked into the eyes of the woman sitting opposite her, and she saw anxiety in them. She decided to use the same answer the harem aga gave her:

"Who didn't she argue with, Gülbahar? Who didn't she argue with? She attacked everyone."

"There's a new one. They are saying she's Ruthenian, and she was the one who had an argument with her."

Sultana Hafsa was shocked that Sümbül Aga hid it from her, but she didn't let anything show.

"You've heard wrong."

"They say that Ruthenian is quite uncouth..."

"Gülbahar, are we supposed to believe the harem rumors?"

How blind she is, thought Gülbahar. *How she protects this girl. She will not hear a bad word about her.*

"Apparently, they could even barely take her to the baths. The odalisques complain about her. Who knows what a dirty girl she is? After all, the giaours do not wash very often."

"You haven't seen Ruslana, Gülbahar?" Sultana Hafsa asked, outraged.

The woman didn't know what to say, but the silence did not last long.

"Apparently, you visited the courtyard of odalisques today," the Sultana resumed. "The girl was there too. You walked past her. You must have noticed her."

The woman apparently wanted to distinguish the Ruthenian girl, suggesting that no one could miss her. Gülbahar tried to keep a stony face.

"I don't know. She did not catch my attention," she replied with a shrug of her shoulders.

"How is that possible? She is now the youngest and most beautiful girl in the harem. You must have seen her."

"How did she come to the Seraglio? I didn't know anything about it. Did she get here as a pirate booty or was she bought from slave traders? You know, Mother, that such girls often spread diseases... God forbid..."

"Gülbahar!" The old woman's soft voice suddenly became loud and rough. "Ruslana was entrusted to us. Sultana Güldane, who is also like a mother to me, before her death, passed her care to her daughter-in-law Aj Bala, and she entrusted her to me. I consider this orphan to be an inheritance from a woman, whom you should also consider a mother."

There was nothing left to add.

Everything is clear, Gülbahar thought. *So that's why she accepted the girl in her room and talked to her for hours. That is why, having forgotten that she is the mother of a sultan, she sat among the servants, and chatted with an ordinary odalisque like a mother and daughter.*

She stood up, bowed respectfully to Sultana Hafsa.

I'm sure she'll push this girl into her son's bed, she thought as she started to walk out. Then her heart burned with anger.

As Gülbahar sat devastated in her room, Ruslana was working to deliver a silk handkerchief in time for Sultana Hafsa. In her haste, the needle repeatedly pricked her finger, and each time she gave a short cry of pain, sucked the tip of her finger, and then returned to her work. Eventually, the purple handkerchief reached Sultana Hafsa just before the evening prayer.

When everyone went to their chambers after the evening prayer, and only the quiet talks of the guards were heard in the seraglio bathed in flickering candlelight, all the palace nooks and crannies filled with Ruslana's melancholic song.

Sultana Hafsa knowing her son was spending this night alone, crossed the harem corridors that echoed with the girl's beautiful voice and went to his chamber.

Sultan Suleiman, lying on a sofa set in front of the window in his underwear only, was surprised, but immediately recovered. He hoped that his mother wouldn't notice the cup with wine on a bedside table, inlaid with gold and ivory. Of course, the woman noticed it right away, but she didn't say anything.

Ever since he'd stayed in Manisa, Suleiman had begun to drink — a constant element of their maternal-filial tradition. Suleiman hid that he drank wine, even though he didn't drink much anyway, and he was particularly fond of the Greek raki imported from the Aegean Islands. His mother, on the other hand, turned a blind eye to the fact that her son spent some evenings with a cup in his hand. And so, it was also this time.

Padishah kissed his mother's hand and put it to his forehead. The woman stroked her son's back.

"You hear it, right?"

"How could I not hear, Mother?"

"Have you ever heard such a beautiful voice?"

"It seems even more beautiful tonight."

"I told her today that our Ruler really liked her voice. If you could've seen how happy she was. Probably it's happiness that makes her sing even more beautiful now."

"Is she as beautiful as her voice?"

"To be honest, I can not decide, son, what's more beautiful, her voice or herself. I thought you could make your own decision."

Suleiman's one jet-black eyebrow arched. He stroked his chin with a frivolous smile. He stood motionless so that Sultana Hafsa couldn't see the cup with the wine. For a moment, mother and son listened to Ruslana's voice. Sultana Hafsa took out the handkerchief that she'd carefully hid under her caftan. Holding it with both hands, she handed it to her son.

"Look what she sent you."

Suleiman stared for a moment at the purple silk fabric in his mother's hands and the red, purple, green, and carmine flowers adorning it. He raised his head and looked at his mother for a long time.

The woman tried to read his thoughts.

Who loves loneliness, oh, who?
Whether mountains or rivers do, I do not know.
I am always waiting for a dark night.
Thanks to the stars, loneliness goes into oblivion.

Suleiman reached out and took the handkerchief from his mother. Subconsciously, he lifted it and sniffed. As he unfolded it, dry petals of the same color fell on his hands.

"Redbuds," said the woman.

"Pardon?"

"These are the petals of the redbuds. Ruslana really likes these flowers. She dried and stored them."

"Her name is Ruslana?"

CHAPTER TWENTY

Ruslana was snatched from her sleep by some tumultuous activity in her room. To wake her up, Setaret opened the shutters, while Merzuka ran back and forth in the sun rays that spilled into the interior.

"What is going on?" Ruslana covered her eyes with her hand to protect them from the irritating light.

"Get up at once, young lady," Setaret's voice was full of excitement.

"Why? It's still early."

Suddenly she heard sounds coming from outside – it was as if the whole harem was already on its feet. Women spoke in raised voices, and there was a whirlwind of energy everywhere.

"The Padishah is coming," said Merzuka.

"What?!" Ruslana didn't even notice when that cry came out of her mouth, and her inner voice didn't stop repeating, *Padishah is coming? He is? My God! My God!*

"You get up immediately and start getting ready, or maybe you want the Sultan to find you in sleepwear?"

If it hadn't been for those words from the Tatar girl, perhaps due to the shock, Ruslana would still be sitting dumbfounded, repeating, *My God* to herself.

After a while, Jafer also ran in, followed by a sweaty Sümbül Aga, with his belly bouncing from the running. As soon as he entered the room, he shouted, clapping his hands:

"Fast, fast, fast! Why are you standing like this?!" Harem aga couldn't even calm down enough to see that Ruslana was dressing.

Without stopping his clapping, he ran out into the courtyard. Now his voice came from the outside.

"What is this laziness? You wish me so bad? In a moment, our Ruler will honor us, and nobody is ready yet."

Actually, everyone was ready – especially Ruslana. Like the other girls, she too had put on her most beautiful dress.

"Does it fit me? Is it good like this? Do I look nice in this?" she incessantly asked Ekaterina and Merzuka, and although she received an affirmative reply each time, it didn't calm her down in any way.

Maybe I should have put on a yellow caftan? Or perhaps I would look nicer in black? Wouldn't it emphasize the color of my hair? This love for purple limits me. Are there no other colors? Not always everything has to be purple. Does the Sultan like this color? What if he hates it? She tortured herself.

It was too late now. The moment of truth had arrived. What is to be, will be.

Our mother, Mary, she thought, *make a miracle. Help me. Make the Ottoman Sultan like me. Let me share the throne and the crown with him.*

She put her hand to her chest as if it would help her calm down her heart, that pounded at a frantic rate.

Jesus, our Father, she continued, *you know that I have not been to a church for a long time. But in the temple that I have in my heart, I am always with You. Now, at this moment, I need your help. Come, fill my heart. Do not leave me alone. Let Suleiman not be able to take his eyes off me. Please, God, help me.*

Ruslana didn't even hear the noise of the courtyard anymore. It seemed to her that the harem girls and supervisors all hovered above the ground. She didn't hear Ekaterina's words. She was afraid that her heart would not endure this excitement.

Suddenly there was a thunder-like sound at the opposite end of the courtyard. She didn't know what it was, but she noticed that the bustling in the courtyard ceased immediately. All the girls and supervisors lowered their heads. She also did the same, but she couldn't help but look out of the corner of her eye in the direction of the noise.

My God! The same voice inside her spoke again. *It's him! It's him! It's him!*

This time, he wasn't wearing that big turban on his head. Nor did Sultan Suleiman wear a caftan either. This time, he wore a loose, red silk shirt, with a leather belt wrapped around his waist, and white silk galligaskins. His shoes were not pulled over his calves, had upturned toes made from the skins of gazelles, and were of the same color as the shirt.

Why doesn't he have a turban? Why didn't he put on a caftan? The questions rushed through Ruslana's mind. *It's stupid. It's his home, and this is his home outfit. Why would he wear such heavy clothing at home?*

She had wondered earlier if he was bald because she couldn't see his hair through the turban he wore. As she now discovered, the Padishah had black, wavy hair. When she'd seen his beard from afar, it had seemed thinner – but in reality, Suleiman had a lush, black stubble.

Is he handsome? Ruslana so often asked herself that question, and now she could easily answer it. *Yes, handsome, and very much so.* And in addition, huge. Like a giant.

Actually, she knew that Sultan Suleiman was not that tall, but she wanted to see him like that. In the future, Ruslana will become as great and immortal as he is. Maybe it was the power of faith, but the voice in her heart, even if it was only a faint whisper, told her the same.

Ruslana saw that Suleiman, whom she described as great, proud, and full of majesty, was absorbed in thoughts. For some reason, he put a bent forefinger to his mouth and mustache.

Is there something that he doesn't want to laugh at? Ruslana wondered. She couldn't see anything more — she'd almost got a squint from looking at him while bent in a deep bow.

As Sultan Suleiman walked along the courtyard towards the harem aga Sümbül and another supervisor, she could hear the sound of his footsteps and those of his servants rushing to meet him. He didn't hesitate for a moment or stop by any of the girls. She turned her eyes again as far as possible to the right. Yes, he was walking straight toward her. She saw red shoes with upturned toes, made of gazelles' skins, on the Persian carpets that covered the courtyard floor... red shoes that were getting closer... Closer... And closer... With each of his steps, Ruslana's heart beat harder and harder as if it was going to jump out of her chest.

However, something happened that she completely did not expect. The red shoes made of gazelles' skin, instead of stopping in front of her, went on.

God, he didn't stop! He didn't even look at me! It's over, everything is over! Ruslana was desperate. Still bent in a bow, she moved her gaze to the left. The red gazelles leather shoes moved away, and with them, her hope faded. Or maybe it was one of those strange Ottoman customs? Maybe this was how they were supposed to meet? Perhaps Ruslana was to see his shoes, and the Sultan the back of a girl bent in front of him in a profound bow?

She realized that her eyes were starting to be covered by rainy clouds.

Do not cry, she scolded herself. *Do not show your despair to anyone. Even myself. You heard? Even myself.*

From what her eyes could see, it looked that the red shoes and the other shoes accompanying them were about to leave the hall at any moment. Suddenly, the red shoes stopped. Why did the Padishah stop? His feet changed direction, and he started walking again. He stepped back and headed toward her.

God, Ruslana prayed in her mind. *Jesus, our Father, our Mother Mary, let him see me. I'll light a candle in the first church I see. No, two candles... No, no, a whole lot of candles!*

The red shoes with their upturned toes approached... They were right next to her... This time they stopped exactly in front of her.

Long live! A shout of joy echoed in Ruslana's head. If she looked up, her eyes would meet Suleiman's eyes, but she couldn't do that. She could feel his breath, but she couldn't see anything but the tips of his shoes and the galligaskins.

Damn it! She cursed inwardly. *Do I have to wait for an order to be able to see him? How can I stop myself? The Sultan will surely hear my heart beating. I'm too excited. Maybe I won't even be able to talk to him. Or maybe my heart will stop. How can my heart endure such a great*

emotion? Why doesn't this man tell me to raise my head?
It seemed to Ruslana that not a few seconds had passed,
but two centuries. She could not stand it.

What is to be, will be, she told herself. She was no
longer able to obey customs, orders, or rules. She decided
to straighten up and look into Suleiman's eyes. She won't
even blink.

"Are you the one singing these beautiful songs at
night?" he asked.

Ruslana wanted to shout. He had a thick but warm
voice, and he spoke in her language. He had used some
words incorrectly, but she could understand what he said.

*Who did this voice belong to? To the sultan or somebody
else?* Once again, she felt a hatred for deep bows. However,
still maintaining her position, she asked quietly:

"Who is asking about it?"

The silence which prevailed among the people
gathered around Suleiman, no doubt wondering how the
Padishah would punish her for this insolence, seemed to
Ruslana to last forever.

"I am the Padishah, and who are you?"

She couldn't stand it anymore – she couldn't wait for the
order. This was the moment, and she straightened up slowly.

Their eyes met.

One black and the other green, maybe blue – Suleiman
could not decide either way. As for Ruslana, she looked for
some kind of feeling in the eyes of the man with lush
eyebrows. Both were silent for a moment.

Suleiman probed deeply into the girl's eyes, and when
Suleiman's dark brown eyes escaped from the depths of her
eyes with difficulty, they slipped onto her golden-red hair.

"Aleksandra. Aleksandra Anastasia Lisowska," Ruslana said majestically.

That's when she first noticed that Sultan Suleiman was also excited. His misty look moved back from her hair to her deep, blue-green eyes.

My God, thought the young Padishah, *can such beautiful eyes exist? They are like the ocean. The ocean in which torches burn, precious stones glisten, stars reflect, and the light of the moon shines.*

"But they call you Ruslana... So, we've heard..."

He spoke again in a thick, warm voice, but this time he could barely utter his words. He couldn't take his eyes off the girl's eyes – and Ruslana looked at him the same way – without fear, with confidence, and even defiance. Suddenly, a smile appeared on the girl's flushed cheeks, and two small dimples appeared at the corners of her mouth.

"I wanted it myself, My Lord," she replied after a moment's hesitation. "It's better than when they called me a Ruthenian." Her smile now lit up her whole face.

"I like the name."

Sultan Suleiman agreed with his mother – he'd never seen such a beautiful smile before. It lit up the inside of a man, warmed it, drove his worries away. No one would be able to resist reciprocating it. This smile distracted all the bad thoughts, whether about problems or even about the Military Order of Rhodes.

"Really? Why?" Suleiman asked, pulling himself together.

"Because it reminds me of my homeland, village, mother, and father, My Lord."

Ruslana was answering, but inside she was continually shouting with joy:

He likes me! He likes me! He likes me! He likes me! Long live!

A smile also appeared on Sultan Suleiman's face; the one who caused trembling and fear so great, that none of those present even dared to lift their head.

"What are we going to do now? How are we to call you? Aleksandra or Ruslana?"

Yes! My prayers have been answered. It didn't even bother her that the man referred to himself as 'us,' even though it seemed ridiculous to her. Sultan Suleiman saw her, and what's more, he liked her. He talked to her like to a friend.

Ruslana was so focused on the Padishah that she still hadn't noticed the surprised and jealous glances of the odalisques and harem supervisors surrounding them. Even if she had noticed them, she wouldn't have cared. Finally, she felt that her life, which from the night when she had been kidnapped from her mountain village and had raced towards the unknown filled with suffering, had now broken out of the darkness, and was going towards the light. In the end, the dawn of her life had arrived. The day was waking up, and if she wants, she can be Aleksandra Lisowska, or she can be Ruslana. It was him. She wanted Suleiman to love her madly.

I'll love him too, she thought. *I'll make him forget about Gülbahar. I will give him sons.*

They still stared at each other. A smile appeared on Ruslana's face, taking away Suleiman's senses.

"What importance does the name of your subject have?" she bravely replied. "Let it be whatever the Sultan wants, what he likes." She fell silent.

Their eyes met again. Padishah noticed that the girl was swallowing.

"You wanted to say something. Do not be shy. Tell us."

"It surprised me that you speak my language."

"For three years we did the duties of Beylerbey in the eyalet of Kaffa, in the Crimea. Many inhabitants of the Crimea know Ruthenian. Our mother also speaks."

The girl struggled to restrain her laughter – the Padishah's Ruthenian was terrible. In order not to laugh, she replied:

"My holy memory Sultana Mother also spoke to me in this language."

"No one here tell your tongue. A little Sümbül Aga, but only a little bit. I do not talk a lot, do not talk, and man forget."

Ruslana couldn't stand it and began to giggle.

"What happened? Did I say something wrong?" he was worried.

As she answered, she looked directly into the eyes of the Padishah with a sparkling smile, and without a trace of fear.

"You said, 'No one here tell your tongue. I do not talk a lot, do not talk, and man forget.' Some words are wrong."

"Really? And how is it correctly?"

"It would be better to say: 'Nobody can speak your language here. When a man does not talk it for a long time, he forgets.'"

Suleiman slowly repeated the girl's words, and she spoke some words with him. Sultan Suleiman did not hide his amusement.

"Tell to you Ruthenian, will not be bad..."

"It will not be bad to talk to you in Ruthenian," Ruslana corrected him.

Suleiman repeated the correct sentence.

"How was it? Not bad, right?"

Without stopping laughing, Ruslana replied:

"Not bad."

Suddenly Suleiman's face became serious.

"The last time we spoke several times in your language during the trip to Belgrade. Ruthenian resembles Serbian language. But we not talked since then. Now for the first time."

In an instant, the Padishah's demeanor became cold. His face took on a grim expression.

"But your Turkish is a bigger tragedy than my Ruthenian."

It was then that Ruslana discovered the childish side of Suleiman. The Ruler governing the State so great that no one knew exactly where its borders were, had in himself something of a joyful boy, willing to learn new things, sometimes joking, and sometimes even dangerously impatient. Suddenly she realized that she should answer something.

"You are right. I think you are very capable. You know my language. And I've been here for so long, and have not learned your language yet."

Suleiman's grim face lit up. Ruslana learned something else. The Padishah liked it when his pride was stroked.

Do not forget about it, Ruslana, she noted it in her mind. *Never forget to praise him often.*

"In that case, we will do this: you teach us Ruthenian, and we will teach you Turkish."

This time, Ruslana did not manage to stifle her laughter. Radiant, she looked at the young man. There was everything in their eyes: acceptance, devotion, love, fear, challenge, pride... and lust.

Does Padishah want me? She thought about it. *Is there really desire in those eyes, or is it just me? Or do I see a reflection of my own desires in his eyes?* she wondered.

But she was right. At that moment he was thinking about kissing her delicate, moist, full lips.

Suddenly, Sultan Suleiman noticed that he had gone a bit too far. He had so much to say to her, he could even sit down and write a couplet, but this was not the right moment. Rumors and jokes are going to appear right away. Even at the Divan, they will whisper whether it's right that the Padishah has shown such interest in a Ruthenian girl. Gülbahar will probably reproach him again. She was probably insulted by the fact that he had not answered her letter that she'd sent him yesterday.

An internal debated raged within him.

What to do? Should I consider now that the bed is ready for conquest? Come on... he continued to ruminate. *But if it is so, then where does this fire, which begins to burn inside me, come from? Why couldn't I take my eyes off the girl's eyes? And her smile? When Ruslana smiled, it seemed that the sun rose on her face, roses bloomed. What is happening to me? Have I been enchanted? The Master of the great world has been enslaved by a fifteen-year-old Ruthenian girl?*

"I must go now," he said reluctantly.

Leaving Ruslana with a trembling heart, he began to walk away. However, he had not even taken three steps, when he stopped and turned back.

"Do not deprive us of the pleasure of listening to your voice at nights. The song you sang yesterday was beautiful. The one on the night before too. How did it go? Ah, *'Pull, huh...'*"

As Suleiman left, Ruslana bowed almost to the ground – and for the first time, she did it with pleasure.

CHAPTER TWENTY-ONE

"Damn it! Damn it! Damn it." With every curse, Ruslana struck the floor with her heel. Two days had passed, and nothing had happened – Suleiman, it seemed, had just disappeared. Sultana Hafsa had also not left her chambers.

After he'd distinguished her with compliments, all the eyes in the harem focused on Ruslana. Needless to say, those eyes were all full of envy.

When Sultana Hafsa first showed her respect for her, and then Sultan Suleiman, a wall of respect and fear arose around her – and Ruslana loved it.

The days of when other girls put on airs and didn't deign to look at her as they passed by belonged in the past now, to be replaced instead by a race for her interest. Whenever she went out to the courtyard, almost immediately a crowd would gather around her, including the Arab servants who now ran around and stared at her, asking if she needed anything.

Even Sümbül Aga's aide, Jafer, came without shame at night and curled up on the pillow in the lobby in front of Ruslana's room.

Ruslana eagerly awaited the day when she would talk to Sultan Suleiman again. After the evening prayer, when night fell, she sang the songs he expected.

Was she singing louder so that her voice, penetrating the grates, corridors, doors, and walls, would reach Suleiman, or did it only seem so to Jafer? She sang even more beautifully and touchingly. In this nightingale song, there was longing, love, hatred, anger, plea, pride, and everything else. Jafer couldn't understand the magic of Ruslana's voice in any way. Many girls in the harem sang in the evenings. True, ever since Ruslana's voice was heard for the first time, they all stopped, but before she appeared, he'd heard many beautiful voices. However, none of them captivated a person like Ruslana's.

Jafer sank into shadows growing in the light of a torch. As soon as the shadows disappeared, the distant, endless red lands of Sudan appeared before his eyes. He saw a boy running in the shade of a date palm tree growing in the middle of a sea of sand. Who was it? Him? He tried to wipe away his tears with his large hand, and at the same moment, he fell asleep, thinking about the boy. The child remained in his dream until the morning.

Sultan Suleiman, who'd been talking all day with the viziers about the preparations for the expedition to Rhodes, had his thoughts filled with the image of the fortress of the Knights of Rhodes, made of black stone – but they quickly disappeared as Ruslana's voice carried all the way to his chamber. He tried to forget the pain his soul had suffered when he learned that the first prince, Mahmoud, had died in Manisa – he was only nine years old, and had been born when Suleiman was a Beylerbey in Kaffa. True, he was a child himself at the time, and he'd not found love for his son, but the death of such a small child had shaken him tremendously.

Fortunately, Prince Mustafa was like a young lion. Padishah raised the goblet to the flames crackling in the fireplace. Listening to the voice of the girl, now growing, now fading, sometimes pained, sometimes caressing, and sometimes joyful, he gazed thoughtfully at the scarlet wings of fire, reflecting in the cup.

My God, what a beautiful voice she has, he thought. *What was her name? Aleksandra... She wanted to be called Ruslana. That's right?* In his mind, the place of the Rhodian stronghold was suddenly taken over by Ruslana's face: She was smiling beautifully, and her smile lit up everything around her. And those dimples at the corners of her mouth? They suited her so much. He remembered Ruslana's eyes. He couldn't decide if they were blue, navy, or green. *What color were her eyes? She had such a deep, penetrating look*.

He drowned in his thoughts. He couldn't take his eyes off the red ribbon of light dancing in the goblet with the wine he held facing the flames in the fireplace. Ruslana's songs were full of longing and complaints.

She had a right to complain, thought Sultan Suleiman. *Someone kidnapped the girl from home. Who knows what she went through? How much did she suffer?*

Padishah fidgeted uneasily.

For the first time, he found himself wondering about the past of a harem girl. He was surprised – yes, odalisques had a family once. They were sent to the Seraglio as gifts, but what were they before that? Most of them were not ask about anything, they were simply abducted. They ended up on pirate ships, with slave traders... It was also right that some of them were given to him by their families, with their own consent; those were the ones who wanted to obtain the Sultan's protection. But how many like this were there?

Why did they have to travel to distant countries, he thought. *That's how it was with my mother. And with Gülbahar Haseki. They came to the palace with the consent of their families. But the others?*

These thoughts made him even more restless. He got up and went over to the fireplace, where the warmth of the flames reached his body. Taking a sip of wine, he listened to Ruslana again and sank back into his thoughts.

Was the girl happy to be here? Why not? Who wouldn't like to be in my harem, the ruler of a vast huge empire, shaking the world? Certainly, she had to be happy that she was here. But if that was the case, why are her songs so moving? What kind of feelings depress her so much, that they pour out of her mouth with a sob? Why do her songs always talk about distant lands?

"Longing," whispered the young Padishah, now laying on the tiger skin from India in front of the fireplace. The girl certainly missed what she left behind.

This is the order of the world, he consoled himself. *If Ruslana were not here today, who knows where she would be. If she is so unhappy, the solution is simple. I will ask her. If she wants to leave, I will send her away. Let her return to her homeland, to her family, if she will be happy this way...*

Suleiman committed his decision to his memory.

While the Padishah wandered the worlds of dreams, following Ruslana's voice, Gülbahar sat in her chamber angry and unhappy. Her anger was unloaded on all her servants, and when the girls opened the door to hear Ruslana's voice better, she went berserk.

"Simpletons!" she shouted. "Why do you open the door?! Who heard of the door to the Sultana Haseki's room being left ajar?! Do you think this is a caravanserai?"

Several servants immediately ran to close the door. However, it failed to soothe haseki's anger.

"Which one opened them without permission? Who rules here, you or me?"

Furious, she rose and began to nervously stroll around the room. The lack of response enraged her even more.

"So, you're all guilty, right? As you wish. You will all get hit, and you will all learn what it means to oppose the favorite of Sultan Suleiman, Gülbahar Haseki!"

She drew a deep breath and shouted:

"Stick!"

One of the girls ran and brought a dogwood stick from another room, and the first blow fell on her. The branch whistled through the air and hit the girl's shoulder – the maid screamed in pain.

Meanwhile, the stick whistled several more times in the air, and every time there was another scream.

"You cheeky women!"

Gülbahar's screams carried far along the corridors. The loud and sharp sounds coming from Gülbahar rooms were the opposite of Ruslana's beautiful voice. Beauty and ugliness. Black and white. Love and hatred. But Gülbahar didn't realize that her anger and envy made her ugly and cost her – losing favors and gaining enemies. Suleiman had already been with many girls, but for the first time, Gülbahar felt such jealousy; and especially so because the ruler did not even invite her to his alcove yet.

Everyone knew why Gülbahar was so angry. Three times she wrote letters to the Padishah, but she didn't receive even one message back. During these three days, the ruler never came to her chamber either. Sultana Hafsa had also stopped visiting her and only sent her a brief message: 'I caught a cold.' And on top of all this, was this thing with that Ruthenian girl. The fact that she joined the odalisques of Sultan Suleiman thanks to Sultana Mother, also enraged Gülbahar.

How is this possible? How is this possible? It kept bothering her. The great Padishah, the father of Prince Mustafa, actually made a personal visit to see some odalisque, and he even talked to her in front of everyone. What was this chat, and that sprinkling with compliments? 'What a beautiful voice you have. Do not deprive the harem of this beautiful voice.' *What was so special about that voice? Before she appeared, my voice had been beautiful too.*

She didn't believe herself in what she was saying; she played the oud beautifully, but her voice was not delightful. She never even sang any song properly. She tried that night for the first time, but she failed. She was ashamed and stopped.

"Envy and worry have changed me into a madwoman. I do things that I should be ashamed of," she murmured to herself.

But what could she do? Something was going on. She felt it.

Gülbahar had horrible dreams at night. She woke up in fear, but oddly enough, she couldn't remember anything in the morning.

She barely recognized herself. She'd never been like this. She was always gentle and patient, and until a few weeks ago, no one had ever heard her scream at servants. But the arrival of this Ruthenian had turned everything upside down. She couldn't see her future anymore – it was strange but true. She didn't recognize Suleiman either. Well, his head was occupied by the affairs of the State, but why didn't he ever want to see his haseki in the last ten days?

And what could she say to Sultana Mother? They hadn't seen each other for a few days, but every time their eyes met, the woman escaped her gaze. It was as if she was feeling guilty. She was guilty. She was guilty because she tried to push the Ruthenian into her son's bed. She was also guilty because she's tried to convince Suleiman to smell a different rose than Gülbahar. She was guilty because she let herself be overwhelmed by the feeling that made the mother of her grandson lose her position.

I can't stand that voice. I don't want to hear that girl's voice. Devilish voice. Yes, that was certainly the voice of the devil. The devil who's come to take my happiness and future. Gülbahar threw herself on the bed and burst into loud crying. She cried and screamed... She cried until she lost her breath. She was desperate.

On the third day, the storm of Ruslana's rage broke out for good. She sang every evening so that Suleiman could hear her voice, and she waited for him every morning, but all in vain. It was about time that she did something about it.

Later, she thought. *They said they gave him the handkerchief, and the Sultan did come the next day. Well, great. He gave me compliments. And later? There has been no 'later.' I've been abandoned,* she told herself. *Or maybe the Padishah did not like me? Maybe he's reproached Sultana Hafsa: 'Mother, how can you think that I will let that country maid in my alcove?' Fine, if he doesn't like me, let it be so, but then why did he compliment me?* Ruslana was filled with pain. Somewhere in the nooks and crannies of her mind, the question arose: *Or maybe he wanted to hurt me?*

"Call Sümbül Aga to me!" she shouted to Setaret and Merzuka.

The Tatar girl realized that anxiety had overpowered Ruslana. She tried to calm her down, comfort her somehow, but to her surprise, she heard only:

"Keep those tips for yourself. Don't forget that you are here thanks to me. Do what I asked immediately. Find Sümbül and bring him here. Immediately!"

Ruslana words hurt Merzuka very much because she considered her a friend, but she did not speak up. To hide the tears that came to her eyes, she turned and ran to look for Sümbül Aga.

Under normal circumstances, the harem aga would grab the odalisque who summoned him in this way, and give her some beautiful blows, but considering what he'd experienced with the Ruthenian under the stairs, and the special kindness of the Sultana Mother and the Padishah for her, he decided to keep his hands off her.

When he entered, the atmosphere became extremely dense. Ruslana nervously walked around the room that was full of dark shadows. Seeing the aga, she immediately turned on him.

"What's going on, Sümbül Aga?"

The man understood at once what the girl meant, but he preferred to pretend he didn't know it.

"What do you mean, what's going on?"

"Someone is trying to stand in my way."

"What way?"

"I do not see either Sultana Mother or the Sultan."

"Whether you see them depends on their will."

"That's what I'm talking about. Does anyone try to harm me? Sending rumors to cool my relationship with Sultana Hafsa, and our Master?"

Sümbül understood that the girl suspected that only he could do something like that.

"Do you suspect that I slander you?"

"Who else could have done it?" Ruslana's voice whistled from rage.

"I would not do something like that."

"Ha! How can I know that?"

"You know I wouldn't do it."

Ruslana looked the man in the eyes. Sümbül Aga was afraid to even mention what had happened under the stairs. Saying this, he meant one thing: 'If I would say something; you would do the same.'

In the darkened room, she clung to the harem aga.

"Don't ever say you're scared of me," she said. "You know that I couldn't do it either. Our future depends on whether we keep our mouths shut."

"What should I do?" Sümbül Aga's voice was so quiet that if the girl weren't standing so close, she wouldn't have heard him. Many years of experience had taught the man that nothing could be hidden in the harem. The walls had eyes and ears.

"Whatever needs to be done. Make the Sultan invite me."

"But how can I do it? How can a harem aga tell the great Padishah what he should do?" the man moaned helplessly.

The girl clung closer to him. Sümbül was stuck between the wall and Ruslana's chest, rising and falling to the rhythm of her breathing.

In the darkness, in which the whites of his eyes seemed even larger, she looked into his shining eyes.

"You know best how to do it," she said slowly.

Suddenly, she turned her back to the man and angrily stabbed a heel into the man's foot, as if she were hitting the floor.

"And do it now!" she exclaimed.

Sümbül's eyes filled with tears from pain, and he covered his mouth with his huge hand to suppress the scream.

Ruslana moved toward the courtyard, drunk with the thought that she'd finally taken revenge on the man for all the beatings she'd got from him.

Serves him right, she thought to herself. How many nights had she plotted and schemed how to soothe that pain? Finally, she'd succeeded.

The giant writhed in pain for a moment. He limped as he walked towards the girl, his face distorted in pain, and as he passed by her, he hissed through his teeth:

"Tremble, Ruthenian wench! If he doesn't take you into his bed, I'll drink the carmine sherbet made of your blood."

Ruslana was aware that she was standing on the edge of the abyss. If she showed even a shadow of fear to his threat, everything would be over. So, she smiled as if those words did not make any impression on her.

"But if he does..." Without finishing the sentence, she looked once more into Black Face's eyes. She saw anger and pain in them. "But if he does, Sümbül Aga will have more akce than he can count."

CHAPTER TWENTY-TWO

Sümbül rubbed the ointment on his foot where the girl stabbed him with her sharp heel and wrapped it with a bandage. He couldn't sleep all night because of the pain and ruminating on how not to sit under Ruslana's thumb. If he tries to do it now, it could have dangerous consequences, especially because the rumors of the sudden disappearance of the Greek woman Despina from the harem hadn't calmed down yet. He couldn't risk another incident now. Also, if something bad happened to a girl in the care of the Sultana Mother and the Sultan himself, it would be a different case than Despina's. So, it was best to do what she wanted. But how? He couldn't go to Sultana Hafsa and say to her, 'Tell your son to invite the girl to his alcove.' Or maybe he should run to the Sultan and ask, bowing lowly: 'Sultan, let this girl into your bed?' What a dilemma this Ruthenian caused!

As soon as the dawn broke, Sümbül had decided. He'd invented a plan with which he would both remind them of Ruslana's existence, as well as take revenge for his injured foot; he would show her that he still ruled here. There was no other way to avoid the girl's constant demands and the danger hanging over his head – and Sümbül always took good care of his head. He had been flattering and kowtowing for years to protect it. He couldn't even count anymore, how many lives he'd taken because of it. Who knows what fish were feeding on the body of the Greek Despina. But apparently, Ruslana had not learned anything from this. He could no longer silence her with a stick or lock her in a room and starve her until she would come to her senses. If she suddenly disappeared, Sümbül would put himself in danger. If she died out of blue, the traces of poison would be sought...

Damn it! he cursed in his mind, trying to keep his heavy eyelids open. *What was so great about those embraces under the stairs? Why did I do something so stupid? Did I become a man during those few minutes of squeezing, rubbing, and licking? If not for that several-minute long escapade, I'd break that thin neck of the Ruthenian girl. But what happened, happened. Now I have to not only assure her the position of the favorite of the Padishah but also to convince her that if I go down, I'll drag her with me.*

As soon as he got up, he went, limping, to the room of the Sultana Mother.

***

Sultana Hafsa worried, seeing the bandaged foot of the man and how he tried to bow before her.

"What happened, Sümbül?"

"A minor accident, Sultana."

"What accident?"

"Nothing important, My Lady. Your concern about the servant made him forget about the pain already."

"Tell me, Sümbül, what was this accident?"

"It's... Sultana... Ruslana... Our..."

The curiosity of the woman grew. When she heard Ruslana's name, her voice became sharper.

"What about Ruslana? Did something bad happen to her?"

"God forbid, Sultana. I would not be caught dead letting anything bad happen to our little girl, so cherished by Sultana Mother and our Ruler. The girl is safe and sound."

"Then what happened?"

"Recently... I don't know how to say it."

In order to arouse even greater curiosity in the older woman, he delayed the response for as long as possible.

"Recently what? Speak, man!"

"She's unbearable, My Lady," Sümbül Aga replied with one breath.

"How come, unbearable?"

"I don't know, just unbearable. She easily gets angry and her anger, mashallah, is dangerous and sharp like a sword."

Sümbül measured the woman with his cunning eyes and tried to assess what impression his words had on her, but he couldn't see anything.

"Mashallah!" he repeated, not taking his eyes off the woman. "When she gets angry, the beautiful golden-haired girl disappears, and a warrior from the northern lands appears in her place. I want to tell you, My Lady, that one can not cope with her."

Finally, Sümbül Aga noticed the long-awaited flash in the woman's gaze. When he compared the girl to the warrior, a light appeared for a moment in the Sultana's eyes.

Yes, the old lady wants the girl to be like that. That's what it is. That's why Sultana Hafsa wants Ruslana to take Gülbahar's place by Suleiman's side, he thought.

Gülbahar was too gentle. No one heard her get angry, shout, or oppose something. She was submissive. Sultana Hafsa immediately saw a strong will in the Ruthenian – the girl was as delicate as a rose, but like every rose, she had thorns as sharp as daggers. She knew how to fight for what was hers. She could be supportive, and she didn't hide her abilities under the blanket. She was feminine, but above all, wise. She was beautiful, but she seemed to know that the mind is more important than beauty.

My son needs such a woman whose strong will, will be a support for him, she thought. *Let her give her heart to Suleiman when he is lonely. Let her lighten up his life and soul.*

"What does Ruslana's anger have to do with your condition?" The woman pointed to harem aga's foot.

"She suddenly got angry again... Shouting her anger, she pressed my foot with her heel."

"She did it on purpose?"

"I think it was an accident, My Lady. That's true, she was angry, but when she turned away, she stumbled on my foot inadvertently."

Sultana Hafsa understood. It wasn't an accident. It was clear that the girl deliberately stepped on the man's foot with a heavy wooden heel.

"Why was she angry? Do you know what caused this?"

"That's what I was trying to find out. Our girl looked sad and thoughtful..."

"Sad? For how long?"

"She was bouncing with happiness after your warm words, My Lady, but..."

"'But' what? Say it, Sümbül. But what?"

"After meeting with our Ruler, she changed. She sat in the corner and meditated. One of the servants mentioned that she stopped eating and drinking..."

Sümbül Aga chose his words so carefully, and pronounced them so meaningfully that everyone would understand that the girl fell in love with the Padishah. Sultana Hafsa also inferred this, and her heart got wings. It seems that everything will happen with the consent of the heart. The girl loved her son. It was obvious. During those few days, she missed him. That was the reason for the lack of humor and anger. That's why she crushed the poor Sümbül's feet with her heel. Could this girl warm up the cooling ashes in Suleiman's heart?

I know my son, thought the woman. *A spark was enough to light a flame of love in him. All that was needed was someone who would enkindle this spark. But now I should be interested in Sümbül Aga's foot.*

"Call her, Sümbül Aga. Call our daughter, let her tell us what caused her anger."

"It's nothing, My Lady. Don't be angry at her," the aga began to mutter falsely, and then hurried out, forgetting to limp.

He'd succeeded. Not only did he cause that Ruslana would get a reprimand, but he also met her request to be seen by Sultana Hafsa.

***

Entering the room, Ruslana bowed to the Sultana Mother. The woman was once again impressed by her beauty and stature. However, she should put on a stern look now.

"Apparently, you've recently become nervous, child. Don't you know that we don't want any disputes in our master's house?"

Ruslana didn't answer. Instead, she acted contrary to what she had been commanded a thousand times, and she straightened herself up without receiving such an order and looked into the woman's eyes with love.

Sultana Hafsa could not take her eyes off the girl.

"Moreover," she said sharply, "I heard that you hurt the foot of Sümbül Aga, who cares so much about you. It is a sin. Aren't you ashamed?"

The Mother Sultana's question was left unanswered again, and this time the woman was sure; it was impossible to not be moved when looking into those eyes.

This look will enchant Suleiman, she thought.

"What made you so angry? Someone did something to you? Did you hear something?"

This time, Ruslana only shook her head slightly to show that this was not the reason. The embroidered veil, covering her hair, waved gently. A lock of her red hair moved with her.

Sultana Hafsa tried to take on a stern posture, but she didn't want to hurt the girl too much.

"Tell me, child, what happened to you?"

Now a motherly tenderness appeared in the woman's voice. Ruslana, without taking her eyes off her, simply whispered:

"It's nothing, Sultana Mother."

"But you know that what you did to Sümbül Aga surprised me a lot. I was sad. Sümbül is the backbone of the whole harem. We expect our girls to respect and obey him."

The girl moved her head again. Again, the white, embroidered tulle twitched slightly. This time, Ruslana nodded her head, as if to say, 'Yes. Whatever you order, My Lady.'

"I am sorry, Mother," she said slowly.

There was no need for Sümbül Aga to further accompany their conversation. The woman moved her head, at which Sümbül Aga, again limping, left the room. Sultana Hafsa stopped making an effort to make her voice sound harsh.

"Are you sad, child?"

"Yhy... Sad and unhappy..."

"Do you miss your homeland, your family?"

When Ruslana shook her head this time, the white tulle slipped over her shoulders. Her red hair was now completely uncovered.

"You are my family now," she replied, and for the first time looked away from Sultana Hafsa's eyes. "Here is my home and my homeland now..."

***

Two more long days passed since she'd talked to Sultana Hafsa, and the Sultan still hadn't shown either but this time Ruslana was hopeful. She could still hear the woman's words she said as she was about to leave, echoing in her memory:

"Love requires patience, child. And it is a woman who must have it." What more could the mother of the great Padishah say? 'Don't worry, I'll make it happen that you will end up in my son's bed?'

As for Sümbül, he still limped, but he wasn't looking at the girl with hostility anymore. It seemed that the Ruthenian finally realized who really ruled the harem until she would become the favorite of the Sultan.

Suddenly, a buzz broke out in the courtyard and shouts could be heard.

"Sultan is coming! Sultan is coming!"

Ruslana was in her room.

"My God," she said and stood up.

She grabbed her taffeta skirts on both sides, ran out into the courtyard, and almost bumped into the Sultan! She bowed immediately. Upon seeing her, Suleiman turned back.

"We aren't bothering you, are we?"

"Your view can only give us happiness."

These words were pleasing to the Padishah. What a beautiful voice this girl had.

"Is something the floor?"

Ruslana smiled.

"Is something on the floor?" she whispered so quietly that only Suleiman could hear her.

"Oh, we'll remember that. Is something on the floor?"

"Pardon? I do not understand."

"You keep staring at the floor..."

She raised her head slowly. She'd been in such a hurry she'd forgotten to cover her hair. Their eyes met.

Suleiman, freeing himself from the girl's eyes, stared next at her golden-brown curly hair. It flowed down her arms all the way to her waist like the rays of the setting sun. Then he stared again into her eyes.

"Everyone should bow before the Sultan, isn't that true?" she said softly.

"But the Sultan should see the eyes of who he is talking to. Especially if they are so beautiful, right?"

Her face seemed to burn with live fire. As if two flaming spheres sat on her cheeks.

"It is a great honor to hear such words." As she spoke, a radiant smile appeared on her face.

"You know..." Sultan Suleiman said suddenly. "We came up with a name for you."

"My Sultan thought about me?"

"Yes. We found a name that will suit the sun."

"Did you say 'sun'?"

"Yes. When you smile, you remind me of the sun."

She almost fainted with happiness. *Sun? She – the sun?*

"We thought: let our sun have a name that suits it."

"Everything that pleases the Padishah suits his slave."

"There is no more Aleksandra nor Ruslana. Ok? From now on you will be called Hürrem."

"Hürrem, sir?"

"Yes, Hürrem."

Sultan Suleiman hastily put something purple he pulled from behind his belt on the girl's shoulder.

My God! My God! the girl with the new name of Hürrem screamed in her mind. *My handkerchief. The handkerchief that I sewed and sent to the Sultan.*

Unaware of the shouts of happiness and joy in the girl's head, the Padishah gazed at her with burning eyes for a moment. She girl immediately read lust and embarrassment in his gaze, reflecting the same feelings she had.

The Padishah turned quickly again and left walking briskly, or actually running, or rather as if he was running away.

Hürrem was alone with a beating heart in the midst of jealous glances.

Hürrem, Hürrem. From now on you will be called Hürrem, she continuously repeated in her mind.

"God, I am stupid, so stupid," she murmured. "It didn't even occur to me to ask the Padishah what Hürrem means."

After the Sultan left, she took the handkerchief off her shoulder as the jealous whispers of the other girls rippled through the courtyard. Her heart was still pounding like mad.

This is the handkerchief that I sewed and sent to him – a cry of terror echoed in her head. *Does it mean he didn't like me? God, he didn't like me?*

Meanwhile, Setaret's joy was unmatched. Her Lady was just becoming the favorite of the Sultan. She couldn't sit still out of happiness. Her huge lips stretched into a wide smile.

"Congratulations, my lovely," she cheered, clapping her hands. "Our Ruler gave you the handkerchief."

Ruslana, drunk with compliments just a moment ago, then surprised by the sudden retreat of Suleiman after he put a handkerchief on her shoulder, didn't understand the reason for this joy.

"What are you happy about here, Kalfa?" she asked, wanting to hear the truth from her lips. "He probably didn't like it. It turned out ugly, he…"

Setaret cut in.

"Of course not! He liked it, he did. And very much so. He liked your handkerchief very much. He liked it so much that in the evening our Master invites you to his alcove."

"What?!"

"He's expecting you tonight, my lovely. It's a custom. He sends a handkerchief to the one he wants to have with him at night. What's more, he brought your handkerchief in person."

Yes, I understood it right! Shouts of joy echoed in her head. This message almost swept her off her feet. After a moment, her doubts returned again. Did she hear correctly?

"Are you telling the truth, Kalfa?"

Setaret approached her, glancing at her playfully with her dark eyes.

"Yes, yes," she giggled. "Don't pretend you didn't understand, my lovely. You got the handkerchief. This night you will meet the Padishah." Then, Setaret left her and ran into the courtyard waving the handkerchief, where the rumors among the odalisques and servants rumbled.

"Don't pretend you didn't hear. Let those who have not heard, hear this now, and those who have not seen, see. Let those jealous, writhe in envy. Our Ruler gave my Lady the handkerchief. He said: 'From now on, you will not be called Ruslana, but Hürrem.' Remember this and make sure you don't make a mistake. Ruslana has left, Hürrem has arrived. Viva Hürrem!"

Setaret's voice echoed under the dome of the harem as she ran from one end of the courtyard to the other, waving the handkerchief.

"There will be a tryst tonight, girls. A tryst! A meeting of my mistress Mrs. Hürrem..."

***

Setaret shouts proclaiming good news to everyone quickly reached the rooms of Gülbahar. Her reaction was just what the servants had expected.

The Circassian beauty, brought up among the harsh winds of the Caucasus mountains, in whose veins flowed blood mixed with ice and ashes, became enraged like a storm. All the maids scattered into the corners, but some could not escape the fury of the haseki. Led by anger, she went to Sultana Hafsa rooms only to receive the response that the Sultana Mother did not feel good and did not want to see anyone.

"Tell her right away that her grandchild's mother, her son's favorite has come!" She raised her voice, but it didn't achieve the intended effect.

The servant came back with the answer to come tomorrow then immediately returned to the Sultana Mother's rooms, her skirts rustling.

Pig! flashed through her head. *She knows well that tomorrow it will be too late.*

"Call the Sheikh of Islam at once," she ordered as soon as she returned to her room.

But it did not work either.

Ali Jemali Zembilli Efendi did not spare his words as he answered Gülbahar's veiled question.

"It is the sole will of our Master whom he honors with compliments, and whom he meets within the harem. It is inappropriate for his servants to discuss it. It has been like this, child, since our great ancestor, Osman Bey, the son of Ertugrul, the legendary chief of Oghuz Turks, the father of Osman the first and founder of the Ottoman dynasty. It is also in accordance with Sharia law."

The man paused for a moment and looked at the woman sitting opposite him. Sparks flashed out of her eyes. In a whisper, he slowly drew the words:

"If... God forbid, it was possible, the life of haseki in a harem would be in danger, even though she is the mother of Prince Mustafa..."

Was there anything more to say?

Oh, what happened to me? thought Gülbahar. The man had just reminded her of her position without beating about the bush. It is true that she gave Suleiman a wonderful son, thanks to which she became the second woman in the Seraglio after Sultana Hafsa – but that was all. She had no right to demand that there was no other woman in the Padishah's life but her. Besides, her life was in danger, even though she was the mother of the heir to the throne. Were they bound by marriage so that she could invoke the law, justice, or Sharia? These were the customs, and it was supposed to be like this – she was a favorite, and the Sultan's heart was pulling him to a new girl. That was all. It will always be like this until she would become the mother of the Padishah.

But maybe she was unnecessarily worried. Padishah will take the girl to bed and satisfy his lust, and then probably will put her out the door.

Not probably, it will surely be like this. Suleiman will not put a favorite over me, she sighed to herself.

She really wanted it to happen, but her female intuition told her something completely different. Whatever Sultan Suleiman saw in this girl from Ruthenia, although it could not be anything special, he liked it. However, it was more than just lust. If it were only lust, she wouldn't be afraid. This was something different – she could feel it. Otherwise, why would the Padishah go to the girl personally and give her the handkerchief?

Were his actions something ordinary? No, because what was Sümbül Aga for? Padishah should have given Sümbül the handkerchief and instruct him to bring the girl to the alcove, and that would be the end of it. But he didn't do that; he showed to the whole harem that he liked the girl. He didn't care that the agas, pashas, and viziers would talk about it. He gave her compliments and, as if that were not enough, he gave her a name. The whole palace resounded with the name of Hürrem.

Annoyed, Gülbahar sat on her heels and stared at the embroidering servants whose backs were still sore after the blows recently received from her.

"What did the Sultan say?" she asked. "How should you call this godless Ruthenian?"

"Hürrem," one of them replied.

All the women in the room, except Gülbahar, heard the grudge from recent torture in the girl's voice. This answer was like revenge.

Gülbahar sank into her thoughts. If it were appropriate for the haseki of Sultan Suleiman and the mother of Prince Mustafa, she would have cried aloud – but she didn't do that. She did not. She wouldn't let anyone say that a girl from Ruthenia forced Gülbahar Haseki to cry.

Hürrem, huh? Oh, that such a thing happened to me, she thought again. She cried silently, her tears sinking into her broken heart.

CHAPTER TWENTY-THREE

By the time the evening prayer was recited, she still wasn't ready. She didn't even notice when the evening arrived – in fact, a day full of bustle had passed in the blink of an eye.

The women in the bathhouse spent hours washing her body with washcloths. Her skin became as smooth as a baby's because they didn't leave a single hair anywhere – her skin almost bled in delicate places, and she couldn't recognize herself. And oh! The pain it caused; tears flowed from her eyes.

She struggled to refrain from shouting and telling them that what they were doing was a torture, but ultimately she decided to remain silent, so she didn't object to anything. Nor did she shout to anyone: 'Don't look at me.' She didn't even scratch the slaves who were touching her all over.

She was so quiet that even Sümbül Aga, who waited outside not knowing what was happening and afraid of an imminent row, entered the bathhouse. The crystal-clear body of the Ruthenian sitting by the pool among the many slaves, whose sight took his breath away, was not enough to overcome his surprise. The predatory Ruthenian cat had disappeared somewhere, and a kind girl had appeared. She joked with the slave girls and her laughter echoed through the bathhouse. She even tried to join the girls as they sang.

How beautiful is a young bride's pageant?
Come on, girls, get on dancing!

Ruslana didn't even notice Sümbül Aga as he opened the large wooden doors and looked inside for a moment because she was so absorbed in her joy and thoughts. She was focused only on looking good. She had to be beautiful. Very beautiful. If they were to tear her skin off for this, then let them tear it off. Later this night, Sultan Suleiman will be waiting for her. She was supposed to become a woman this very night – and what's more, Sultan Suleiman was supposed to make a woman out of her.

I have to make him lose his head, I must enchant him. I can not be a love for just one night. I have to reciprocate with all the feeling that is dormant in me. Unfortunately, I know nothing about the art of love. God, help me. Let me, in the eyes of my Sultan, be as pure as an angel, but as sensual as a belly dancer.

Rinsing her body with fragrant waters, she repeated in her heart the same words hundreds, and perhaps thousands of times:

My name is Hürrem. I'm Hürrem.

Okay, but what does Hürrem mean? She already asked everyone, but they couldn't answer her.

When Sümbül Aga entered her chamber, they'd just finished dressing her in white underwear made of Chinese silk – and she wore nothing else apart from this. She didn't know if it was because she was ashamed of her nakedness or the cold, but her face burned with a living fire. Her naked body trembled from the touch of the cool silk; it was as if thousands of needles were digging into her skin. One could even see her nipples under the thin fabric, hardened from the cold. The front of the underwear had a long slit from her neck to her stomach, revealing her naked skin. At the slightest step her jiggling breasts, capable of depriving any man standing in front of her of his senses, could slip out through this slit. Her curly red hair, raised from the long combing with ivory combs, fell to her shoulders.

She liked the Nomad style cape she was supposed to put on top. Large branches and flowers were embroidered on it with silver threads on a silky fabric in a shade of purple. A delicate Trabzon belt squeezed her already narrow waist.

I won't be able to breathe with this belt, she thought, but the army of servants, pouring out sweat trying to get her ready, didn't worry about it.

"You'll regret it if I drop dead out of breath at the feet of the Sultan," she'd threatened, but to no avail. She had to put up with this belt somehow.

Setaret and Merzuka looked at the girl, pushing aside the dressmakers, seamstresses, and bustling servants.

"Tfu, tfu, tfu," spat Setaret, as always when she liked something. "Mashallah, Mashallah." She was delighted.

Merzuka reacted with a long silence at the sight that appeared before her.

"You are beautiful, Aleksandra," she whispered as if enchanted.

Noticing the sparks of anger in the girl's eyes, she hurriedly tried to fix her mistake.

"I wanted to say, Ruslana..."

When more sparks flashed, the Tatar girl shook her head.

"I should say Hürrem, right?" She paused for a moment. "What can I do? Your name changes every day. I don't know which one to remember anymore." The girl turned away, her skirts rustling.

"Don't forget about Hürrem," she announced. "The Ottomans and the whole world will remember Hürrem. You will see."

Leaving the woman reciting prayers behind her, she headed, full of majesty, toward the vestibule where Sümbül Aga waited impatiently.

"Hurry up! Go on! If you are any later, the Sultan will order to cut the heads off all of us."

She followed Sümbül, ignoring the praying servants and the odalisques throwing jealous glances, who stuck their heads out of their rooms. She didn't feel the need to hide, nor did she even care about the scornful words of the odalisques:

"Where are you going, Ruthenian trollop?"

To calm down her throbbing heart, she repeated in her heart:

What do you mean where? Hürrem is going to a meeting with the Ottoman Sultan.

The long corridors seemed endless to her. Each of her steps was accompanied by a loud heartbeat. Finally, the harem aga stopped before a door in front of which stood menacing soldiers armed with sabers and shields. One of the guard's thick, black as coal whiskers hanging down to his chin, reminded her instantly of Tacham Noyan.

Actually, his mustache was not that black. Looking at it from a distance, it seemed as if there was snow on it, but in spite of that, it looked the same as this one. When one of the stern looking guards slowly opened the heavy door, a question appeared in Hürrem's head:

Where are you, Father Tacham? He'd turned her life upside down, put it in darkness, and then gave it a fresh start. Her heart was pierced by the pain of longing, and her eyes began to fog. In panic, she tried to pull herself together.

"Listen. Don't you dare cry," said one of the women preparing her. "If you cry, the coal that we've blackened your eyebrows and eyelashes with will flow down your face in black smears. Your face will turn into a piece of coal, and our Master will put you out the door."

When the door opened, Hürrem opened her eyes wide to get rid of the tears. Now another corridor appeared before them with big torches blazing on both sides. She moved silently with Sümbül toward the door visible at the end of the corridor. Hürrem kept looking straight ahead, just as she'd been ordered, but she still noticed out of the corner of her eyes, the guards in even intervals. They stood in the shadows, where the torchlight didn't reach; their eyes glowing like coals in the darkness.

When Hürrem prayed that the door she could see was the last obstacle on her way to Suleiman, an elderly woman suddenly appeared before them, seemingly from out of nowhere. She'd never seen her before. Judging by the fact that Sümbül greeted her, bowing with respect, she must have been someone important. The woman acted as if Hürrem wasn't there, but she could feel the old woman's eyes on her, carefully examining every inch of her body, from the top of her head to her toes.

"Daje Hatun," Sümbül whispered slowly. "Our Sultan's nanny. She was the one who took care of him and raised him. She still serves him. Our master treats her like a mother..."

Hürrem understood what he wanted to tell her. Without waiting for Sümbül Aga to finish speaking, she bowed respectfully to the old woman, lighting her face up with an unbearably beautiful, loving smile.

Daje Hatun responded to her greeting with a slight nod of her head. She was just like they described her. The nanny had never seen such a sincere and beautiful smile before.

No wonder the girl had made a great impression on Suleiman, Daje Hatun thought. Then she noticed with surprise, that she was overcome by a feeling that she had known this girl for a long time. She felt sympathy for her. Without taking her eyes off Hürrem, she said something to the harem aga.

The nanny's voice was like a whisper, but Hürrem understood that the person to whom her words were addressed was not Black Sümbül, but herself.

"What does she say?" she asked in a whisper.

"When you enter the room, you will immediately fall to the ground and greet the Sultan. When he tells you to get up, you will rise and go straight to the bed. You will kiss the quilt in the foot of the bed and cover your head with it.

"What?"

"You will kiss the quilt and cover your head with it."

"Why?"

Sümbül Aga didn't know why either, but this was the custom.

"Do as you are instructed," he said slowly.

Daje Hatun looked unhappy that they were speaking in a language incomprehensible to her, but for some reason, she liked this whispering. Looking again at Sümbül, she spoke to Hürrem.

"When our Lord lets you go, leaving the bed, you will not leave immediately. They will come and take off the bedding, then they will take you and the sheet."

"The sheet?"

"Yes, the sheet. Don't ask questions, just do as you were told."

Hürrem showed her respect to Hatun, bowing her knee a little, and giving her the sincerest smile.

"Don't worry, Hürrem will not make you ashamed," she said.

The old woman realized with astonishment that she was stroking the girl's hand. She'd never done anything like that before. Who knows how many girls she'd let through this door? But it was true that she'd not felt such closeness with any of them.

A guard appeared at the woman's sign and began to open the door. Then Daje Hatun turned and walked away. Sümbül Aga followed her for two steps, then turned and looked at Hürrem.

"I can not accompany you further. You're on your own now."

***

Hürrem walked over the high threshold. Hearing the door slam shut behind her, she did precisely the opposite of what she'd been told. Instead of falling on her face and waiting for Suleiman's order to let her get up, she stood upright.

On the opposite side of the room, she could see a cone fireplace where a log burned with a loud cracking. In the trembling light emanating from it, she noticed that the interior was painted yellow. There were also candles burning in front of a huge mirrored console. The light of the fireplace and candles reflected off yellow, red, blue, and white little glass windows opposite, and the tiles covering the walls. Amber to yellow flames gave the green tiles a red hue or the color of a beech. A bit further away stood a large bed, and in front of the window, a large, wide sofa, a table covered with numerous documents and maps, and several chairs. On the table in front of the sofa, there was a carafe reflecting the light, a few bottles, and a large bowl full of rare winter fruits. That was all. Was this the chamber of Sultan Suleiman, before whom the whole world trembled? Where were the gold, diamonds, emeralds, rubies? Was the place where the Ruler lived, whose power was praised by poets, so ordinary?

Suddenly, she noticed a huge shadow with a turban on its head, standing motionless in the twilight, at the bed head.

Mother of God, she thought hastily. *It's him. Him!* She immediately bowed gently. *Have I upset him because I didn't fall on the ground before him as soon as I passed the threshold?* she wondered. *If he doesn't speak, he must be upset. Now he'll put me out the door. Why doesn't he say anything? Should I hurl myself at his feet and beg for forgiveness? Come on, talk. Say something. Be angry, shout, but don't be silent! Speak up, damn it!*

"Will my Sultan, forgive me?" she whispered, straightening up.

The majestic shadow in the big turban did not even move.

Hürrem, trying to use the sweetest voice possible, continued:

"I'm just a simple country girl. I see a Sultan's chamber for the first time. Please ascribe my impropriety to a surprise. Forgive me."

At the same time, something she didn't expect happened. While the majestic shadow in the big turban was still silent, Sultan Suleiman came out from behind the mirrored mother-of-pearl console.

"Is it how you imagined the Sultan's chamber?" he asked.

She didn't know what was going on. Without taking her eyes off the huge scary shadow in the big turban, she gasped.

"You! You! I thought you... I mean he..."

Laughing, Suleiman put aside the towel, which he used to wipe his hands.

"Did you confuse me with this fright that was dressed in my caftan and turban?"

Trying to get herself together and to fix her slip, Hürrem threw the words hurriedly.

"Yes, I... I mean, no..."

Suddenly she remembered that she still had not bowed to the Padishah. When she bowed, mumbling something that she could not understand herself, Suleiman's laughter sounded louder.

"Look, there's nothing to be afraid of. The Sultan is a turban and a caftan. It's in them that the power is. It doesn't matter what's inside."

Still bent in a bow, Hürrem was indignant.

"How is this possible? What's a turban and a caftan? Just a few meters of fabric, some gold threads, and stones. In my opinion, it's what is inside that counts."

"Really?"

"If my Master does not get angry, I will say what I think. The caftan and the turban are worthless."

Suleiman looked at Hürrem's hair, blazing in the red glow of the flickering fire, and at Hürrem, who was still bowing. He inhaled her scent. Because the glow of the fire illuminated her from behind, the contours of her figure could be seen under the thin underwear.

"Really? I will not believe it unless you raise your head and say it while looking at me. Raise your head, let me see your eyes so that I can understand if you're telling the truth. The tongue is hypocritical, but the eyes do not lie."

Our father, Jesus, she cried silently with joy. He wasn't angry. Suleiman was not angry at her.

She raised her head immediately. For a moment, she watched the young man in front of her, clad in white underwear, just like her. Without a caftan or turban, he looked completely different. He wasn't such a giant at all – you could even say he was slim. Also, without a turban, he was much more handsome because now his jet-black eyebrows and eyes that flared with lightning were clearly visible.

The young Padishah watched her magnificent, silk-covered shapes, which were clearly visible now that she'd straightened up. The deep cut of the shirt revealed her quickly moving breasts. Turning his gaze with difficulty away from the plump, firm breasts appearing and disappearing under the shirt, Suleiman concentrated on her gaze. When he was about to sink in those eyes, shimmering with all shades of the sea, Hürrem suddenly ran to the sofa.

"What happened? What are you doing?"

Instead of answering, she knelt by the sofa and did what she had been told by Daje Hatun. She kissed the satin quilt and covered her head with it three times.

Padishah approached Hürrem, reached out and helped her up.

"I see that Mother Daje taught you that. It has been done since the time of our ancestors, and it's become a custom. If a woman does not kiss a man's quilt, the bed will not yield heavy crops."

When Suleiman led her to the sofa set in front of the window without letting go of her hand, Hürrem heart fluttered like pigeons' wings.

What did Suleiman say? Crops of the bed? Or did I hear it wrong? Did the Sultan suggest that he would beget a child with me on this bed? She thought she would faint from joy. If there was something that she should not be doing at the moment, it was to faint or to cry.

"Does my Sultan believe that?"

"It's a divine will. It is as He wants. You see, he took so quickly from us Prince Mahmud, whom he had given to us. Neither my power nor the knowledge of my medics was enough to save him. Therefore, if he wants to give his servant a descendant, he will do it, if he does not want to, he will not. I would like to say that fate has nothing to do with kissing a quilt."

"The death of the Prince made me very sad, too. May God give our Master a long life. Fortunately, you have one more son."

"Thank God, my Prince Mustafa is growing and blossoming every day. May God protect him from evil. May He give him a long life."

"I wish that all will be in harmony with my Sultan's heart."

Hürrem tried to keep her mouth shut, but it was certain she wouldn't manage to do that. She knew the answer basically, but she couldn't help it. Padishah noticed her confusion at once.

"Does Smiling Face want to say something to us?"

"Let my Sultan forgive me for my ignorance. After all, it is a rural girl standing before you. May God give you a long life, but who's after you... How to say it... Prince?"

In no way could she express in words what she felt, but Suleiman understood. He seemed to like her shyness and innocence contained in her question. He smiled unknowingly.

"You want to ask who will lead the Ottomans after me. This is obvious. My successor is Prince Mustafa. But he is only six years old."

He suddenly fell silent. He looked into her concerned eyes, and a perverse smile appeared on his face.

"What is this? Did Hürrem get bored with us so quickly that she would like to put our successor on the throne?" And as he said this, Suleiman noticed that for the first time since the death of Prince Mahmoud he was so full of joy.

Hürrem looked as if she would die from fear that she'd just insulted him with her audacity, but his smile seemed to ease her worries, and as he smiled, he looked into her eyes. The young Padishah was sure he could once again see embarrassment in them.

"Calm down. Don't be afraid. I told you already. Padishah is standing there." Laughing, Suleiman pointed to the caftan and the turban, to which she'd been bowing with respect just a moment ago, saying: 'My Sultan.'

Hürrem turned away, muttering something.

"Do you still have a question?"

"Yes," said Hürrem, holding her breath.

"In that case, ask."

"Why did you change my name?"

"Ruslana or the other one... What was it... Something starting with 'A'..."

"Aleksandra. Aleksandra Anastasia Lisowska." There was a grudge and even anger in her voice.

"Yes, that's it. It did not suit you."

"What does Hürrem mean? I don't even know."

"Why didn't you ask about it then?"

The girl lowered her head.

"I..." she began slowly. "I was ashamed. Seeing you, I was so excited that I forgot to ask."

Sultan Suleiman looked at her with understanding. He liked her honesty.

"You're so beautiful... Your eyes are so beautiful... And when you smile, it's like the sun is rising. I thought that the name would suit you. It describes all your beauty. It will be yours only – so that even the sun will envy you."

She almost fainted with happiness.

Am I really hearing this, Blessed Lady? she thought. *Is this Sultan Suleiman telling me all this?*

She paused, moving her gaze from the floor to the man.

"Forgive your slave girl for complaining, but you still have not said what it means," she smiled.

"It's this smile," said Sultan Suleiman. "The smile that takes my breath away. That is what Hürrem means. Hürrem means beautiful, smiling, with beautiful eyes. Each separately and all together."

Padishah could barely look away from her, and his look made her feel that she was ready to spread her wings and fly away.

He leaned over the table and poured some red liquid from a bottle with a narrow neck into a crystal goblet that flickered with a thousand stars in the light. He raised it and turned to the fire. Hürrem admired the glow of the crystal.

"Rhodes," Suleiman said, handing her the cup. "They say that the best wines in the world are those from the Rhodes grapes."

Hürrem jumped up hastily. The great Sultan served her while she was sitting on the sofa and looking at the man with a dreamy look. It was unthinkable."

Suleiman noticed her sudden anxiety.

"What is this? Is my beauty with beautiful eyes afraid of wine?" he asked.

"I'm not afraid of anything," she replied.

"Really? Not me either?"

"Why should I be afraid of you? You are not even angry at my inappropriate behavior."

"If so, why this anxiety then?"

Hürrem looked at Suleiman, ashamed.

"While I sit here, you are filling my cup. If the Sultan permits, your maidservant will serve you."

Sultan Suleiman appeared to like her answer very much. He sat on the sofa. He bent one leg at his knee and slipped it underneath the other. Filling the second goblet, Hürrem felt the Padishah's eyes on her. She tried very hard not to spill the wine out of excitement, but she couldn't stop the trembling of her hands. She eventually managed to fill the cup, go over to the sofa, and hand the cup with wine to Suleiman. As she bent in a bow, Hürrem noticed that the young man couldn't resist looking at her breasts, which were ready to slide through the deep slit of her blouse at any moment. Her cheeks blushed again. Caught red-handed, Suleiman also reddened with shame. He took the goblet from her small hands with a smile.

"You're not drinking?"

"I've never drunk before."

"Would you like to try?"

"Does our Ruler want your slave to get drunk?"

The Padishah would have preferred that the girl had not discovered his intentions.

"I just wanted you to try. I said it was Rhodian wine. Very rare and tasty. The best wine in the world."

"Even if it's not tasty, Hürrem would have drunk poison from the hands of her Padishah."

She lifted the goblet to her lips. She took a small hesitant sip. She felt the red liquid leaving a slightly sour taste in her mouth, running down her throat and warming up her body.

Without taking his eyes off Hürrem, Suleiman took a sip of wine.

"So? Do you like it?"

"It seemed that a fire was filling me," she said. She couldn't stop herself anymore and started coughing, ashamed.

Suleiman smiled happily.

"This is the secret of wine. It warms you up and makes you cough."

Hürrem wondered why her head had started spinning. She'd just drank some wine for the first time in her life and didn't know if one could get drunk with one tiny gulp. Could excitement, happiness, joy, anxiety, fear, and desire be the reason for this? Why did her lips seem dry?

Suleiman took a large red apple from a bowl and gave it to Hürrem. When she reached out, Suleiman offered the fruit to her full, embers-red lips. As soon as he touched her lips with the apple, she felt a tremor in her body – Hürrem was on fire. She bit a small piece. Their eyes met again.

They froze, looking at each other.

Suleiman, staring at her beautiful, captivating eyes, tried to arrange the words galloping in his head into sentences. Hürrem, in turn, tried to find a flash of love in the eyes of the man who would become her lover.

When is this supposed to happen? Who should make the first move? Does the Padishah wait for me to move to actions – was that the tradition? What if it's different? Ekaterina didn't mention anything about it. As if it were not enough that they did not know each other at all, her lack of experience in these matters made everything even more difficult. It left her without breath, with no way out, and she didn't like having no choices. Even that night when the barbarians had kidnapped her, she hadn't felt so helpless.

She took another sip of wine; this time a lot bigger. Without taking her eyes off Suleiman, she drank the next one.

"Wait, don't be so fast."

"Why? Doesn't my master want me to get drunk?"

The Padishah laughed.

"He doesn't want to, because he would like to hear that beautiful voice, which even the nightingales envy, my beautiful."

"But I don't have my instrument..." Hürrem said quietly.

Suleiman got up immediately and disappeared behind the screen made of mother-of-pearl. Then he quickly reappeared, surprising Hürrem. She barely stopped herself from clapping her hands and jumping with joy.

"My God, it's so beautiful."

"I'm glad you like it. It's yours."

Hürrem took the saz slowly and gently from the Padishah's hands as if afraid that she would break its long griffin.

"Thank you... Thank you..." she stammered.

She couldn't resist. She hugged the balalaika – and it seemed to her that she was holding her homeland: steppes, meadows, snow-capped peaks, roaring mountain streams. She felt as if she was embracing her mother, whom she would never see again, and whose scent and face she missed so much. She sniffled and her eyes filled with tears.

Suleiman was moved by the girl's happiness and tried to read her thoughts. He had to stop the impending flood immediately.

"Now that Hürrem has her own instrument, we can listen to her songs."

Grateful, she tried to fall on the floor in front of the man, but he stopped her. He pressed the girl's filigree body to his chest.

"How do you think, Hürrem, why did we like you? Just because I could not get enough of the view of your beautiful face, your beauty, and this look?"

Before she answered, she nestled and hid her head in Suleiman's chest. The young Padishah deeply inhaled the scent of her hair.

"There is another equally important reason why we liked you – your pride and your head held high."

"But I have not raised my head since I arrived here. That's why, during our meeting, when bowing I saw mainly your shoes."

At first, the Padishah wasn't sure whether he should respond to this complaint with laughter or a concern.

"You are like the steep peaks of snow-covered mountains. Mountain peaks can not bow," he said slowly.

Gently lifting the girl's chin, he looked into her eyes.

"Now that we are alone... Go ahead, go ahead and sing... Let the whole palace hear you."

"What song does my Master wish?"

"Hm... First, sing a song full of love."

A moment later, Hürrem's voice began to carry out along the walls of the seraglio. People opened windows and doors to listen to her. Only the windows of Gülbahar's room remained closed tightly. If she could, she'd build a thick wall around herself to not hear the sound; it burnt her ears. The voice of that damn Ruthenian odalisque who took the father away from her son, and her man from her, was engraved in her mind and did not want to become silent.

Hürrem sang and sang, and Suleiman listened to her, sipping red wine.

Volga girls, Volga girls,
Hold their heads high like mountains.
Wielding a sickle in their hands, they cut the golden ears,
How beautifully they dance and sing among the fields.

After some time, he stood up slowly. He turned off the lamps that had brightened the chamber so that now the interior was lit only by the red glow of the conical fireplace, whose crackling flame spread a pleasant fragrance around. He approached Hürrem. He gently took the balalaika from her hands and set it aside, then picked it up.

"Thank you, my beautiful... I know that I hurt you, moving you into the land of memories, but your voice brings me relief."

He didn't let Hürrem answer anything. He took her into his arms. Their breaths accelerated and their lips united. A long, fiery kiss took their breath away. Then another and one more. They kissed and bit passionately. Padishah could no longer restrain his wave of desire, fueled by the girl's inexperience. He picked the odalisque up and walked toward the bed.

"My Lord, My Lord..." she softly pleaded.

He covered the girl's lips with his lips.

CHAPTER TWENTY-FOUR

Hürrem felt like she was floating above the clouds. Could everything really change in one night? Because that's what happened. It was as if a door opened before her, through which she'd entered into a completely different world. Her body still trembled from the kisses and hugs, and she couldn't forget how she writhed with lust under Suleiman's body.

Blessed Lady, she shook, *forgive me for my sin. Suleiman does not believe in our Father, Jesus, but I confess. I am a young girl. I had great pleasure in his arms. I reached the peaks, I burned, I lost myself.*

And that's how it was. When Suleiman's firm lips slid down her neck, Hürrem seemed to be consumed by fire; the Padishah's thick beard and mustache made her tremble, and his breath, hotter than fire, slid down her neck. From time to time he would take the petals of her ears into his velvet mouth. And then, touching her with his tongue, he moved toward her shoulders.

My God! My God! My God! I'm about to go crazy. Then she remembered Ekaterina's words:

Do not hold back. Let everything that wants to come out of your mouth come out. Speak, moan, purr, whine, but never be silent. Men like women who stay silent during the day and talk in the evening.

Hürrem could not be quiet, even if she wanted to.

At first, she moaned for some time, "My Lord, My Lord..."

Her female intuition told her that she should show the animal pleasure she was experiencing in a subtle and sophisticated manner like a work of art. Small shouts and soft giggles slipped out from her lips before she let herself be carried away by a storm of senses. Their tongues met in his mouth, and then she'd circled her tongue around his ears and neck. She noticed her lips became increasing swollen from his delicate bites, which only kindled an even bigger fire in her. The touch of the powerful Padishah's hands on her firm breasts turned her moans into a scream. Her body stretched in spasms, and she embraced the man tightly, and then suddenly, when the Padishah's mouth wandered over her breasts, there was an explosion. Hürrem, amid her screams, began to writhe like a mountain stream.

"My Lord, My Lord..." she moaned continually. As she'd twisted with pleasure, another wave overtook her body. Suleiman's head moved lower, all the way to her groin. His lips that burned like fire drove her crazy. Her delicate body fluttered like pigeon's wings.

At that moment, Hürrem stopped thinking about anything. Let it be what is to be. Neither the man lying on her was the Ruler before whom the whole world trembled, nor was she a defenseless slave. Now they were simply servants of love — he was a man, and she was a woman – that was all. Things that happen between a man and a woman happened. There was no room for orders and rules in the bed, and at that time she didn't listen to the rules, but to her inner voice. She went where her lust led her. At that time, she rejected all bans.

Suddenly she grabbed the Suleiman's penis. Her wheezing breath mixed with Suleiman's groans. It was so hard and pulsated in her hand. It was at this moment in the storm of their passion, Ekaterina's voice echoed through Hürrem's mind.

'Be scared,' said the girl. 'When you see his tool, you should be scared. And it doesn't matter if it's small or large. They love it when we say it's big.'

"It's very big," said Hürrem.

She didn't know if she had said this to apply Ekaterina's advice, or because it really was. Interestingly, this was when she noticed that Suleiman was out of his senses with pleasure as she slowly moved her hand, so she did it again and again... The young Padishah's chest began to rise and fall rapidly.

Suddenly, Hürrem made a decision. She bent to the man's penis. First, she touched it with the tip of her tongue. Then, her tongue began to wander. Then, with her lips burning like fire, she kissed his protruding masculinity.

Now the Padishah took her head with both hands and pressed it. Feeling his hot, thick penis pressing on her, she obediently opened her mouth. She understood what he wanted from her. The sound that Hürrem made got mixed up with the man's groan and suddenly... it was as if a volcano erupted. Suleiman's body shook with a powerful spasm. His moans turned into a cry:

"Don't stop, don't stop!"

His breath echoed from the walls. At the same moment, Hürrem was also taken up by this whirlpool. Strong fingers wandering between her legs led her to the heights of pleasure.

That moment passed like a storm.

Relieved, two bodies rested side by side. After a bit, Suleiman rose and drank a sip of wine. He also gave a sip to Hürrem. Then pouring some wine on her body, he slowly licked the liquid from her lively, fragrant breasts. He dried the trickle flowing down her belly with his tongue. Tracing the blood-red drops heading towards her womb, he arrived at the treasure. Hürrem answered him with a loud groan. She grabbed his head and held it.

"Don't stop, my Syleiman," she moaned.

When she was about to reach the top, he suddenly stopped. While Hürrem, who was close to losing her senses and writhed with pleasure, Suleiman entered her – the moment had come.

"Have mercy, My Lord," murmured Hürrem. "Have mercy."

Her pleading voice was so inviting at the same time that Suleiman noticed that she wanted to say, 'Come on, don't stop. Don't interrupt. Take me. Have mercy.'

So, he did. Possessed with lust, he once again looked into the girl's eyes.

"Don't be afraid," he whispered.

Holding her by the hips, he pushed. As he filled her, he listened to the scream that came out of Hürrem's mouth, so he waited a moment. He felt his thick masculinity pulsing inside her. He entered deeper.

Hürrem looked at him. She wanted to see his reaction. *Am I giving him pleasure? Have I succeeded?*

However, his eyes were closed as he went in and out of her.

"Yes…" murmured Hürrem. "My Lord. My Syleiman. My man."

Suleiman opened his eyes – yes, Hürrem noticed that the man was looking at her with pleasure.

What's happening to him now? she wondered.

They couldn't stop, but the storm had to last.

When the first pain began to pass, she wrapped her legs around the Padishah's waist. She pressed the man to herself with strong arms.

Suleiman went deeper and deeper with every thrust. Suddenly moaning, he lowered his head, and with a great sigh reminiscent of a scream, reached his climax. He didn't stop despite being tired. Pulling the girl's hips to himself, he kept moving.

So that was it, thought Hürrem, convinced she was walking among the stars – so that was what passion was.

Neither Ekaterina's stroking nor Sümbül's withered touch had caused such a storm in her body. The pleasure spreading from her groin to her brain, from her breast to her heart, reached every corner of her body. She found the man's lips with her lips. While they kissed, she caught up with Suleiman in the pleasure race.

She didn't remember what happened after that first event. She spent the whole night in Suleiman's arms. No, she spent it in the clouds. How many times had this storm of pleasure raged that night? She lost count. At dawn, they still made love. The young Padishah couldn't get enough of her fresh, flaming body. And Hürrem, having overcome the anxiety of a novice, passionately led him to madness.

With the last drop of pleasure, the Padishah fell beside her. She was also tired. Because of their exhaustion, they could barely pull the silk cover over their sweaty bodies. Before the sleep overtook them, she checked her crotch with her hand. She knew what the warm liquid between her legs was – it was blood. The little country girl who'd greeted life as Aleksandra Anastasia Lisowska was now in the bed of the Sultan Suleiman, and she'd just taken her first step towards femininity as Hürrem. Hürrem was a woman now; the woman of Sultan Suleiman. There were his life-giving juices in her.

She let the rain of tears which she held back all night, now flow from her eyes. She cried silently as she stroked the hair of the man lying beside her. She didn't know why she cried. From joy or from fear? Or maybe out of remorse because she'd slept with a man of another religion? She didn't know. She just did not know. The only thing she was sure of, was that she was the Padishah's woman.

But what will happen if my fate is similar to the fate of Ekaterina? she worried. *If after a one-night storm of passion, Suleiman forgets about me and abandons me in some corner of the harem? No, I will not allow it*, resolved Hürrem. *I will not let him forget about me.*

While Hürrem surrendered her body, tired of climbing the summits of pleasure, to the warmth of sleep, Suleiman circled between a dream and awaking. While awake, he combed her hair with his fingers, and then he realized that he genuinely enjoyed the presence of Hürrem. This feeling surprised him. He couldn't remember any of the girls visiting his bed giving him so much pleasure before, and although this had been her first time, she'd stunned him with her courage.

What had she done? She'd showed me everything she felt. She said whatever she wanted, he realized. Her voice, whispering, moans, murmuring, screams took away his reason.

Then he noticed that completely unknowingly, he'd been comparing Hürrem with Gülbahar, his son's mother. It was a strange feeling. He'd never done that before. What was that supposed to mean?

And there was something else that surprised Sultan Suleiman – previously, he'd always felt an uneasiness because of sleeping with another woman other than the mother his son – but this time, there was no guilt.

***

The day began with the words:

"Get up, get up. Get up immediately and go straight to the room of Sümbül Aga."

Hürrem opened her eyes and noticed a soft but accusatory look of Daje Hatun. She looked around. Suleiman wasn't there, and several servants were cleaning around.

While Daje Hatun pulled a satin quilt from her, Hürrem tried to find her underwear in a hurry. She was ashamed. She didn't want the woman to see her nakedness. In fact, the rush was unnecessary because one of the servants, even before the quilt was raised, wrapped her in some fabric.

Hürrem then felt her stomach twist with hunger. Just after she took an apple from the bowl and had taken a few steps towards the cone fireplace, she heard Daje Hatun give her some instructions.

"Quickly, pick up this quilt. Take the sheet and put it in a purple bundle so that the Sultana Mother will know that Hürrem has become a woman." Then the woman gave Hürrem a meaningful look. "I saw the sheet. The girl was clean. The Ruthenian girl became a Ruthenian woman in the Sultan's bed. And you, my woman, hurry up," she told Hürrem. "You have a lot of work today. First, you will go to the bathhouse, and then you will move."

"You have not heard it from me, my dear," said Daje Hatun softly as she watched the servants roll up the bloodstained sheets and pack them into a bundle, "but our Master decided to reward you. From now on, you will get money for your expenses."

"Money for expenses?"

"Yes, that's the custom."

Hürrem quickly moved close to Daje Hatun and whispered in her ear:

"A custom? Any girl who spent the night in the Sultan's bed gets money for expenses?"

The old woman turned red and after a moment quickly moved her head back.

"Of course not," she snorted. "I will assign these bold words to your ignorance, Hürrem. Padishah rewards whom he wants." Then a playful look appeared on her face.

"Do you want to hear something? If everyone who comes here were rewarded by the Sultan, the treasury would be empty."

Daje Hatun resolved the crisis with laughter, but this situation did not please Hürrem. So... there were so many girls passing through this bed? And she was one of them.

"That will end," she murmured through clenched teeth.

"Pardon? What did you say?"

"I said it would end, Mother." She leaned over the old woman. "It will end. No other girl will pass this doorway."

She turned and started toward the door. Sümbül Aga was expecting her.

Once she arrived at Sümbül's rooms, the two lines of his enormous lips stretched into a nasty smile reaching to his ears. His embarrassed assistant Jafer stood beside him.

"Your stuff has already been moved," said the aga. His voice, which hid a delicate hint, continued: "The rooms of Gülbahar Hatun are at one end of the corridor, yours will be at the other. We'll see if you like your new home."

***

She liked it. Her apartment consisted of four rooms, including one large one. One of the bay windows looked out onto the rose garden and the other onto the sea. She could even see a white tower standing in the middle of the sea like a bride with a veil.

Hürrem was now to be recognized as a 'Kadin,' a woman of higher standing in the Sultan's harem and the Sultan's favorite, or wife. Although she wasn't a bride, for some reason, the next morning after the odalisque had reached maturity in the Sultan's bed, people had begun to call her that.

Merzuka and Setaret embraced her, shedding tears of happiness. Two other women stood by the door – one's skin was black and the other's white. The black woman's name was Kamer, and the white woman was Emine. She also saw Jafer again – he was now in Hürrem's service. As he stared at her, the whites of his eyes and his white teeth that resembled pearls, gleamed in contrast with his dark face.

Her time in the bath was very pleasant. According to custom, Gülbahar Haseki was supposed to be in the bathhouse that morning, but she didn't come to see Hürrem, the Kadin. As far as Gülbahar was concerned, her going to the bathhouse would mean that she accepted the girl's status. Even if she had to pay with her head for it, she did not intend to do anything like that. She did not want to listen to the giggle of this godless Ruthenian.

Despite the absence of Gülbahar in the bath, Hürrem jumped with happiness. In fact, she didn't care that haseki didn't show. She was even pleased. She didn't think that she could bear the woman's contemptuous glances anyway, the morning after such a beautiful night. Gülbahar's reaction was a good sign – it meant that the woman was jealous of her, and it was clear that she considered Hürrem her rival.

It's strange, the girl thought, *after last night I don't consider her my rival anymore.*

The small family of Hürrem, consisting of Merzuka, Setaret Kalfa, Kamer, and Emine, met Jafer at the door of the bathhouse. In order to ruffle the other odalisques, Setaret Kalfa screamed to put everyone on their feet. Her voice echoed under the dome of the bathhouse.

"Uuu! Open! The bride Hürrem goes to the bathhouse! Make the way! Make room for Kadin Hürrem by the main platform. In the evening, she will go to the private rooms again."

Hürrem's head spun from happiness. On the one hand, she tried to get rid of the love fatigue and gather her strength to face the next storm of passion, and on the other, she prayed to the Blessed Virgin that she'd protect her from the envious eyes of the other odalisques.

As she passed one of the bathtubs, she saw Ekaterina pouring water over her head. The girl's eyes were also turned toward her. Hürrem was surprised to see the same jealousy in her friend's eyes, and when she waved cheerfully to her, the girl didn't even respond – she just stared at Hürrem. Spending the night with the Padishah was important, but it was not a guarantee. She'd also shared the bed with Suleiman, but she'd been forgotten. Now she waited for the day when they would remove her from the palace to put her at the mercy of some somber, old man.

Who knows, maybe Hürrem will face the same fate? However, for now, the Padishah had assigned a room for her, and it was right under the nose of Gülbahar Haseki. So, this little village girl, having learned a few tricks from her, won Sultan Suleiman. It was clear.

This was confirmed later by the official news from Sümbül Aga.

"Our master expects Hürrem tonight."

***

On the second evening, Hürrem was dressed up like a dream. Her clothing was once again purple, and with the accompanying yellows, reds, greens, blues, and roses, made her look like a flower garden this time. Her hair was braided into two braids, then gathered up into a magnificent bun. Her eyes were filled with the will of love and hunger for passion. She bit her lips all day to give color to them, even though they were still swollen from the kisses and bites of Suleiman the night before. Her arms, breasts, and crotch were full of signs of the man's loving bites, and although she had no chance to show them, she proudly displayed the purple spots around her neck.

Suleiman waited for her, sitting at a huge, richly set, copper tray.

She passed the doorway and went inside. She was about to bow humbly but changed her mind. She remembered the words of the Padishah: 'We liked you not only because you are beautiful, but also because you are equally proud and hold your head high. You are like the steep peaks of mountains covered with snow. The mountain peaks can not bow.'

So, that's what Hürrem did; this time she did not bow when she saw the man.

Sultan Suleiman stood up and took Hürrem by the hand. They embraced with passion as if they'd missed each other for a thousand years; as if it wasn't them that had extinguished the fire of love last night, intertwining their bodies, burning with passion. Hürrem yielded to the strong arms of the young Padishah.

"My Sultan," she whispered. Their lips met, and they shared a very long kiss.

"If we don't stop, I'm afraid we'll be hungry this evening," Suleiman said.

"My master's love is all I need."

"Doesn't Hürrem know my name?"

Hürrem looked carefully into the eyes of the Padishah.

"I know it."

"Then tell me. Look, the caftan and the turban are over there again. There is no Padishah or Master here. It's just you and me. There are only the two of us. Your name is Hürrem, and mine?"

"Syleiman."

Sultan Suleiman, laughing, almost spilled the wine he held onto her.

"Oh, long live, my girl. What did you say again?"

"Syleiman."

Hürrem was aware that she couldn't pronounce the name of the Padishah correctly, but what could she do? Was she supposed to answer the Sultan who insisted that she say his name – that she couldn't? She looked straight ahead, ashamed, and the man stopped laughing for a moment and repeated:

"Syleiman, Syleiman," he repeated. "You said that last night, too, but I was so overwhelmed with delight that I thought I must have heard wrong." Then he burst out laughing again.

"I'm not laughing at your mistakes," Hürrem said suddenly. "And you make, ho, ho, a lot of them..."

"Really? Do I make many mistakes?"

"Yes. A lot." She pursed her lips.

"For example?"

"For example, you say: 'I udore.'"

"I udore... Yes. Where's the mistake here?"

"It's not 'udore.' I adore."

"I adore. I adore, right?"

The Padishah's face seemed a bit clouded to her, so Hürrem decided to appease him.

"Syleiman, my man. Syleiman, my man," she chatted.

A wave of joy flooded over him again.

"Syleiman udores Hürrem."

Their lips met again.

***

Cheerful laughter echoed from the rooms of the Padishah late into the night. Suleiman drank wine from Hürrem's hands, and Hürrem tried the best dishes from the hands of Suleiman. They laughed happily and sipped Rhodian wine.

For the second night in a row, Sultana Hafsa sent servants to the Sultan's floor:

"Go and see what's going on there."

The girls brought back the news to the Sultana Mother that the Padishah was joyful for the first time since the day he'd received the news of Prince Mahmoud's death.

The pale face of the older woman lit up even more. That was it. It was the breath of freshness she had expected and wanted for her son. Freshness is a great force that every human needs, especially for the Ruler of the world – it was as important as the army.

Soon, Hürrem's songs echoed through the corridors. One could even hear the unskilled, deep voice of the Padishah trying to accompany some of the songs. Torches and lamps began to go out, and the corridors emptied. Silence seized even the chamber of the great Ottoman Sultan. From inside, you could only hear their love whispers.

"I love Syleiman."

"Hürrem takes Suleiman to heavens."

"Syleiman is mine, only mine. True?"

Happy and joyful, the Padishah responded with a nod of his head.

That night and the next, and the next one – four nights in a row, the tired body of Hürrem found relief in the man's arms. From time to time, she'd wake up, to check if Suleiman was next to her. When she touched the man's body, she thought:

He's mine. Only mine.

But on the fifth night, she realized it was not so.

On the fifth night, Sultan Suleiman did not call her to him. Neither on the sixth... Nor on the seventh...

This is the end, Hürrem cried in her room. *He threw me into a corner like he did with Ekaterina.*

Love occupied her head so much that she didn't even notice the nervous hustle and bustle that had started in the palace corridors.

***

Sultan Suleiman, the Grand Vizier Piri Mehmed Pasha, and other Viziers held endless meetings at the Divan. Suleiman spent many hours poring over maps and talking with his good friend from the time of his stay in Manisa, the falconer Ibrahim. Rumors circulated around the palace that the Padishah had gone down to the Golden Horn.

"Apparently, the Sultan has done a fleet check," the rumor went. "He goes into galleys at night and talks with the Levantines."

But Hürrem didn't hear those whispers, even though the rest of Istanbul was boiling.

The Ambassador of the Venice Republic, Marco Ketto, sent a report to his government:

"Something is going on here. It seems that young Suleiman is preparing for his next trip. I am afraid that after the defeat at Belgrade, a new Turkish storm awaits the Christian world."

But where was this army going to go? Galleys, galleons, and other ships were moored at the Golden Horn.

Marco Ketto couldn't get any information from the spies sent around the city. Istanbul was like a powder keg, but no one opened their mouths. In the end, he decided that he would take care of it himself. He left the ambassador's residence in Galata. Out of his carriage window, he watched the small and large ships of the Ottoman fleet, which surrounded the Golden Horn like a forest. He mingled with the crowds in the hope that he would overhear something. It was then that Marco Ketto heard rumors that the girl from Ruthenia had taken over the Padishah's heart. Stories about Suleiman's love conquests did not interest him at all! Where were these ships preparing to go? As an ambassador to the seaside state, he had to find out.

The preparations that made the Venetian ambassador lose his senses out of curiosity did not interest Hürrem at all. Her eyes were swollen from crying. Merzuka and the other servants tried to comfort her, telling her what was going on around them, but Hürrem didn't care.

"I want Syleiman," she just sniffed and shrugged.

She wondered what she should do to remind him of herself.

One evening during the prayer, Hürrem finally found a solution. She stood up slowly, then she fell down as if she'd fainted, in front of the stove in the middle of the room. As she fell to the floor, she turned the stove over. Lying between the coals glowing on carpets and rugs, she prayed:

Take care of me, Blessed Lady. Let somebody come in here. Let someone come in here.

The glowing kilim quickly caught fire. The flame, writhing like a snake, enveloped the silk cover of the sofa. Hürrem was to burn in her own chamber. The fire spread to the curtains. As more and more flames moved toward the place where she lay as if in fainting, the smoke that seeped outside drew Jafer's attention. His scream was the first one to sound throughout the harem.

"Fire!"

Then one could hear the scream of Setaret:

"Fire! Will anyone save us?! Lady Hürrem is burning!"

When the door was opened, the flames were already crawling under Hürrem's skirts. Jafer hurried toward her. Hürrem opened her eyes as if she'd just regained consciousness, and she shouted terrified, seeing the flames. Jafer pulled his mistress out of the flames. She put her arms around his neck in fear and gratitude.

While the harem residents tried to extinguish the fire burning in the chamber, Hürrem's forehead was sprinkled with water as the servants tried to revive her.

"You should have left me there," were her first words. "You should have left me there, and then my soul, consumed by the pain of love, would mount the flames and leave this world."

Chapter Twenty-Five

The harem was a-buzz with rumors, and everyone was saying something different.

Some claimed that the girl had set herself on fire – which was partly true. Others denied it, saying it was an accident and the girl accidentally caught her skirt on a stove – which was a lie, of course. There were even rumors that it was Gülbahar who'd set the fire. Fortunately, the Ottoman palace, which had suffered from many fires over the years, was saved this time. This time, the fire was quickly extinguished, and the area secured. Nothing happened to anyone. The only consequence of the fire was the smell that lingered in the harem. Despite the winter cold, the windows and doors were opened wide and left open so that the bad odor would disappear.

But Hürrem's fire still burned. Despite the episode that put the whole harem on its feet, ten days had now passed since Suleiman had met with her, and he still had not sent any message.

Sümbül Aga said that he saw the Sultan sometimes stop with the falconer Ibrahim Aga at the pavilion in Sarayburn. Who was this Ibrahim Aga? What was so special about him that while she waited for Suleiman filled with all-consuming love and lust, he spent time with that damned man?

So, even the fact that I almost burned here, did not remind our Master about his slave, Hürrem, she constantly agonized.

In time, even the odalisques began to gossip behind her back. To further scoff at Hürrem, they shouted at each other from afar:

"How many days has it been?"

"Ten, or maybe fifteen?"

"A year, my beautiful. A year."

In fact, every night is like a year to me, Hürrem thought.

"How does this strumpet warm up at night? Nobody adds wood to her stove."

"The fire of love is all I need. Look, the flames are coming from me."

Laughter would then fill the air after an exchange of words like these, to be followed by the angry voice of Setaret:

"Enough! Get back to work! Get back to work!"

Later, even Jafer joined in. His voice was thin, but his powerful body and his matching threatening gaze made the odalisques that were mocking his lady scatter like a flock of wild birds.

Now even the gaze of Ekaterina, who had previously looked at her with envious eyes, changed. The girl smiled seeing Hürrem, as if to comfort her: *He abandoned you too, just like me. Don't worry, sweetie. You'll see, he'll call for you. Be patient.*

***

There was joy in Gülbahar's chambers upon hearing the news that Suleiman had not summoned Hürrem for many days. Her servants enjoyed it with her, no longer having to fear her anger and the dogwood stick. Their old lady was back. Gülbahar got up early, she waited for the maids to dress her, and left to a rose garden surrounded by few of them. She laughed, talked, and even gave gifts to her servants as before. Her appetite also was back.

Everything was just as she'd expected: Suleiman had sniffed the Ruthenian rose and then threw it away. It was true that he still didn't call her to himself either, but never mind. The day of the expedition the Padishah was preparing for was quickly approaching. Who'd ever seen the Sultan leave the army and pashas for a woman on the eve of war?

On the eleventh day, Gülbahar visited Mother Sultana.

"I came to see how our Sultana Mother is."

The older woman knew what the intentions were for this visit, but she didn't say anything. Cordial and smiling, she greeted the mother of her only grandson. She ignored Gülbahar's look that said, 'Here, you, old witch! Did you see? Your son left your godless Ruthenian girl. How do you feel now? Are you happy?' and she pretended that she didn't understand the allusion hidden in her words.

The two women sat next to each other and while embroidering, talked about the army preparing again for the expedition.

"I miss seeing my son's face," Sultana Mother said suddenly.

Gülbahar did not let the opportunity slip away.

"Who doesn't miss him, Mother?"

At first, the old woman thought that she would let it go. However, after a while, she decided that she should show Gülbahar, who was clearly possessed by jealousy, where her place was. She looked deep into the eyes of her grandson's mother.

"Longing is difficult, Gülbahar," she said. "You know it best. You have not seen your man's face for so many months."

Haseki shuddered as if stabbed in the chest with a knife.

You... old witch, she thought, *the day will come when you will leave this world, and I will still be here. When Mustafa takes the throne, Gülbahar, forgotten for months, will become the Sultana Mother.*

Gülbahar felt that a storm raging inside her as she left Sultana Mother's chamber. The first thunders hit the gossiping servants who waited outside for their lady. Haseki moved resolutely, loudly tapping her heels.

"Don't stand here like fools!" she shouted as she passed them.

What could have happened? Why was their beautiful lady boiling with anger again?

Gülbahar barely managed to calm down. The old witch had managed to throw into her face that Suleiman did not want to see her anymore. Well, what could she do? The truth was obvious. For now, she had to be content with the fact that the Sultan had also abandoned the Ruthenian giaour. Sooner or later, the day will come when he will return to her – to the mother of his only son.

***

However, things did not go as Gülbahar had expected. After a long fourteen days had passed since their last night of passion, Sultan Suleiman finally invited Hürrem to himself.

When the message reached Hürrem, against all expectations, she didn't jump with joy. She watched in silence as the servants prepared her for the evening. She didn't even feel the pain when Kamer pulled her hair while combing it. Hürrem had sunk deep into her thoughts.

No one has the right to put me aside, she'd repeated to herself over and over in those forgotten days. *I'm not Ekaterina. Nobody has the right to push me away. Nobody, even if he is a Sultan.*" Undoubtedly, these thoughts had filled her mind during her sleepless nights. She was so absorbed by them that she didn't see what was going on around her. Words didn't reach her. She'd stopped eating and drinking, and she had not wanted to get out of bed. When Merzuka, holding the balalaika that Hürrem received as a gift from the Padishah, asked her to play, she looked in the eyes of her friend with a blank stare. What would she play? What would she sing? For whom? Who was to listen to her songs?

Despite the insistence of Merzuka, Setaret, and even Sümbül Aga, she never once sent a pleading message to the Padishah: 'Call for me. I missed you.' Why would she beg him? She held her head high like snow-capped peaks. Didn't Suleiman say that's why he liked her? So, what happened? She couldn't find an answer in any way. What did she do that the Sultan suddenly moved away from her – and without a word of explanation? Maybe it was because he'd got angry that she'd laughed at his Ruthenian? But it didn't look like that. After all, he laughed with her. Didn't he say: 'Hürrem takes Suleiman to the heavens?' If so, why did he leave her now? Did he have the right to humiliate her in front of the whole harem?

What should I do? she wondered as the rush of thoughts overwhelmed her during the evening darkness. *He is Sultan Suleiman, and I was just the daughter of mountains, steppes, and rivers.* She felt hurt, very hurt. She suddenly realized that she meant nothing in this great palace. Her childhood dreams ended here, and she'd finally come to terms with the thought that all her dreams were gone.

I was supposed to be the lady of this palace. A rural girl from the Ruthenian steppes, Aleksandra Anastasia Lisowska, was supposed to give birth to the successor of the Ottoman throne. One day, Suleiman's throne was to pass to his son, in whose veins my blood would flow, and I would become the Sultana Mother. Although my village and mountains had forgotten me, the whole world was to remember the name Hürrem.

So, why would he call me again now – just to have fun and abandon me again? Was I to become a love toy of the Turkish Sultan who will remember me from time to time? What would Daddy Tacham do if he heard about it? My giant wolf who protected me even against the wind and treated me like his daughter. What would he say? What would he do when he learned that I'd become the love toy of the Ottoman Ruler? How could I look into the eyes of the man who'd told me, 'Go and become the wife of the Padishah?' At the thought of it, she smiled to herself.

As if I ever were to see Daddy's face again, she sighed.

Yes, love was great, and she couldn't get enough of it. She loved being a woman of the Padishah, but that was all. She wanted to be loved as much as she loved, and she wanted to be the only one, not a toy that is hugged first and then thrown away.

No, I won't become a love toy. Not anybody's – not even Suleiman's. I will tell him. I don't know how to do it yet, but I will do it, she resolved in her mind.

Walking to the Padishah's room, she noticed that for the first time her heart didn't beat so loudly in her chest from excitement. She proudly passed Daje Hatun, and when the big heavy door was opened, she equally proudly passed the doorway and faced Sultan Suleiman.

The ruler was sitting at the table still wearing his caftan and turban. It meant that he too had recently arrived. When he heard the door open, he looked up from the documents and maps and looked at Hürrem. Seeing her, his thoughtful face brightened, and he stood up and moved toward her.

"Hürrem, for whose shine my eyes have been longing for so many days, who brightens my heart, I am glad that you came."

She slowly raised her hand and stopped him.

"I know a slave girl has no right to demand anything from her Master, but this slave girl has something to say to the Sultan."

These words surprised the Padishah. A smile crossed his face, and he looked at her with interest.

Nobody so far, and in particular no woman, had ever dared to speak to him in such a tone. Even the very old Great Vizier Piri Mehmed Pasha when wanting to oppose some of his ideas, did not disrespect him. He would say: 'It is up to you, Master, our Ruler, but if you allow, I would like to say something...' And yet, here was this beautiful young girl, addressing him in a tone he'd never heard, and who was ready to reproach him. Was it this eccentricity, the boundless pride, and steadfastness that attracted him to Hürrem? She didn't kiss his hands or clothes, nor did she bow down – she just said what she had to say. In all his life, only Ibrahim addressed him without beating around the bush, and now this Ruthenian beauty. He was thirsty for her honest face and words.

"Express what you want, Hürrem," he encouraged her. "I hope that thanks to your words I will understand the reason for the sadness in your beautiful eyes. If this happens, your smile will again give me the opportunity to laugh."

"The first thing I wanted to say was that our Master would first take off the turban and caftan."

Padishah was even more surprised.

"The turban and the caftan? Do you want me to take them off?"

"Yes," said Hürrem. "Was it not Syleiman who claimed that the Padishah was that turban and caftan? What I have to say I want to say to my man, Syleiman, not to the Padishah."

The Sultan was about to burst into laughter because, despite all the effort, angry Hürrem was still unable to pronounce his name, but he refrained from it. He recognized that she was being serious, and the way she pronounced his name excited him. So, he did what she wanted; he removed the turban and the caftan and hung them on their stand, then turned to Hürrem.

"Syleiman is ready to listen to you."

Hürrem pretended not to notice that the Padishah was trying to turn everything into a joke. After all, her life was at stake. Either she wins, or she will lose. There was nothing in between.

"I wanted to say that today is the fourteenth day."

"Fourteenth day of what?"

"Since you abandoned me."

"You missed me." Suleiman tried again to give his voice a sweet tone, but Hürrem still did not pay attention to it.

"What is the meaning of my longing for our Master to him? I wasn't called. I was exposed to the mockery of the harem. It means that my Sultan did not miss his slave whose name he changed."

"You didn't call me either."

"Does an odalisque have the right to do so?"

Sultan Suleiman approached Hürrem. He took her face in his hands, bent a little, and gave her a penetrating look. He saw sorrow in those charming, deep eyes.

"Aren't you Syleiman's Hürrem? Of course, you can call me and send me a message. Even if Syleiman doesn't answer, he will be happy that his Smiling Face thinks about him."

The clouds in her eyes disappeared, but Hürrem did not intend to lower the sails immediately.

"I heard that the meetings with some falconer or pigeoner Ibrahim were better than the company of Hürrem. The Sultan spent all his time with him."

The Padishah could not restrain himself anymore and laughed.

"You have not heard everything. There was also Piri Mehmed Pasha." He embraced Hürrem and hugged her to his chest. "Ah, my beauty, the greatest love of a Ruler is the State. The State is even jealous of you, but it can not be neglected. It immediately grabs you by the collar and draws the consequences. The judgment of the State does not look like yours. The punishment is much worse."

Hürrem, cuddling into the man's chest, preferred to be silent. She'd confessed everything to him already, and he didn't get angry. On the contrary, he hugged her.

"Don't think that during those fourteen days, we stopped thinking about you for a moment. But the affairs of the State are the most important. Do not forget about it and never expect from us to be otherwise... And do not forget about one thing: Syleiman adores Hürrem. He doesn't want her face to be gloomy, or her eyes to look sad. We would like you to know that. That's all."

It seemed ridiculous to Hürrem that the plural was constantly used in the palace. What could be funnier than saying 'us' instead of 'me?' But that was the custom. At first, it had surprised her and made her laugh, and she even got a few blows from Sümbül Aga because of it; but in the end, she got used to it. That's why it didn't seem funny to her when Suleiman often said 'we' about himself.

She raised her head and looked into his eyes. There was no hypocrisy in them – Suleiman said what he thought – just like her. Their eyes met. When the Padishah stroked her hair, her bitterness slowly gave way to love.

"And I thought you forgot about Hürrem."

Suleiman took her by the shoulders and moved her away from him. Again, he stuck his serious gaze into her eager eyes.

"I give you the word of the Sultan. Syleiman will never forget about Hürrem."

***

Gülbahar didn't believe it when she received word from the servants that the Sultan had once again summoned Hürrem to himself. But that night when she heard the songs of the Ruthenian odalisque and the accompanying laughter, she was enraged. She couldn't control her anger.

She didn't sleep or let the servants sleep, and her strong Caucasian character had made itself felt again.

I can't take it, she repeated to herself. *I can't take it that some girl from Ruthenia has taken my son's father away from me.*

And this day had begun so beautifully. In the morning, she'd visited the little prince's chambers. The energy and joy of the future Padishah made Gülbahar forget about all worries and troubles.

Am I exaggerating? she'd wondered. Perhaps she'd paid too much attention to the Ruthenian odalisque. After all, that was the tradition, and that was the law. Padishah could invite to his bed any woman from the harem that caught his attention. It was nobody else's business. *That's how it has always been until now. I didn't say anything about the Greeks or the black beauties. Why do I now feel such aversion to this godless Ruthenian? After all, she's still a girl.*

Gülbahar had no doubts about the feelings the Padishah had for her.

"Suleiman loves me," she whispered.

Suleiman, who now gave this girl the name Hürrem, once named her Gülbahar.

'From now on you will be called Gülbahar,' he'd said. 'Gül means rose, my sweet, and 'bahal' spring. And you are as beautiful as a rose and as fresh as spring.'

I gave him a son, she mused. *Had it not been for my Mustafa, Suleiman would have no successor after the death of Prince Mahmud. I am the woman, thanks to which people do not call him 'the sterile Padishah.' Even before he took the throne, Suleiman had taken his prince into his arms.*

These thoughts partly extinguished the fire that burned in her heart. Likely she had nothing to worry about. She was the second woman in the Ottoman palace – and when Sultana Hafsa says goodbye to this world, she will be the first one.

Well, but if it is so, why do I feel such anxiety? she began again. *Why am I afraid of this snotty Ruthenian wench?* For the first time, Gülbahar could finally identify and name her fear. *And what will happen if this ungodly Ruthenian girl also gives birth to Suleiman's son?*

That was the fear that had tormented her for so many days.

She was aware that the girl was different from other odalisques. She didn't know what made her stand out, but it was a fact. She enchanted the Sultan.

Suleiman has already placed her under my nose, she thought. *Who knows what he will do if the girl gives birth to a son?*

At night she tossed around in bed, dreaming nightmares. She couldn't confide in anyone. Every night she saw a dirty, oily rope in her dreams. Around whose neck will this wretched rope wrap?

She could no longer control the anger boiling in her.

Earlier, she'd instructed one of the servants to ask Hürrem if she was afraid of Gülbahar Haseki. When the girl reported the response, she was overcome by unbridled fury. According to the maid, the girl first asked, 'Why should I be afraid of her?' And then she'd added: 'I am young, and she is old. If my parents waited for two or three years, I would be the age of haseki's son. Young people should benefit from the experience of the elders. I respect her, in the end, she is older than me.'

What insolence?! What audacity?! Gülbahar repeated all night, tossing from side to side. *My prince just turned six years old. An old wench – and she pretends to be a little girl.*

For the first time in many years, she was screaming and cursing in Circassian. By dawn, she'd made her decision. She could not give up. She will fight for her and her son's future. The blood of Tomyris, the legendary Queen of the Massagets, who defeated the Persian army and sent the Persian ruler Cyrus to hell with her sword, flowed in her veins. Was she to be defeated by a Ruthenian godless wench?

As the sun approached its zenith, she took her most trusted servant and went out into the corridor. The girl noticed that Gülbahar's look did not bode well, and tried in vain to lighten her mood, proposing to go to the rose garden. But the Sultana haseki started angrily toward the end of the corridor. She arrived at Hürrem's door.

Jafer, unaware of what was happening, bowed to her with respect and opened the door wide. What's more, this visit even pleased him. He thought that this meant that Gülbahar had finally accepted Hürrem's position.

But it wasn't like that at all. Gülbahar started the argument immediately.

"Where is this Ruthenian bedbug?!" she yelled through the doorway, then passed through three rooms like a storm and reached Hürrem's bedroom.

"You godless Ruthenian! You...!" She started to pound the girl ruthlessly with a dogwood stick.

Oddly enough, Hürrem didn't oppose it. She just stood there and didn't even shout. It was only on her face one could see pain.

Gülbahar could not relieve her anger in any way.

"I'll kill you! You will die!" she shouted as she continued to hit Hürrem with the stick.

No one could stop Gülbahar. The strong Circassian beauty easily pushed away the servants that tried to separate them with one hand, while lashing out with the stick with the other one. Finally, she threw away the dogwood stick and began to pound Hürrem with her fists. She grabbed her hair, dragged the girl onto the floor, and kicked her. She scratched the girl's face and eyes, and a lock of hair was left between her fingers.

Hürrem still did not react. She didn't move or make any sound. She surrendered to this terrifying attack in silence, and just looked at the face of the angry woman with a lock of her red hair between her fingers.

Gülbahar, you will curse the day when you met me, Hürrem repeated over and over in her mind.

When the woman left, leaving the beaten Hürrem behind, the girl tried to get up, and then passed out and fell to the floor.

CHAPTER TWENTY-SIX

Sümbül Aga was furious.

"I've never heard of such a thing before!" he shouted in anger. "This is unacceptable!

"Unacceptable! You hear me?"

Hürrem didn't care about anything. She just looked out her favorite window. It had a view of the sea, and because no one could peek in through it, it was one of the few windows in the harem without the bars.

If it had happened a few days earlier, Sümbül would bruise the places missed by Gülbahar, hitting her back with a stick – but now he was helpless. How could you dare beat a woman who shared a bed with the Sultan?

The aga noticed that he couldn't gain anything by shouting, so he tried to get through to her by assuming an official tone instead.

"Mrs. Hürrem."

He used the name the Sultan had given her on that first night in his chambers, and the one the Padishah had repeatedly called for her with ever since – so he'd stopped calling her Aleksandra too.

"Have you lost your mind? Who dares to reject the great Sultan?"

When the girl still did not say a word, he turned to the servants.

"Say something. Have you lost your tongues? Can a woman reject the Sultan's invitation? Is this acceptable?"

The women present in the room looked ahead helplessly. Harem aga was right, but Hürrem kept refusing. Merzuka and Setaret shook their heads gently, but none of them had the courage to speak up. Everyone was shocked. The Padishah had sent aga to her room to invite her, and she insisted she would not go. Never before had anything like this been seen or heard of.

Suddenly, Hürrem turned her head to the man who was begging her. It was then that he saw the bloody marks of Gülbahar's fingerprints on her face, and her cheeks that had become black and purple from the blows she'd received.

"I think it's obvious why it is impossible," she finally spoke. She stood up and started toward Sümbül Aga. She approached him so closely that she could smell the stench from his mouth.

"Do you see this?" she asked. "You see, in what condition I am. My face and eyes are massacred. I have scratches, scrapes, and bruises all over my body."

Suddenly, she angrily hit the floor with her heel.

"How can I stand before him in this state?! Do whatever you want. Tell whoever you want. Mrs. Hürrem has a reason. She can not go. End of story."

Sümbül Aga couldn't bear the look of Hürrem's scratched and bruised face, but he still could not stop insisting.

"Please, Mrs. Hürrem, don't do it. Our Lord will be angry because of you. Maybe you don't value your own life, but what about us?"

His question remained unanswered, but the servants gave out quiet murmurs, admitting he was right.

"What will happen if I go and say: 'Mrs. Hürrem will not come. I insisted, but she was stubborn. I begged and begged, but she would not come,' and our Master will call Black Ali and order him to put a rope around my neck? He will do this to me, as God is my witness!"

Whatever he did, and however he begged, he failed. Even the threat of dragging her there by force did not help.

"Just try it, aga," Hürrem hissed, looking directly into the man eyes. "Just try it, and you will see what will happen then."

Sümbül knew exactly what that threat meant.

What devil tempted me then? It must have crossed his mind for the thousandth time. *Look what you've gotten yourself into because of one moment under the stairs.*

The harem aga was in a difficult situation. Somehow, he'd got stuck between this inflexible, crazy Ruthenian girl and the will of the Padishah. He was between a rock and a hard place. Muttering something under his breath, he left Hürrem's chamber.

Having rejected the invitation, that night Hürrem did not go to Sultan Suleiman room.

Sümbül Aga did not dare to stand before His Majesty and tell him that she would not come. Fortunately, he found a solution. He leaned over to Daje Hatun, and whispered it in her ear. If the Padishah gets angry, he won't punish his nanny.

Waiting for beautiful Hürrem, Suleiman was surprised when he saw his seventy-year-old nanny instead.

The old woman, carefully choosing her words, explained that she was very sorry, but Mrs. Hürrem did not comply with the order of the Padishah, and she had a reason not to appear in front of His Majesty, despite his insistence.

"What is this reason, Mother Daje?" he asked slowly.

The woman was silent. What was she to say to the great Padishah – that Gülbahar Haseki had massacred the face of this beautiful girl?

When the Padishah saw the look his nanny gave him, his face grew grave, and he began to walk around the room angrily. Daje Hatun knew Suleiman well enough to know that this response did not portend anything good. Before making important decisions, the Sultan always circled like a tiger around a cage, as he thought about something. When he accelerated, it meant that his anger was rising.

"Let them pass the message again!" the young Padishah suddenly shouted. "Hürrem is to appear in front of me immediately. Since when does anyone dare oppose the will of the Padishah?"

The second invitation was also rejected. Hürrem, even though she wanted to throw herself in his arms with all her strength, did not go to Suleiman's chamber. The Sultan boiled with anger before he helplessly went to sleep alone in the bed, which he'd shared with Hürrem just yesterday.

Rejecting the invitation of the Padishah twice shook the harem. The message first reached Sultana Hafsa, and then Gülbahar.

Sultana Mother, who'd heard the argument, wasn't too surprised by Hürrem's reaction. She knew how proud and unyielding the girl was; she wouldn't appear in front of the Padishah with the marks of blows, telling him, 'Look what state your son's mother put me in.'

It was possible that the girl intentionally did not oppose Gülbahar. As she was beaten, she never said a word, and now she sat in her room – she was a victim. Her fair son could never bear the suffering of victims – especially when it came to a beautiful and young girl who did not leave his bed.

"Oh, my Gülbahar..." Sultana Mother sighed deeply. "Is it jealousy that pushed you to this mistake? Not wanting to lose Suleiman, you have pushed your future into the abyss..."

Meanwhile, in the second room, there was a completely different mood. When she heard that the girl did not go to the Padishah, Gülbahar couldn't believe it.

"Are you sure?" she asked her servant. "If this is a lie, know that you will regret it."

"Yes, and not once but twice. Our Master sent her a message twice, and that cheeky girl disregarded him twice."

Well, well! thought Gülbahar. She hadn't expected anything like that. On the contrary, she was convinced that the girl would complain to the Padishah about her, exaggerating what had happened.

On the one hand, Gülbahar was happy. Now Suleiman will surely get mad and throw that insolent girl out of the palace. Maybe even banish her from Istanbul.

Yes, that's what he'll do, thought Gülbahar all night.

***

But Suleiman did not do that. The next day he sent for Daje Hatun. Of course, he'd also heard about Gülbahar attacking the girl.

Why does she sadden us? Why won't she come and reveal her sorrows? We expect her. Or maybe our beautiful thinks that her face will not make us happy? he lamented to himself.

During all the years spent in the seraglio, the old woman had not experienced anything like this – the Padishah had invited one of the odalisques to his bed, and she'd refused him. Furthermore, the Sultan, instead of getting angry, sent a humble request to her.

"The judgment day is close. God, take care of us," the nanny constantly prayed as she traveled slowly through the narrow, sun-thirsty corridor.

Before she went to see Hürrem, she decided to talk with the Sultana Mother about everything first. The two older women consulted in a whisper.

"Daje, tell me how it will end?" she asked.

"Sultana Mother," said the experienced nanny. "There is no doubt we are dealing with love here. And this is how it should be understood."

A spark appeared in the darkened eyes of the Sultana Mother. So, the mother of the Padishah, like her, approved the feeling that Suleiman had for this girl from Ruthenia.

Next, Daje Hatun went to Hürrem's room. Entering her chamber, she felt much calmer. The girl, seeing the old woman, immediately jumped up and humbly kissed her hand. She indicated her a place for her to sit down, and to make her more comfortable, she put pillows behind her back.

"Oh, my child," the old woman sighed, seeing the scratches and bruises on the girl's face.

She told Hürrem how sad the Padishah was having not seen her for so long, and in place of one of Suleiman's words, she neatly wove in five.

While her heart fluttered with joy, Hürrem embraced Daje Hatun, trying not to show her feelings.

"How can I appear before His Majesty the Sultan?" she said slowly. "I am ashamed of my condition. I can not look him in the face. What if he sees my bruises and scratches? What if he is disgusted with me?"

The nanny, seeing how the girl's eyes filled with tears, was sure that she was overcome by love, and she returned to Sultan Suleiman with this conviction.

The Padishah, waiting hopefully for a message from Hürrem, decided after hearing her answer:

"So, the reason for everything is the argument between Gülbahar and Hürrem!"

There was anger in Suleiman's voice.

"That's sure, my Sultan. But know that it was not a quarrel."

"What then?"

"I don't know how to say it... I'm afraid..."

"What are you afraid of, Mother Daje? You're close to me. You raised me. Can a mother be afraid of her son? Tell me. If it wasn't a quarrel, what happened between Hürrem and Gülbahar?"

Actually, the woman wasn't afraid at all, but because she knew that what she was about to say would direct the Padishah's arrows of anger towards Gülbahar, she weighed her words carefully.

"I am not saying what I heard; I saw it with my own eyes. There was no argument. Gülbahar Haseki cruelly beat the girl. The poor girl's face is covered with bruises and scratches."

"Hürrem did not pay her back?"

"She did not even raise her hand. To those who asked why she allegedly answered: 'Would I dare raise my hand to the prince's mother?'"

Judging by his response, it appeared he'd heard about the disturbance — but had he heard how Hürrem had just stood there and watched as Gülbahar pounded her with her fists? — that she didn't make even the slightest movement, open her mouth, or even scream in pain.

Daje Hatun saw that Sultan Suleiman continued to wait anxiously for her further words, but she couldn't do it. If she told him about that, she would cause a sentence to be placed on Gülbahar. She didn't want to fuel the anger of the Padishah and become the cause of that misfortune.

Sultan Suleiman noticed the hesitation of his nanny.

"Tell me, how does Hürrem feel? What did she say? What does she think? Does she want us to punish Gülbahar for her cruelty?"

"I heard with my own ears, as her heart fluttered in her chest, wanting to break free and fly to our master," the old woman began. "I saw with my own eyes the tears of longing that she poured out. But please understand, my Sultan, Mrs. Hürrem is ashamed to appear before your face so bruised and wounded. She said she can not come to you because 'Our master can not see me in this condition.' But..."

"But what?" asked the Padishahs when the woman fell silent.

"But you can not say that Gülbahar didn't have her reasons. After all, she loves you too. Love does not obey orders. The poor woman was blinded by jealousy... A man possessed by jealousy is capable of anything." Daje Hatun tried to justify Gülbahar's actions somehow.

Supporting the old woman, Suleiman helped her reach the door.

He had to think, to reconcile his heart with his reason, consider truth and falsehood, and make the right decision. His name was Suleiman. Suleiman's law and justice had to be unwavering.

Suddenly he stopped his deliberations.

"Syleiman," he said to himself, smiling. "Syleiman..."

***

"Where is my wife?" Sultan Suleiman roared as he walked inside, his caftan skirts flapping like a thunderstorm.

Gülbahar expected that the Sultan would call her back to him, bored with the moods of the unholy Ruthenian. When she heard the raised voice of the young Padishah, she made haste to see him. Her heart trembled with excitement. It was clear that her man had come in person to invite his son's mother to him. This Ruthenian witch should see this.

However, there was something strange about it, and panic seized her.

At first, she hadn't noticed that her court ladies had suddenly disappeared somewhere. After all, it wasn't the first time the Padishah had visited her rooms. What was going on here that made the women hide in fear? She moved quickly in the direction from which the voice came.

At precisely the same moment, Suleiman roared again:

"Tell me where my spouse is! Is she afraid to stand in front of me, ashamed for this primitive act she committed?!"

Oh no! These were the first words that Gülbahar thought. *Oh no! It's not love, but anger that's brought my son's father to my door.*

She opened it and went into the spacious living room. The last few servants ran away in panic to save their lives. Gülbahar saw him so angry for the first time – he didn't wear a turban so she could see his hair raised with anger, and his facial muscles quivered with rage. The mustache above his shapely lips was rising and falling. He kept his hands on his waist and circled the living room, screaming like crazy. He appeared so lost in his anger that he didn't even notice Gülbahar standing in the door.

"Tell the mother of our prince to come here immediately!"

The arrow is shot from the bow, Gülbahar thought. Her jealousy had led to a point where nothing could be done anymore. Apparently, such was the fate. *What's meant to be, must be,* crossed her mind. *I will either survive this storm thanks to my love, or this wind will push me into the abyss. But under no circumstances will I be suppressed.* She was determined, regardless of what price she would pay. *I am the mother of Prince Mustafa. The mother of the future Padishah.*

Trying to take on a calm expression, she went inside.

"Our master wanted to see our Prince's mother?"

Hearing the woman's voice, Suleiman spun around. His steel eyes looked like glowing coals.

Immediately, Gülbahar realized she was lost. She shivered at the sound of his voice, thundering like cannon balls.

"Since when does the mother of the Prince, instead of taking care of her son, go to an odalisque's chamber to publicly beat a helpless girl?"

Gülbahar thought it would be better if she left this question unanswered: *We'll see what Suleiman continues to say.*

"Does law, tradition, custom, education allow such a thing?"

The Padishah was breathing through the nose. Gülbahar felt his breath furiously hit her in the face.

"Or is our haseki trying to destroy the order of the Sultan's harem?"

"I did not try to make things right, but I gave her a lesson," Gülbahar said slowly.

"A lesson? What lesson?"

"A lesson that was supposed to teach the one, who, after spending the night with the Sultan, began to put on airs."

"You went to the chamber of the odalisque, and not only you pulled her hair, but you also punched her with your fists, and kicked her. You call this an education?"

"I thought it was the right thing to do, My Lord."

"What are these words, woman? Is haseki to guard order, and give lessons to those who behave inappropriately? What are the harem supervisors for then? Or maybe this is the ambition of haseki?"

Gülbahar swallowed. She looked at the man with loving eyes, trying to ease his anger. She even tried to smile at him gently.

"My Sultan probably knows that sometimes the anger gets ahead of the reason. You said it yourself. Remember? One day in Manisa..." Gülbahar's attempted to remind the young Padishah of their loving days in Manisa was in vain.

"What anger?! What reason?!" he shouted. "You don't know what you're talking about! Does a woman in the Sultan's harem have the right to show her anger? In the race of anger and reason, it is our right to decide whether the reason will win, not the right of the woman who, after sharing a bed with us, gave us a prince."

How sharp were those words? There wasn't a trace of love in them.

"What your maid did, she did out of love for you, my Sultan. But I see that you have been deceived cruelly."

"Silence, woman! It's a sin! Don't try to slander anyone. They're already calling you 'Punching Haseki,' at least don't let them talk that you vilify others as well."

"Did you say Punching Haseki, My Lord?"

"That's what we said. What did you expect? An innocent girl who did not even raise her hand at you..."

Suleiman was so angry he had to take a short break to try and bring his feelings under control, but after a while, he started even more firmly.

"Did you expect that they would call differently the haseki who, in the middle of the harem, madly beat the girl whom we invited to our bed the night before?"

"Wouldn't Haseki-In-Love be more appropriate?"

"Aren't you aware of the embarrassment you have brought upon us? That from now on, the inhabitants of the seraglio will remember the mother of our prince, the heir to the throne, Mustafa, as the Punching Haseki? And when this bad fame leaves the walls of the palace, that's how the world will associate the mother of Sultan Suleiman's son."

Gülbahar was close to losing the war that was going on inside her. To hold back the tears, she opened her eyes wide.

"In that case," she said, looking deeply into Suleiman's glowing eyes, "give my head to the hangman. This way, we will not only save our life from shame but also avoid living life without your love. Whoever knows the truth, will say that love was behind us. The one who does not know it will laugh at the end of the Punching Haseki."

The woman's tone of voice, full of complaint, but unbending and firm, made an impression on Suleiman. He saw Gülbahar in such a state for the first time.

'How could I force my love to listen to reason?' his son's mother had just tried to tell him. 'If so, take my life.' She'd challenged him instead of falling on her knees and asking for forgiveness.

And now what? he hesitated. *If I forgive her, saying: 'Go away to your duties. Do not commit such boorish acts anymore,' people will ask if this is Suleiman's justice. Even if no one has the courage to say it aloud, Hürrem will face me with the question: 'Where has your famous justice gone?' Gülbahar herself has set a punishment. In fact, even though she is the mother of the prince, it was a punishment she deserved and was in harmony with her wishes. But what will happen when Mustafa grows up? If he asks whether he sacrificed his mother's life for an odalisque, how would I look my son in the eyes?*

We have also spent many beautiful days with Gülbahar. Those enchanting days full of childish joy appeared before Suleiman's eyes. How happy they were when they kneaded fruit with their bare feet during the grape harvest, holding hands. 'Do you think they are drinking wine from grapes that we crushed with our feet?' he'd asked Gülbahar, kissing her feet with juice dripping from them. He didn't want to lose her, but he couldn't fail to punish her either. Grand Suleiman should not succumb to a jealous haseki.

Oh... the Padishah sighed deeply. *Keeping the pans of justice in balance doesn't always resemble a sword fight, throwing bullets, or stringing the bow. But what is to be, will be – justice is justice. We need to find a place for her.*

The father of his grandfather, Mehmed the Conqueror, established order in this country with his laws. His father – Selim the Grim – introduced it with a sword. Suleiman was to be remembered thanks to his conquests, but the world was to remember him as the Legislator. If the conquests were to become his domain, justice had to be its foundation. Suleiman suddenly broke free of the storm that raged in his head.

Gülbahar noticed that the flame in the man's eyes had begun to dim, and hope awakened in her. Would it mean that her love won? Are they going to fall into each other arms? Will they wake up together from this nightmare?

Placing his hands behind his back, the Padishah started walking towards the window. He looked out at the sea and the hills opposite, between the branches of the snow-covered trees, whose greenery met with the white of the Bosphorus, and standing with his back to her, he explained his decision.

"Gülbahar, the mother of the heir to the throne, will go to the territorial unit of Saruhan sanjak, tomorrow at the latest. Taking her son with her, she will look after the education and upbringing of the young prince in Manisa, so that he becomes our worthy successor. This is my last word.

He turned around and, without looking at Gülbahar, who was shaken by the decision of her exile, walked out in a determined step with his hands crossed on his back.

***

The next day, coaches were prepared to take Prince Mustafa and his mother from the palace courtyard to the place of their exile. Gülbahar relieved her pain with the hope that one day she would come back here as the mother of the Padishah, but she never turned back.

"I will not pray for you anymore, Suleiman," she murmured. "You will live the rest of your days sleeping with a scorpion."

Padishah watched the sad scene until he lost sight of them. He'd acted in accordance with the law, tradition, and justice. All princes, once they reached the proper age, were sent to be educated in places far from the seraglio.

So now he's done it too. Will not his mother take care of the prince best?

He gave Gülbahar her life, but he'd killed her love.

That's how the sword of justice cut.

Suleiman felt something inside him break, and his heart bleed.

He also knew the ointment for this wound – a war and Hürrem – and both were at his fingertips.

CHAPTER TWENTY-SEVEN

Hürrem cured Suleiman's wound very fast. Not even a week passed since the departure of Gülbahar Haseki from Istanbul before she was already forgotten.

Finally, the evening arrived that he could meet with the smiling muse who'd been rejecting him for so many days. When Hürrem entered, she seemed like a sunrise to the young man who'd waited for her with impatience and excitement for so long. Hürrem had not covered her head, so the Padishah saw the girl's hair so exposed for the first time. She wore it tightly braided on both sides, with the plaits then fastened on the top of her head in the shape of a red crown.

How well it suits her, he thought. Suleiman felt the blood in his veins boiling.

Oddly enough, Hürrem was amazingly calm. She bowed her head without looking at him, and she looked as if she was going to cry under his touch. Suleiman could not understand the cause of this suffering. Shouldn't she be happy, smile, fill the space around her with laughter, distract his thoughts from worries? Did she realize that for the sake of her, he'd dismissed the mother of his only son, the woman who had been with him for ten years?

To ease the atmosphere and hopefully bring a smile on Hürrem's face, Padishah immediately jumped up.

"Thank God that I have the opportunity to see your beautiful face again."

Hürrem's face did not even flinch. On the contrary, sadness, like tulle, covered her eyes, of which he could not get enough.

"I know I have slighted Your Majesty, Your Highness Sultan, but I am ashamed to say what caused it."

"You don't need to say anything. I know everything. And the one who committed this primitive act against you has been punished."

Hürrem raised her head for the first time and looked into Suleiman's eyes, then stared at the floor again.

"But she's your son's mother," she whispered hurriedly.

"That's right, and that's why, as the mother of Prince Mustafa, she received a mild punishment. Otherwise, the penalty would not be the same. Besides..."

"What guilt, sir? Could a woman, who gave you a son, giving a soul from her soul, be guilty, no matter what she did?" she whispered in a barely audible voice.

Suleiman was surprised.

I probably misunderstood, he thought. *Was Hürrem defending Gülbahar from him, the woman who did not just beat her up as much as she massacred her?*

"She raised her hands to you! She beat you!" he protested immediately.

"She had her reasons."

"What reasons? No reason justifies raising a hand at a woman who shares a bed with the Sultan. The hand raised at you is a hand raised at us."

She almost burst out laughing at hearing again the term 'us' being used during such a serious conversation, but she stopped herself from it. She had to play her role well all the way to the end.

"If I faced the threat of losing you, I would behave differently."

Hürrem reminded Suleiman of the sea: One time you look at it, and it's stormy; then you look another time – and it is calm. She'd just defended Gülbahar a moment ago and now says that she would have behaved differently than she did.

"How would you behave?"

The girl looked up again and looked deep into the Sultan's eyes.

The man shivered.

"I... I would not beat a woman who would try to take you away from me..." she whispered. "I would kill her..."

Ignoring the sparks of pride in the Padishah's eyes, she stretched her fingers like claws and extended them toward some phantom.

"I would rip the devil's heart from her breast with these hands," she added.

The girl's gaze and voice made Suleiman tremble, but after a while, his pleasantly stroked male pride took over. He took Hürrem in his arms and kissed her eyes and face for a long time. The girl broke free from his flaming arms.

"I want to say, My Lord, that Gülbahar Haseki's anger can be considered light. Furthermore, I did not intend to take you away from her."

How was this possible? It surprised the young Padishah even more. Just when he was supposed to ask what she meant, she added:

"I was happy that I could stand in the shade, somewhere to the side. It was enough for me to be close to the scent of the skin and the voice of my Sultan. And when my Master said, 'Come,' I flew into his arms as if on wings. That was enough for me..."

Sultan Suleiman again grabbed Hürrem in his arms. This time he held her stronger so she wouldn't run away again. Trying to escape the man's kisses, she wriggled in his iron grip of her waist and continued to recite her well-practiced speech.

"Therefore, my Sultan, if I knew that you would punish Gülbahar like that, I would've stood before you and begged you. Didn't you compare my head to the steep peaks of snow-covered mountains? I would not even mind your words: 'Mountain peaks can not bow, don't lower your head either.' Not only would I have lowered my forehead, but I would have fallen to your feet so that you forgave haseki. Just as I accepted with humility that my Master changed my name because he did not like it, so I would have endured with submission the few blows, which the mother of our Prince gave to the godless Ruthenian girl. My Sultan's love would be the cure for my hurt pride."

Hürrem still didn't speak Turkish too well. Sometimes she lost some letters or sounds, but the Sultan felt drunk with her words. Despite her young age, she proved that her heart was huge. Kissing the girl, he held in his arms with love, desire, and admiration. He began to take her aroma into his lungs again.

That's enough, thought Hürrem.

She didn't want Suleiman to understand that she had done it so that his feelings for Gülbahar would cool down; that she didn't raise her hand at the woman who was beating her and rejected the invitations of the Padishah only to turn his anger on Gülbahar.

I should drop the part of the girl grieving the banishing of a woman from the seraglio already. What will I do if he says, 'in that case, I'll bring her back,' she wondered?

And suddenly she gave in to Suleiman's arms like a dove with a broken wing. Her heart beat again with excitement. This difficult role she'd played for so many days exhausted her. She even believed herself in the dramatic mood that she'd created in the last scene. If she didn't know better, that at the news of the woman's exile the drums of joy thundered in her, bells rang, and trumpets sounded, she would have believed herself that she was sorry for Gülbahar's departure.

She gave Suleiman her full lips, quivering with thirst. This time their lips united with love and longing.

"My Suleiman, my venerable Sultan," murmured Hürrem, and the young man filled with joy.

"You said 'Suleiman'... You said 'Suleiman'..."

Yes, she'd finally pronounced his name correctly. How else did they think she would not go crazy from anger when she'd locked herself in her chamber, full of shame and pain? Maybe a thousand times, ten thousand times, no – indeed millions of times – instead of 'Syleiman,' she tried to say 'Suleiman.' Millions of times, Merzuka engraved in her the words, 'His Majesty Sultan.' And she finally succeeded. Now, she would always address Suleiman like that.

"My Hürrem!" he stammered and embraced her again.

Their thirsty lips merged again.

It took minutes before the Sultan slowly moved the girl away from him. He reached to his belt, looking for something. With a smile, he pulled out a ring which shone in his hand. It was a huge ruby surrounded by diamonds and emeralds.

He took the girl's tiny hand and put the ring on her slim finger. Hürrem didn't even bother to look at the ring that sparkled in the flames dancing in the fireplace. Now she was only busy putting kisses on the man's eyelids.

"Do you know what I did today?" Suleiman asked. "If Sultan Suleiman calls his sun Hürrem," he continued, his voice quivering with lust, while Hürrem's red-hot lips wandered around his neck, her tongue caressing his ears, "everyone should call her that. We have ordered that from today on at the Divan, in the harem, and into every corner of the Ottoman State, the sun of my heart will be called Hürrem. You are now my soul mate, the beloved of my heart. You will share joys and sorrows with me. It seems that you, Hürrem, are the longing I have always felt, although I could not give it a name."

Having freed herself from the arms of the Padishah and the rain of his kisses, Hürrem flowed on her tip toes as she had learned in the Crimea. She lay down on the large, silks-and-satin-covered bed. In white satin underwear, under which the outline of her hips was clearly visible, and with her breathtaking legs exposed in a deep cut in the red glow of the fire that burned in the fireplace, she looked like an ivory sculpture.

***

That day Suleiman forgot what they had gone through. While Gülbahar, banished from the seraglio, was heading along with the prince in a carriage jumping along dusty roads for Manisa, the place of her exile, Suleiman was opening a whole new chapter in his life. Padishah felt younger and stronger now – and more powerful. He was now ready to raise his fist and wipe the enemy off the hill. Neither the indestructible castle of the Knights of Rhodes, nor the Hungarian valleys, the fortresses in Temeshevo, Buda, Shigetvar or Vienna could stop him.

Storms and typhoons raged inside Suleiman. He saw huge armies before his eyes. He imagined a triumphant march.

Just as my great-grandfather was called Mehmed the Conqueror, and my father, Selim the Grim – the whole world will glorify me as the conqueror of Europe, he shouted with passion in his thoughts.

Hürrem, lying on the bed beside him, first thought that the fire burning in Suleiman's eyes was a reflection of the flames of the fireplace. Then she realized that this fire was different. It was a fire she'd never seen before – a fire of passion.

We will be a wonderful couple, she thought. *The two of us will become one and shake the whole world.*

Suleiman took a goblet and went to the fireplace. He directed the crystal vessel towards the fire and gazed for a moment at the dancing flames through the red veil. When he turned back to Hürrem, he held a piece of paper.

"Mrs. Hürrem should not think that on the dark nights spent without her, our thoughts did not turn toward her.

You were right with us. Since you refused to let us see your beautiful face, we brightened the darkness of the night, dreaming about you. We put our feelings on paper."

"Beloved, the most beautiful of beautiful..." He began to read the letter he'd written to Hürrem. His voice rose and fell, one moment wistfully lamenting, only to change into a whisper after a while. Raising his hand that held the goblet, he looked into Hürrem's eyes.

"You are my life, the Source of Abundance,
the spring..."

Suddenly the Padishah fell silent. They stood for a moment, looking at each other.

"For the time being, I've only managed to write a single, two-line verse of poetry, which we call a bayt. This is my first poetic piece... a 'ghazal,' and it's dedicated to you. Did you like it?" Suleiman asked in the light of the dancing flames.

She liked it. She didn't understand anything, but those words delighted her. She felt that this poem was more valuable than the ruby ring Suleiman had put on her finger. She was charmed by the man's voice, the feelings on his face, the rhymes, and the rhythmic music of the words, even if she didn't understand their meanings yet. This poem... ghazal... was written for her – from the Ruler of the world to Aleksandra Anastasia Lisowska or Ruslana. And now Hürrem... What will happen to her tomorrow?

"Your Excellency, My Sultan."

She approached the man seductively. Each of her kisses was like a thousand words of thanks to Suleiman.

Hürrem had risked and won. She'd already learned that to win, one had to face danger. Her fate was in the hands of the man who was standing in front of her. His one word could raise a man to the stars or sweep him off the face of the earth.

I don't want to turn to dust, thought Hürrem as she glanced at the young man staring at her passionately from behind the goblet of wine.

I was born to live among the stars. And so it will happen. Now she believed it. Just as she believed that Suleiman gave her love.

Do I love this mighty man? she asked herself.

Of course, she thought – because she loved greatness, which she was just beginning to understand. She also loved power. Suleiman had both of those features.

She slipped her underwear off her shoulders, letting the thin fabric stop at her waist. She extended her bare arms to Suleiman.

Taking another sip of wine, Suleiman threw himself in her arms.

Hürrem saw fire in the Padishah's eyes. She felt her heart pounding in her chest.

You, my Ottoman – rule the world and I will be your mistress. Let the whole world lie down at your feet, and fall at the feet of a rural girl from Ruthenia, she thought, lustfully embracing the man.

Chapter Twenty-Eight

The next morning, Jafer rushed out of the palace with impetus. The black boy was sure that happiness was beginning to light up the darkness. This feeling was spreading throughout him. With the growth of Hürrem's position, the door of fortune will also open for him.

Who knows, he thought happily, while he climbed the alley that led to the Grand Bazaar. *Maybe someday you'll take the place of Sümbül Aga, and you will become the harem's aga, Jafer.*

Hürrem Haseki was exceptional. He'd understood this immediately when he saw her for the first time. He sank in her eyes, in the light that shone from them. She was nothing like the other girls. She was crazy, but at the same time clever and cunning. He knew that the Padishah must have been enchanted by her because even disregarding the fact that she was the mother of the prince, or the pleading and begging, he still banished Gülbahar far away. Who would have thought that the girl, who'd received a beating from Sümbül Aga in the courtyard of the pavilion for the novices on her first day in the harem, would one day become Hürrem Haseki?

As soon as haseki had received her first money, she gave Jafer a rich bakshish and said:

"Look, Jafer! Run to the bazaar and buy fabrics in my favorite color."

Hürrem wasn't allowed to leave the harem. That was the custom. In fact, it would be good if Merzuka or Emine went with him, but the boy would rather do it himself. That's why he didn't even want a carriage.

I'll run quickly, and I will be back soon. After all, the bazaar is not far away, he thought.

Passing through the Imperial Gate, Jafer mingled with the crowd. He climbed the narrow street leading to the Hippodrome, where the obelisk was located.

It was a clear day, but the winter sun did not warm bones. Torn from his homeland of hot suns and thrown to Istanbul, Jafer always felt cold, but now he was warmed by an inner excitement and happiness. Suddenly, he remembered his childhood. He'd left behind him the sun he now looked at with blinking eyes. Now his shadow fell right in front of him. For a short time, he tried not to stand on his own shadow and walked in a strange, staggering pace. It is as if he saw the shadow of happier days. He used to play like this with Nyjama in the endless sunny steppes of his homeland. Nyjama... With a high forehead, big black eyes, and a slender neck; she was beautiful, like a doe. Jafer imagined the girl was walking beside him. He thought he heard her voice:

'You lost! You lost! You lost! You stepped on your shadow!'

Jafer turned abruptly. He didn't notice anyone except an elderly man; big like an oak, and the hair sticking out from under his hat waved on his shoulders as he walked. He had thick raven-black eyebrows and big eyes, black as coal. If his slightly grayed beard left a sliver of free skin on his cheeks, he could have sworn the man was as black as himself. It was obvious with the first glance that he didn't come from around here. His body was covered with a large fur wrapped by a thick belt. He wondered what kind of fur it was.

It is what it is, what do you care? Jafer scolded himself. It's important that it kept the man warm.

He turned back and resumed his game. He remembered the rhymes he sang with Nyjama, laughing happily when playing.

One step to the right,
One step to the left.
Don't stand on your shadow.
And if you lose, don't shed tears.

Nyjama always won, because Jafer would deliberately take a wrong step and step on his shadow. He adored it when the girl danced happily, crying:

'You lost, you lost! You stood on your shadow!'

Jafer reached the place where the street turned slightly to the left, and he noticed that the old giant was still following him. He was probably going to the bazaar.

It didn't take long before he realized that it wasn't so. He looked gently over his shoulder. The man was still behind him.

Could he be following me? he wondered, but he smiled inwardly. *Why would an old man follow me?*

Suddenly Jafer shuddered. Maybe this man is a thief or some kind of thug? He hastily reached into his belt and checked if the pouch Hürrem gave him was still in place. Once he'd made sure it was, he calmed down, but he didn't take his hand away from his belt. If the man had bad intentions, this gesture would scare him. He might think Jafer had a knife at his belt.

He walked quickly toward the square. The old man also accelerated. Now he had no doubt that the man was following him. Jafer suddenly turned right and found himself in a side street. He quickly regretted what he'd done because now he was utterly alone. However, it was too late. If he turned back, he would surely run into the man. He almost broke out into a run. Around the corner of one of the houses, he turned into another street and clung his back to the wall.

He listened to the sound of footsteps – they were getting closer. But suddenly the sound stopped.

What happened? Jafer thought. *Did the man melt into the air?*

Pressing his back against the wall even harder, he waited, holding his breath.

Suddenly something happened that he had not expected. On the other side of the wall, a thick voice spoke.

"Don't be afraid..."

"Are you a thief?"

"I told you not to be afraid."

The force of his voice would scare anyone. Nevertheless, he didn't bend under it.

"Why are you following me? If you're a thief, know that I have no money. I have a big knife instead."

Standing against the other end of the wall, the man reached out with his hand.

"Look," he said, "my hands are empty. I don't want to hurt you. I do not want your money or your life."

Jafer stared at the claw-like hand for a moment.

"In that case, what do you want, old man? What do you want from me?" he asked.

"To talk to you."

"Talk?"

"Yes. Just talk. I wanted to ask you about something."

The large, claw-like hand of the man was still extended. Jafer calmed down, but he didn't cease to be vigilant.

"In that case, ask."

"We will talk like that, without seeing each other? It's time to end this clownery, isn't it?"

Without waiting for an answer, the old man found himself on the other side of the wall to which Jafer's back was glued.

The boy was big, but he felt like a child next to this man. He had never seen such broad shoulders in his life.

"Are you from the palace?"

The black boy shook his head.

"Don't lie. I saw you leave the palace gate. I've followed you since then."

"So, what?" Jafer jerked. "This gate is open to everyone. All who have something to do in the palace pass through it."

A small smile passed over the old giant's face.

"But not black boys whose faucet of life has been closed," he said, staring at the boy. "Tell me, you live in the harem?"

This time, Jafer nodded.

"Do you know all the girls there?"

"Let's say I do. So, what?"

"I'll ask you about one of them. If you lie this time…"

Jafer didn't even notice when it happened. With lightning speed, the man took out a curved dagger he had at his belt and put it on his throat.

"I won't say anything. I will give the voice to this dagger. Once it realizes that you are trying to lie, it will slit your throat immediately. This is its nature."

Jafer opened his eyes wide in fear. His body instantly covered with cold sweat. It was clear that the man was not kidding. Slowly touching the sharp end of the dagger resting on his neck with his forefinger, and trying to move the knife away from him, he whispered:

"About whom?"

"About Aleksandra..."

"What?"

"Aleksandra, a girl from Ruthenia. Have you seen her?"

Jafer, squinting, looked with a tremor at the iron sharpened on both sides, wandering between the tip of his nose and the throat.

"I've seen her."

The old man looked relieved and took back the knife. The curved dagger disappeared behind the red belt as quickly as it had appeared.

"Really? How is she? Is she doing well?"

Jafer thought he should answer, 'Why do you care, man? Do you have anything to do with her?' But he didn't intend to meet the curved dagger again. Besides, he was very curious about who this man was and how he knew the girl. He decided to reply truthfully.

"Aleksandra is doing very well. She is healthy," he started to say.

"If you're lying, I will not interfere. Besides, how do you know Aleksandra?"

Jafer smiled despite himself.

"Nobody knows her better than me," he said.

"Why is that?"

"Aleksandra is my mistress."

Suddenly, the old man hugged the boy with joy. Squeezing him in his strong arms, he raised his feet off the ground.

"Blackie, you ensured my heart's peace. May God protect you from evil."

Jafer didn't expect this sudden gesture of love. It was only with some difficulty that he managed to free himself from his crushing embrace.

"Also know that my mistress is no longer called Aleksandra. Now she's called Hürrem."

"How? Hür-rem? What does it mean?"

"I don't know. This name was given to my mistress by our Master – Sultan Suleiman Khan."

For a moment the old man's mouth remained open. Jafer, proud with the impression he made, continued:

"Since it pleased you so much, I'll tell you something else. Mrs. Hürrem is now the only favorite of our Sultan. Padishah loves her. He doesn't talk about anyone else but Hürrem Haseki."

The huge old man suddenly collapsed to the ground. He grabbed his head and cried loudly. Were they tears of happiness or despair?

He must be crying from joy, thought Jafer. *Is it possible to cry because one has become the favorite of the Padishah?*

He sat down by the old man.

"Now you tell Jafer who you are. Just don't think I was scared of you. I will tear the insides of anyone who will try to hurt Mrs. Hürrem. How do you know My Lady? Are you her friend or relative? But your face is not like hers, jigit."

The old giant wiped the tears running down his cheeks with the back of his hand, and from there down the beard sprinkled with grey. He looked deep into Jafer's eyes. He rose as suddenly as he fell to the ground.

"Do as you said. Take care of your Lady. Protect Aleksandra..."

"Hürrem, old man, Hürrem. This is the order of the Padishah."

"Well, good, protect Mrs. Hürrem. And if someone is her enemy, tear his guts out." The old man then let out a big sigh. "I don't care if you're black or white, you're a good kid."

"I'm not a kid. Let's not spoil this nice conversation."

The old man burst out laughing. Not that he took the boy's threat seriously, but nevertheless, he mitigated the situation.

"Don't mind my words. Of course, you are not a child. Otherwise, would I entrust Aleks... Hürrem to you?"

"Wouldn't you?"

"Of course not. You must protect her, Black Boy."

"Either you are deaf, or you don't listen to me. I told you, she is now haseki. Hürrem Haseki has got the jigits and soldiers who protect her."

"A soldier protects following an order... A loving jigit follows his heart. I looked into your dark eyes. When you mentioned Hürrem, your eyes flashed immediately. You love your mistress, true?"

A smile appeared on Jafer's face.

"How could I not love her? She is the only one in this great harem who treats me like a human being. She talks to me and shares her worries with me. She has a really pure heart. If I were not so black, we would be like siblings."

When he mentioned the worries, the old man suddenly became serious.

"What did you say, jigit? Worries? Is your mistress

worried about something?"

"Relax, don't reach for the sword, huge man. I just blurted out something. Could Hürrem Haseki have any worries? But in the first days after arriving at the harem, she suffered a lot. A lot..."

Jafer did not finish.

"Tell me," the old man insisted. "Did she suffer a lot?"

"She got a lot of beatings."

"What?! Do you know what you are talking about? Beating?!" the giant roared.

Jafer's heart leaped into his throat. Could this terrifying voice belong to this old man? Sparks sprinkled from the giant's eyes.

"Beating? Was Aleksandra beaten in the palace of the Ottoman Sultan?"

"Yes..." muttered the boy. "And with a stick. For many days. But My Lady did not give up. She didn't bend her head."

"This is a Ural girl. Would she bend her head? Tell me who this pig is who dared to raise his hand to Aleksandra."

"It's harem aga. His name is Sümbül Aga – a black eunuch like me. With a big belly."

Seeing the expression on the giant's face, Jafer shivered in terror. In fear, he didn't even dare to say that she was beaten even more by Gülbahar Haseki.

"How many times I wanted to snatch the stick from his hands and lower it on his back..."

"Don't do this, they will skin you," said the man. "I need you. Leave it to me."

Suddenly, he stopped and looked deep into the boy's eyes.

"Do you want to do a good deed, and at the same time earn some money, my jigit?"

The boy looked at him suspiciously.

"Who wouldn't want to?" he said slowly.

"I don't want anything bad. Just meet me every Friday at this corner, in front of the bakery. You will bring me news about your mistress. Each time you will get two akce," he said.

He was about to turn around and leave when Jafer called after him:

"As you wish, old man, but when I'm talking Hürrem Haseki about you, who can I say you are?"

The man turned angrily and grabbed Jafer by the throat with a claw-like hand.

"Don't you dare open your mouth. Don't mention about me to Aleksandra or anyone else. If you don't listen to me, dear jigit, hiding in the palace will not help you. Even if you run to the other end of the world, I'll find you, cut that long tongue off and throw it to the dogs."

He let go of him as quickly as he'd grasped him and began to walk away with a heavy step.

Jafer did not give up.

"Who are you, man?"

The huge old man looked over the shoulder at Jafer. There was a strange smile on his face. A smile that made you tremble.

I am the Azrael of those who do and want to do evil to Hürrem Haseki, Jafer thought as he stared after the departing man.

"Your goose is cooked, Sümbül Aga," he murmured. "Soon your Azrael will set out for the road."

CHAPTER TWENTY-NINE

The next morning, Hürrem appeared before Sultana Hafsa. Sultana Mother, having heard that the girl was coming had made special arrangements. She wanted the servants to dress her in her grandest and most expensive outfit, including wearing a large bonnet decorated with pearls. Finally, she placed herself majestically on the magnificent sofa by the window. Girls, one white, the other black, sat at her feet. The preparations were complete.

The elderly woman hadn't slept all night. She didn't know what to think about it all.

On the day of Gülbahar's departure from the seraglio, after the evening prayer, she'd walked the dark corridors to visit the rooms of her grandson's mother. The chamber had been filled with Mustafa's chirping until that morning, but now it was overcome by silence. Everything looked like before, but the walls, curtains, sofas, everything, had lost their soul. For a moment, Hafsa sat still in the voiceless darkness. There was no trace left of Mustafa's joyous shouts and running that always embarrassed the harem residents.

Emptiness is lurking from every corner, she thought worriedly.

Gülbahar was now just a subject of rumors in the harem. She knew that in just a few days the girls will find a new topic – it will become as if neither Gülbahar nor Mustafa had ever lived here; as if it was not her who parted the curtains or was lying on this sofa as if Mustafa did not play here.

A shudder shook the older woman. How quickly a person can disappear into oblivion, and it was this thought that aroused doubts in Sultana Hafsa.

Have I made a mistake? That question did not leave her alone.

"No, my dear, nothing like that," she whispered to herself.

The interior was so quiet that her whisper echoed like a scream from the walls, that still carried the scent of Gülbahar Haseki.

She didn't contribute to the fact that her son's feelings towards Gülbahar had cooled. It wasn't her who caused Suleiman to move away from the Circassian beauty, day by day.

And Aleksandra? she thought – and promptly got upset. She couldn't get used to calling the girl Hürrem in any way. She remembered her as Aleksandra, and later she became Ruslana, but now the girl from Ruthenia was Suleiman's Hürrem. Like everyone else, she also had to get used to it.

Yes, it wasn't her who helped cool the relationship between her son and Gülbahar, but she recommended Hürrem to Suleiman. She praised the charm of her voice and she who urged him to listen to her song. It was she who paved the way for Hürrem.

How could I know that Suleiman would lose his head for this girl? she wondered. When things started to get complicated, shouldn't she have said, 'Listen, son, Gülbahar is the mother of your son and my grandson. If you don't forgive her, God will not forgive her either. After all, you know that your mother also...' But she didn't do it. If that had happened, maybe everything would have unfolded differently.

Meanwhile, while Gülbahar sat over her needlework, wilting somewhere far away, Hürrem led a happy life as a new favorite in her chamber in the harem.

She couldn't turn back time with a few words, but she should at least force Suleiman to settle his conscience. And what was supposed to win in this settlement was not lust, but conscience. Not Hürrem, but Gülbahar.

"If so, why were you silent, Hafsa?" muttered the old woman. "Don't try to deny it. You played the main role in Gülbahar's exile and the promotion of Hürrem."

Well, but what would have happened if I'd remained quiet? Would that joyous laughter have come from my son's chambers down the corridors that had witnessed so many sufferings, crimes, and sins? Would Suleiman, who at such a young age took on the burden of the world, be so full of vigor and strength then? Would he be able to raise his head as if he wanted to touch the clouds with it? she continued to ponder.

Expecting Hürrem, the new favorite of Sultan Suleiman, Sultana Hafsa allowed herself to get lost in her thoughts. She looked into the distance. Sometimes it seemed to her that she could see the spring Crimean meadows covered with yellow flowers of the greenweed, sometimes her grandson Mustafa in the arms of Gülbahar. Was the prince crying?

"Sultana Mother, Hürrem Haseki has come."

The sound of the voice brought Sultana Hafsa back from her brooding.

So Hürrem had officially become the favorite.

The girl greeted her with a humble bow, as she had learned in the Crimea from Aj Bala Hatun. She waited like that in the doorway. She did not raise her head until she got a sign from Mother Sultana.

"Come here, child."

Hearing the order, she moved forward. She knelt before the woman, kissed her robe, and remained motionless. Was the voice of Sultana Hafsa cold, or did it just seem so to her? Would Suleiman's mother, who had shown her love until today, have turned into an iceberg overnight?

"I heard that my son officially announced your new name to everyone. I also heard that they are calling you haseki.

Yes, it certainly was that way – the woman was as cold as ice. There wasn't even a trace of sympathy and warmth in her voice. Hürrem bent over Sultana Hafsa's dress again. She shook her head, her shoulders shaking.

"You are not happy, child? Why? I think you should be. You have become my son's only favorite. How many girls have managed to get the Sultan's favor? I think you must be God's chosen..." The woman suddenly fell silent, leaned over, and looked at the girl's shaking shoulders. "Fate is like that. It condemns some to exile while pushing others forward."

In response, Hürrem's sobbing resounded in the room. Sultana Mother looked around, without changing her dignified position. She did not dismiss the servants so that they could see this scene. The new favorite of Sultan Suleiman poured tears, falling to the feet of Mother Sultana. Let them see who has power in the harem.

"Are you crying, child?"

"Yes, Sultana Mother." The quiet voice of Hürrem came among the sobs from where she still kneeled.

"Why? Shouldn't this day be your day of joy?"

"I didn't know it would happen, Sultana Mother."

"What didn't you know, child? Raise your head already."

Hürrem slowly got up.

The woman shuddered, seeing deep pain in the watery eyes of the girl. She couldn't understand it.

"What didn't you know, Hürrem Haseki? Why are you crying?"

"If I had known... how things would happen..." Hürrem cried and then fell silent.

Sultana Hafsa felt satisfied with the show she had prepared to demonstrate which woman in the harem is the most powerful. It was enough for her. Clapping her hands, she gave the servants a sign to leave.

After the two servants, who sat just like Hürrem at the foot of Sultana Hafsa, had risen hastily and left the room, the girl continued, pouring out another stream of tears:

"If we knew... we refused to face our Sultan ashamed to show our face... If we knew it would arouse so much anger in him that it would push him to make such a decision..." She burst into tears again.

The elderly woman thought that the girl was biting her lips because it was difficult for her to share her worries. In reality, however, Hürrem was chewing her lips so that she wouldn't laugh at the fact that, in the Padishah's style, she used the plural when she spoke of herself.

Calming down, she finished her speech, sobbing.

"We would not have let the Sultan send Gülbahar Haseki and our prince away, Sultana Mother."

The older woman was surprised.

"You wouldn't agree? How come?"

"I would have begged my Sultan, sprinkle salt on the wound of my love, I would have explained that it is not our haseki who was guilty, but his slave Hürrem..." she sighed and continued, sobbing: "If it were necessary, I would give my life."

"Guilty? But you are not guilty. What Gülbahar Haseki committed is unforgivable."

The conversation had taken the turn desired by Hürrem – the ice in the woman's voice seemed to melt away.

"Forgive me, Sultana, but this is what love is like. It can force you to do anything. You can see that Gülbahar Haseki also loved our Master so much that she was even ready to face his anger.

After these words, she turned her gaze for the first time to the side where the woman sat in her full majesty. Their eyes met. From behind her curtain of tears, she saw the haughty look of Sultana Hafsa begin to disappear.

"Yesterday evening, when His Highness Sultan called me to himself, I told him the same. Just as I accepted with humility that my Master changed my name because he did not like it, so I would accept with submissiveness a few blows, given by our Prince's mother to the godless Ruthenian. My Sultan's love would be a cure for my hurt pride.

"Do you really think so, Hürrem?"

As she spoke, her voice seemed to soften. Hürrem could see the faded, steel-cold eyes of the Mother Sultana piercing her face.

"Yes," she replied and sobbed again. "At dawn, after the night I was honored by our Master's favors, I ran to you. Isn't it you, that in addition to my mother in the Crimea, are my mother, in whose love, compassion, and wisdom I found refuge, Mother Hafsa? If instead of singing joyful songs, I am pouring out bitter tears, it is because I want the advice of my mother. I am a young girl. I'm a stranger. I don't know how to behave. Tell me what to do, what to do to connect Gülbahar Haseki with her family, my Sultan with the Prince, my mother with her grandson?

After these words, Hürrem fell to the woman's feet, shaken by a new wave of weeping. Sultana mother looked at the young shoulders, trembling in front of her. She calmed down.

I did the right thing, she thought. *These tears show that she has a big heart. One who has such a heart, whether from Ruthenia or Persia, deserves everything. My son also needs a woman with a big heart. If these tears are false, then there will be nothing left for me but to beg God to forgive me for the sin I committed.*

"Get up, child," the old woman said slowly.

It was at this moment that Hürrem gained a new life experience. Now she understood that a woman who plays her role well would not be stopped by anything. She can do whatever she wants, and make others do what she wants.

"Don't cry, Hürrem Haseki, don't cry. Come and sit by me."

When the favorite heard it, her heart filled with happiness. She could have shouted with joy. Since the mother of Sultan Suleiman called her 'haseki,' it meant that she'd accepted the fact that Hürrem was the new favorite of her son. Otherwise, she wouldn't have called her that, even if someone put a knife to her throat.

Hürrem hid her joy and rose slowly, sniffing. She prayed that there would be no glimpse of victory in her eyes. She sat down shyly by Sultana Hafsa. She took her hands and kissed them, then put them on her forehead.

"Please advise me," she said.

Sultana Hafsa looked deep into the girl's eyes, as if she wanted to read what was inside her, and spoke firmly:

"You create your own destiny, not me. Nor my son, the Sultan, despite his power. He can take life with one order, but in reality, it is not his will but the Highest God's. It is God who created us all, earth, heaven, and stars."

She stroked the girl's wavy hair. She wiped the tears streaming down her cheeks. She took her chin and gently lifting her head, looked deep into her eyes.

"Everything happens with the will of God. Only He knows what is written for us. We are but a miserable tool in His hands. Whatever we do, whatever we do, we can not change our destiny, we can not erase it. That's what was written for you, and what was written for Gülbahar."

Hürrem breathed a sigh, as if of relief. The woman felt a tremor even in her breath. No, she couldn't be pretending so well – she believed Hürrem. In Crimea, mother Aishe Güldane Hatun also believed her, as did Aj Bala, and her son the Sultan, ruling the world, who could recognize the bad intentions of the viziers and pashas. This girl was speaking with her heart. The sadness in her eyes was real.

"One day Gülbahar will come back," said Sultana Hafsa. "After all, she is the mother of the heir to the throne. One day she will come through this door as the mother of the Padishah."

Hürrem didn't focus too much on the words of Sultana Mother. There was only one sentence in her mind: 'One day she will come through this door as the mother of the Padishah.' She wondered why, but the answer came immediately: *She gave Suleiman a son.*

She kissed the old woman's hands and put them on her forehead. She said good-bye and went out into the corridor. When she was among the servants, she felt like she was floating. Nobody noticed the strange flash in her eyes.

If so, Sultana Mother, she thought, *Hürrem will also give Suleiman a son, and we will see what happens then.*

The day will come, that the fates will change, and Hürrem's son will sit on the Ottoman throne.

***

For many days, Hürrem managed to keep her joy of the victory secret. She didn't even smile once. She had many fiery nights of love in the Sultan's bed, but she tried not to show her happiness. No one in the harem could say that the new favorite celebrates Gülbahar's banishment.

On the contrary, everyone said: 'We treated this girl unjustly. She is honest to the bone. Such a favorite is suitable for Sultan Suleiman.' But in truth, Hürrem celebrated in the innermost recesses of her heart.

She even forbade the servants to show excessive joy. Under no circumstances were they allowed to laugh. She instructed them to tell everyone in the harem about her sorrow and torment, about the fact that she stopped eating and drinking, and they obeyed this order diligently.

Setaret Kalfa, in particular, was most concerned.

"Oh, I'm afraid that something will happen to Hürrem Haseki, God forbid," Setaret said, and rolled her eyes. "I've never met an equally good person. If she had not been an angel, would she despair so much after the exile of the woman who had massacred her face? If it goes on like this, she'll get sick."

Setaret praised the great heart of the new favorite so zealously that the news about it went beyond the walls of the palace. It was a topic of women's conversations in Istanbul houses. They loved her so much that even the Janissaries, who blamed Hürrem for having contributed to the departure of the prince from Istanbul, changed their mind and praised her:

"We were wrong. Haseki interceded for our prince with the Sultan."

Hürrem also refused to move to larger chambers.

"Do we need luxury and wealth now? Better tell me how our Gülbahar Haseki and our Prince are. Are they in good health? Have they arrived happily?"

A few days later, when she was told she would move to the chambers abandoned by Gülbahar, she started to scream. She stamped her heels again, loudly hitting the floor.

Sümbül Aga, whose toe had already suffered once, was terrified. The huge man jumped away in fear.

For a long time, Hürrem's songs were not heard in the harem either.

One day, Sultana Hafsa visited her.

"We've missed your beautiful voice, child," she said, stroking her hair, and Hürrem's eyes went foggy.

"Something broke in us, something's gone, Sultana Mother. How can I sing and play now?" she complained.

Then one evening Sultan Suleiman also said he missed her singing.

"Beloved smiling muse, my pomegranate fruit. For so long, there has not been a smile on your face. What do you want? What should I do to make you smile at least once? How many days your nightingale voice has not been heard in our home? Give up your sadness. Sing our song and save our heart from darkness and worries."

She gave him a similar answer. She looked surprised at the young man as if to ask: 'How can you demand this from me?' before she replied.

"My Sultan's wish is an order for me, but the wound after the exile is so fresh that your slave can not sing. However, if you insist, I will do it. If this is My Lord's wish, I will sing, but know that my heart is bleeding..."

Suddenly she fell silent and looked the man in the eye.

"I know that His Majesty Sultan will not do this to me. Let your servant Hürrem's heart burn with the pain of separation she unconsciously contributed to. Let her punish herself."

In response to these words, the young Padishah stood up and started to comfort Hürrem, showering her with the rain of kisses.

What a good choice I made, he thought.

Meanwhile, Hürrem put her head on the strong arm of the man.

"Oh, My Lord, oh! How big is my longing and my sorrow?" she sighed deeply, as he savored the scent of her hair.

CHAPTER THIRTY

How fast the severe winter went! Floating with happiness, Hürrem Haseki didn't think that when she reached her goal to become the favorite of Sultan Suleiman, that time would stop. However, nor did she expect it to pass so fast.

Hürrem's despair after Gülbahar's exile lasted two months. One day she obediently moved to her chambers. By then, she had not failed to convince everyone that it was the Sultan's insistence that forced her to do so.

"Every day we think that we see our Sultana haseki and our Prince Mustafa Khan. We hear their voices. Our heart is bleeding," she said at every opportunity.

However, it didn't take long before she stopped, either. In the end, everything was forgotten, or so it seemed to her.

The evenings passed quickly.

Every morning Hürrem went to the bathhouse. In spite of all the insistence, she always refused to let the army of servants accompany her in the bathhouse. When she washed, only Merzuka and Setaret Kalfa could be present. She sat at the top of the pool, poured cold and hot water on herself, and savored the taste of various dishes and chilled sorbets that Setaret brought her.

The next stage after the thorough washing was the depilation — she hated that the most. It was a Turkish custom to which it was most hard for her to get used to.

Should I mention that to Suleiman? If a woman should not have hair, why did God create her like this? she reasoned.

When all those activities were completed, she had lessons. Teachers came and went. At least Suleiman didn't laugh at her Turkish anymore. Or maybe he'd got used to it? While she began to speak Turkish more fluently, her writing it was still a nuisance; in fact, this fancy writing had become Hürrem's nightmare. She'd fall into despair when sometimes in the evenings the Sultan took an inkwell and a pen and tried to teach her writing. She was driven crazy by the fact that although she focused all her attention on it, she could not do it. Besides, she preferred when Suleiman taught her love.

She was second to none in music lessons. She played kanun wonderfully, but these few songs she played did not express Hürrem. They were so depressing and somber. The Kanun was a great instrument, and Hürrem loved to play it. Her fingers flew along the strings like birds. The songs she performed herself seemed more beautiful to her than the ones the music teacher tried to teach her, which is why she'd often say:

"The Sultan loves these verses. They are not only joyful but also full of life."

In addition to the lessons, there were two other things that Hürrem did not forget about.

Every day, without exception, she went to the odalisque's pavilion and sat and talked with the girls. Initially, it was accepted somewhat reluctantly. Well, why was the only favorite of the great Sultan Suleiman visiting the odalisques? Could she be coming to eavesdrop? To check on them? However, when Hürrem helped to solve the problems of several girls, their suspicions disappeared.

"Hürrem Haseki turned out to be completely different. She's nothing like Gülbahar," the girls began to say, including those who until recently had slandered her in jealousy.

In fact, Hürrem's intention was both to arouse sympathy around her, and to get to know the newcomers to the girls' harem – especially, to check if there was a beauty among them that could draw Suleiman's attention. If a potential rival appeared, she would have to find a solution.

The second place that Hürrem visited every day was the chamber of Sultana Hafsa.

She kissed her hands and put them to her forehead. She asked about her health.

"Does Sultana Mother have any wish?"

The woman's answer always sounded the same.

"The peace of the State and our son, the Sultan. Let his rule, health, and happiness last."

The woman knew that Suleiman was happy in Hürrem's arms, and Hürrem was doing her job well. She made Sultan Suleiman grow wings out of happiness.

One evening the young Padishah, kissing her, and savoring Hürrem's scent, started talking while sipping wine from her hands.

"You know, Hürrem..."

Haseki looked at the Sultan with her charming eyes, that always distracted him, as if to say, 'I'm listening.'

"Today at the Divan, Piri Mehmed Pasha said such a thing, that I didn't know if I should've laughed or got angry."

"No one has the right to upset my Ruler, even the Grand Vizier. Whatever he said, he was probably joking."

Actually, she was curious, but it wasn't her style to unmask and cry out: 'What did he say? What did he say?' Sooner or later the Padishah would reveal it to her. Slowly, Hürrem mastered the art of making him talk.

"I thought so too. Piri Pasha is old, but the tongue of this sea wolf is unruly. Nothing escapes his eyes."

Padishah took another sip of wine. In the place of a snack, Suleiman kissed the voluptuous, pale-pink, naked arms of Hürrem.

"While discussing an issue at the Divan, we told the viziers and pashas that we liked the preparations very much, and we are full of admiration. Then Piri Pasha took a step forward." Trying to remember the words of the pasha, Padishah fell silent for a moment, then continued: 'We, who while serving our Padishah and the Ottoman State, try not to miss anything, have become very happy since Hürrem Haseki appeared in the path of our Master. Now both our Sultan and the State are happy,' that's exactly what the old wolf said."

"Am I to understand from this joke that I make you happy, my Sultan?"

In response, Suleiman took Hürrem in his arms and laid a hot kiss on her lips.

"Yes. Is there anyone who hasn't noticed my happiness yet? They talk about you and praise you in every corner of the seraglio. Everyone talks about your beauty. If I sometimes appear drunk to you, know that the reason is not wine, but the love of Hürrem and the happiness she gave me."

At those words, Hürrem stretched her lips in a smile and thanked him.

"Only the falconer complains about you, Hürrem Haseki."

That man again! That man again! Ibrahim, with whom Suleiman is seen more often than with her. Despite the jealousy and anger that he aroused in her, the girl acted surprised as if she had never heard this name before.

"Who is this, my Sultan?"

"Ibrahim, my falconer. Ibrahim, who reminded me of your traditions."

If Hürrem saw the falconer that day, she would have kissed him.

***

One day, Suleiman rushed into her chamber without warning.

"What day is it today?" he asked.

"Thursday."

"I'm not asking about it. Today should be special for you."

The girl did not understand.

"For me, only one day is special. That was the day when His Majesty Sultan gave me love."

How beautifully she talks, thought the Padishah. *She can take my mind away with a few words.*

He stroked the girl's waving hair.

"We did not know that either. Ibrahim reminded me of that. Apparently, it is Christmas today?"

Hürrem suddenly became sad.

"Get ready," Sultan Suleiman said happily.

"What does His Majesty the Sultan want me to do?"

"You go to church, Hürrem. Aren't you a Christian? You must go to a Christmas mass."

Hürrem couldn't believe her ears. To church? Instantly, tears flowed from her eyes. Regardless of the rules, and much to the surprised looks of the stunned servants, she embraced Suleiman.

"It's been so long... so much time..." she whispered.

How many years had it been since the last time she was in a church? Three? Five? Or maybe a hundred like it seemed to her?

"I knew, but I did not have the courage to mention it," she said as she sprinkled Suleiman with a shower of grateful kisses.

"It's unacceptable. Quick, get ready. Suleiman goes to the mosque, Hürrem to the church."

That day, Hürrem kissed Suleiman's hand with real gratitude for the first time – and it felt strange.

She got ready quickly. She put on a large, black hooded cloak over her clothes – she didn't want anyone to recognize her. When it started to get dark, the carriage left her in front of the Byzantine church in Balat, the part of Istanbul that belonged to the Fatih district, on the Golden Horn.

Suddenly her heart shrunk with fear that she might get lost, but then she recognized Jafer in the crowd in front of the church, and later the commander of the Chaush and several guards, all of them incognito. It meant that her beloved Sultan had taken all the steps necessary to make Hürrem feel calm and safe.

For the first time in many years, Hürrem prayed not to the broken icon she took from her bundle, but in a church from the time of the East Roman Empire, staring at the image of Jesus on the cross, and the Holy Lady, made of colorful pieces of glass, decorating the altar.

Jesus, our Father, and beloved Mary, our Mother. Look, I came. Do you recognize me? Aleksandra... The daughter of priest Nikola from Ruthenia... Aleksandra from mother Ilona..." She calmed down in her mind as if waiting for a response from heaven. If someone slipped off the hood hiding her face in the darkness, they would have seen large streams of tears spilling out of her eyes.

She lit the candles thanking for the fact that Sultan Suleiman liked her.

Forgive me. I did not keep my word. Jesus, our Father, and beloved Mary, our Mother, I can not light you a million candles, but let each of these candles be not one, but a thousand.

She still prayed as the touching melody of the Ave Maria hymn rose beneath the magnificent church dome.

Now they call me Hürrem. Some people call me a Ruthenian odalisque. For them, I am the Ruthenian favorite of Sultan Suleiman. Take care of me. Let me not have the future like the future of Gülbahar. Do not let me lose my place by Sultan Suleiman's side. Do not spare me the love of the Ottoman Ruler.

Her own voice, echoing in her head, went silent for a moment. Did she move her mouth? She didn't know. With her eyes wet with tears, she stared at the statue of Mary holding the little Jesus in her arms. It seemed to Hürrem that calm Mary was smiling at her. The voice of her heart sounded again:

Most beloved Mother Mary, I am the same little girl who kneeled before you and prayed every evening before going to sleep in the country house. Thank you for always listening to my prayers. Now I have one more wish, Mother Mary. Fill my arms. Give me sons. Give me good luck.

Make it so that the throne and the crown of the Ottoman State will be given to Hürrem's son. Jesus, our Father, bring the son of Hürrem, the daughter of the country priest Nikola, to the throne.

That evening, Hürrem returned to the palace full of inner peace and purified.

Suleiman was expecting her. She embraced him with gratitude, then began to stroke his body, making him lose his senses. However, the Sultan slowly moved away from her.

"Let us devote this night not to love, but to prayer, Hürrem. You pray in your own way, and I pray in my way. In your prayers, do not forget to mention me, the Ottoman State, and the army. Pray for the victories of our soldiers."

So, until she fell asleep, she prayed for everything and immersed herself in thought, especially about falconer Ibrahim. She wrote the name of this man who spent more time with the Padishah than herself, in her memory. The man had shown her how much influence he had on Suleiman, allowing her to go to church on Christmas Day. It was, in a sense, a message to Hürrem that she should be careful – it was not a good sign.

Jesus, our Father, she prayed that night as she fell to sleep. *Yes, I know that it's thanks to that man that I could come to you, but he is dangerous. Do not let him turn Suleiman against me. Make Ibrahim fall out of the Padishah's favors. Only I should have an influence on Sultan Suleiman. The Padishah should only listen to Hürrem. Just me and nobody else.*

CHAPTER THIRTY-ONE

Spring 1522

People talked everywhere about the love of Sultan Suleiman and the Ruthenian odalisque Hürrem.

In the harem, divan, Enderun, military barracks, houses of pashas, viziers and agas, bathhouses for women, and Istanbul wine bars – the talk was only about their love. It was compared to the fairy tales written by the Middle Eastern protagonists in poetic, romantic literature about Kerem and Asla, Yusuf and Zuleica, Ferhat and Shirin. The young Padishah divided his spare time after fulfilling his State duties between his two loves – Hürrem and hunting.

Hürrem got angry whenever Suleiman took the falconer Ibrahim and went hunting with him. It was true that the Padishah was also accompanied by many pashas, viziers, and State officials, but the fact that Suleiman and Ibrahim spent time together was enough for Hürrem to boil with anger.

Hürrem got some information, pulling the tongue of the harem aga.

"The man was a Croatian who turned Turkish. These Croats dislike the Serbs very much," Sümbül Aga said between the lines.

"What do I care, Sümbül Aga? If they want, they can like them, if not, then no."

"I thought it was important information. Apparently, I was wrong."

"What's so important about that? Tell me, let me find out."

"Serbs are the Slavic people, Hürrem Haseki."

The black man fixed his black eyes on Hürrem's face. He appeared to search her face for some reaction but didn't notice anything. Haseki, however, had immediately understood the importance of the matter, but she didn't let it show.

"During the migration of the tribes, part of the Slavs crossed the Danube and Sava rivers, reached the Adriatic coast, and settled there. These people are Serbs. They are southern Slavs. Serbs are your relatives, Hürrem."

Hürrem's face remained expressionless.

If Sümbül Aga didn't know how smart and clever the girl was, he'd have thought she still didn't understand. The harem aga leaned closer to her and whispered in a fox voice:

"The point is, that I was afraid that Croats who do not like Serbs, don't like Ruthenians either."

"What are these words, Sümbül Aga? All we need is our Master's love. Why would we need this Croatian? Also, who has the right to undermine the intentions of a friend of our Ruler?"

When Hürrem noticed that when talking about herself, she'd begun to say 'we' instead of 'me,' just like Sultan Suleiman, a smile crossed her face. All those who occupied high positions and came from noble families in the Ottoman palace talked in that manner – especially when, having abandoned communication with signals, they found the courage to speak. Since she too joined the elite, she had to adhere to the rules.

Sümbül Aga read the smile on the girl's face as a sign of calmness, and that she didn't take him seriously.

But he was wrong. Hürrem took the Croatian-turned-Turk Ibrahim very seriously and she'd become very vigilant. In fact, from the first day of her stay in the harem, Hürrem had been very vigilant with everything and everyone who could stand between her and Sultan Suleiman. Ever since she learned that he talks with the Padishah for hours, in the Mehmed the Conqueror Pavilion, the only place in the palace that overlooked the sea on both sides, her vigilance towards falconer Ibrahim was high.

"What else do you know?"

"They say he is the son of an Italian fisherman and a Croat woman. He was born in Parga. As a child, he was brought to the empire as part of the devshirme. Nobody knows his real name. For some reason, our Master moved him to Manisa while he was a beylerbey there. There he was given to a rich widow. Because he was very handsome, the woman named him Ibrahim.

"He was in service of this woman?"

"Yes. In time, Ibrahim began to manage the woman's house, vineyards, and gardens, providing her services of all kinds..."

Hürrem interrupted the harem aga.

"Services of all kinds?" she asked in a suggestive voice.

When he saw the flash of a naughty girl in Hürrem's eyes, a smile appeared on the man's face. The big lips parted, revealing his white teeth for a moment.

"That I don't know. He was young and handsome, and the woman had been a widow for many years. Can fire and powder stand side by side? Probably something was on. But it's their sin – I don't know anything."

Hürrem nodded with satisfaction, wondering whether this information would prove useful one day.

"Ibrahim became very famous. All the rich agas went to the woman's door, asking her to give him to them. But the woman was unyielding. Eventually, the praises of Ibrahim reached our Master's ears. One day he went to the vineyard where he worked, and he acquainted himself with Ibrahim. He liked the brightness and diligence of the boy very much. They were a good fit, and they liked each other. Eventually, the woman reluctantly agreed to give Ibrahim to the Prince. In the end, one should not say no to the heir to the throne. From that day on, Ibrahim became a close companion of our Master. How to say it... They are close to each other like friends. They are close to each other like brothers."

Sümbül took a break to breathe.

"When the day arrived that Sultan Selim Khan left this world, our Master rushed to the city of Istanbul as fast as his horse could take him so that the State would not be left without a Ruler. Guess who accompanied him..."

"Ibrahim..." said Hürrem slowly.

Aga nodded.

"Two riders. Sultan Suleiman and the falconer Ibrahim. The viziers and agas who went out to greet them were stupefied."

Sümbül tried to assess what impression his words had on the girl. Not finding any sign, he leaned over her ear again.

"They say our Master does not make any decisions without Ibrahim," he announced and looked around. After making sure there was no one around, he whispered: "Let no one hear it. It's unnecessary. I only repeat what I know."

That made her think. If there were those who said that, 'Our master does not make decisions without Ibrahim,' it meant that their closeness bothered some people. This possibly proved that Hürrem had silent allies in the palace. Who were they? She had to find out.

But now let's not scare the man, asking him about that too. Otherwise, he might clam up, she decided.

Harem aga looked around again.

"Do you know what the viziers call the falconer?" he asked.

Hürrem shook her head.

"Ibrahim the Chosen, they say. Ibrahim the Chosen," the Aga said, rolling his eyes.

***

It didn't take long, but Sultan Suleiman acquired another hunting companion, apart from Ibrahim the Chosen – Hürrem.

Actually, it went really smooth for her. From the day she decided she wouldn't leave the Sultan alone with Ibrahim during the hunts, she created a master plan, and with equal perfection, she brought it to life. The proposition did not come from her, but from the Padishah.

One day, when Suleiman embraced her once after he'd returned from the hunt, Hürrem immediately realized that something was bothering him.

"Has anything happened, God forbid, that troubled my Sultan?"

"We have not hunted even one hare for three days."

Hürrem looked at the Padishah in disbelief.

"While the whole world praises my Sultan's talent for hunting, you can't expect me to believe those words?"

"Believe me, we have not hunted even a single hare. True, we returned with a few wild boars, and a deer, but no one was lucky enough to shoot a hare. What do you say to that, the most beautiful of the beautiful?"

"I will say that our Lord deigns to joke or..."

Padishah noticed that Hürrem broke off at the last moment.

"Or?" He made her understand that he wanted her to finish the thought.

"Or... My Ruler checks us – his slave..."

When Suleiman shook his head, Hürrem decided that it was time to get to the point.

"In that case... Forgive me, but the friends accompanying Suleiman in hunting are good for nothing."

The Padishah was very surprised.

"Did you say that they are good for nothing, Hürrem?"

"Yes. Otherwise, would a master hunter like my Ruler return after three days empty-handed?"

The Sultan smiled under his mustache – a hint that he didn't take her words seriously.

"They are all masters of hunting. They are unmatched."

"But they didn't find a hare?"

If it were not for the unruly, childish smile on the girl's face, Suleiman could have been offended. His eyebrow, after rising for a moment, returned to its place. He asked half-jokingly:

"If my companions did not find a hare, maybe Hürrem would find the place where it hid?"

"Of course," she answered with the same unruly smile.

"Really? How would you do it?"

"I would fool the hare."

Suleiman laughed.

"Oh, you. How would you manage to do that?"

"Dad Tacham used to say: 'Listen, Aleksandra. Do not underestimate a hare just because it is small. When its life is in danger, it'll outsmart you. If it smells your scent, it will not leave the burrow, no matter what you do. That's why you have to hide your scent first so that the hare doesn't notice you until you get closer.'"

Sometimes in the evenings, Hürrem would tell the young Padishah about her adventures with Tacham Noyan. For Suleiman, those adventures were like a fairy tale – that's why the term 'Dad Tacham,' was not foreign to him.

Hürrem mentioned the Cossack jigit's trick for a hare as if it were something very ordinary. On the one hand, she was bending over her needlework, while on the other – she was saying such things. Her voice never sounded instructive. Hürrem already knew that Suleiman hated it when somebody was clever with him.

Sultan Suleiman and his hunting companions knew a thousand ways to effectively lure a hare out of a burrow, but none of these tricks had worked over the past three days.

"How did your father Tacham hide his smell?"

"We took a handful of brushwood and smoked it, and then we walked in a cloud of smoke..."

Padishah suddenly put his finger to his lips and cut her off mid-world.

"Wait a second, wait a second. Did he take you hunting, too?"

"He also taught me how to string a bow."

"Impossible. You strung a bow and shot arrows with these beautiful, delicate hands?"

Hürrem felt hurt by this disbelieving question, but she didn't let it show, she only nodded her head.

"How did you manage to do it?"

Hürrem replied, trying not to bore the man. She never bragged, and what's more, she invented funny scenes, as if nothing really unusual happened.

"The first time I didn't even know how it happened that the arrow shot."

As a result, she had now managed to create an image for Suleiman of not a hunter, but an unruly girl wandering by the side of a highlander.

Suleiman couldn't stop laughing.

"How did you string this bow? How did you string it? Tell me again," he demanded the details.

When Hürrem joyfully jumped up and began showing how she strung the bow, he took the girl in his arms, kissing and stroking her.

"You must go hunting with us," said the Padishah.

Even though she'd just done everything she could to entice this invitation, she nevertheless, managed to make herself look very surprised.

"What? Me?"

"Of course. We will see how the hunt for a hare with the help of brushwood will go for us."

"But all those men..."

"It will be great fun. You will remain in disguise while hunting."

So, that's what she did. She put on a man's outfit, covered her face, and set off with him on the first hunt. She amazed both Suleiman, the falconer Ibrahim, and other agas and beys. The mastery with which she mounted her horse, strung the bow stroke, followed the game, embracing the steed by its neck as it sped along like the wind, and hiding her face in its mane, surprised everyone. Even the experienced riders were impressed. Especially after, following her advice, they lit up the brush and spread clouds of smoke around them, and they caught some three or five hares – the humor of the Padishah significantly improved. But what most delighted Suleiman was the moment when Hürrem, dashing on a horse, racing with the wind, shot an arrow and took down a roe deer. First, all the participants of the hunt sighed loudly:

"Oooh!", and then voices full of admiration could be heard: "Mashallah."

The young Padishah, who rewarded the success of the beloved woman with applause, said to Ibrahim:

"Look, falconer, such a young kid, and he has already become a rival for you."

Ibrahim knew, like all other participants of the hunt, that the rider whom the Padishah called a 'young kid,' was actually Hürrem Haseki, but he pretended he didn't know anything so that he wouldn't have to fraternize too much.

"I always say it, My Lord, 'Our Sultan makes the most accurate decisions.' Forgive me, but I didn't expect you to choose your hunting companions so perfectly."

Having given the Padishah joy with those words, Ibrahim slowly turned to Hürrem, who'd been listening attentively to their conversation from the back of her mount.

"Those chosen by our Master are not our rivals, if anything, they are our companions. We will not compete with each other by thought or knowledge."

Even with the incomplete knowledge of the language, Hürrem understood the allusion, threat, and superiority coming from these words, but happy Suleiman nodded his head in satisfaction – or maybe he just pretended not to understand.

Her face was covered, which is why Ibrahim couldn't see the antipathy in her eyes. If he's seen it, he would have understood immediately that he'd gained a sworn enemy, and that would have shaken him deeply.

We will see, Croat, thought Hürrem, letting the horse trot. *You'll see how valuable Hürrem's thoughts and knowledge is. Will the Sultan be guided by your judgment or the words of the Ruthenian odalisque?*

That night Sultan Suleiman was like a storm of passion. He looked her in the eyes for a long time, thinking how lucky he was. He drank the beautiful smile from her lips as if it was wine.

This is my woman, he thought, *full of love, fiery and brave. She knows how to hug and how to kill.*

Ibrahim was right. Suleiman knew how to make a choice. That day, he'd seen once again how right he had been to choose Hürrem over Gülbahar. He took the girl's hands. He couldn't believe that those white dove-like hands were strong enough that they could release an arrow that took life. He kissed them with love – and then came a storm of passion that continued until dawn.

But things were not all going Hürrem's way.

Padishah did not give up on his nightly talks with Ibrahim in the Mehmed the Conqueror Pavilion, overlooking the green islands of the Marmara Sea on one side, and the unique beauty of the Bosphorus on the other. Hürrem spent many nights sitting in front of a crackling fireplace, waiting for Suleiman, and boiling with anger. But she didn't give up – she didn't let sleep overcome her. Nor did she show anyone how angry and disappointed she was. As soon as the Padishah returned, she'd throw herself into his arms, and shower him with a rain of kisses.

She didn't complain once: 'Has my Master gotten bored with me that he spends more time with his favorite Ibrahim?'

What do you want? Love or power? she asked herself one night. And she found her reply. *Power and authority!* But power, like love, required patience. *If so, I will be patient,* she promised herself. *Power is worth this bitterness.*

CHAPTER THIRTY-TWO

One lonely night Hürrem jumped out of bed to the sounds of shouts:

"Sultan! Sultan!".

The harem corridors filled with anxious voices. The screams were mixed with the clanging of swords. She understood that the Sultan's guards were among the bustling people, too. It meant something significant had happened – the presence of the army in the harem was not commonplace. What was happening? Her heart squeezed with terror. Among dozens of screams, she recognized the voice of the commander of the Chaushes.

"Sultan! Sultan!"

Merzuka and other servants also woke up. While Setaret Kalfa tried to light the lamps, the other girls ran around the chambers aimlessly and shouting.

The bustle outside was getting louder, bigger, and closer. The harem aga Sümbül's feminine calling could be heard among the many voices.

"Shhh! Leave! Get out right now! Do not violate the silence of the harem! The wrath of the Sultan..." The man's fearful, thin voice appeared and disappeared among male murmurs.

"Stop yelling!" Hürrem scolded the girls as she climbed out of bed. Emine immediately dressed her in a sheer, translucent dressing gown, gifted to her by Sultana Mother.

"We have news from Crimea!" someone shouted in a thick, male voice.

From Crimea? Instantly, Hürrem's heart beat so loudly that it could have drowned out all other voices. *From Crimea?* She was surprised. *They have news from Crimea!* Crimea was so close to her thyme-scented homeland.

The commander of the Chaushes said again:

"The messenger of the Crimean Khan awaits your permission, My Lord. What he'd really just said was, 'Let me lose my head, if the message I came with is not worth waking up the Lord of the World from his sleep.'

Hürrem put her ear to the door, trying to hear and understand their words. What could be important enough to wake the great Sultan Suleiman in the middle of the night?

At the same moment, Hürrem recognized the voice of the falconer Ibrahim.

"Silence, fools!"

There was silence. When Hürrem heard Ibrahim, her heart froze. While she'd been there lying here alone, he'd been by the Padishah.

"Damn Croat," she murmured.

She was furious when she realized that Sultan Suleiman and Ibrahim were pouring over the maps in his room again. The falconer didn't shout, but the words he spoke almost in a whisper cut like a whip.

"Do you have no shame?"

Sümbül Aga tried to answer the question.

"I warned them, but..." he began with a weak voice before Ibrahim cut him short.

"How dare you come like this before the Sultan's door? What is this scandal? The punishment for destroying the privacy, silence, and peace of the harem is your head. Don't you know that? If the message from the Crimea does not alleviate the anger of our Master the Padishah, I wouldn't like to be in your skin. The anger of the Padishah will reach you all."

The commander of the Chaush said something that Hürrem couldn't hear. Ibrahim was silent for a moment, then spoke again.

"Notify Piri Pasha immediately." Now there was an indefinable commotion in his voice also. "Awake also Ferhat Pasha. Don't forget about Ahmed Pasha and Pijal Pasha. The Sultan will go to the audience room to hear the news."

The talks stopped. Some door closed. Probably Ibrahim returned to the Padishah.

Footsteps and hushed voices drifted away, and the harem was overwhelmed by an unbearable night's silence.

Hürrem couldn't shut her eyes all night. What important news could come from the Crimea to Sultan Suleiman that couldn't wait until the morning?

Could Mehmed Khan have died? If so, what will happen to me? she asked herself. *If Suleiman throws me out of here, with whom will I find refuge, if not with Aj Bala?*

Again, she was swallowed by the same paralyzing fear that had haunted her since the first day she'd arrived in the Seraglio. What if Suleiman throws me out?

Until now she'd hid this anxiety, even from herself. Now, she felt afraid for the first time, even if only inside, that she would be left without a roof over her head. Dad Tacham wasn't there to protect her either. If he were, he'd throw her on the back of Hope, and rush to the mountains – to freedom.

No, she thought, *the Khan hasn't died. The commander of the Chaushes said that the message was sent by the Crimean Khan. Don't worry.* At this, the Devil in her said with a terrifying laugh: *Wait. Don't be so fast with this joy. The man did not say it was Mehmed Girej. Maybe Mehmed Girej has died, and someone else has become a Khan and taken his place.* That thought was enough to make Hürrem shudder.

The death of Mehmed Girej would mean that Aj Bala was gone too.

Maybe Sultana Hafsa will leave me then too? she thought, *and she already has one foot in the grave. Then I'll be left with nobody in this world. God, I'm all alone! Completely alone! I don't have anyone!* she lamented.

In the early morning hours, Hürrem directed her steps toward the courtyard of the odalisques in the hope that she might find out what the news was that the messenger had brought.

If Ekaterina were there, she would have certainly heard something.

However, that wasn't an option. On the day when she'd caught the girl's jealous gaze, she'd decided to expel her from the palace. Ekaterina was very dangerous to her. If she started talking, it would have meant the end for Hürrem. So, when on Christmas evening, the Padishah had asked her, 'What would you like to get as a gift from me?' Hürrem decided it was the perfect opportunity to get rid of the girl.

"The health and peace of His Majesty Sultan are the greatest gift to us."

"No, Ibrahim reminded me that it is your tradition to give gifts for Christmas. Tell me, what would you like?"

Again, playing the role of a small, innocent girl, Hürrem wished that His Majesty Sultan would bring freedom to her beloved friend.

"If it's possible, I would ask you to arrange a happy marriage for her. It will be a good deed." Saying this, she did not forget to bow down humbly.

Not even fifteen days passed before Ekaterina was sent out on her way to Kütahya, promised to an aged pasha. In fact, the girl didn't go to her husband, but into exile. Oddly enough, Ekaterina was happy with that situation. She was glad that instead of leading a prison-life like Hürrem, enclosed among four walls, she would be the wife of a pasha, even if he was old. She showed her gratitude by kissing Hürrem's hands before leaving the palace.

Now, however, without Ekaterina, the courtyard of the odalisques seemed deaf. The girls had not even heard about the commotion during the night. Hürrem, who hurried excitedly to the courtyard of the odalisques, accompanied by the flapping of her skirts, came back empty-handed.

So, she immediately sent Jafer to Sümbül Aga. She couldn't run to Sultana Hafsa and shower her with questions: 'What happened last night, Sultana Mother? What message was sent to our Sultan by Mehmed Girej Khan – the brother of your companion?'

As she waited for Jafer, her stomach ached with anxiety and impatience. There was a strange atmosphere in the palace. As she peeked out from behind the bars, she saw the guards embracing each other. She'd never seen soldiers behave like that before. At first, thinking that it was a coincidence, she didn't pay attention to it. But, the same scene was repeated with each guard as if they were celebrating something. What could it be?

When Jafer ran in, her patience was almost gone.

"Have you found out? Have you?" she asked nervously.

"I haven't found out much, but there is a celebration in the seraglio. They send messengers to the four corners of the world with good news."

"What good news? Speak up!"

"Crimean Khan Mehmed Girej Khan..."

When Jafer began to speak, there were shouts of joy inside her: *He's alive! He's alive!*

"... gave his regards to our Ruler and, assuring his loyalty, sent good news about the victory of the Crimean jigits."

Was this black boy doing it on purpose? He obviously knew how curious she was. He talked and talked. Hürrem absorbed his words.

"There is a place – the Grand Principality of Moscow. The Crimean troops conquered it."

She couldn't believe her ears: *The Crimean riders entered Moscow?*

The boy, as if hearing his mistress's question, continued:

"Now Tatar jigits with turbans and their red-felt börks on their heads and sabers in their hands roam the streets of Moscow. The Crimean Khan sent such a message to our Sultan: 'I put the white flag of the Golden Horde in the

Kremlin, and the red and green pennants of my brother Suleiman Khan flutter next to it. The young prince, called Ivan the Terrible, barely saved his life...'"

Hürrem didn't listen to him anymore, and even if she listened, she didn't hear. Her mind roared – her country had been invaded. It was true that Moscow didn't belong to her homeland, but Ruthenia was located exactly where the borders of the Grand Principality of Moscow ran, and the Polish lands began. Now, it seemed that not only her village had been plundered, but it seemed that the whole country, long and wide, was undergoing a siege. Who knows how many more girls like her had been thrown onto a horse's back and taken to the mountains by Cossack and Tatar riders?

She turned her head to hide her tears.

What a misfortune, she sobbed soundlessly. *My village, my home is gone. I don't have anyone. I don't have a homeland. How can I still exist, God?!* The silent rebellion that intensified in her made her question herself: *Who am I? Am I Ruthenian? Ukrainian? Polish? Who am I? All of them? Which one of them?*

In fact, who was she? If she didn't even know who she was exactly, why did she cry at the news of the siege of Moscow? She saw Merzuka hanging onto Emine's neck in happiness. The Tatar girl celebrated Tatar victory.

Maybe I'm Tatar too, she thought suddenly. Didn't she live for six years in the Crimean land, in a palace in the Crimea? It was true. Wasn't Hürrem, the spiritual daughter of Sultana Güldane, the wife of Khan Mengli Girej, the heir of the Golden Horde?

She suddenly sank in thoughts to consider all the questions and answers. Almost immediately, she raised her head, straightened her arms, and wiped her eyes with the back of her hand – she had already solved the problem of her identity.

No, she thought. *I am neither a Ruthenian, Ukrainian, nor a Polish woman. I am Turkish now. I am Hürrem Haseki, beloved favorite of the Ruler of the Ottoman Empire, Sultan Suleiman. Let them say that and talk about me that way.*

Hürrem, who just a moment ago had been pouring a sea of tears, now rose with vigor, while Jafer looked on astonished.

"I have to get ready and immediately go to Mother Sultana," she said. "I will not let anyone say, 'Look at this godless Ruthenian. How despaired she was after hearing about the siege of Moscow. I wonder if our Sultan will let her into his bed again.'"

Walking with a determined step, Hürrem ordered herself:

Get used to rejoice in the Ottoman victories. You are an Ottoman Queen now!

CHAPTER THIRTY-THREE

Over the winter there was an avalanche of news. The palace, which couldn't shake off the suffering after the passing away of Prince Mahmud before seeing his ninth winter, was now full of joy.

"Sultana Mother," said Hürrem shyly. "Something happened to us."

Seeing her shyness, the old woman guessed what it was even before the girl began to speak, but she still asked:

"What happened, child? Are you sick?"

Hürrem stared at the floor and did not look up. Her face was chalk-white.

"Tell me, child. What's wrong?"

"I think we've got a cold," she said.

"Not something else?"

There was silence.

"And also... something... is... is... late... Sultana Mother," Hürrem stammered, barely audible.

Sultana mother had been waiting for this message with great anxiety for so long.

"Are you sure? For how long?"

Hürrem nodded.

"Almost two months already."

Sultana Hafsa immediately clapped her hands and summoned the servants.

"Call the midwives immediately."

At the news that the odalisque was pregnant, the harem became overcome by an unprecedented commotion. After all, the Sultana Mother had called for the midwife herself.

Usually, when some odalisque was pregnant, Sultana Hafsa limited herself to only visiting her.

"May God give you a successful birth," she'd pray — and that was all.

But, this time she was very moved.

Hürrem wasn't like the other odalisques. She was now the second woman in the Seraglio; the second woman after the Padishah's mother. Ever since Sultan Suleiman had invited her to his alcove, he had not smelled other rose than Hürrem. Until Gülbahar was sent to Manisa, the Padishah's pain after the death of the prince was softened by prince Mustafa's joyful playing. Now, instead, it was replaced by love, Hürrem's smiling face, passionate deep eyes, and her songs that they tried to sing together.

The midwives came running. They thoroughly examined Hürrem Haseki, whom Sultana Hafsa had arranged on the sofa, placing pillows under her back. Putting their ears next to her belly, they tried to hear a sound in it. While Hürrem and Sultana Hafsa eagerly awaited their diagnosis, the women stepped aside and whispered something to each other surreptitiously, then proceeded to re-examine. Hürrem looked anxiously at the women who leaned over her belly, touching it and nodding gently.

Was something wrong? How is that possible? she thought. Merzuka had already made a diagnosis. Didn't she tell her Lady this morning that the child had started to move? In that case, what was going on? Why weren't the midwives giving her good news?

Hürrem had long ago guessed that she was pregnant, but she didn't confide in anyone until she was sure.

God, she continued to say to herself, *Holy Mother Mary, you gave me a child. Thank you*.

However, soon the problems with her stomach couldn't be hidden. Merzuka watched her every move suspiciously.

"My mistress seems to have cravings," she'd said bluntly.

Hürrem also felt movements in her stomach, somewhere near her womb; something like a flutter. All night long, she could only think that she was carrying life inside herself. She was scared first. It was an entirely new feeling for her. Hadn't she been praying to become a mother? God had finally answered her prayers. During the nights, she caressed the child, rubbing her belly. She tried to get used to it, give it warmth. Together with Suleiman, she was bringing a new life into the world. With Suleiman, the Ruler of the world. Could there be a greater miracle? She will give birth to the prince, and when the time comes, the prince will become a padishah.

The midwives' meticulous examination exhausted the patience of Sultana Hafsa.

"What is this long examination? Why can't you make a decision?"

The chief midwife straightened. First, she directed her blank look at Hürrem. While the other midwives still examined her belly, the expressionless face of the chief midwife moved. Her eyes softened. She looked at Hürrem with a gentle smile, then the woman turned to Mother Sultana.

"Sultana Mother, I have good news," she finally said. "Your son, the Sultan, will be a father again. Mrs. Hürrem is in the third month of pregnancy."

While Hürrem was filled with shouts of joy, Sultana Hafsa rose and walked toward her.

Should I be happy or scared? Of course, happy that my son will have another child. Also, I love this girl. Hürrem, who was a child herself, will become a mother in a few months – the mother of my grandson. But what will happen if it's a boy?

Two princes to one throne meant danger and even death. How much suffering of the unfortunate princes had this palace seen? Fathers killing sons. Princes acting against their father. For years, didn't she try to protect Suleiman, so that he wouldn't suffer any disaster at the hands of his father? She thought she would faint in fear when one day her husband, Selim Khan, called for Suleiman to come to Istanbul. How could she know that he wanted him to stay in Istanbul, and become the head of the State while he set out on an expedition? No one had any idea about the fear in which Hafsa lived.

Now things were complicating again. If Hürrem also gives birth to a son, she'll consider Prince Mustafa, the son of Gülbahar, a rival. Yes, luck smiled upon Mustafa – he was the eldest son. It was he who should hold the throne. Only will a younger prince listen to that? And when the time comes for Mustafa to sit down on the throne, will her elder grandson leave the prince, the son of Hürrem, alive? That was the order of the world. It was terrifying, but that's how the Ottoman dynasty had survived since the time of the Conqueror. The State was eternal. When it was necessary, father, son or brother had the right to shed blood for it.

Oh! The Sultana sighed in horror at the thought of future events – but right now wasn't the time to ponder over them. *Leave it, Hafsa*, she said to herself. *Look, this orphan Hürrem carries your son's child. Stop it, let her live her happiness. Besides, you never know. Maybe it will be a girl*. Sultana Hafsa tried to smile, distracting her anxious thoughts.

She took out a purse from the pocket of her caftan and tossed it to the head midwife. The woman caught it, kissed it, and put it to her forehead. She prayed for the happiness of the father, child, and mother.

Sultana Mother approached the head of the bed, and bending over, wanted to kiss Hürrem.

Seeing that, the girl got up and embraced her. There were butterflies of happiness in Hürrem's eyes. There was also pride and gratitude in them. The sources of her blue-green eyes filled - those were the tears of joy.

Sultana took the girl into her arms, embracing her around the waist. Kissing Hürrem's forehead, she felt her eyes fill with tears.

Could these be tears of happiness? How much time has passed? Sultana Hafsa thought suddenly. *I've even forgotten how to cry from joy.*

"Be happy, Hürrem," she said slowly. "Give me a reason to be proud. Give my son, the Sultan, a healthy and happy child. I hope that happiness will come to your child as it came to its mother."

Hürrem kissed the woman's hands three times with real gratitude and put them on her forehead three times. The Sultana Mother wrinkled hands became wet with the girl's tears. A single tear flowing down her own cheek also dropped on Hürrem's hair.

"You opened my way to happiness, Sultana Mother," she whispered. "My mother Gül, my rosebud, who took in a girl torn out of her homeland. My sister Aj Bala, who sent me here with the words: 'Go and find your happiness.' And the beautiful mother of the Master of my heart, the father of my child, my Suleiman, Sultana Mother. If it were not for you, happiness would not have smiled at the unfortunate Hürrem."

The woman looked with love into Hürrem's eyes, wet with tears. She wiped her cheeks with an edge of a handkerchief.

"It is God who gives and takes back happiness. It's him who writes our destiny on our forehead. We are only His tools. If he did not write on your forehead that you would give birth to a child of the Sultan of Sultans, Suleiman Khan, whatever we did would be in vain. I want to say, Hürrem, you are also a tool. God has appointed you to give birth to a child of my son, the Sultan. Have courage, Hürrem, you can do it."

She stroked Hürrem's hair for a moment, then rose.

"Why are we standing like this?! Let the preparations begin now!" she ordered. The love and compassion disappeared from her voice, and their place was taken by a composed and harsh tone. "Mrs. Hürrem will give my son, Sultan, a child. You must ensure her peace and take good care of her. Let the midwife stay in her chamber every night. If the need arises, bring in a court medic in readiness. Let new servants be assigned to her. Be careful with what she eats and drinks, and every day, let us know about the health of Hürrem and her child."

In this happy and joyful moment, two important things did not escape Hürrem.

Speaking of her, Sultana Mother did not say 'haseki' anymore. By calling her 'Mrs. Hürrem,' she'd placed her in a different position. She couldn't determine what position it was, but it seemed to her closer and warmer than haseki.

The second one was more important. Sultana Hafsa kept saying that Hürrem would give birth to a 'child.' She might as well say that 'Mrs. Hürrem will give our Sultan a son,' but she did not. Why? The answer hit Hürrem like a slap.

She is afraid that I will give birth to a boy! Of course, she knew that if Hürrem gave birth to a son, he would become Mustafa's rival.

Whoever heard of fear standing in the way of destiny, Grandma? she thought. Exactly. Sultana Hafsa was about to become her son's grandmother soon.

The die is now cast, she resolved. *I will give Suleiman a son. The son of Hürrem, not Gülbahar's, will sit on the Ottoman throne. I swear it will happen.*

***

"Hürrem is pregnant! Hürrem is pregnant!" These words spread like wildfire all around the palace, so it was neither Hürrem nor Sultana Hafsa who passed the happy news to Sultan Suleiman. The young Padishah was at the docks of the Golden Horn, where he was admiring a newly built galley, and he received the good news from the falconer Ibrahim.

At some point, a man had approached them and whispered something to Ibrahim's ear. The falconer didn't look surprised. Then he approached the Sultan who was talking with the captain and said:

"Congratulations, My Lord."

The Padishah, who was just discussing the risk of reducing the control of the galley by the huge size of its sails, was surprised. He turned his head and looked at his friend with a questioning gaze.

Ibrahim immediately bowed humbly and kissed the edge of the Padishah's robe.

"May God give you a long life, and make your State eternal. Let your seed yield a rich harvest. Let your offspring multiply."

"What are you talking about, falconer?"

"My Sultan will soon be a father again. Congratulations."

My Hürrem! A shout of happiness sounded in Suleiman's soul. *A girl or a boy?* He suddenly noticed that this question did not give him peace. God has already given him the happiness of having a son twice. *A girl*, he thought. *Will God offer us a Sultana this time? She must be beautiful like Hürrem. A Sultana with eyes, gaze, and voice as charming and intoxicating as hers, and with a smile that even the sun will envy her.*

A shout rose up from the mustached Levantines, dressed in knee-length trousers, bustling like ants on the boat's bow, stern, and both sides.

"Long live the descendant of the Padishah! Long live the Sultan!"

They climbed, and after a moment rappelled down the ropes that stretched from the sails fixed to the masts so large that even six men could not embrace them.

Sultan Suleiman's eyes filled with tears. He embraced the viziers and the pashas, one by one. He patted the backs of the Levantines who approached him, kissing his hand.

Then everyone went back to work. Huge bronze cannons were rolled into the belly of the galley with even bigger zeal. Trunks with cannon balls were carried on the shoulders so easily, as if they'd suddenly become lighter.

At the same time, the moving voice of a swarthy Levantine came from the stern:

If I ask you for a smile, for a smile,
I'll slip a sunny crown on your head.
Even if the hell freezes over,
I will not give up my rose.

The other Levantines joined in this song. Strong male voices echoed over the calm waters of the Golden Horn. The melody was accompanied by the cries of the gulls circling the sky.

Suleiman also hummed this sincere song for a moment; a song ringing out for him and Hürrem.

If I ask you for a smile, for a smile,
I'll slip a sunny crown on your head.

***

It was already late when Suleiman returned to the harem, after having said a thanksgiving prayer. He'd prayed for the health and long life of the child, whom he would soon take in his arms, and for the expedition he was about to set out for, to end in victory.

He entered Hürrem's chambers. He silenced the servants, who'd begun to run in panic wanting to inform their

Lady about the arrival of the Padishah. He quietly opened the door to Hürrem's bedroom. She was sleeping on a magnificent bed set under the window. There was no sound inside but a cracking of logs burning in a large fireplace. Her face was lit by the faint light of a lamp with a shortened wick. There was peace, joy, and smile painted on it.

She smiles even in her sleep, thought Suleiman.

He began to believe that Hürrem was his blessing. She was so fresh and beautiful. When he was at her side, he forgot about the worries, sadness, afflictions, and war plans – and his inside filled with peace and joy.

What more can a man want from a woman? He asked himself. *A descendant? Hürrem will give me that, too.*

He could talk to Hürrem about any topic. For example, he recently mentioned the wrestling in Edirne, where the players' bodies are lubricated with oil before the fight.

Hürrem had opened her eyes wide and exclaimed:

"How is it possible?! How will players fight when their bodies are covered with oil? They will slip."

"That's what their mastery is all about, my beauty. Until they see the stars..."

Hürrem couldn't resist. Hearing those words, she'd begun to giggle. That was what Suleiman loved in her: being herself, free, unrestrained, the easygoing conversations.

"What does it mean to see the stars? Do they fight at night?"

Suleiman had started laughing.

"Oh, God bless you," he'd said, calming down. *What night? Of course, they fight during the day.*

"Then how can they see the stars?"

"It's just a saying. This is said when the defeated wrestler lies on the ground and looks at the sky."

This time it had been Hürrem who was overjoyed.

"A wrestler watching the stars," she'd said, and burst out in laughter.

Her joy was like a splash of a stream. It brought freshness and relief.

"Not watching, but seeing the stars." Suleiman tried to correct the girl between their successive bursts of laughter.

Once they'd calmed down, Hürrem then began to describe what wrestling looked like in her homeland.

"What? You know all about wrestling too? I must say that Gülbahar was lucky. You could have caught her in an iron grip and knocked our Prince's mother down."

How could he have said something like that? Padishah regretted his words. Was it the right time for such words?

Boor, he'd scolded himself in thoughts, but nothing that he feared happened.

Hürrem had felt confused hearing the name of Gülbahar from the Sultan's lips, but she didn't let it show.

"Oh no," she'd replied. "What can your slave know about wrestling? We were once at a fair with my father Tacham. I saw them there."

Suleiman picked up immediately:

"There's probably no such place that your father would not take you to."

She'd then nodded her head and began talking about the wrestling she had seen.

"Wait. I did not understand. You must show it to me," said Suleiman.

Hürrem then jumped up and showed the Padishah how the wrestlers knocked each other down and pulled each other to the ground.

The wrestling of the Padishah and his favorite soon turned into a battle of passion.

"I surrender!" Suleiman was defeated. "Oh! You threw me to the ground. I saw the stars."

Remembering back to that evening, Suleiman smiled while he looked at Hürrem sleeping peacefully. She was so charming in the light of the fireplace.

The girl stroked her belly, where his descendant, a life from his life, was growing.

He leaned over. His lips touched the girl's forehead. When Hürrem opened her eyes, he couldn't resist. He kissed her sleepy eyelids.

"The happy news has reached me, Hürrem."

The girl embraced the man's neck with affection.

"I wanted to tell my Suleiman about it myself, but in the Sultan's palace the news spreads faster than the wind."

"In the palace?" Padishah smiled. "Even my soldiers found out before me. They are celebrating in the barracks."

"Is our Master angry?"

The Padishah silenced Hürrem with kisses.

"How can I be angry with the one who carries life in herself, Hürrem? Our palace will experience a miracle. The sun will give birth to the sun. We were happy that we had the sun, now we will have two."

The girl led Suleiman's hand to her stomach.

"Look, the baby seems to be moving."

Suleiman could not feel the movements of this new being, but he didn't want to hurt Hürrem, so he put his hand on her smooth belly and stroked it for a long time.

Combing through the Padishah's hair with her fingers, Hürrem spoke in a sleepy voice:

"Our prince is naughty already."

"Prince? What if it's a Sultana? Beautiful like you…"

"No," Hürrem cut in without stopping playing with the man's hair. "Hürrem will give His Majesty Sultan a son. He will be handsome like his dad. Is there anyone who is just as strong, powerful, just, full of goodness and love?"

***

The palace was so preoccupied with Hürrem's pregnancy that no one even noticed the sudden disappearance of harem aga Sümbül. One day he left through the palace gate and never came back – and no one saw or heard of Sümbül Aga again. Those who went to search for him returned with empty hands. Sümbül seemed to have been swallowed by the earth.

At first, he was suspected of stealing something and escaping. However, when eight bundles full of treasure were found under his bed, those assumptions were dropped – he hadn't even taken his money. So, clearly, that meant that one day he would come back. But Sümbül did not come back.

As the days went by, the hopes diminished, until finally he was completely forgotten.

This turn of event disturbed Hürrem the most. How was this possible? One day a person existed, and the next day, they did not? And then they fell into oblivion so fast.

It was as if he'd never walked through those corridors, he did not open the door. The same thing had happened to Despina. One day was enough for everyone to forget about her. And Gülbahar? The great Mahidevran Gülbahar Haseki, the mother of the son of the Padishah, had ceased to be the subject of palace talks long before she'd even reached the place of her exile. And now it was Sümbül Aga. So, it was so easy to forget someone. And to not be forgotten? What did she have to do to save herself in human memory, and not to pass like a dry leaf?

Jafer, just like me, is sad because of the disappearance of Sümbül Aga, she thought. *He has probably suffered a lot of pain because of Sümbül's stick, but all the same.*

"Don't be sad, Jafer," she said to the black young man. "We both got a good beating from him many times, but he was your aga after all. We also lost someone who led us by the hand."

The boy said nothing and just sat there with his eyes fixed on the distance. At first, when he heard about the disappearance of Sümbül Aga, an image of the terrifying giant, Tacham Noyan, had appeared before his eyes.

Did Azrael give Sümbül a punishment for the beating that our mistress got from him?

He knew that even if he asked him about it, he wouldn't get an answer. He raised his head and looked at Hürrem.

The fire in Jafer's black eyes made Hürrem change her mind.

No, he's not sad at all, she thought. *Should I be sad?*

Suddenly that question brought to her the terrible memory that had not occurred to her before. Yes, she lost her support, but the one who knew her dangerous secret had also disappeared. Thanks to this turn of events, an embarrassing adventure had been erased from her life. Ekaterina also knew about it, but she'd agreed to accept a bribe. Besides, even if she said something, who would believe her?

Many days later, the body of a black giant with a large head was found on the other bank of the river, by the estuary. Someone had ripped his stomach with a saber.

CHAPTER THIRTY-FOUR

On a moonless night, a dark figure sneaked down one of the steep slopes leading from the Galata harbor to the Yoros fortress. He hid in the shadow of the walls. He stopped and look around, and looked back for a moment to make sure he was not being watched. He was wrapped in a black cloak, whose flaps were tossed by a strong wind blowing from the sea. His head was hidden in a huge hood. He took a few steps forward, stopped again, pressed his back against the wall, and listened. With one hand, he firmly grabbed the dagger hidden under his cape.

For a moment, a pale light seeping from one of the windows of a house seemed to illuminate his face, hidden under the hood, just in time to capture a blood-chilling, ominous flash in the man's eyes. He stared at the direction he came from as if he wanted to penetrate the darkness, to see if anyone watched him. There was no trace of a living soul - nothing moved. The only thing that could be heard was the mumbling cry of some drunk. Only such a soak, or a robber ready to take a life, would be out in the streets at this hour. Or someone who had such an important task to do that he was willing to risk his life. The man in the cloak was someone like that. Or maybe both?!

He breathed heavily for some time, and then he began to climb up the path again as if he was to never reach his destination. The dark shadows of the tall buildings on both sides turned into a wall of darkness. The shadow of the Yoros fortress ended with a pointed dome, and stood strong, despite a large part of it being destroyed during an earthquake two years earlier – and that added horror to this silhouette that could make people shiver.

He waited on the corner of the street that overlooked the road and listened to the silence again. His eyes penetrated into the darkness. Everything was fine. He quickly turned into an alley and knocked on the door of the stone building on the right.

Two quick taps, one slow, and again two quick, a short break, and one more tap.

Moving uneasily, the man in the cloak waited in the dark. He constantly looked from side to side so that he would not be unpleasantly surprised at the last moment. It took a long time to hear voices behind the door. A streak of light finally filtered through a hole in the heavy wooden door. Someone put his eye next to it until he saw the face hidden by the hood in the dim light. Then a husky voice said:

"Did you bring the fan of *donna* Sophia?"

The mysterious visitor moved toward the light coming through the small hole in the door.

"No," he answered. "I only have *donna* Alba's mask."

There was a sound of the key turning in the lock, and a twang, which could only be caused by taking down a very long chain. This noise broke through the silence of the darkness that enveloped the street. Eventually, the heavy door opened slightly, and a cat slipped out through the gap, while the cloaked shadow quickly slipped inside. He followed the man with a round, bald head, and dragging left foot, who'd opened the door for him, along a stifling, cramped corridor, that smelled of mold. They climbed some creaky wooden stairs to the second floor.

The two men entered a small room. There was nothing inside but a few broken armchairs, chairs, and tables, and a large wardrobe which covered almost the entire opposite wall.

The man with the large, bald head turned his bulging eyes onto the newcomer and extended his hand. The guest, without hesitation, placed a long dagger on the man's hand.

The cold steel flashed for a moment in the room lit by the flame of a single candle.

Limping, the man directed his steps to the wardrobe that covered the whole wall. The man in the cloak didn't notice which place the man touched when one of the edges of the wardrobe gently moved forward. The bald man then stepped aside slightly, so that the newcomer could squeeze through the resulting crack. After a moment, the wardrobe took its former shape, and again covered the wall of the small room. Now a secret passage separated the bald, limping man and the other cloaked man.

The newcomer threw his hood back onto shoulders, revealing his face. It was none other than the Ambassador of the Venetian Republic – Marco Ketto. While he tried to look around, a door opened nearby and, with the flapping of a cassock, a priest hurried toward Marco.

"Signor Ketto, we already thought you would not come."

"I had to take a detour to make sure no one was following me, dear Father."

"His Eminence even began to worry about your life."

Ketto didn't like this reproach, but he didn't show it.

"I was afraid to make a mistake, which would reveal the secret journey of His Eminence."

"Of course, I understand. Of course."

The Reverend rubbed his hands and looked at the young man standing in front of him. Even in a crowd of thousands, seeing this dark-eyed man with a long face and a delicate beard surrounding it, he could swear that he was a Venetian. Not to mention the suspicious, crafty, and dangerous look typical of the Venetians.

"The most important thing is that you came," he said suddenly. "Let's go. Let us not make His Eminence wait any longer."

The Reverend turned abruptly, throwing a rope he had tied around his waist into the air, then walked toward the door with a soft, even supple step, utterly incongruous with that abrupt movement. He opened it and announced:

"Marco Ketto, Your Eminence."

The moment Marco crossed the doorway, he was blinded by the light. It was a huge, richly lit hall, where all objects took on a yellow-gold hue. The opposite wall was covered with a huge tapestry depicting the Last Supper of Jesus and his apostles. Many candles burned in the room. In the right corner, the frail body of Jesus hung on a cross that reached from the ceiling to the floor. A statuette of the suffering Mary was placed on the console by his feet.

A tall man stood with his back to the door. He wore a red robe that reached all the way to the ground and the red miter headwear that indicated his status as a dignitary, which contrasted with the ubiquitous yellow-gold color of the room.

The man turned toward them.

This must be the Bishop of Rome, coming from the Netherlands, His Grace Adriaan Florenszoon Boeyens,

Marco Ketto thought. *The closest assistant of Pope Leo X.* His Grace had thick, black eyebrows and equally black eyes. His slender face with protruding cheekbones was complemented by an eagle nose, a narrow mouth, and a sharp beard dangling from the tip of his chin.

The Ketto's report, *'Ottoman's Preparations for War,'* worried Europe. Leon X wanted to turn this danger into an opportunity. It could be an excuse to organize a new Crusade. First, they will stop the Turks, and then they will take over Anatolia and save Jerusalem. If Jesus was the founder of Christianity, Adrianus was to become its savior.

The European kings did not support his plan. Having learned his true intentions, everyone was afraid of invoking the wrath of the powerful Suleiman on himself. For this reason, the Pope was forced to send Adriaan Florenszoon Boeyens to Istanbul despite the risk of capture by the Turks. The news he would bring was going to ensure the creation of an army of crusaders.

However, the Pope had no idea about the secret plans of his assistant, whom he trusted so much. Adriaan Florenszoon Boeyens did not intend to help Pope Leo X become a savior. On the contrary, Boeyens was preparing to take action to prove that the aged Pope was too old to serve Christianity – to spread the belief that he was beginning to lose touch with reality, and his fantasies will bring danger on the Church. It was only a matter of time before he would sit on the papal throne. Besides, even though he had been in Istanbul for a week already, he hadn't noticed any preparations for war. That was the reason for summoning Marco Ketto to this secret papal palace.

"Signor Ketto," said the Cardinal slowly. The cold in his voice made people tremble.

"Your Eminence," the ambassador said and kissed the great papal ring on the man's extended right hand.

"You're late. I hope the news you are bringing is worth waiting for. You know why His Holiness sent me on this dangerous journey, right?"

"I know, Your Eminence."

"Really?" His tone was enough to suggest to the ambassador that he was not sure of his knowledge. "The fall of Belgrade," continued the Cardinal, looking at Ketto, "has become the fall of the entire Christian world, Signor Ketto. Europe can not agree to the strike of another Attila. Such a tragedy could lead to the annihilation of Christianity."

Marco Ketto listened respectfully, nodding his head. The Cardinal took an apple from the table and bit it. He pretended that he noticed only now that the ambassador was still standing.

"Oh, why are you standing? Sit down," he said, chewing the apple loudly. "What was I saying? Yes... We definitely have to stop this Turkish procession. Yesterday it was Belgrade, and what will it be tomorrow? Vienna? Rome? Hungarian plains?"

Ketto tried to open his mouth to answer him, but the Cardinal did not give him the opportunity.

"If war breaks out, it must be a war all over Europe. That's what His Holiness Pope Leon X thinks. You understand me, Signor Ketto? The whole of Europe. The war of all Christianity."

He plucked another large piece of the apple. He labored for some time to chew it. This was when Ketto noticed huge, disgusting black holes in the man's mouth –

and it was because most of his teeth were rotten, that he had difficulty chewing. That's probably why his lips were usually closed tightly.

"Only such a force can stop Suleiman," he continued. "We must be ready, but to prepare ourselves, we must find out where the Sultan will strike. Isn't that so?" The man did not see the need to wait for Ketto's answer. "You say the war is close. But that's all. You say they make preparations, but you do not give us any other information. His Holiness sent me to Istanbul to learn the truth. Could it be that you raised a false alarm, Signor Ketto?"

From the expression on the man's face, Ketto understood that he wished it were so.

"No. Suleiman is preparing for war. And I believe that this war is already very close, Your Excellency."

"How can you be so sure of that, Signor Ketto?"

"From the day he sat on the throne, Suleiman has been expanding his fleet. Even when his army was fighting in Belgrade, people worked like ants on the docks."

"I saw these docks," interrupted the Cardinal. "That's true, they're quite crowded, but most boats are small and not powerful."

"They also built large galleys and galleons."

The Cardinal shook his hand to silence the ambassador, trying to object.

"Next to the Venetian fleet, they are very weak."

"But fast," he insisted.

"What did you say?"

"These are very fast boats. In comparison with our great galleons, their maneuvering abilities are excellent."

"Eh!" The man waved his hand in a sign that implied what he said was irrelevant. "I am with those who believe that wars are won not by maneuvers, but by a large amount of fire. And tell me, Señor Ketto, what is the reason for your belief that the war is near?"

"The fleet moved from the Golden Horn to the Bosphorus."

"Those boats with big sails? There aren't really many of them."

Marco Ketto began to lose his patience. This stupid man had no idea about the world.

"The ships are disappearing, Your Excellency."

"They are doing what?"

"The ships that sail out from the Golden Horn, moor for a few days at the shores of the Bosphorus to later sail out towards the Black Sea and disappear. In the deep nighttime darkness, without lighting any light, they sail into the Sea of Marmara."

"Can I know who you have this information from?"

"I got it myself, Your Excellency. A watchful eye can see these activities."

"And your eyes are very watchful..."

Ketto ignored the mocking tone of the Cardinal.

"Yes, Your Excellency, it's true."

This time, the Cardinal pretended not to notice the firmness in the man's voice.

"Where are these ships going, Signor Ketto?"

"They disappear!"

The Cardinal's mouth remained open. He wanted to ask something, but Ketto continued.

"I have not heard from any of the Venetian merchant ships that they have seen Ottoman warships in the Aegean

Sea. Big... ships... disappear." At this point, Marco Ketto made a strange gesture with his hands. "Poof!" He made a sound to describe it.

"What do you mean?"

"They hide their destination. During the day they hide in shallow bays, and set off on their journeys at night."

"It's quite an absurd tactic. Like a child's play. Will they finally show up?"

"Yes, but by then it will be too late – they will be right under our noses. We will not have time to prepare. They will crush us."

Adriaan Florenszoon Boeyens moved uneasily in his seat for the first time. He tried to swallow a bite of apple that he had in his mouth. As he thought about it, he stood up and started pacing around the room, stroking the cross hanging on his neck.

"Do you have any information about Suleiman's target, Signor Ketto?"

The ambassador also got up.

"Unfortunately, not. I have some suspicions though."

"Ah, that's great!" The Cardinal's voice was as sharp as a knife. "When I return, if I manage to return to Rome without being caught by Turkish corsairs, I will say to His Holiness: 'Your Holiness, Signor Ketto has no information about Suleiman's destination, but he has suspicions. Apparently, Turkish ships are disappearing at night.' And the Holy Father, based on the suspicions of Signor Ketto, will call the kings to set off on a new Crusade. Right?"

"Right." The ambassador did not know what else he could answer. *Stupid man*, he snorted in his thoughts.

"All right, and if we take these suspicions into consideration, what will Suleiman attack? Signor Ketto?"

"Venice!"

It was as if Cardinal Boeyens was hit in his face with a fist. He tried to recover as soon as possible after what he heard.

"You must have lost your mind," he said.

He devoured the Venetian ambassador with his eyes. Venice was the gate to the Vatican. Whoever gets to Venice will easily reach the Vatican.

"Suleiman would never dare to do something like that," he murmured.

"That's what we said about Belgrade, Your Excellency."

"What are your suspicions based on?"

"Two things. First, Suleiman strengthens his fleet day and night. Secondly, and more important, the tray that was placed in front of me yesterday, when I was called to the palace."

"The tray? What tray, Signor Ketto?"

"The one with a severed head on it."

The Cardinal's hand went unknowingly to his neck.

"A head?" That was all he could say in a trembling voice.

"Yes. A severed head. Can you guess who this head belonged to?"

Noticing that the man looked at him blankly, he continued without waiting for an answer.

"It was the head of Janbirdi al-Ghazali, whom we helped to incite the uprising in Egypt. Remember him? The ambassador of the Damascus Province, under the rule of the Ottoman Empire. One of Suleiman's most trusted people, Ibrahim, set the tray in front of me yesterday and took off the fabric covering it. He just said: 'For the Ottoman State and the Ruler of the world, Suleiman Khan, this is the end of the uprising.' Can there be a clearer message, Cardinal? Is there anyone who does not know that Venice gave al-Ghazali support? They're telling us: 'We punished al-Ghazali, now it's time for Venice.'"

The Cardinal filled a goblet with wine from a carafe made of Venetian glass.

If the ambassador's suspicions are correct, the European kings will support Adrianus' plan, he thought. *At least most of them.*

"Did you send this last message to Venice?"

"Your Excellency is the first to know," said Marco Ketto.

At that moment, Adriaan Florenszoon Boeyens decided to keep this knowledge to himself. There was no need to strengthen the Pope. He suddenly changed the subject.

"You claim that the war is close; meanwhile, it seems to me that in Istanbul everyone is talking only about the new favorite of Suleiman."

"So, you've heard about it, Your Excellency."

The man wanted to say that the Church hears everything, but he gave up.

"Apparently, she is a Ruthenian?"

"It's not entirely clear. That's what the Turks call everyone living north of the Crimea. This girl is probably not a Ruthenian but a Ukrainian girl."

"But Slavic blood flows in her veins. Tell me about her."

"She is young. She's only fifteen years old. The Padishah has some serious feelings for her. Furthermore, he sent Gülbahar Haseki, the mother of the heir to the Ottoman throne, Prince Mustafa, away from the palace to be alone with the girl."

"Impossible! Who is this girl? Is she very pretty?"

"She must be. Apparently, her name is Aleksandra, but when she came to the palace, they called her Ruslana as a sign that she came from Ruthenia. The Padishah liked the girl so much that he changed her name. Now they call her Hürrem."

"Hürrem? What does it mean?"

"Something like smiling, beautiful-looking woman. Suleiman's eyes can't see any other odalisque now apart from Hürrem."

"What is she like? What is her character? You know something about that?"

Ketto didn't react to the cynical tone of the Cardinal.

"They say she's unbridled. She goes hunting with the Padishah, rides a horse, shoots a bow. Until the Sultan got his eye on her, she fought to the death with all the girls in the harem. It is true that some say that Gülbahar Haseki beat her, but I don't believe it. I think it was the other way around."

The Cardinal laughed briefly and took another sip of wine.

"If you want to know my opinion, Signor Ketto, Sultan Suleiman gave Hur... How was that?"

"Hürrem."

"Right. I think he gave the girl a wrong name. If she is both beautiful and predatory, she should be called Roxolana... Rose... And this is a rose with thorns."

The Cardinal sent Ketto a suggestive, lewd look, and his laughter echoed from the walls.

"During my visit to the palace yesterday, the Padishah's confidant, Ibrahim, whispered in my ear that the girl was pregnant. Roxolana is pregnant, Your Excellency."

Boeyens stopped laughing and turned to the ambassador. He looked at him slyly.

"I think you want to say something, Signor Ketto."

"Just think what happens if Roxolana gives him a son."

"What will happen?"

Ketto refrained from laughing at the man's stupidity. He stood up and walked over to the Cardinal.

"Just think, two princes to the Ottoman throne. The son of Gülbahar against the son of Roksolana."

The cunning on Cardinal Adriaan Florenszoon Boeyens' face gave way to a mockery.

"I cannot believe it, Signor Ketto. One of the children is not even born yet, and the other is about six or seven years old, and you calculate the odds in the fight for the throne, which will take place in forty or fifty years."

"Children grow fast, Your Excellency. And the ambitions even faster."

"No, my dear, no. The atmosphere of Istanbul has made you a fantasist. You see wars, conspiracies, and intrigue everywhere."

***

That night, Marco Ketto returned home, just as he had left – hiding in the shadows of the walls. He sat down immediately and wrote an encrypted report to Venice.

'Contact was made with His Excellency. He does not seem to believe in the Ottomans preparing for war. The Cardinal Adriaan Florenszoon Boeyens was more interested in the new Ruthenian favorite of Suleiman than the approaching war. He even named her Roxolana.

Meanwhile, Ibrahim, whom I mentioned to you earlier, gave me two important messages yesterday. The first one is the head of Janbirdi al-Ghazali shown to me on the tray... This is a very clear message. It says: "It's your turn." The second is the information that Roxolana is pregnant. The Ruthenian will soon give Suleiman a descendant.'

Hürrem didn't know about it, but from that night on, the Christian world would always call her Roxolana. The Ottoman bride Hürrem had changed her identity again. Ketto checked the notes. To make it clear who was the author of this letter, which – no one knows when – will reach the hands of a competent person in the palace of the Republic of Venice, he pressed an encrypted stamp to the hot red wax poured on paper.

A sword and a shield.

TO BE CONTINUED ...

IN BOOK II

HURREM - THE POWER BEHIND THE THRONE

Book IV of the Magnificent Century Series

GLOSSARY

Bahar – means 'spring' in Turkish.

Balat – part of Istanbul belonging to the Fatih district, on the Golden Horn.

Bayt – a two-line verse in the genres of lyrical poetry of the Middle and Middle East.

Beyaz – means white in Turkish.

Börk – a red-felt headgear, typical for Janissaries, the sultan's guards, and the servants in seraglio.

Chaush (Turkish: çavuş) – a herald, a court official in the Ottoman Empire.

Devshirme – A system that began in the late 14th Century when Christian boys were recruited by force to serve the Ottoman government. Boys were usually taken from the Balkan provinces, converted to Islam, then tested for their intelligence and capabilities. Also known as the 'blood tax' or 'tribute in blood'.

Dzezve (Turkish: **cezve**) – a kitchen utensil used to prepare coffee in a traditional 'Turkish' way.

Ertugrul – a semi-legendary chief of Oghuz Turks, who lived in the second half of the 13th century, the father of Osman I, the founder of the Ottomans dynasty.

Eyalet – a primarily administrative division of the Ottoman Empire, from 1453 to the beginning of the nineteenth century.

Falaka – originally a Persian tool of physical punishment resembling stocks, immobilizing a person who was beaten with a stick, so-called foot flogging.

Giaur – a person who is not a believer in Islam, who Muslims find offensive.

Ghazal – a poetic lyric piece, popular mainly in Persian literature.

Gül – means a rose in Turkish.

Güldane – a name of Persian origin, meaning 'a bud of a rose.'

Hadrian VI – Adriaan Florenszoon Boeyens adopted this name when he became Pope.

Haram – everything that is forbidden in Islam.

Haseki – at the Sultan's court a woman belonging to the harem, who gave the ruler a descendant.

Hateful Croat - according to historical sources, this was Sokollu Mehmed Pasha, who was probably of Serbian descent.

Hotoz – a kind of headdress for Ottoman women.

Ibrahim Pasha – according to historical sources, Ibrahim Pasha was Greek, and he came from Parga. Became Grand Vizier of the Ottoman Empire after June 1523, succeeding Piri Mehmed Pasha.

Janbirdi al-Ghazali – the first ambassador of the Province of Damascus under the rule of the Ottoman Empire. He served his function from 1518 until his death in 1521. The Ottoman army crushed the al-Ghazali army insurgents, and his head was sent to Sultan Suleiman as a trophy.

Jigits – in the Turkish language refers to a skillful and brave equestrian, or a brave person in general, sometimes spelled as **yigit, zhigit or igid**.

Jochi – the eldest son of Genghis Khan, the father of Toka Temur.

Kadin – a woman standing higher in the hierarchy in the sultan harem, sultan's favorite, wife.

Kaffa (Turkish: Kefe) – an old city in the Crimea. The seat of the Ottoman governor of the province.

Kalfa – a slave in a Turkish harem, a maid, often acting as the manager of the harem.

Kanun (Turkish: kanun) – a zither-like stringed instrument used in traditional Middle Eastern music.

Kerem, Asla, Yusuf, Zuleica, Ferhat, and Shirin – the protagonists of romantic poems in Middle Eastern literature.

Lala Kara Mustafa Pasha – the Ottoman chief and politician, the beylerbey of Damascus, and later the Grand Vizier.

Mahidevran – means 'always beautiful.' The origin of Mahidevran arouses a lot of controversy. Many historical sources state that she was Albanian.

Mashallah (Turkish: Maşallah) – a phrase derived from Arabic, expressing admiration, joy, pride, or gratitude.

Miter or Mitre – a high headgear, a sign of the dignity of Christian church dignitaries.

Mount Kaf – in Persian mythology the mountain where djinns, good spirits, and other mythological creatures live; currently a synonym for a distant place.

Oud (Turkish: ud) – a stringed instrument, called the Arabic or Persian lute, very widespread in the Middle Eastern and Mediterranean countries.

Piri Mehmed Pasha – Grand Vizier of the Ottoman Empire until the end of June 1523. Ibrahim Pasha took over this office after him.

Pope Leo X – according to historical sources, Pope Leo X died on December 1st, 1521 in Rome. His successor as Pope was Hadrian VI, or Adriaan Florenszoon Boeyens.

Sanjak – a territorial unit of the Ottoman Empire, headed by a bey. In the 15th and 16th centuries, the Serengian Sanjak with the center in Manisa was managed by Ottoman princes.

Saz – a stringed instrument, reminiscent in shape of a lute with long fretboard, very popular in the Middle East.

Selim I The Grim – also acquired the nickname 'Cruel.'

Shah Ismail I – the ruler of Iran in 1501-1524, the founder of the Safavid dynasty.

Sokollu Mehmed Pasha – according to historical sources, was also known as the Hateful Croat, and was probably of Serbian descent.

Tomyris – half-legendary queen of the Massagets, who in 529 defeated the Persian army, headed by Cyrus II the Great.

Tugra (tuğra) – a monogram in Islam, a sign of the reigning monarch, sometimes serving as a coat of arms, an emblem of Turkish rulers.

Tumanbaj – the last ruler of Egypt, from the Mameluk dynasty. He ruled in 1516-1517.

About The Author

Demet Altınyeleklioğlu was born in Ankara.

She obtained a degree from Ankara University's Faculty of Political Sciences and Journalism and a master's degree from Haceteppe University in Educational Communications.

From 1980 onwards, she worked as a producer for TRT Turkish Radio and Television Corporation and was a director on various levels. She has translated a few novels and continues to translate. Demet Altınyeleklioğlu lives in Istanbul with her family.

ABOUT THE PUBLISHER

Royal Hawaiian Press is a publishing house located in Honolulu Hawaii. It was established in 2005, primarily to promote the works of author and founder, Maria Cowen. Since then, it has expanded to encompass an assortment of other authors from around the world.

Royal Hawaiian Press specializes in providing books in a variety of languages and genres, including translating and publishing existing European-language books into English for the English-speaking market.

To learn more about Royal Hawaiian Press and the books it represents, please visit:

www.royalhawaiianpress.com

To receive an alert when new books are released, subscribe to the Royal Hawaiian Press Mailing List:

http://tiny.cc/rhp

Printed in Great Britain
by Amazon

31039554R00260